BEYOND DERRYNANE

BEYOND DERRYNANE

A NOVEL OF EIGHTEENTH CENTURY EUROPE

The Derrynane Saga

Kevin O'Connell

The Gortcullinane Press

Copyright © 2016 Kevin O'Connell
All rights reserved, including the right to reproduce this book, or any portions thereof, in any form.
ISBN-13: 9780997407600
ISBN-10: 0997407603
Library of Congress Control Number: 2016905431
Gortcullinane Press, The – P.O. Box 157, Severna Park, MD

Published by The Gortcullinane Press

For Laurette –
with incalculable love and immeasurable gratitude.

In addition to being my dearest friend, the love of my life, she has become a
unique,
much kinder, far gentler version of the mythical Gaelic muse,
Leanan Sidhe ("My Inspiration").

Without her, this work would never have been conceived – much less
written.

Go raibth mille maith agut!

ACKNOWLEDGEMENTS

I FIND IT WONDERFULLY COINCIDENTAL that a debut novel – with a memorably-strong, colourful female protagonist – and written by a male, in no small part owes its existence to a group of, each in her own way, colourful, memorable women – none of whom I had ever met prior to beginning *Derrynane*, shortly after the turn of the new year of 2012. To each one is owed an awesome debt:

Carole Sargent, director of faculty publishing at Georgetown University, was the first professional to read what was at the time the first perhaps fifty or sixty pages that I'd written. When we met after she'd done so, she said bluntly, "You need to take this seriously, because I am . . . I can visualise the settings, I can hear the people speaking . . . ." At that point, she urged me to "write on" and has continued to encourage and support me in countless ways to do just that during these ensuing years.

Laura Oliver, who, in addition to being a gifted published author and a recognised teacher and authority on writing well, has been the consummate mentor. When asked early on in the process if and how she might help me, she said "I believe I'll just let you write." She did so – all the while encouraging, nudging, criticising, commiserating and educating – and I have. This book is the result.

Randy Ladenheim-Gil, my editor, who, I am pleased to say has also become a dear friend, has been and is nothing short of brilliant and awesome. Originally faced with what was, at the time, a massive raw manuscript, Randy skilfully assisted me in treating it as the genesis for *Derrynane* and for the books that, as the *Saga* unfolds, will follow. She has edited my many words with skill, sensitivity, humour, good cheer – and a not-insignificant degree of patience with her novice author.

Vanessa Fox O'Loughlin, the creative writing, literary doyenne of Dublin, who, in addition to being a brilliant published author in her own right, has fostered countless aspiring Irish writers through her various endeavours and enterprises, significantly the unimaginably-wonderful and helpful site *Writing. ie*, which, as much as anything, has become a virtual community, a safe place to come, learn and share. With wit and wisdom, and near-instantaneous responses to my numerous questions and concerns, she has done much more than she knows to help me reach this point.

Derrynane—County Kerry, Ireland— Autumn 1760

The early October sun and the soft blue ocean current-warmed breeze, which had been blowing southwesterly off of Derrynane Bay much of the day, had combined to make the mid-afternoon almost hot. The waters of the bay shone, then sparkled, then lay still, the tide being almost out and the wind becoming spare.

The small, sturdy river ship now completing its journey down the Kenmare River towards the bay, located off of the barely accessible Iveragh Peninsula, at the remote tip of southwest County Kerry, was one of a number of vessels in the variegated fleet belonging to the O'Connells of Derrynane; the craft typically carried butter and other produce, messages and, less frequently, passengers. This day, the ship held no cargo and only two rather singular travelers: an arresting young woman and the massive black-maned, black-tailed chestnut stallion she called Bull.

The vessel rounded Lamb's Head, the ebbing outgoing Atlantic surge nevertheless still patent. Shortly thereafter, reaching its destination, the shallow-draft boat's pilot eased its bow onto a tidal-bar of soft, pungent sand. As the boat was coming to a gentle rest, the enormous, red-headed mariner came forward from the helm and, with surprising grace, stepped off the bow, his bare feet splashing, then squishing onto the soft shore. Immediately, he turned and held open his arms.

"M'lady . . . please," he called with a smile to the very tall—six feet, and perhaps an inch—willowy girl of sixteen. A thick, gleaming mane of hair tumbled over her shoulders and down her back to her waist, as black as the full-skirted, hip-padded wool dress she wore, the hem of which she lifted ever so slightly, partially baring her calves as she stepped off the bow. Her bare toes just skimmed the water as the sailor caught her and, as they both laughed, swung her around, setting her gently down onto drier sand.

Eileen O'Connell, the fifth of eight still-living daughters and the ninth of thirteen still-living children—there had been twenty-two in all—of the late Donal Mór Ó Conaill and his wife, Maire ní Dhuibh ("Big Daniel," a name appropriate for the massive man he was, or the "Elder Daniel," and "Mary of the Dark People," which referred to her own colourful family, the "Fighting O'Donoghues of Glenflesk"*)*, was returning to Derrynane.

Still on deck, the wind-and-weather-worn, smooth planking warm beneath his bare feet, the young mate handed the pilot several battered leather satchels and a magnificent hand-tooled, Spanish-made saddle, which he set softly on a low grassy dune. Eileen hoisted the saddle over an arm and began to sling a bag over her other shoulder, the boat's master taking it back. Still barefoot, and lugging her saddle now, she began to walk up the strand. The sailors then called, "Along we shall be shortly," and as she nodded in understanding, both men, leaving the remaining luggage on the sand, hopped back aboard to lower a gangplank so as to bring the now-whinnying horse ashore.

The breeze catching and playing with her hair, the young woman trudged across the warm sand, around a tide pool, over low dunes, through sea grasses, and up onto the rough grass, lawn-cut and emerald green, striding purposefully towards the cluster of buildings ahead, dominated by the massive, dark, rambling structure that was Derrynane House itself: the location, if not the building in its present form, home to the O'Connells since the first years of the eighteenth century.

The feel of the warm, rough sand on her wet feet, the coarse dune grass scraping her bare legs, the sensation of the damp lawn beneath her feet, these—along with the salt-and-seaweed-laden air, itself spiced with more than a suggestion of dead fish and low-tide bay bottom—all made Eileen conscious of the reality of *home*.

By this time her arrival had been noticed, and as she crossed the lawn, Eileen gazed on a mix of O'Connells, along with retainers, tenants and craftsmen, household and kitchen help and others who had begun to gather. Standing apart was Denis, the eldest O'Connell son, of taller-than-average height, fair of countenance, dark of outlook, and, at his side, a diminutive, middle-aged woman, the mother and matriarch of an extraordinary family, dressed in a rough, flowing gown of dark blue wool, her greying blond hair worn loose, below her shoulders.

As the broad-shouldered girl reached the level ground where the group had gathered, Denis, his pale blue eyes now squinting against the afternoon sun, called out, "Why, *Nellie*, you are here!" stiffly, unemotionally, and with a deliberate, calculatedly bitter measure of sarcasm.

Eileen winced visibly; how she *loathed* that nickname. She never had understood its origin, it made no sense to her, and she was grateful only a very few of her relatives seemed to favour it, despite knowing how intensely she disliked it. In a flash, however, her expression became a grateful smile as her mother burst from the little crowd and, as Eileen dropped her saddle, enveloped her tall daughter, murmuring in a mixture of English and Irish, burying her face in her daughter's bosom, sobbing.

After long moments her tears slowed, then stopped, and Maire stepped back, her hands in her daughter's, her eyes lifted, looking deeply into the girl's—just looking—and then tears, though now quiet, streamed yet again down her tanned cheeks. "You are home, my girl, home."

Eileen nodded in silence and silently mouthed the phrase *"Tá . . . mé sa bhaile"* – "I *am* home, yes, indeed."

Just at that moment, Denis O'Connell, his expression one of utter contempt and total disdain, stepped next to the emotional pair and leaned towards Eileen.

"How *dare* you come here?" he hissed callously.

With the hard, bony fingers of his left hand, he appeared to be reaching for her left arm, his intent unclear, his raspy voice icy, as he continued. "You shall not be remaining, girl. Do you understand me?"

Her eyes suddenly wide, her expression venomous, Eileen unexpectedly released her mother's hands and wordlessly shook him off with a quick, abrupt motion, as she would any loathsome creature.

Undeterred, the basis for his seething rage now to be made fully apparent, he finished. "You shall return to whence you have come, and you shall there and then *do precisely what is expected of you.*"

Without waiting for a response, he quickly moved away, thus not hearing Eileen's muttered "Bastard!"

Her mother had, and glaring in her son's direction, Maire stretched out to drape her left arm around her daughter's waist, as Eileen did the same to her mother's, and the women walked slowly away from the little gathering.

Halting some distance from the women, Denis's hard eyes glared at those remaining, as though to say *Enough, be about your business now*, and they quietly dispersed.

Mother and daughter made their way into the house and up to Maire's rooms, located at the far end of the second floor. Within moments, the sound of women's voices, though muffled by heavy doors and thick walls, resonated in the upper corridor, in a jumble of Irish and English, raised in high emotion, enveloped in a sense of anger, fear, and more tears. Eileen's husky voice was raised now, dominatingly, *"Nil, Nil!"* – "No!" and then she actually screamed at her mother, now in Irish, "You would not understand – you *could not* understand! I cannot, I *shall not* tell you. . . . !" One of the inside doors in Maire's rooms slammed and the hall echoed with wrenching sobs as Eileen pounded a wall with her fist, again and again.

Suddenly, there was silence.

Eileen had stopped crying. She found the dressing room's basin—kept filled, as were those in all of the house's occupied bedrooms, with fresh water—washed her face and bathed her eyes, and quietly, slowly, turned and walked, still barefoot, back towards where her mother sat in a cushioned window seat, gazing out to sea.

Reaching her mother, Eileen knelt silently at Maire's feet and sat back on her heels, her hands resting in her lap—on her left one the simple gold band gleaming sadly—the folds of her widow's weeds lying about her on the worn rug, her hair tumbling over her shoulders, front and back.

Her eyes red and swollen, she looked up at her mother, whispering *"Tá brón orm,"* "I am sorry," and, her shoulders shaking, she began to cry again. Her mother turned to face her, and the somehow delicate fingers of Maire's tan, rough hand gently gripped and lifted her daughter's chin. Looking down at the girl, she slowly nodded from side to side, her face set now. *No more. Enough.*

"Eileen, my darling, what has happened has happened and you are now again . . . and safe . . . at Derrynane."

"But Mama, Denis said . . ."

"I shall tend to Denis. 'Tis at a time like this that I wish your dear father could have lived forever." She shook her head. "For now, my girl, you must rest. You will take my bed and I shall see to it that your room is opened."

Her arm at her daughter's back, Maire led her to the huge canopied bed she had shared with Donal Mór Ó Conaill for so many years and, in a fluid motion, the girl climbed up, sat and then lay, scrunching her legs up. Maire kissed Eileen's forehead, and by the time she reached the bottom of the stairs, Eileen was asleep.

It proved to be a sleep that was as fitful as it was needed as some of the events of the last eight months raced through her mind.

Derrynane—February 1760

That Eileen was to be wed had first been made known—in a deliberately off-handed manner, almost in passing—by her eldest brother one stormy, desperate evening in early February, whilst the family was at table; it surprised her siblings, shocked her mother – and, in addition to both, numbed Eileen.

It had, ironically, occurred within days of the first of that month, which was St. Brigid's Day, the Christianisation of the pagan feast of *Imbolc*, being a "female" holiday of the old Gaelic calendar, a time of hoping and planning celebrated as the first day of spring. As the Irish adopted Christianity, Brigid of Kildare seemed to have miraculously spanned the distance from bearing the same name as the Gaelic fertility goddess to becoming an abbess and saint of the Church.

As more of the facts and circumstances of the proposed match became known, there had ensued numerous heated discussions amongst mother, eldest son and other sons. Only once, at the initial meeting that very evening between Denis and their mother, was Eileen present, behind closed doors.

"Who is this man?" Maire had demanded coldly following the tumultuous scene that had just ensued in the dining room upon the announcement. She and her eldest son now sat by a blazing though smoky fire in what had come to be called "the library," two of its walls being bookcases filled from floor to ceiling. Denis had pointedly seated Eileen alone on the periphery, in a high-backed leather chair by the shelves, away from the fire.

"A fine gentlemen, John O'Connor of Ballyhar, near Firies, a man of property and standing," Denis drawled in reply, his long clay pipe still in his mouth.

"Will he come to pay me court, brother?" Eileen asked softly in her throaty voice from across the room.

"He will be coming to take you *home*," he said abruptly, without even looking at his sister, whose eyes grew a bit wider.

"And when is this to happen?" asked Maire.

"Quite shortly . . . he may perhaps even now be en route," said Denis, starting to stand.

Eileen's mouth fell open, while Maire's jaw set. "Eileen," she requested gently, "leave us, please."

Shaken, the girl did as she was told, closing the door with a gentle click. She retrieved her long green cloak from the hall chair where she'd left it and drew it about her; pulling the hood over her head, she stepped outside into a heavy rain shower.

She began walking slowly and then abruptly stood still, her arms folded beneath her bosom within her cloak. She knew these types of things were arranged for a variety of reasons. "Alliances" was the term she'd heard used—political, commercial, even religious; they were the bases of many a marriage in Ireland in these sad, troubled times. She just hadn't thought . . . Walking again, she whispered into the by then soft mist, "But not to me, not now. The O'Connells have no need of alliances . . . or do we? . . . and where is Firies?"

Eileen shook her head gently and resumed walking, her mind somersaulting. . . . *How is it, why is it . . . that I have been chosen to wed this man? . . . What possibly could the reasons be?* she mused, again walking in silence, her thin-soled, delicate French slippers having immediately grown damp from the thick grass, already wet before the rain had begun to fall.

Some steps more, the rain was falling heavily now, such that Eileen could feel the drops as they *thwopt* onto her hood.

She suddenly stopped again, this time smiling ironically, nodding now, her racing thoughts reaching, settling for the moment in ancient Ireland. As she knew the lengthy poetic tale well, she recalled that at the beginning of the *Táin Bó Cúailnge*, Queen Maeve speaks to her husband, Ailill, of the six daughters of Eochaid Feidlech, listing the sisters by name, then saying, ". . .

and myself, Maeve, the highest and haughtiest of them. I outdid them in grace and giving battle and warlike combat. . . ."

With this thought, Eileen reflected, *I am indeed frequently compared to Queen Maeve, am I not? . . . Her stubbornness, her pride, her arrogance, her "un-ladylike behaviour."* She laughed softly. *Though in her clan there were but six sisters, the daughters of Eochaid Feidlech, and we O'Connells are eight in total, daughters of Donal Mór. . . .*

As Maeve spoke in relation to hers, am I not myself, Eileen—she smiled beneath her hood, the rain again having become a subtle mist—*"the highest and haughtiest of them," the daughters of Donal Mór? Considering my own, I surely and with no question "outdo them in grace" . . . and there is no doubt at all that 'tis I and I alone of all of us who would "give battle," and engage in "war-like combat."* She laughed aloud again, then stared into the blackness before her, slightly turning her hooded head towards the lighted windows and then again, gently biting her lower lip, she returned her gaze to the seeming void of the night.

As she did, the thick, outwardly sodden woollen cocoon of her green mantle embracing her, she briefly pictured her three eldest sisters, Nora, Joan and Alice, all well married now with seemingly good husbands and each with many children and "away," though none all that far from Derrynane; two in Kerry, the other in Cork. Whenever she'd seen them, either separately or together, each seemed primarily concerned that Eileen be aware they were expensively gowned in the latest high French fashion, *which impresses me not,* she thought dismissively, *the work of the Jesuits with each of them having been for naught,* her condescension—even in her mind—deliberately cruel.

Considering Abigail, whom she adored and to whom of all the family she was the closest, Eileen thought, *But she is perhaps too kind, too temperate . . . perhaps even too good, though I love her more than any of my siblings.*

And whenever Eileen thought of her twin, Mary, she was immediately reminded of what their mother frequently said of her daughters: "No twin girls ever have been less alike, more distinct from each other than my darlings." *Mild to the point of being passive, Mary is . . . she will take a horse for her own only if it is no more spirited than a child's pony. She is a dear girl, but . . .*

Eileen shook her head again dismissively in terms of Mary, half a foot shorter, blond, quiet, oft-times distant, even aloof—so different from herself.

She briefly considered the little girls, Elizabeth, only nine, and Anne, ten, who shared a mischievous demeanour. Thinking of them, she laughed but withheld a final opinion, as *potential, I believe they indeed may both have.* . . .

Though she knew herself to be outspokenly opinionated and, she felt, all too frequently criticised for being out of place in her remarks, Eileen was certain that she was bright—"brilliant," she had heard the priests say, and "strong," most definitely strong—of that she had no doubt, and with all of these characterisations she was fully comfortable. Additionally, she was impatient with the hesitancy of others to act, and harshly disdainful of what she saw as most people's reluctance to speak honestly.

"So then, if this be the case . . . why should not I be the one chosen to wed this man . . . whoever he may be?" Eileen concluded aloud, as she smiled archly. Why not indeed? She turned then towards the unsteady glow cast by the flickering candles within the house.

Before walking in their direction, she bent and removed her now soaked silk shoes, the grass cold but embracingly soft beneath her bare feet. She moved towards the looming door, her slippers dangling from the fingertips of her left hand. As her right fingers rested on the latch, she momentarily considered rejoining her mother and brother—*perhaps I should tell Denis how wise a decision I believe he has made,* she thought with a laugh. Tugging the latch, she decided aloud, "Perhaps not!" Her wet feet padding silently, drying quickly as she traversed the thick Chinese rugs in the hall, and barely sounding as she ascended the stairs, she quietly went to her room and was soon albeit not wholly peacefully asleep.

As—and after—Eileen had walked, reflected and concluded, the conversation in the library had continued, at best genteelly combative, at worst angry and accusatory.

At one point, almost immediately following Eileen's dismissal, Denis had looked icily at his mother, drawn deeply on his pipe and exhaled a thick cloud of bitter smoke. "'Tis a matter of business, Mother: O'Connor has much property. He has been widowed these seven years, has spent his life assembling and preserving his lands and properties and wishes . . ."

"And wishes what?"

"He wishes a wife, a young one; indeed, he *very much* wishes a very pretty, very young wife."

"How is this a concern of yours, son? How is it in any way *ours?*"

Denis sighed and glared sharply, impatiently, at his mother. "It is very much our concern—mine especially now that Father is dead—in that O'Connor is, as I said, a man of lands, in Ireland and the New World, of vast wealth. He also maintains significant relationships in Dublin and London, relationships we do not have, relationships which can be used to 'protect' us.

"Additionally, he has a great deal of something else we do not have, something the critical importance of which neither Father nor you seem to understand. . . ."

Her resentment immediate, Maire brusquely interrupted. "And what is it that you feel the O'Connells lack, knowledge about which somehow eluded Donal Mór and now seemingly myself as well?"

Denis shook his head incredulously, his eyes wide, "'Tis *money*, Mother: pounds, shillings, gold. What you and the great Donal Mór have *never* understood is that we live much like the poorest of tenants, the peasants. . . . Basically, all too often *we barter*; the only difference is that we barter French wine for Alsatian lace, Spanish leathers for Syrian brass, instead of a load of potatoes for a load of turnips . . . and, indeed, we all too frequently *do* trade produce, butter, hides for French fashion." He sighed in dismissive disgust.

Maire, was further reflexively enraged by her son's arrogant, caustically expressed disrespect for his father, but all the more so because, deep within herself, she realised that Denis was, at least in part, correct: Their enterprises, whilst resilient and growing, always were in need of currency were they to become even stronger and more extant. Despite this reality, Donal Mór had refused to engage in the type of alliances that Denis was now suggesting, using a daughter as a pawn in order to secure a continuing source of such capital.

"We are not the Habsburgs, not the Bourbons," Donal Mór had declared on more than one occasion. "We do not prostitute our daughters. We are better than that. We are better people than they are!"

It was true that in their continuing successful efforts to thwart the Cromwellian-imposed though by now unevenly enforced prohibitions against significant land ownership by Catholics, the O'Connells had created and maintained a complex system of silent and well-disguised unrecorded deeds, leases and subleases, carefully cultivating both personal and business relationships with accommodating neighbours who had themselves turned Protestant to protect their own property. The results of this strategy had enabled the O'Connells to better secure the sometimes tenuous grip with which they held onto their lands, as well as to constantly expand what were carefully referred to as the family's "commercial interests."

For a number of years, from the safe haven of Derrynane, the family had conducted a sophisticated and highly profitable smuggling operation that revolved around a complex trade/countertrade system, effectively connecting Ireland with all of Catholic Europe, North Africa and the Eastern Mediterranean. Goods regularly "imported" into Ireland via the remote and largely secure though still carefully guarded harbours in South and West Kerry, included French wines, brandies, silks, laces and fine men's, women's and even children's clothing, Spanish leather goods, as well as things rare, many virtually unknown in Ireland, such as brass and bronze metalwork from Syria, elegant furniture and other exotic wood products from Egypt and artworks, including mosaic renderings from Jerusalem. Even an Old Testament in Hebrew had been brought from the Levant and now rested on a striking Italian mahogany bookstand in the library in which mother and son now sat.

The O'Connells had even taken to bringing into Ireland a variety of exotic horses—strong, strikingly powerful, regal Andalusians, ghostly white Arabians, cloaked with an aura of mystery, invariably displaying an unsubtle disdain for all those about them, equine and human. Eileen's treasured Bull was, for example, a Frisian—of an ancient breed that had originated in Friesland in what had become under Emperor Charles V the Austrian Netherlands. The O'Connell children were enthralled when they learnt that these horses' ancestors were said to have carried knights into battle during the Early and High Middle Ages.

Donal Mór had originally acquired an exemplary all-black Frisian stallion after seeing him being ridden by a young officer of the Imperial Austrian Dragoons, returned to Iveragh from Vienna on leave. Judging the imposing animal to be *in perfect proportion to my own bulk*, the patriarch purchased the horse almost immediately from the surprised, suddenly-prosperous subaltern; so pleased was the elder O'Connell with the horse's size and agility that he'd almost immediately set about acquiring a mare, they would together become sire and dam to Bull and several other O'Connell horses, as well as being the origins of a long line of fine, sturdy Iveragh draft as well as saddle animals. It was the subtly chestnut mare who was responsible for Bull's striking appearance: the classic long, thick and wavy black Frisian mane and tail, offsetting his deep chestnut coat and distinctive leg "feathers." The horse's presence had become even more dramatic by that he had ultimately reached a size of some seventeen hands.

The principal "customers" for the goods the O'Connells brought into Ireland were wealthy families of the Protestant Ascendancy, principally in the provinces of Leinster and Munster.

Records—particularly the spoken ones, passed from generation to generation by the itinerant poets and harpers, each in their own way being chroniclers of Gaelic Ireland—indicated that the O'Connells had attained positions of varying degree and consequence in the lower-to-middling ranks of the Gaelic aristocracy of Kerry as early as at least the late thirteenth century. The most significant title held appeared to have been that of hereditary constable or warder of Ballycarbery Castle, located some nineteen miles to the west of Derrynane, this under the Lords of Desmond, the MacCarthy Mór. Despite that, as one of the smaller clans in County Kerry, the O'Connells had at some point been absorbed into the more powerful MacCarthys (as the result of which they would possess no clan pedigree) during Elizabethan times, one of the O'Connells, named Morgan, served as high sheriff of Kerry.

In the mid-1650s, as the cataclysm unleashed by Cromwell's invasion engulfed Gaelic Ireland, Ballycarbery, as were so many other castles, was sacked and virtually destroyed, although its haunting, starkly beautiful ruins remained, high on their grassy hill, still challenging the limitless ocean beyond.

Following this loss of status and home, whilst some of the O'Connells, confronted with Cromwell's decreed alternative of going "to hell or to Connaught" chose the latter (primarily the starkly-green, ocean windswept hills of Clare) and thus departed both Munster and the pages of history, others were more fortunate. Following Ballycarbery's destruction, the last warder, Daniel MacGeoffrey O'Connell, along with his wife Alice, had quietly settled on lands near Waterville, several miles east of the ruined castle. It was their oldest son, Captain John O'Connell, who, having fought through the Williamite wars with the armies of James II but not departing with the "Wild Geese" for France following the king's defeats at the Boyne and Limerick, had positioned himself such that he was able to secure the lease of a significant—said to ultimately come to consist of some tens of thousands of acres—tract of land, the inescapable remoteness and perceived poor quality of which appeared to have rendered them wholly undesirable. In 1702 he and his own wife, Elizabeth, there built the first rough structure, the house now called Derrynane—*Doire F'hiondin*, or *the oakwood of Saint Fionain*—which his first son, Donal Mór, and Maire continued to renovate and expand, beginning the process of siding it with slabs of slate.

The dwelling, sprawling yet as one drew close to the massive, iron-banded, gleamingly varnished oak doors, somehow inviting, continued to face inland and north, the family's security virtually assured by the fact that most of Derrynane's lands lay between a fortuitous combination of looming hills, cliffs and mountains, several of the latter rising two thousand feet and more out of the stony soil and deep green glens, and the Atlantic Ocean. Not only was the trackless area remote, it was virtually inaccessible, even the entrance to the harbour at Derrynane Bay being all but invisible from the sea.

Never doubting that the location was the perfect one from which to operate their risky—indeed, at times, distinctly dangerous—enterprises, the O'Connells left little if anything to chance, it being commonly said that "The O'Connells trust only the O'Connells," a tight circle of relatives and friends, sons of fathers who themselves were sons of fathers who had given and proven their loyalty to the O'Connells.

Men and women, children of the extended family, cousins and retainers alike, were all skilled in the use of firearms, the children—the girls even—being taught that, on the remote chance of coming upon a stranger, they were to "Fire first a warning shot, and only then inquire as to the man's purposes." It was well known that more than a few suspect individuals, unable to provide a credible reason for drawing near to the sanctuary at Derrynane, had paid for it with their lives. The people had long understood that the O'Connells cared only for themselves; they protected themselves and their own. To them, the life of a stranger was regarded as being valueless against the need to maintain Derrynane secure. It was equally well known that the same fate would befall anyone who even threatened, much less caused harm to any of them or theirs.

Within their sea-bound, rocky stronghold, the constant roar of pristine mountain streams challenging that of the Atlantic's waves, the O'Connells lived well, in what was largely a self-contained environment, those necessities they could not themselves produce there, along with significant luxuries, were brought in by their own ships.

The O'Connell children—boys and girls alike—were educated from an early age by a succession of, it always seemed, handsome young Jesuit priests, who also arrived aboard the O'Connells' ships. It was through the efforts of these talented men that the children quickly became highly literate, numerate and minimally trilingual (Irish, English and French); the brighter ones, of whom there had been many, were also schooled in Latin, and a number in Greek as well. The young O'Connells were especially well acquainted with the works of Shakespeare and other leading English authors and playwrights, and acquired a significant understanding of world geography, European history and Catholic teachings. Spanish riding masters taught the O'Connell children to ride, as well as instructing them in the many complexities of equestrian care, in the course of which imparting to a number of them a working knowledge of Spanish. Art teachers were regularly in residence, as were music and dancing masters.

It was from their parents, as well as from the bards, the peripatetic *seanachie* (story-tellers) who, their ranks greatly diminished, still visited, occasionally remaining for weeks, that the children learnt the tales and poems of ancient Ireland, becoming familiar with, amongst many others, the *Ulster Cycle,* including the heroics of Cúchulainn and the Red Branch Knights and the arrogance of Queen Maeve, as well as the exploits of Niamh, Fionn mac Cumhaill and the Fianna, and of Oisín and his journey to *Tír na nÓg.*

The children periodically journeyed aboard the family's ships, their destinations largely determined by the politics of Europe; a number travelled to France, Spain or Portugal, others to Italy, whilst the more adventurous sailed as far as North Africa and the Eastern Mediterranean.

All of this notwithstanding, the fact remained that the O'Connells, as secure, even as powerful as they were in the world they had created, indeed continued largely deficient in the areas of hard currency and influence, just as Denis had said.

"'T'woud all be much tidier if the O'Connells had simply accepted the Church of Ireland," he pronounced rudely. "We would have none of these burdens."

Standing abruptly, Maire flared, "How dare you suggest that any of us turn our back on Holy Mother Church? I cannot believe that any child of mine would . . ."

His interruption abrupt, immediate, Denis raised his right hand dismissively and sighed yet again, this time with an air of yet greater annoyance. "Fine, then, we are devout Irish Catholics. We have kept our lands despite Cromwell and those and what he spawned; good for us, then. We still have insufficient money with which to conduct our business. We require funds—and we need to be joined with someone like O'Connor of Firies, who can do more for us than simply help us hold on to . . ." he spread his arms open, "this . . .

"'Tis quite simple, Mother; O'Connor is prepared to transfer to us a substantial sum of money, to cede certain valuable properties—not in Ireland—to us and to provide us entree to Dublin Castle, not to mention Court in

London, and form a strong, continuing alliance with us—something we have never had."

"'All this' in return for . . . ?" she said, her voice now trembling, for she was certain of the answer she would hear.

"Eileen," he said curtly.

Whilst Maire leaned her elbows against her chair's high back, Denis continued, his tone now approximating what it would sound like were he to be discussing a transaction involving horses, his voice a mixture of impatience and condescension: "Let us be honest here. Unlike her twin, Eileen is a headstrong and difficult girl, though at the same time—and I do not necessarily agree—she is said to be quite a good deal prettier than Mary. Odd is that not, as they shared your womb for some nine months?

"At twenty, Abigail is aging rapidly, and though she is more pliant than Eileen, she has what the men call plain good looks, rather than what your dear *Eibhlin Dubh* apparently offers—the hair, the eyes." He sniffed, his own eyes rolling. "It seems some men find these features, and what I would have to say is her inordinate height, as well as her tiresome degree of intelligence, somehow attractive—at least I am told." He took a deep breath, "I find her irksome, at best.

"In the event, John O'Connor apparently believes that he is amongst those who look favourably on all of these attributes. God knows why he would, but this gives Eileen far more value than I have ever placed on her. She is now worth something significant to us. *Now* do you understand, Mother?"

Shaking her head, taking some steps away from where she had been standing, Maire turned back, visibly trembling, steadying herself with her right hand now gripping the high back of the chair, and with the index finger of her left hand she pointed at her tall, spare son. "Denis, you are your father's and my firstborn child, our firstborn son. Hard as it is to do so at this moment, I love you. To a degree, I have come to respect your judgment, at least until now, though I am loath to ask this next question."

The man drew on his pipe, his eyes focused on the bowl. Without waiting for the question, his face expressionless, he exhaled pipe smoke and said simply, "At his last birthday, which was only recently, he achieved sixty-two years."

Maire stood frozen, her left hand too now gripping the chair back. "The girl is barely sixteen. How could you ever agree to this?"

"I agreed to nothing." Denis waved his left hand dismissively, "'Twas *O'Connor* who agreed, indeed quite immediately, with *my* proposal, Mother. I approached him with this offer some months ago, when first I became aware of the opportunity."

"Holy Mother of God, son o'mine, how *could* you?!"

Denis rose abruptly and stepped closer to his mother, only the wing chair behind which she now stood separating them, towering over her, his tone now coldly cruel. "As I have said, Mother, 'tis simply a matter of business. Substantial sums of money—some quite soon, actually—and some valuable properties will come to our family as a result. And, of course, certain doors will immediately open to us in both Dublin and London, behind which sit men who will see to our continuing security. There is nothing more to be said here," he drawled dismissively, "'Tis my decision alone and I have made it. The agreements have been written by the lawyers and already executed."

He turned suddenly and resumed his seat, dropping heavily into the solid leather chair.

Her breathing marked, her eyes squinting coldly, Maire did not move.

Staring in seeming disbelief that his mother yet remained in the room, Denis flicked the fingers of his right hand in the delicate upward motion all knew he employed when dismissing a servant. "As I have said, this conversation is now ended . . . *Madame*." His words hung frigidly in the silence.

Finally vanquished, her cheeks scarlet, Maire turned sharply and stalked silently out, the explosive sound of the door slamming behind her echoing throughout the rambling house.

Denis turned slightly in his seat, looking deeply into the now merrily dancing fire and relighting his pipe, he smiled, nodding his head.

Derrynane—Autumn 1760

Though what the little ship's master had called a "pleasant float" down the Kenmare River from Kenmare to Derrynane had been that, Eileen had nevertheless travelled by horseback over rough ground for five long days from Firies to reach the boat at Kenmare, there being no actual roads to speak of—the few "easier" parts of the trek being over tracks, themselves very rough versions of nothing more than what would come to be known as bridle paths—she was truly weary, so she did sleep some, if not soundly.

She was nevertheless partially awake, gazing into the gathering dusk, when her mother returned. A welcome touch of humour had been provided by a massive grey wolfhound who belonged to her youngest brother, Hugh, now five, whom he had named simply Madramór ("big dog" in Irish), who'd found his way into Maire's rooms and climbed up on the bed, nuzzling next to Eileen as she was sleeping most deeply. At some point she had awakened to see his big, heavy head resting on her hip, causing her to startle and then to laugh softly.

When Maire entered the room, the dog had resumed his sound sleep and was snoring softly; seeing this, Maire could not help but smile.

Hearing her mother's soft steps, Eileen slowly sat up, rousing the sleepy dog and eased her feet into the soft leather slippers her mother had set next to the bed. Whilst Eileen stood quietly, Maire softly brushed the girl's gleaming black tresses, smoothing some down her back and some over her shoulders and breasts. *Eibhlin Dubh*—"Dark Eileen," she whispered and kissed her daughter's hair. The girl smiled albeit weakly at the name given to her by her mother when she was a small child; with her unique features—her hair as well as her piercing, deeply blue eyes and near alabaster skin—all come to her from her mother's "dark people," the O'Donoughues at Glenflesk, Eileen was then and remained the only dark one amongst the largely blond, ruddy O'Connells. It was by some ironic twist of fate that amongst her original family, Maire—blond, fair and petite—was the exceptional one.

"Do you wish to join your sisters and brothers at table, my darling?"

Eileen pondered for a brief moment and sighed. "I am unusually weary, Mama. I do not think I wish to see anyone—not even Abby—until tomorrow."

Maire nodded. "They will most certainly understand."

As the women sat quietly conversing, there was an unexpected sharp rap, the door opening immediately, and, unbidden, Denis O'Connell stepped into the room, not bothering to close the door behind him, his face flushed, his eyes watery.

An instantly strained silence replaced what had been the women's gentle voices.

Denis grimly, quickly eyed his sister and then his mother, avoiding eye contact with both before speaking into the room, directing his words to neither woman.

"I simply wished to formally welcome *the Widow O'Connor*," he announced, his eyes scanning the walls, the ceiling. "I trust that she will enjoy her *visit* here," he continued slowly, coldly.

A bitter smile creasing her face, Eileen shook her head wearily and turned away, stepping towards a window and looking into the darkness, her back to the room.

Maire abruptly grabbed the left lapel of her son's dusty brown coat. "Was that really necessary, Denis? Is it not enough that she has been through what she has, without you . . ."

Wordlessly, the man slowly removed his mother's fingers from his garment, his own fingers hard, his touch not gentle, his eyes looking searingly down into hers as he bent to speak. "A *visit, you* will understand . . . and *she*—" he gestured with a bony finger, as if he were thrusting a knife towards Eileen's back—"will be *made* to understand, that is all this is to be: a *very . . . brief . . . stay*; nothing more," he drawled and immediately turned and walked through the partially open door, leaving it open wide.

The women simply looked at each other, puzzlement on both of their faces.

Wordlessly, Maire extended her hand to her daughter, and silently Eileen took it. Mother and daughter left the room, though Eileen turned and pointedly closed the door behind them.

As much she loved Eileen and wanted to listen, to care for, to help her begin to heal, Maire was weary. As promised, she'd seen that Eileen's room had been opened, that her bed had been made with fresh linen and coverlets, that a fire had been laid and was now blazing, even flowers placed on a dresser, and as she and the girl reached the room's closed door, Maire stood on tiptoe to kiss her wounded child. Reaching up and placing her hand on Eileen's head, she blessed her, kissed her again and returned quietly to her rooms.

Entering her room, Eileen slowly walked about. The air *was* fresh albeit, as expected, evening damp, the fire in contrast being both bright and warming and the crisp bed linens smelt of sunshine and sea air. She smiled at the flowers, including orchids and palm fronds from Maire's always exotic gardens. Her battered leather satchels were lined up against a wall, open and empty, her clothes and belongings already placed in drawers, on hooks, on shelves.

The room was peaceful, and at that moment she felt wholly safe for the first time in a long while, there in the steady light of two barely flickering candles. She stepped towards a dresser and from the drawer where she had always kept them, she noted with a smile, retrieved a long nightdress, tossed it on her bed and then wriggled out of her dusty and—now looking at the mud spattered across the skirt, caking the hem in places—dirty black dress. She held it up, then letting it drop to the floor. "*You* shall be burnt in the morning." She shed her chemise and cotton hose and, as she slipped the nightdress over her head, laughed bitterly. *'Tis the Widow O'Connor I am . . .* she thought, blowing out one of the candles, *come home.*

She climbed onto her high bed, and with just a single candle now burning on the nightstand, leaned back against the down pillows.

The Widow O'Connor: Eileen had grown accustomed both to the reference and the reality it embodied whilst she was still at Ballyhar, but here, now, it suddenly seemed more a condemnation, a sentence. *Holymotherofgod, what is to become of me?* She blew out the candle and before the tears she'd shed dried on her cheeks she was asleep.

Eileen slowly came awake in her still almost dark bedroom. The bedclothes were smooth; she'd barely moved during the night. She rolled onto her back and rubbed her eyes, and as she did, warm female lips bent and gently kissed her forehead. It was Abby. Eileen stretched and smiled.

"Good morning, sister," she murmured and, yawning, "It *is morning*, is it not?"

"And a good morning to you, my darling—and yes, 'tis morning of a new day," said Abigail as she sat on the bed, and as she did so, Eileen scrunched up, her back against her pillows.

Abby cast a glance at and gestured towards Eileen's dress of yesterday, now a puddle of dusty, mud-spattered black fabric on the floor. "I take it you shan't be wearing *that* today?"

Eileen draped her legs over the side of the bed. "Nor any other day," she said wearily, untying her hair and shaking her head so it tumbled over her shoulders and down her back.

She slipped off the bed and, now standing, noticed that Abby, who had clambered down from her perch on the edge of the high bed, was dressed for the saddle. Her sister, four years older than she, was at least four inches shorter than Eileen, and with her hair, softly curly and reddish-blond, lying just past her shoulders, much more than possessing what Denis had always said were plain good looks. Indeed, much more than being merely pretty, Abigail's light, sky-blue eyes sparkled, a smile or the warmest of laughs was always close to the surface and her complexion was glowing, healthy, with cascades of faint freckles over her nose and down her cheeks, her manner elegantly casual. She possessed an outlook and appearance that radiated warmth, exuberance, sunshine itself and an infectious laugh. Eileen had always felt that Abby truly loved most people and disliked very few things in life. She sang (adequately), played the harpsichord (quite well), painted (poorly) and, like most of the siblings, was a strong, athletic rider. This morning, a flowing grey woollen cloak covered a padded cotton dress, and she wore thick black hose, a pair of boots having been left at the door.

"Are you going somewhere so early?" the younger sister asked.

"*We* are going *somewhere*. Do you require clothing, my love?" Abby responded matter-of-factly, without turning away from the window, as her eyes continued to follow the arching flight of a pair of gulls.

Eileen stretched, shook her head in the negative and, pointing at it, walked towards the armoire, casting only a quick look at the face in the looking glass on the door. She peered in and retrieved a chemise, along with a long, heavy brown woollen skirt, a white linen shirt and a hip-length black jacket of the same rough wool as the skirt. Tossing the clothing on the bed, she lifted a pair of yesterday-muddy, now-gleaming boots, into which a pair of hose had been stuffed, off of the floor of the armoire and walked back towards the bed, where she dressed quickly.

"'Tis sorry I was and am that with you I did not speak last evening, my love," Eileen began, and before she could continue Abby waved her right hand in an elegantly dismissive gesture.

"Ah, my darling, I could tell even from a distance how weary you were, could only imagine how long and difficult was your journey. I only regret that it was with our eldest brother alone you did speak . . . and Mama," she added softly.

Eileen responded with a gentle nod and a weak though grateful smile. *"Ta . . . agus mamái."*

Carrying their boots, the sisters quietly traversed the lengthy corridor and padded as quietly as possible down the immense staircase, hastening along a thick carpet running down the middle of the hall to a massive, iron-banded door at the rear of the house. As Eileen began to push the portal open, using her left shoulder, Abigail reminded her, "It creaks on closing. Just leave it."

The door left ever so slightly ajar, they strode quickly, the broken stones and crushed shells of the footpath cold and sharp on their unshod feet, the air moist, sweet with a mixture of smoke from a number of turf fires and the complex maritime aromas wafting up from Derrynane Bay at high tide.

As soon as they reached it, they sat quickly on a wrought-iron bench; then booted, their long skirts sweeping the damp grass, they quickly made their way through a magical, sun-dappled mist to the stone stables. Constructed much like the kitchen building, which they'd just passed, but higher and larger, the lower part of the stable's walls were either slated or panelled with rough wood. The floor was hard-packed earth, flecked with or in some places completely carpeted in sweet-smelling hay. Stalls for as many as two dozen horses lined both sides of the main part of the stable building, each fronted by a gleaming, heavily varnished gate, with brass fixtures, several sporting lustrous brass plates, engraved with the name of the resident animal.

As they stepped into the building, a young groom called William was just beginning his day, filling buckets of oats for his dozen or so charges, a muck rake awaiting him as soon as the buckets were hung. The mud and clumps of dung on his otherwise gleaming boots indicated that he'd been outside with some of the younger horses already. The odours from his boots mingled with those of the barn: the fresh hay, the as yet unmucked stalls, the low turf fire from William's quarters. To Eileen, it smelt just like a barn was supposed to.

"Ladies!" He smiled and pointed.

The massive chestnut Bull and a dusty grey mare, both already tacked up, were just emptying their oat buckets. "Daisy," he gestured to the mare. "You remember Daisy, Lady Eileen, yes?"

As she mounted her stallion, Eileen smiled ironically, remembering the day she'd finally broken the spirited, in some ways obstinate Daisy to the saddle, William having been charged by their gregarious older brother, Morgan, to "keep the fool girl from killing herself."

Reading her mind, he continued, "Ah, and wasn't Mister Morgan wrong, m'lady?" He laughed as he took Abby's left hand whilst she swung herself up onto the soft-eyed mare. "The way he spoke, you would have thought this sweet girl a stallion," he went on, shaking his head as he gently stroked Daisy's withers.

Both women now sat mounted astride, neither of them owning a side-saddle. "'Tisn't wholly ladylike to be astride," Maire always said, "but 'tisn't always safe in this rough country to be too ladylike."

William opened the back barn door, which opened away from the house, onto an open space and a rough trail leading out of the immediate Derrynane close.

The girls guided the horses out as quietly as they could, their hooves softly thumping in the moist earth, their bridles jangling, but neither loud enough to be heard at the house.

They rode quietly around Maire's gardens and up a gentle rise, where the trail switchbacked several times as they climbed relatively quickly up and away and out into the open, if *open* could describe the still sharply tilted, gorse-covered, rock-strewn terrain over which they continued to ascend until they were above the lower hills and the few tall treetops and were able to turn and look out to sea.

Eileen sat quietly, her leather-gloved left hand gently stroking Bull's neck, the palm of the other flat on her muscular right thigh. Her legs were warm beneath the thick wool of her skirt and she adjusted her feet in the stirrups. She turned her face to try to catch the warmth of the rising sun, just now glinting off her shining stirrups and Bull's brass fittings, and then back to the ocean.

"My God, 'tis good to see this view," she said softly as she gazed at the ruins of what had been St. Fionin's Abbey, the beach and the islands, many of them being simply familiar large rocks in Derrynane Bay. Since she was a very little girl, Eileen had always loved one grouping of islands—which today she could make out—referred to, by size, as being the "Bull," the "Cow" and the "Calf," from the largest of which she had, fittingly, taken her beloved mount's name—even as a colt, it was apparent that he would be a very large horse.

The panorama before her embraced so much of her own life and history, in many ways defining and distinguishing, at least in part, the unique person she was, as it did all the O'Connells of Derrynane. Her beloved father, those brothers and sisters who had been born and died before her own birth, unknown to her but prayed for nevertheless, and other O'Connells lay beneath the sandy soil by the ruins of the Abbey. The endless sky, at the moment a dazzling blue, and the equally illimitable sea, so unpredictable: gentle as it was when it brought her home the day before, wild, seemingly boundlessly powerful and awe-inspiring as it was more often.

After silently scanning the horizon, Eileen's eyes looked almost straight down on Derrynane House itself, plumes of largely turf smoke rising slowly straight up from some of the main house's six chimneys, until the soft breeze from the Bay caught them, playing with them and twisting them. The same was true of the other blue ribbons of smoke ascending from the much smaller but still substantial scattered white lime-washed houses. These buildings, some thatched-roofed, other shingled, belonged to those families some referred to as the *lesser O'Connells,* as well as the much more humble cottages of the tenant families, most in good repair, several not. All of the dwellings, and the people who dwelt within them, in many ways different, yet intimately connected, shared the vividly emerald-green, rock-punctuated panorama upon which Eileen gazed.

Eying the expanse of water again, Eileen noticed the small craft that had brought her home appearing from behind one of the larger islands.

Turning to Abby, Eileen sighed and gestured towards it. "I must tell you, sister, I have *never* been more joyful to see any boat in my entire life than I was when I saw ours and, with it, good Master Dennehy at Kenmare."

Abby eased up next to her younger sister and rested a leather-gloved hand on her knee and squeezed it. "I can only imagine." She smiled.

Eileen shook her head sharply, such that some of her hair tumbled about and over one side of her face. With her own gloved hand, she pushed it back over her shoulder, her facial expression suddenly grim. "No, my darling girl, you cannot *ever* imagine . . . but let us find a spot and sit awhile, and I shall then tell you all that it is that you cannot imagine."

She gathered the reins in her right hand and gently nudged Bull forward, using her knees, Abigail following.

Following an unseen switchback pattern they'd used for as long as both girls could remember, they continued to climb for perhaps another five minutes until they were finally on generally flat albeit still rock-strewn and gorse-covered ground, and Eileen reined Bull in.

As Abby settled both horses, Eileen clambered up onto a large flat rock, stripping off her gloves and sliding further so her back and shoulders rested against the now sun-warmed outcropping behind, her right leg stretched out in front of her, her left drawn up, so her hand rested on her knee. Seeing her sister approaching, with her right hand she patted the space next to her, and Abigail joined her.

Eileen took a deep breath. "So now, I shall tell it all . . . once and then never again. You recall when they came for me?"

Abby did, all too vividly, so she nodded silently and rested her head against her sister's shoulder as Eileen took a deep breath and began to speak.

County Kerry, Ireland—February–
March 1760

A small, strange-looking party had arrived at Derrynane one dull, grey Tuesday morning in mid-February, the only notice of which was that one of the tenants, returning from an errand for Denis and riding one of the stable's younger and faster horses, had passed them on the rough track and advised him they would be arriving shortly.

"'Tis a young man, finely dressed, sir, and two women, not at all well dressed, sir, and them leading some weary and sad-looking animals, sir," the man had advised, twisting his rough felt hat in his gnarled hands, his eyes averted from his landlord's typically disdainful gaze. Though Denis had arched his eyebrow at the mention of a "young man," he had nodded and, waving the man off, gone to locate his mother.

Following a brief, tense conversation with her son, Maire had sought out Eileen and brought her to her rooms, the girl wearing a heavy, dark blue wool dress.

The women sat in armchairs by the fire.

"Denis advises that Squire O'Connor, or perhaps someone on his behalf, and others are approaching."

Eileen sat silently, her eyes welling with tears, and looked at her mother.

"My darling, you are packed and as ready to depart as possible. I regret they have chosen to come overland, but . . ." Her voice trailed off and she drew her chair closer to her daughter. "We have spoken much these weeks, but I must say some things to you, my darling girl. You must listen carefully. I shall say what I must only once, so you must keep it all in your heart and mind." She paused and looked into Eileen's deep blue eyes.

The girl nodded.

"You must never forget who it is you are: the daughter of Donal Mór Ó Conaill."

". . . and of Maire ní Dhuibh, of the 'Fighting O'Donoughues of Glenflesk,' proud denizens of Robbers Glen," Eileen, her husky voice strong, certain, nodded in her mother's direction, her expression warm.

Maire smiled back and very gently nodded. "Very well, then, *two* strong bloodlines you have." Pausing, she continued. "But 'tis the O'Connells from whom you come, to whom we both belong and of whom we both are—and 'tis the O'Connells who will protect you, as they have protected me these many years, daughter.

"Should you find yourself in peril, *we* shall protect you—and if by God's will 'tis ever necessary, so too shall we *avenge* you—in both, even to the taking of life."

Eileen's eyes grew wide, and her full lips parted ever so slightly.

Maire paused, then asked, "Do you understand, Eileen?"

Her eyes still wide and her lips parted, the girl nodded ever so slightly.

Reaching beneath her chair, Maire retrieved a leather bag that had been hidden by her skirts. Sitting back up, she said, "I have waited until the moment of your departure to give you this, my beloved child." She passed the satchel to Eileen, who, receiving it gently, sat back in her chair as Maire said in barely a whisper, "Open it, girl."

Holding the soft glove-leather bag on her lap, Eileen slid open the gleaming brass catch and removed a deep blue velvet sack. Maire gestured, and from the velvet Eileen withdrew what was neither a small nor a large pistol but one quite sufficient to kill a man, and placed it in her left hand, looking at it.

"'Tis beautiful, is it not?" her mother asked.

Without looking up or immediately answering, Eileen studied the weapon. The barrel was a deep, dull gunmetal grey, delicately filigreed, as were the sideplate and the hammer itself, the gleaming walnut stock strikingly gold inlaid. Eileen's long, elegantly thin fingers rubbed it slowly, almost reverently. She turned it in her hand and rested it in her lap.

"'Tis beautiful indeed."

"*This*," Maire gestured, "is in the event that we are unable to reach you in any peril, so as to permit you to protect yourself."

Eileen silently nodded.

"*This* is why you and all the girls have been taught how to use a pistol—and a rifle." Eileen nodded again. "In these sad and troubled times," her mother added. Maire passed an ample sack of ammunition and powder from her lap to Eileen's.

Then, tapping her right forefinger into her left palm, Maire continued, her tone forceful. "Make certain, Eileen, that only you know that this is in your possession. You must journey with these in your right front saddlebag and never allow them out of your sight. Once arrived at Firies, you must always maintain access to and regularly care for the weapon, as you have been taught." She reached over and covered her daughter's hands, Eileen still holding the pistol in her own. "May you never have to use this, my darling, but if you do, shoot to kill."

Eileen suddenly nodded her head in the affirmative, tossing her hair softly. In a suddenly steely voice, and a tone Maire had never heard used by her daughter, and looking directly at her mother, she said firmly, "My darling Mama, please rest assured as you rise each morning and retire each night that I know *precisely* who I am. You and Papa have taught me well from an early age. I know what I must do and, perhaps even more importantly, what I may have to do."

She patted the weapon. "And, yes, I believe I do possess the wisdom to know when to use this and, if ever necessary, the courage to kill with it . . . so, should the time come, kill I shall . . . of *that* you may be assured as well." She sighed deeply and tears welled up in her eyes yet again but did not fall. "I am indeed as ready as I can be to go, so let them arrive and let me be gone with them."

Maire leaned back, amazed but in some—*perverse*, was it? she wondered— way proud of her beautiful daughter. *After all, she is an O'Connell, is she not?* she sighed to herself, *and wasn't it the near-perfect response to what I have just this moment said to her!*

Once the strange little party had finally arrived, they spent an awkward afternoon and evening amongst the O'Connells, with much side chatting on the part of the younger O'Connells, behind hands and fans and in the course of their repeated stepping outside and away, to speak amongst themselves.

Where was Squire O'Connor himself? Who was this young man? Who were these girls, and why are they so sad and so shabbily dressed? Will these horses survive the trek back?

The young man, who introduced himself as John O'Connor the Younger, was of average height and size, dressed in expensively tailored travelling clothing, his boots supple and soft, his long blond hair tied with a flowing ribbon. He seemed quite affected, speaking English in a soft voice, and appeared to be trying to give the impression that he spoke Irish hardly at all, both with much fluttering and emphasis on his snuff box and handkerchief. He seemed patronizing to Eileen, and strangely drawn to Daniel, one of Eileen's younger brothers, less gregarious, more serious than some of the others, who immediately pronounced him odd.

"My father, the squire, has many important affairs with which to deal," he told Denis, Morgan and Daniel, "so he felt it best for me to come for the Lady Eileen. I am, after all, the eldest son."

"And these girls?"

"Oh, just girls." He smiled weakly. "I wished to bring my equerry but 'twas felt, by my father—the squire, you know—more appropriate for Lady Eileen to have servant girls with her."

"Very odd," Morgan said directly to him, using Daniel's choice of term.

"Sir?" he fluttered, dabbing his nose with a silk handkerchief.

"I said it is odd . . . *you* are odd, the whole bloody goddamned thing is odd, *sir*," said Morgan, turning away in disgust.

He then stalked back and grabbed his eldest brother's sleeve and pulled him to him. "And you, you greedy bastard, you are responsible for this. If anything—I mean *anything at all*—happens to Eileen, you will answer to all of your brothers."

Denis looked archly at Morgan; he said nothing but turned his back and walked away . . . quickly.

The meal had been generally awkward and unpleasant, the visitor attempting to be every moment at Daniel's side, the servant girls spending it in Brigid's kitchen, where whilst she fed them, she could elicit virtually nothing from them, other than a steady stream of "Thank you, mums," spoken in obviously rarely used and barely understood English, their eyes lowered. Once Brigid had lifted one of the girls' chins up, saying harshly, "Speak Irish if you wish, girl, and look at my face, not my feet."

"Beaten puppies they are," said Brigid to Annie, her pretty daughter and chief assistant in the kitchen and in helping Maire run the house.

Annie looked at the two, inhaling their food. "Indeed they are, and ill-fed as well. If Eileen . . ."

"Hush, girl! Do not even think much less say it!" her mother hissed, but then she stepped back, took a breath and said softly, "Eileen can take care of herself. Pity anyone who tries to harm her in any way." She closed her eyes; *Please God that I am right.*

Early the next morning an array of leather satchels containing Eileen's belongings were slung over four still somewhat weary-looking—though less so than when they'd arrived at Derrynane—packhorses. There were hugs and tears and a special moment during which Eileen knelt on the damp grass hugging little Hugh and rocking the both of them, whispering only to him as he sobbed softly after trying so hard to be brave. After draping her saddlebags across Bull's shoulders, with her mother's parting gift resting vigilantly in the right one, inches from where her hand would hold the reins, she took a deep breath, stood and lifted a solidly booted left foot into the gleaming stirrup of her Spanish-made saddle and swung herself effortlessly onto her beloved horse's broadly ample back.

Standing next to the horse, John O'Connor looked up at her, observing, "Such a *large* mount, Lady Eileen . . . or should I now say 'Mother'?" He giggled.

"Lady Eileen, Mistress Eileen will suffice," she replied coldly. Abruptly, she leaned over from her saddle and firmly grabbed his left lapel, and so shocked was he that a seemingly spontaneous girlish squeal filled the air as he involuntarily for a moment stood on his toes. "Indeed, you will call me nothing else," she said through clenched teeth. "Do you understand me, you weak little . . ."

"Eileen!" came sharply from Morgan, who was standing right next to John, who, smoothing his lapels, smiled feebly and climbed aboard his own mount.

She settled back into her saddle and smiled down at her brother. "Ah, 'tis well, dear brother, 'tis well," she said in her strong, husky voice, fully believing that nothing at all was well, nor was it necessarily going to be . . . at least not soon.

And finally off went what Morgan again pronounced a "totally odd" group of travellers. Maurice, the second O'Connell son, who'd been until only recently in France and, whilst sharing his siblings' contempt for their eldest brother, had remained largely quiet during the whole time, draped his lanky arms over Morgan and Daniel's shoulders. As the three walked towards their mother and sisters, he said, "I fear the only real *man* in that group is Dark Eileen herself." And he laughed; *bitterly*, Morgan immediately thought.

Eileen eased Bull into the lead even before they were out of sight of Derrynane House, glaring at John O'Connor as she slowly passed him. As he tugged his own horse to one side, permitting her to pass, she smiled sweetly at him and purred, "Good boy."

Eileen rode in silence for the first rough miles, her mind wandering to her childhood, the good times and not. She thought long about Donal Mór and, as regularly occurred when she did, tears streamed down her cheeks.

As prearranged by the younger O'Connor on the trip from Firies, a rugged young man had joined the group as a guide. Though John had handled the introductions and logistics, as he had when he'd travelled to Derrynane, as soon as the group assembled for travel the next morning, the lad—a handsome, rough-hewn boy named Patrick O'Mahony, who spoke only Irish in a gravelly voice—instinctively understood that it was Eileen who, in actuality, was in charge. He himself was immediately enthralled with the girl.

As he recalled later, *Six feet tall she stood, she did, straight and regal as a queen, like Maeve herself, she was.* Her mane of the blackest hair he'd ever seen had shone brilliantly in the morning sun, *so long and thick it touched her saddle, it did*, and he had audibly gasped as she flashed a dazzling smile at him, indicating with a cock of her head that he should fall in next to her as they set off.

And so they travelled, the young man and his Irish warrior queen in front, and John O'Connor behind, followed by the two girls, both named Kate, who led the packhorses.

It would take them nearly seven days of hard riding to reach Firies, in the process covering some of the roughest ground in Ireland that took them over and through a craggy mountain range that would become known as MacGillicuddy's Reeks, circling aside Carrauntoolhil, ultimately recognised as being Ireland's highest mountain peak and up, into and through Bearna Dhuna Loich, the rugged and desolately, strikingly beautiful Gap of Dunloe, which Eileen correctly pronounced as being "truly magnificent."

The track—and it was no more than that—was narrow, rough and in a number of long stretches virtually nonexistent. Especially through the Gap, trees and vegetation were sparse, many of the rocks abutting their route black and smooth from centuries of rain and snow; but, on the good days, the skies were magnificently blue, the late February sun warming.

Eileen and Patrick chatted amiably, this daughter of one of the few remaining intact families of the old Gaelic aristocracy, fluent in Irish, English, Latin and French, who played the harp and broke horses, and this handsome, illiterate son of peasant parents, who, along with him and his seven siblings, at times shared their mud-walled cottage with their livestock. Nevertheless, the two spoke easily of the scenery and the sky, and the stories of their childhood, Eileen telling him to his amazement that her mother was "*bean caointe,*" a poet in the oral tradition.

Patrick gasped and said, "But when she dies . . ."

Eileen nodded. "Aye, a banshee she may well become, in our mountains and glens, wailing of our deaths and those of others."

By the third day, Eileen was fully enjoying the company of this boy, in background so utterly different from her brothers but in so many ways—his flowing conversation, his marvelling at what they were seeing and at the world, seen and unseen, about them and his rollicking laughter—so like them; well, so like them, except for Denis. *No one is like Denis,* she mused, *thank the good Lord God.*

As they rode, they alternated between conversation and silence, the periods of the latter growing more frequent as the days passed, their arrival at Firies growing closer. Eileen's thoughts raced about: *What will this be like? Am I in real danger? Is that why Mama gave me the pistol? What is being mistress of a grand house like? What will being a wedded woman be like?* As the last thought came, as it did more frequently, she could only nod and smile: *But a few weeks ago, I was being told when to retire; soon I shall not be alone. in bed*, and she surprised young Patrick with a hearty laugh.

By the night of the fifth day, she'd slept flanked by Kate and Kate for four nights and had come to know them a bit, though the only time they'd had to speak together was at bedtime.

They were both in service to "the squire," they told her, becoming more comfortable each time they sat or lay next to this very tall girl, having been put at ease by her fluid Irish. They thought they might be somehow related, but neither had seen their family for "oh, I don't know how long," said the quieter Kate. At Ballyhar they slept on straw mats and heavy blankets on the floor of the kitchen cabin, and each had two dresses. The boots they were wearing they would give back when they got to Firies. They never wore shoes either, and Eileen marvelled at the leather-like feel of their soles, which they had her touch, one of them taking a burning ember from the campfire and laughingly holding it to her heel with no effect. Neither could read or write, and they could hardly fathom that Eileen could. "Master John there," the chatty Kate whispered, "he can barely do so, though the squire, yes, yes, he can. . . . He even has books."

Eileen confirmed that John was the eldest, that the next brother, David was "a few years" younger and both girls had whispered to her in the softest of tones that "He's much given to the drink at times, mistress. It so troubles the squire, it does." They said no more about David.

"And what of the third boy, then?" Eileen asked.

"'Tis Peter he is, Mistress," and Eileen gasped and then laughed, the girls puzzled and their moths agog.

Realising their wonder, she quickly explained: "Oh, 'tis my eldest brother that is Denis, I was recalling he was almost named Peter instead!" She laughed.

"Och, the one who doesn't smile, Mistress?"

"Indeed; the one who doesn't smile." She nodded: *or laugh or feel or care or . . .*

"Well, then, what of Peter O'Connor?" she asked of both of them, whom she now called the Kate girls.

"'Tis very sad, that one, Mistress," said chatty Kate. "He doesn't say much, doesn't speak hardly at all, actually, Mistress, though he has the sweetest of smiles and he loves his kittens."

That night, the fifth night, as she stretched out on her back under the cold, brilliantly starry Kerry sky, Eileen rested her head against her saddle, padded by a blanket and her own hair, bunched up and tied behind her head, and sighed after she'd bid the girls a good night.

A weakling, a drunkard and a God-knows-what kind of sad boy; no wonder O'Connor feared for his lands, his estate, were her last thoughts as she drifted into a deep, blessedly dreamless sleep.

After they passed a large beautiful lake to the east of where they rode and moved through and finally beyond the Gap, the ground became less rough, flatter, and they were able to move a bit quicker.

Midmorning on the sixth day since they left Derrynane, John eased his mount up next to Patrick. "When we reach that grove of trees, ride west." He pointed with his gloved right hand. "You shall from there see the *manor house,*" he added breathlessly. And he then fell back in the column.

Reaching the grove, which stood starkly alone, Eileen and Patrick reined in their horses and turned to see the house, which, as was the estate, Eileen had learnt, called "Ballyhar," a massive structure, looming about two hundred yards ahead to the west. It appeared built of dark local stone, the roof slated, it seemed constructed to overwhelm and daunt as opposed to welcome the visitor.

Eileen gently booted Bull and cantered towards what was to be their home. Approaching it, she could see it stood virtually alone, save for the usual out-buildings, but few trees, and as she rode closer now, it was indeed huge, dark—forbidding even. She shivered slightly to herself. *Derrynane House: 'tis big and dark and slated, yet it welcomes, seems to reach out and embrace one; this place . . . it could make one wish she were going elsewhere. . . .*

John cantered up next to her. "Home! *M'dear,* we are *home!*" he announced, "Ballyhar . . . it awaits!"

Eileen reached for his horse's bridle and, pulling the animal up short, cast a piercing look with her deep blue eyes. "To whom are you speaking? Whom are calling 'your dear,' little man?"

John caught his breath. "Um, *Mistress Eileen*, we are approaching now our home."

Eileen audibly *hmff*'d and released the horse.

"Now, if I may," said John, and without waiting rode ahead.

A bell clanged from one of the outbuildings flanking the dwelling and the house's front door was flung open.

A tall, trim man wearing a dark blue knee-length justacorps and matching breeches, white hose and silver buckled shoes, a white shirt open at the neck, emerged from the house and, clearing the steps, walked briskly towards the travellers, his thick greying-brown hair carefully tied in a long black-ribboned queue.

"Father!" called John. The man ignored him, walking straight for Eileen, noting that she was astride an extremely large and powerful-looking stallion, *No sidesaddle for this one*, O'Connor nodded in silent approval.

Eileen drew up and the man took Bull's bridle. "Mistress O'Connell," he said in English. Not wishing to use her given name, he had without thinking advanced her in the complex hierarchy of the Irish aristocracy.

"Squire O'Connor," she replied, and, her right hand holding her dress against her thigh, deliberately, effortlessly, swung her right leg over Bull's neck, slid off his back, landing softly in front of and facing the man who would be her husband. As she did, he took note of a pair of fine leather saddlebags casually held in her left hand.

O'Connor took her right hand and quickly brought it to his lips in the swiftest of kisses.

Eileen smiled and, without being asked, fell in beside him, as he looked up at Patrick and instinctively asked in soft Irish, "You, young man, you are from beyond the Gap, yes?"

"Yes. Yes, Squire, I am. Patrick O'Mahony I am, sir."

"Well, then, thank you for bringing . . . my . . . yes, my bride safely through such rough country."

Patrick dismounted and stood quietly, bobbing his head respectfully.

"You girls, you and Patrick here take the horses and see to them."

As the three of them began to walk away, O'Connor added, "Patrick O'Mahony, you shall stay the night. 'Twill be a happy evening here. We shall dispatch you in the morning, fed and rested and . . ." he smiled, his eyes actually twinkling, "oh yes, and well paid," and he laughed.

John O'Connor again approached the squire. "Hello, Father."

O'Connor eyed his eldest son, an expression of thinly veiled contempt coming over his face. "Your journey was satisfactory?"

"Oh, yes! And are you pleased with what I have brought you?" he said, gesturing towards Eileen, standing now at O'Connor's shoulder.

O'Connor's jaw set. "You accomplished what I sent you to do." He flicked his left hand at the young man, disdainfully indicating that he was dismissed, and, his arm gently—if somewhat presumptuously, Eileen thought—reaching around her waist, he turned the two of them towards the house, climbing the steps and going inside, noticing again her saddlebags now draped over her right shoulder.

Anticipating his inquiry, Eileen said softly, "Some of my wee treasures from Derrynane. 'Tis no bother for me, sir."

O'Connor smiled somewhat uncertainly. Chancing that she understood what he was feeling, Eileen displayed an awkward sheepishness she did not at all feel, adding quickly, "Including my favourite doll, sir."

Now O'Connor smiled broadly. *The brother promised a very pretty, a very young bride . . . and so she is, with a dolly, it seems!* At that he chuckled softly, nodding almost affectionately at her, and thought no more of the fine leather satchels.

He gestured to a large, richly furnished parlour, and to two high-backed chairs facing each other in front of a massive hearth, a turf fire burning low but steadily, making the room smell sweet, though it was not overly warm.

He gestured at Eileen to sit. Taking his own seat, he leaned back and crossed one long leg over the other and nodded at this tall young girl who within hours would become his second wife.

Eileen folded her hands in her lap.

A servant approached with a pot of tea and cups, as well as a decanter of whiskey and glasses. With his right hand, O'Connor indicated to her to place the tray on the low table between them and, as he had with his son, then gently the same hand in a silent dismissal.

"Your pleasure, my dear?"

"Ah, tea, please, sir," she said in response, "and perhaps a drop later, then."

"Perhaps, indeed," he said. "And 'John' will do quite well," he added, pouring the scalding, nearly black tea.

"Kerry tea. Thank you . . . *John*," Eileen said softly.

"Indeed, even though you are no longer on your wild Iveragh, 'tis in Kerry you remain."

Eileen lifted the delicate cup to her lips and sipped, as did O'Connor.

O'Connor spoke softly in a relaxed, sometimes slurring manner, describing the house and the estate, mentioning his two sons whom Eileen would meet later. She interrupted only a few times with unchallenging questions, using the time and opportunity to focus on John O'Connor.

He was just a bit taller than she, Eileen noticed; *trim, straight, distinguished*, she thought. As she had not noticed on her arrival, his greying brown hair was thick, worn in a carefully gathered and tied queue. Though he wore no waistcoat, his well-tailored clothing was as formal, *as appropriate*, she thought, as his manner. She found nothing about him terribly unattractive, though she tried not to think about his age.

They spoke of her journey. He noted with approval her choice of a large stallion as her mount. "Bull is my dear friend, as well," Eileen allowed with a soft smile.

He shared the fact that he had learnt much about her; he knew of her love of books and reading, her equestrian skills, her trips abroad, allowing, "My own journeys have been largely through my books . . . and from maps. . . . I have many, if only to provide me a sense of the lands in the New World that I possess but shall never see," he said, not quite wistfully, adding that he was regularly in Dublin, where he advised that he had attended Trinity College, and less frequently in London.

Eileen felt appreciably more comfortable, coming to know now what she had. "John, if I may," she began at one point, "you spoke to Patrick of this evening as being a happy one. Am I to assume then . . . ?"

"That we shall be wed this evening?" He leaned his head back against the high back of his chair, the teacup on his knee. "Yes, we shall. I thought it not inappropriate and less awkward than to have you stay here or have to be elsewhere until . . . I assume that is what you were asking?"

"It was."

"And is it satisfactory to you?"

Eileen took a breath. "It is. Wholly satisfactory, sir, very much so." *After all, 'tis the purpose of my coming, is it not now?* she thought, smiling her warmest smile.

O'Connor put down his teacup. "Very well, then. Father MacCarthy is already here. 'Twill just be my sons and my people here. My parents, of course, are dead, and my siblings as well, save for one in Dublin. Of the neighbours, a goodly number, so 'twill be festive."

"Understood, John. 'Tis quite fine, sir."

O'Connor stood. "Well, my dear, if you will excuse me. Maire will be in shortly. Your belongings have been taken upstairs, I am sure. She will assist you to prepare your dress and all." He turned and walked out of the room, Eileen taking note that his strides were long, not unlike her own.

As he was leaving, Eileen picked up her finely tooled saddlebags and stood, gazing down into the fire. *Yes, husband. No, husband. Whatever you wish, husband,* she thought, smiling ironically.

She was looking out the window at a green and not unattractive vista, open land and low hills, as a thin, efficient-looking woman of middle age entered, her red hair tied back and pinned up. "Lady Eileen?" she said in English.

Eileen turned and extended a hand as the woman half-curtseyed, reciprocating with one of her own, she took her hand and drew her up. Still gently holding her hand, she asked, "You are Maire, then?"

"Yes, Mistress, though I prefer Mary. We primarily speak English in this house."

"Oh, very well then, *Mary*, though my own dear mother is Maire," Eileen said. "But very fair and tiny," she added, holding a flat palm down.

Smiling and looking up, Mary could only say, "Given my lady's height, much of the world is tiny, is it not?"

And the two laughed.

Eileen declined the woman's offer to carry her saddlebags. "Please . . . then?" Mary gestured Eileen towards the stairs and followed her through the hall and up the steep staircase.

"To your right, m' lady," she said softly, gesturing to the sole door at that part of the hall and leaned around Eileen to push it open onto a large, bright room, the drapery blowing very gently in a cool breeze. "Is it too chilly? Would you like a fire, Mistress?" she used what would, within hours, be Eileen's proper title.

"No, no, 'tis fine, thank you," Eileen answered, noting as she draped her locked saddlebags over the back of a side chair, that her luggage had already been largely unpacked and many of her belongings put away. She also took special notice of the heavy off-white dress of silk and satin which, along with petticoats, hip pads and a simple corset lay on the chaise at the foot of the bed, and the new French leather slippers on the floor.

"'Tis a lovely dress, Mistress. The squire will be most pleased."

I should hope so, Eileen thought.

"If you should like to rest?" Mary gestured to the bed, and Eileen nodded.

Within moments, the bed had been turned down, the pillows fluffed. "Does Mistress desire anything further?"

Being unused to anyone helping her dress or undress, Eileen shook her head, and Mary advised, "I shall return by five o'clock then," she indicated a dainty clock on the dresser, "to help you dress for . . . this evening." She smiled with a curtsey and withdrew, closing the door with a click.

Eileen wriggled off her boots and dropped onto the big bed, bouncing a little and thinking it comfortable, and wondering if *it* would happen *there*? She shook her head and sighed.

She removed the soft, brass-clasped leather case containing her pistol and ammunition out of her saddlebags, placing it against the wall, under the headboard of the bed—and her soft rag doll, whom she had years ago named *Maeve*, she placed on a wing chair. She then stretched out, noting the dressers, a small ladies' desk and chair, two armoires, the chaise with what she could finally think of as her wedding dress on it and the separate dressing room.

Eileen awoke with a start and glanced at the tiny clock face, noting it was almost five. She lay still, looking up at the smooth ceiling. Her mind was racing: *wedding, my wedding*, she thought. She'd been to several, so she knew the vows, the toasting, the eating, the revelry and the good-natured ribaldry. It had sounded like it would be smaller than those she'd attended at and around Derrynane.

"M'lady?" said Mary.

"Oh, nothing. I was just thinking of something at Derrynane. . . ."

Within a few moments, Mary had helped Eileen shed her travelling clothes, had gently sponged her face, hands, arms, legs and feet with warm moist towels and had offered—and Eileen had declined—to sponge the rest of her body. Instead, Eileen took the small pail of warm water and the towels into the dressing room and, shedding her chemise, washed and briskly towelled herself, wriggling back into her chemise and quickly re-emerging.

Holding the dress, Mary eyed the girl's solid, trim figure. She set the dress down on the bed and, stepping forward, said "If I may, m'lady," and, without any response from Eileen, stepped behind her and drew her palms gently down the front of Eileen's chemise-clad body, from her throat, over her breasts and stomach, onto her hips and her bottom. Stepping back in front of her, she smiled. "M'lady requires no significant corseting, it appears."

Eileen could only shake her head.

After she fitted Eileen's hip-pads, light corset and petticoats, picking up the dress, Mary stepped onto a small stool and, holding it over Eileen's head, said in a much warmer tone, "Arms up, please." Eileen complied, the silk and satin smoothly slipping onto her body. Mary smoothed it over her breasts and hips, then down her legs, asking her to "sit please," and helped her on with her hose and slippers. The woman turned Eileen to the long looking glass on one of the armoires and smiled as she looked and smiled at herself. "Lovely, very lovely," Mary said.

She then stepped in front. "Your hair, dear? Do you wish it dressed, combed, pinned? I used to care for Mistress O'Connor's. It was long, though nowhere near as long as yours."

Eileen gazed into the looking glass and then turned sideways. "If you could gather it behind and tie it, I think that would be lovely, thank you."

"The squire will be most pleased," the woman said softly as she brushed Eileen's mane with two hard brushes so it gleamed in the soft light of the candles. She tied it with a white satin ribbon and then turned the girl to the looking glass one last time. "It would appear you are now ready."

Eileen nodded, and Mary laid a sheaf of wildflowers in her arms. Stepping through the open door, she said, "I shall return in a moment."

Eileen stood, *like a statue*, she thought. She slowly shook her head and sighed. She was just whispering to herself, *Is mise Eibhlin Maire Ni Chonaill . . . an inion na Donal Mór agus Maire. . . ./*I am strong and beautiful . . . I fear very little in this or any other world, I . . . when Mary returned, smiling warmly, and said, "All is in readiness . . . please," gesturing her to go down the stairs, following a step or two behind.

In the hall at the bottom of the stairs, Mary said softly, "This way," leading her to a very large formal room Eileen would later learn was considered and called the ballroom, crowded with guests and ablaze with candles, across the hall from where she and Squire O'Connor had visited earlier.

Eileen stopped and could only smile. The squire stood at the far side with a short, cherubic priest at his side. The squire was regal and solemn in an elegant black suit, a white shirt with ruffs at the front and cuffs, fresh stockings and gleaming black pumps with gold buckles, and the priest, smiling warmly, held a small leather book and wore a simple black soutaine, an embroidered stole draped over his shoulders and hanging to his knees.

She recognized John, her erstwhile travelling companion, standing next to another young man; their suits were almost identical. John waved with his fingers. Eileen looked away. Nearby stood a tall, somewhat pale young man, standing alone; not unattractive, though his face was flushed and his eyes were somewhat dull, looking at her yet not. David, she concluded correctly.

Near the window, with the chatty Kate—in a clean dress, beneath which Eileen noticed her travelling boots, and her hair tied back neatly with a red ribbon—standing with him, stood someone Eileen immediately thought of as a sweet boy, stroking a grey cat. His eyes met hers, and he smiled at her. Eileen smiled warmly back at Peter O'Connor, though all present thought the smile was for his father.

Mary gently nudged her back and Eileen walked to the squire and the priest, the latter taking her hand and bowing his head. "My dear girl . . ."

The next few moments were a blur; Eileen never fully remembered them.

The priest announced the bans, spoke briefly about the sanctity of marriage in the eyes of Holy Mother Church and moved quickly to the vows. She listened; she'd heard them before and she said what was asked of her. Suddenly, the squire was slipping a gold band onto the third finger of her left hand, and the priest made the Sign of the Cross over their hands joined.

Still holding Eileen's hand, the squire turned to face the little priest, and Eileen turned slightly as well.

He raised his hand over their heads and, making a broad Sign of the Cross, intoned the familiar "In the name of the Father" as his hand traced the air from the top of their heads, and reaching the level of their chests, "and of the Son," and finally as it moved in the air in a line from Eileen's right shoulder to the squire's left, "and of the Holy Ghost. Amen."

Eileen stood in place. "'Tis finished!" The priest smiled. "You are a wedded couple. Congratulations," he bowed, "Squire, Madame; God bless you both."

The room sounded with genteel applause and the squire leaned to her, placing a very soft but firm kiss on her lips. She must have looked surprise as he stepped back and gently stroked her cheek and nodded.

Mary entered the room, leading a small coterie of serving women with glasses of what Eileen soon knew was fine French champagne. "Your family may well have brought this to Ireland," the squire said as he toasted his young bride. Eileen smiled and their glasses gently clinked. The squire downed the contents of his glass in a single swallow; Eileen took a sip. It tickled her nose; she took several more.

Everyone's glasses were quickly and regularly refilled, as they were directed towards the large table, set with fine china, gleaming silver and platters of meats, fish, pies . . . a variety of food, all in abundance.

Eileen was grateful when David O'Connor offered her a carefully arranged plate and silverware. "Thank you." She smiled warmly.

"You are very welcome, and I welcome you here as well. I am David."

She nodded. "And I am most pleased to meet you, sir," she said, noting only the slightest suggestion of poteen on his breath.

He added, "I shan't be making any jokes about 'mother' as I know how very awkward this"—he gestured around the room—"must be for you."

Holding his hand, Eileen said, "I am grateful for your understanding. We shall be good friends." David appeared genuinely shocked, as if no one had said anything like that to him for a long time—as, she would later discover, actually, no one had.

Eileen ignored John and the young man she presumed to be the equerry of whom he'd spoken but made a point of walking to the chatty Kate and Peter O'Connor. She extended her hand to the young man, whom she guessed was perhaps twenty-five and gently handsome, with soft blond hair and fair blue eyes. Smiling, she said softly, "I am Eileen."

Still cradling his fluffy grey cat in the crook of his left arm, with Kate gently holding his left elbow, he tentatively reached for Eileen's hand with his right one. Taking it, he said, "I . . . am . . . . . . Pee . . . tur. I am Peter." He looked at Kate, who nodded and squeezed his arm gently.

Eileen held his hand, smiling warmly at him. When she said, "I am so very pleased to meet you, Peter," his head bobbed with delight.

Pointing at Eileen, he looked at Kate and said, "Eye . . . leen."

Kate nodded her head. "Yes, you will be good friends."

"Frens," said Peter, smiling again. "Eye-leen . . . m-m-me . . . *frens*. . . ."

Tears came to Eileen's eyes, and the chatty Kate nodded a thank-you and slowly led Peter away, the cat looking back at Eileen, with a quizzical expression.

Sighing, she thought, *My family, ohmygawd . . .* as she walked across the room towards her husband. *Husband? My husband? Ohmygawd!*

Reaching his side, she instinctively slipped her arm through John O'Connor's and smiled at the short, distinguished-looking, white-wigged gentleman with whom he was speaking.

"Oh, my dear, this is Lord Moyvane. Though some degrees distant from here, his lands adjoin ours on the . . ." he thought, "north and west, aye. . . that way," he gestured.

The nobleman bowed to Eileen, kissing her hand. "Mistress O'Connor, my pleasure . . . and my sincere congratulations, m'lady."

"My lord," said Eileen, as she executed a perfect, deep curtsey, raising her eyes to Moyvane as she lowered herself and only beginning to stand after he'd acknowledged her, and raised her himself.

Lord Moyvane was perhaps three inches shorter than Eileen, a bit heavy, with a ruddy complexion and rough hands. His title—he being George, sixth Earl of Moyvane—had existed in some form since late Elizabethan times. He was O'Connor's age or a bit older, a blunt-spoken, no-nonsense landlord, a non-theological Church of Ireland communicant and, she would learn, her new husband's closest friend and counsellor. Lady Moyvane was said to be infrequently in Ireland, seemingly preferring her mother's family's extensive holdings in Surrey, elegantly well settled and in proximity to London. This arrangement, as he would laughingly say in all-male company, permitted him to "indulge in the hunt—for four-footed males and two-footed females," a comment he, at least, always found to be amusing.

Holding Eileen's hand and looking into her eyes, Lord Moyvane addressed O'Connor. "'T'woud appear that at least one Kerry girl knows how to curtsey well, Squire?"

"Yes, m'Lord," O'Connor said softly, gently nodding his approval to his bride.

"Well done, young lady; I trust that we shall be seeing much of you."

Smiling, Eileen slowly nodded her head and, in response, half-curtseyed. "That would be my hope, as well, my lord."

She heard him softly exclaim "Extrord'nry" as he ambled away, deftly accepting a proffered glass of champagne whilst walking. Later in the evening, the affable nobleman would circle back to the bride more than once, amongst other things engaging her in a brief conversation in French and a lengthier one in English, from both of which he took away several basically correct albeit preliminary impressions of the young girl. She was extremely bright, much more mature than she appeared, and most definitely a person not to be trifled with. *Just like the rest of her family, from what I understand; I should so advise O'Connor*, he mused, but he did not do so, at least not this night.

O'Connor lifted two glasses off the same tray and offered one to Eileen. He held his glass up. "Slainthe!" he said, "health!" The glasses clinked and he raised his and swallowed; she sipped first, and again—and then swallowed.

They repeated this three or perhaps four more times, and Eileen found herself laughing and feeling just a bit light-headed—Abby had told her about champagne—and actually began enjoying herself a bit more. She still avoided John and his equerry, although in her more relaxed mood she now permitted herself to think, *Equerry my hat. They are—what did Morgan say once, "poufs" or "puffs"? They like boys!* and she laughed out loud.

Hearing her, O'Connor turned to her. "You are enjoying yourself, Mistress O'Connor?"

She lowered her eyes, playfully—at least she hoped she appeared play-ful—and smiled. "Oh, yes, very much so, Squire O'Connor."

She also recalled Abby had advised her to stop taking champagne once she felt "a wee bit giddy," so, though setting down her glass, she nevertheless continued to enjoy herself, mainly in flirting with her new husband.

The evening passed more quickly than Eileen thought it would. There had been music and some dancing, though not as much and none as loud and as prolonged as the weddings she'd attended at Derrynane. Eileen and O'Connor had whirled about the floor in several round dances; during each, the groom was light on his feet, his eyes and his smile only on and for his beautiful new wife, who appeared to glow, her smile dazzling, her flowing hair stark against her wedding dress, as she danced effortlessly, her ath-letic body agile. She had spoken with most of the guests, including a brief exchange—partially in Latin—with Father MacCarthy that was overheard by the evening's seemingly ubiquitous Lord Moyvane who, again correctly, concluded that Eileen's command of the language was markedly superior to that of the clergyman's.

The younger John and his companion and Peter and chatty Kate had departed and already now stood near the front door of the house. David, clearly not taken with drink, Eileen was pleased to note, approached his father and his stepmother—it seemed as if he and Eileen had had the same thought at just that moment and smiled broadly—and bowed his head to both of them. "I shall take my leave and find a place in the hall, but God's blessings on you both," he said softly, warmly.

The elder O'Connor seemed genuinely surprised and took his son's hand and looked into his eyes. "Thank you, my boy. Thank you."

"Good night, David," Eileen said.

It was not quite ten—Eileen had taken note that the large clock in the hall had the most lovely, deep *bonnnnnng*—when Lord Moyvane and Father MacCarthy approached the bridal couple with handshakes for the squire and bows and hand kisses for the new mistress and stepped into the great hall, signalling that it was time for everyone else to do so as well.

After all the guests had found a spot in the hall and some of the gathering had stepped outside of the large double doors, the couple entered the hall and acknowledged their guests as they filed out. Some of the men whispered slightly ribald remarks, Lord Moyvane being the loudest with a smiling, "The time for this evening's true festivities has arrived!" as he pointed at the staircase and with wiggling, walking fingers, playfully traced the route for the couple to follow upstairs. Everyone, even the ladies, laughed, some clapping and cheering.

The squire turned to his new wife. "Well, my dear, shall we . . .?" and gestured up the stairs.

Eileen smiled and turned as well. Unexpectedly, and with surprising strength and, to Eileen, remarkable ease, he swept her up in his arms, her own arms most naturally draping his neck, as if she were used to being lifted up by a man. "Well done, girl!" He laughed, and Eileen, her legs swaying slightly and laughing softly, began to climb the stairs, the guests now lustily cheering, laughing and waving at them.

As they reached the second or third step, a loud crash echoed in the high hall, an audible *sproinnnnnnng* following immediately. The group grew abruptly quiet.

O'Connor—and with him, Eileen—turned slightly, and they both saw that the large classic Irish harp—gleaming, beautiful and old—that had been standing on a high pedestal in the corner of the hall opposite the grand old clock, seemingly for no reason had crashed to the floor, several of its strings now asunder.

Eileen gasped. "So beautiful! So . . ."

"Ah, 'tis nothing, my girl, *nothing*; we shall see to it tomorrow. You play the harp, I know. You shall play that one very soon, then—and frequently thereafter, of that I am certain."

Holding Eileen in his arms, O'Connor turned and repeated loudly for all: "'Tis *nothing at all*; we shall see to it tomorrow. Good night, good night, my friends!"

As they resumed their ascent of the long staircase, the guests, led by Lord Moyvane and the priest, began to drift away, still laughing and cheering.

Though Eileen did not reflect on how significant it might or might not prove to be, being Maire ní Dhuibh's daughter, she immediately realised that, with the sudden fall of the ancient harp, *something* had definitely just happened.

As the final guests filtered out into the black Kerry night, the O'Connors continued upstairs. Stopping at the top landing, O'Connor's mouth found Eileen's and he kissed her powerfully; she moaned very softly and instinctively—not because her mother had told her to do so—she kissed him back.

Setting her gently down on her feet, O'Connor gestured to the bedroom where Eileen had napped and dressed, and they walked the few steps together to the door.

O'Connor paused and took a deep breath, her expression suddenly business-like. "I am assuming you and your mother, or you and one, some or all of your many sisters, have spoken?"

"Concerning tonight?" Eileen responded softly.

"Concerning tonight, yes, in terms of precisely what is . . . what shall be expected of you."

"We have, sir, yes. I understand." She nodded.

"Very well, then," he said matter-of-factly, casually reaching around to un-do the hooks of her dress. "You will please enter your rooms, remove your wedding dress and undergarments and hose, your slippers of course, and then don whatever garment you find hanging on the dressing-room door." He softly stroked Eileen's face and then her hair. "You will please leave your hair tied as it is. It pleases me very much." He smiled. "Thus attired, you may await my return, seated on the bed should you wish, but when I knock you will please stand, step to the foot of the bed and face the door."

She nodded again, standing in front of her doorway.

"I shall now briefly retire to my own rooms," he gestured, Eileen's eyes following his left hand as he indicated a partially open pair of doors, on the other side of and perhaps twenty feet farther along the hall than her own.

He opened the door and, taking a pair of backwards steps through the doorway, she entered her room; backing into the hall, with a partial bow, he closed the door gently.

Candles were lit on the dresser and on each nightstand; the room was inviting. A low turf fire burned, so it was comfortably warm, one window ever so slightly open. The large bed had been turned down, with puffy Austrian quilts at the bottom and a mound of down-filled pillows at the head.

Looking at the bed and smiling wickedly, jesting sardonically with herself —*Well, well now . . . what is it that will happen there? Will it hurt? Will it be wonderful? Will it be horrid?*—slipping her arms free of the sleeves, she wriggled out of her dress, shed her petticoats and undid her hip pads. She sat on the edge of the chaise at the foot of the bed, kicked off her slippers and removed her stockings. In her chemise, she walked towards the dressing room and opened the door. A single candle burned on a stand. Looking on the back of the dressing-room door, she saw an empty peg.

She shook her head, laughed ironically and doffed her thin chemise. She shivered slightly and, as the bedroom was warmer, closed the dressing-room door and, nude, stepped near the fire. She saw the flames playing on her smooth fair skin, looking down at her feet, her calves, her thighs, her hips, the soft patch of black hair and her full breasts, the nipples erect.

She stepped in front of the armoire with the long looking glass in which she saw a very tall, very naked girl. She laughed softly. *I understand.*

As truly she did, Eileen and her mother having spoken more than once, not only in preparation for this night. Her more recent conversations with Abby, though containing only second- and primarily third-hand information, all punctuated by much giggling and blushing, had added a bit more to her knowledge.

Yet, the truth be told, Eileen was fully aware of what to expect, even more than what was merely expected of her, and had been for quite some time. She had grown up surrounded by a massive extended tribe, plus tenants, hangers-on, not to mention the life all about her in the barns, the glens and on the mountains. The mechanics of sex were no mystery to Eileen. As did her parents, her siblings and most about her, she saw it as natural, as much a part of *being* as the deaths and births she had witnessed since she was a little girl.

She recalled that at Derrynane, as in much of Gaelic Ireland, the very beginning of life . . . as well as its ending . . . *they are not hidden, not kept from children as perhaps they are elsewhere . . . even in the Irish stories of old, of Maeve and Aoife and the others, such as the naughty conversation between Cúchulainn and Emer in the Táin Bó Cuailnge, they were very open, even the particulars of the very act, the very process of which I shall soon be a part, these things, they are far more commonly understood at a much, much earlier age, and spoken of even lightly, almost playfully in the manner of Cúchulainn and Emer.*

Reflecting further as she awaited O'Connor, she recalled that she had been very free to roam about Derrynane from at an early age, and *saw things* in the barns, in the fields, and stags and does on the mountainsides . . . and that, whenever she had asked about them, the animals, Maire would say, *'Tis all part of God's world!* And she explained that people are, in some ways, not all that different from the stags and the does, the siring stallion and the dam. . . .

So, far from being apprehensive, she saw tonight as marking the time when she, too, would advance naturally to the next stage of her own life;

if it hadn't been John O'Connor on this night, it would have been another man, in another house, on another bed, on another night. For her, the focus was solely on the physical. Had any thought of romantic love come to her at this moment, she would have easily dismissed it, for "love" was not what this was all about. Though she had witnessed the obvious affection between Donal Mór and Maire, she felt this was perhaps something that came to some couples with time.

As she stood now in front of the looking glass, her fingertips played gently over her full, firm breasts, her throat, down her sides, and then slowly rubbed her trim hips, her bottom with her palms. As she did so, she felt a sensation, a tingle perhaps? She was much intrigued by what was to happen, what it would feel like, wondering how she would feel afterwards. She smiled at herself in the looking glass, her fingers moving from her breasts to her soft mound, pressing, teasing herself. It felt good; she felt . . . natural, expectant.

Additionally, perhaps at least in part because she had spent her entire life in that singularly magical place—at least for those fortunate few, like the O'Connells, who did not have to struggle to wrest their daily existence out of the land alone—that was far southwest County Kerry, Eileen was actually already a highly sensual being. Though her environment was often harsh—craggy rocks, stony soil, too often refusing to yield sustenance for those who depended on it the most, steep mountains, deep green glens and winter gales, and seemingly endless weeks of rain blown in from the Atlantic—it was also a unique location, as offsetting the harsh physical realities of the place, the phenomenon of a vivid blue stream, said by some to flow from warm waters in the New World, also served to make southwest Kerry a semitropical place, which accounted for the palm trees brought from Spain and even from the far-eastern Mediterranean thriving at Derrynane, as well as Maire's lemon trees and orchids. The exotic smells floated by a warm breeze on a soft, wet summer evening were in many ways erotic in themselves.

At that moment, there was a firm knock.

Eileen took a few steps so she was facing the door. She put her hands behind her bottom, deciding this was no time to try to retain modesty, or was it dignity?

The door opened and in stepped the squire, wearing a heavy dressing gown. He closed—and locked—the door gently.

"My, my . . ." he began, as he stood facing Eileen. "Aren't you . . . the lovely one," he said softly as he slowly walked in a circle around where Eileen stood. He stroked her gleaming hair, stopping to untie the white ribbon and letting it fall to the floor. Parting the hair on her back, he kissed her bare skin, his fingers delicately touching her bottom, her arms, her hips and, ever so softly, with the knuckles of his right hand, her soft patch of black hair, which made her gasp.

Facing her, then, looking into what he realized were her amazingly deep blue eyes, he lifted her hair completely back over her shoulders, baring her breasts. He gently teased her nipples and Eileen smiled for the first time. His surprisingly smooth palms cupped her breasts, squeezing them gently, and then slid down her body to her firm buttocks, cupping then pressing her to him.

As he did, his mouth covered hers, and Eileen felt his urgency as her husband forced her lips open and his tongue into her mouth. He moaned as her hands wrapped behind his neck, and she opened her mouth wider, feeling she would otherwise gag.

O'Connor's hands played deftly over her bottom, her hips, his tongue still gently teasing her mouth, his palms then pressed into her breasts, and she moaned softly now, feeling his rigid member hard against her. Their lips, their tongues teasing for several minutes, their hands moving over each other's bodies, Eileen suddenly experienced strange new sensations in her psyche and her body. Though no specific thoughts entered her mind, she had come to share O'Connor's urgency as she embraced him more tightly, and as she kissed him, flicking her tongue more ardently.

He slid his tongue out of her mouth and stepped back, slipping off his dressing gown, which he tossed onto the chaise. He stood naked, and her eyes immediately went to his rigid penis. He smiled wickedly but playfully, saying, "You've not seen a cock in this condition before?"

Grateful for apparently having had just enough champagne, Eileen tossed her head back, widened her eyes and laughed. "Oh my, no sir, never! Indeed, sir, *never* have I seen a cock in *any* condition, sir!" she finished saucily.

Obviously pleased with her unexpected degree of playfulness, he stepped back to her. His hands on her bare hips, he writhed against her; her mouth falling open, she instinctively teased his tongue with her own. He very gently, playfully, pushed her onto the bed and, stepping away, watched her fall onto her back. She scrunched herself up onto the bed, and—whether it was instinct, desire, champagne or a combination of them—Eileen smiled wickedly and stretched her arms above her head, arching, slowly writhing her bottom seductively.

O'Connor's eyes locked on her full breasts, her smooth belly, her partially open thighs, and with a broad smile, he fell on her. Her arms enveloped his back, her long legs quickly wrapping around his own, as his lips found her left breast, licking and sucking the hard nipple.

They rocked gently, Eileen's own sensations, as unfamiliar to her as they were, becoming powerful, and she moaned aloud. Her husband drew back and spread her legs, not roughly. Bending his mouth to hers, he murmured softly, "You know, girl, yes, you know?"

Eileen nodded, her lips barely touching his, whispering, "I know," and she stretched and opened herself to her husband.

He sighed as he slowly—she sensed gently—eased himself, just his cock-head, into her.

"Ahhhhh," she moaned, unexpectedly delighting in the strange new feelings.

"You're wet, girl, so wet, so good," O'Connor was murmuring.

"Wet," responded Eileen.

She arched herself to her husband and immediately felt the pressure inside her.

"Good girl," he said approvingly, then softly, "Go easy, girl, it may hurt—it *will* hurt—just for a moment; it . . ."

Though she had heard him, Eileen arched up. By reflex, he thrust, harder and deeper than he meant to, and Eileen screamed, "Ohhhhhhhmyyyyyyyygawwwwwddddd!"

O'Connor now took possession of his new wife. He thrust powerfully, deeply, noting her eyes wide as she screamed again. He knew not what—if anything—she was saying, nor whether it was in pleasure or in pain.

He then thrust again, now with a deliberate, near brutal force . . . and again . . . and yet again and again and again and . . . each thrust made with barely controlled violence. From deep in his throat there now emitted a guttural, "Fuck—fuck—fuck."

The blindingly sharp initial pain having passed, Eileen now willingly, fully surrendered to the powerful passions that had already been so close to controlling her. She thrashed and arched and moaned, her smooth nails digging into O'Connor's back, almost meeting each thrust with one of her own, what pain she had experienced now eclipsed by the potent mix of passion, of pleasure. . . . "Yes!" she began to cry, nearly each time O'Connor plunged into her and, using her muscular thighs, she began arching sharply up, now meeting his thrusts, writhing about his cock, the never-before experienced sensation intoxicating to her.

She even thought she might have perhaps heard herself cry out, "Fuck! Yes! *Yes*"—at least once, perhaps more than once—as for Eileen, time had ceased to matter. . . .

O'Connor thrust deeply into her, his body suddenly rigid, and cried out, "Ahhhhhhhhhhhhh, Gawddddddddddd!" as his body shuddered.

Eileen felt immediately, unexpectedly warm and very wet inside herself, at virtually the same moment experiencing a powerful explosion in her brain as she herself shuddered with repeated convulsions deep in her loins. She raked her nails down O'Connor's back and wrapped her long legs around the shuddering body on top of her, herself screaming, "*YESSSSSSSSSSSSSS! OHHHHHHHHMYYYYYYGAWWWWD, YESSSSSSSSSS!*"

Long minutes passed and they lay entwined, their passion ebbing, breathing slowing, their bodies gleaming with sweat.

Eventually, O'Connor gently kissed her throat. "Good girl," he murmured, quite matter-of-factly, and rolled off Eileen, who, in turn, slowly rolled onto her right side, stretching her quivering body, her head resting on her outstretched right arm, her fingers gripping a pillow.

Turning her head sideways, facing him, she smiled and looked at her husband—now truly, really her husband—through half-closed eyes, the continuing sensation between her legs, though now again painful, deep within herself she felt . . . *extraordinary*!

Sitting up, O'Connor reached for the puffy, down-filled coverlet folded at the bottom of the huge bed and drew it up, partially covering both of them.

Now lying on his side, facing her, he softly echoed her thoughts. "Extraordinary . . . truly extraordinary."

"Mmmmmmmmmm," Eileen whispered in response, stretching her long body again, moving closer to where O'Connor lay, arching her mouth, desperate to kiss her *husband*, her amazing old man, seeming to her so now like a boy. Her husband . . . she started to reach for him; experiencing strange desires, she felt herself wanting him again, wanting more, oh yes, very much wanting more of *that* . . . even though she felt sore *there*.

Though she hadn't at first really been listening to what he was saying, Eileen realised at some point that O'Connor was speaking; as he had begun, it had sounded to Eileen as a voice from a distance. ". . . and you fuck like— oh no, better than, *much* better than!—the very *best* of the best whores ever I have had, and many, indeed, *many* have there been. How could I have known? How could I have even hoped . . . ?"

Eileen's mind cleared quickly and, her eyes opening wide, she lifted herself up on her right elbow. "What did you just say, John?"

"You heard me, girl," he drawled. "I was saying that I knew I had made a sound business arrangement with your brother. Worth every shilling it was indeed." He laughed caustically, yet not deliberately so.

Rolling onto his back now, his head resting on the mounded pillows, his eyes looking up at and following the pattern of flowers and vines on the cream-coloured canopy, he was unable to see the sudden shock, the revulsion, indeed the rage on Eileen's face as she raised herself up by the palm of her right hand.

Half-sitting now, some of her hair falling over her shoulders and her bare breasts, the quilt only covering her legs and just barely her thighs, she heard him continue: "I was certain that in the process I was getting the prettiest of the great Donal Mór Ó Conaill's little girls, but now I find she is the most extraordinary fuck. I must mention this to your good brother Denis when next we speak, although perhaps he was already aware of your talents. My God, girl, *you* are the most extraordinary fuck! I cannot believe you were a virgin, the way you fuck, you sweet bitch," his voice was soft, his manner—although not to Eileen—almost playful.

O'Connor rolled slowly back on his side, stretching and moving his body towards hers.

Looking now at Eileen but not comprehending her facial expression, he laughed. "Ah, perhaps there is a chance you were not one after all? Perhaps you are just a good actress, eh?" He laughed again, just a bit louder, continuing, "Come, you may tell me, girl . . . how *did* you ever learn to fuck like that? Was it a few times, or even more than a few times, with some solid young bucks from the neighbourhood, or did your married sisters school you in the finer points of . . ."

Before he could say any more, Eileen pulled sharply away, in a single motion succeeded in grabbing the coverlet as she stood up, leaving O'Connor lying naked and shocked. She stepped away from, then immediately turned back to the bed, directly facing O'Connor, holding the quilt gathered in front so only her head was visible. She trembled beneath it, but to O'Connor displayed nothing but rage. "You arrogant, filthy bastard!" she screamed. "You miserable, foul excuse for a man, much less a gentleman, much less an *Irish* gentleman. . . ."

She stepped farther away, backing up. "Have you forgotten who it is that I am? How dare you speak to me, *Eibhlin Ni Chonaill*, in such a manner, *Squire* O'Connor?! How *dare* you?! I never expected to feel, much less revel in, the sensations, the desires as I did. Perhaps 'twas the champagne after all and, stupid little girl, I *enjoyed* it, I *enjoyed YOU*, you bastard, and I was happy to have pleased you. I wanted more, yes, more . . ." she paused, ". . . of something I had *never* experienced before. How *dare* you even suggest . . ."

She was by then stalking dramatically around the room, the coverlet having slipped, baring her shoulders, before she tugged it back up. In front, the material barely covered her breasts, her hair having fallen free. Now she *did* appear like Patrick the guide's image of an ancient Irish warrior queen, the firelight dancing on her face, the flames glinting against the blue of her eyes, her blue-black mane gleaming.

O'Connor continued to sit, stunned, a rage the depths, the boundlessness of which he had rarely if ever before experienced now rising within him.

Eileen should have stopped right then, but she didn't. Rather, first drawing herself up to her full height, she then accusingly, commandingly pointed her long, elegant right forefinger at O'Connor and continued, "Do not ever, do you hear me, *never*; *do . . . not . . . ever . . .* speak to me like that again!"

Walking away, she turned, at first not realizing her bare back appeared as the coverlet slipped farther and, noticing it, pulled it again about her. She abruptly turned back, facing him, her hands clenched at her sides, unaware, or by now uncaring, that the quilt had completely fallen open, now just barely draping only her left shoulder.

"Do not ever touch me again, *do you understand, Mister O'Connor?*" she stormed.

She stepped closer to the bed, bending ever so slightly, her hands on her bare thighs. "*Answer me!*" she screamed.

As O'Connor flew wordlessly from the bed, the back of his right hand forming a fist, he brought it forward. She never saw the blow coming, but even had she, it came with a velocity such that she would have been unable to react. As the fist connected with Eileen's outthrust jaw, she let out a cry and, staggering back, fell to the floor in a half-sitting position, still somehow managing to clutch the quilt partially to herself. Her world momentarily went black and was now a fast-moving, terrifying blur.

Get up; I must get up!

As she was unsuccessfully struggling to stand, her vision cloudy, O'Connor kicked her in the jaw with his right foot, and she sprawled onto her back, her arms opening and the coverlet falling off completely, her nude body gleaming with sweat, her firm, athletic thighs, now apart, smeared with both O'Connor's semen and her own blood —from the rupture of her maidenhead.

He stood over her, momentarily wondering if she were conscious, and then kicked her in the chest, her upper arms, her thighs.

I must get up; I cannot simply lie here. . . .

Eileen stirred and struggled to get back up, blood running onto her chin out of the right side of her mouth. She was remotely aware of the pain, sensed that she was now naked and that she must, yet again, attempt to stand.

O'Connor stepped back, his chest heaving, his eyes wild with rage, deliberately allowing Eileen's struggling attempt to regain her footing. As soon as she unsteadily stood, instinctively, though weakly, forming her hands into two impotent fists, he smashed her brutally across the face with his own fist. As her head twisted to the other side, he hit her a second time, this time knocking her to the floor.

His rage far from satiated, he dropped heavily to his knees just at the point at which the thick carpeting gave way to the worn-smooth wood of the floor. O'Connor wrapped his fingers around her throat. Though barely conscious, by some means sensing that to do otherwise could quite possibly cost her her life, by the same means, Eileen now summoned the strength to dig her nails into the backs of his hands. . . .

"You *BITCH*!" Surprised rather than hurt, he nonetheless reflexively released Eileen's neck. He grabbed a handful of her hair off her shoulders, twisting it as he stood slowly, pulling her to her feet. Using her thick hair as if it were a rope, he flung her so violently across perhaps a third the length of the room that she crashed into the wall. She sank to the floor, blood now running out of both sides of her mouth as well as from her nostrils, her lips split, her cheeks red and ablaze, her left eye already becoming ringed with purple. He had propelled Eileen into a totally black place; she sensed nothing, felt nothing.

Seeing her against the wall, nude, bleeding, her legs open, her hair fallen about, seemed to cause O'Connor to stir. "I should fuck you again, *you bitch*," he roared. "I should do things to you—make you do things that you do not even know about . . . although perhaps you *do*, you worthless slut, you common whore!" His laugh was manic, otherworldly, satanic. It would have terrified Eileen had she been conscious.

Having apparently decided against raping his wife, he turned, picked up his dressing gown and calmly drew it on, and then looked back at Eileen, stepping closer to her. Staring down at the girl he had just wed and now beaten into insensibility, he spoke in a guttural tone: "Not a gentleman, bitch? If I were not a gentleman, I would . . ." He spat on her instead.

Shaking his head, he opened the door, closed it with a gentle click and walked slowly down the empty hall to his bedroom.

Eileen was never certain how much time had passed. It was still dark outside, and, as the candles had guttered, in the room as well as she slowly regained consciousness. Shivering slightly, she became aware that she was naked, her skin clammy despite the chill in the room, the fire having almost gone out.

She felt herself lying on her side, sprawled on the floor of what she sensed without looking about was her bedroom, her bare back and bottom resting against the cold, rough wall.

She pushed her hair back out of her face and struggled to sit up straight, a low moan escaping her split lips and echoing in the silence as she finally reached a sitting position, her back and shoulders resting heavily against the chill plaster wall, her bruised legs straight out in front of her.

She sat still. She hurt; everything hurt, it seemed. Thoughts of the times she'd been thrown from horses she was trying to break flooded her foggy brain; how it had felt when she'd gone to bed, or even the next day.

She felt much worse now.

Closing her eyes, fuzzy, disjointed images slowly began to appear: sweating bodies entwined and, yes, her desiring more, reaching to him, to kiss . . . then the foul language, his vile accusations, her rage building, grabbing the coverlet, stalking about the room, speaking, yelling, gesturing. . . . She shook her head as she pictured herself, finally standing at the bedside, barely draped in the coverlet. . . . *"Do not ever . . . Answer me!"*

Then the first blow, and trying to stagger to her feet, and the kick that had left her sprawling on her back. Regaining her footing, only to be smashed once and again in the face . . . and then the sense of her hair . . . *no, then he tried to strangle me, he tried to kill me! . . . that was when I fought him, I did—thank God I did! . . . Then he pulled my hair . . . ah, my hair . . . was it that he used it to . . . ?* She nodded weakly, fuzzily recalling being flung violently, as it turned out, into the wall, where she now slumped, her mind groggy, her memory uncertain, suddenly, randomly thinking, *Trinity College*, and she gently shook her head, a movement she found painful.

She felt a swelling around her left eye and, tasting blood in her mouth, uncaringly spat weakly into the darkness. Her head hurt, her jaw hurt, her back hurt; her *body* hurt.

Chilled, she fell back the first and second time she tried to stand, but finally, by first kneeling, Eileen managed to struggle unsteadily to her feet, her eyes now accustomed to the dark, seeking cover and warmth. She stumbled to the bed and felt suddenly repulsed, so she pulled another puffy, down-filled coverlet, still somehow folded into the dishevelled bedclothes, and, the pain sharp, tugged it free, clumsily wrapping it around herself. She grabbed a pillow and settled into the high-backed chair by the fireplace.

As she did, she noticed a low flame on the turf; moaning aloud, with great effort she eased off the chair and, her muscles screaming, knelt, feeding smaller bits of very dry turf into the low flame, blowing gently on it until they all caught and, having succeeded in getting an actual fire, minute but burning brightly, its low shadows dancing on the walls, she slowly added more turf and, her body throbbing, finally settled back into the coverlet and pillow.

As its light and, more importantly to her, its warmth began to reach her, she rested her head against the chair back, closing her eyes. *'Tis a dangerous time for you, girl. You must remember who it is that you are, the people from whom it is that you have sprung. . . .*

She sat silently, staring blankly into the bright, low fire, though after a time she recalled that Donal Mór had always told his children, *when you are not certain what to do, do nothing. Bold, unthinking steps can lead one over a cliff or into an abyss. Standing still will not.*

"'Tis nothing then I shall do until I am sure, Papa," she whispered . . . "but when I am certain, I . . ." She fell asleep.

It was full daylight by the time Eileen awoke. The fire was almost out. Still wrapped in the bed quilt, she was cold, stiff and her body ached. Rising from the chair, falling back once, she stood painfully, with extreme difficulty and, after first shakingly balancing herself against the chair back, she stepped unsteadily towards the looking glass on the door of the armoire with more than a bit of apprehension.

Resting her left hand heavily against the tall cabinet, she pushed her hair back and heard herself gasp as she saw her reflected image. Her left eye was ringed with purple, both of her cheeks significantly bruised, her lip split and her jaw an ugly shade of black and blue in several places. Her shoulders, upper arms and chest appeared badly battered. Her neck showed evidence that she had been choked. There was dried blood about her nose and, smeared on her face and chin, additional streaks on her breasts. Her thighs were smeared with dried blood, as well as what she concluded was dried semen. Her legs were bruised but not badly.

Aren't you a sight now, girl? she thought half-aloud.

She could only move her head slightly from side to side; it pounded, and her neck hurt horribly. There was a sharp pain in her jaw, though, as she rubbed it, it felt intact, and her cheeks stung.

Letting the coverlet drop from her shoulders to the floor, she walked in a small circle and very tentatively, just barely moved her shoulders and arms; they both hurt. She gingerly wriggled her wrists: not broken. She was standing and walking, so obviously her ankle and leg bones were not damaged, but the pain in her muscular thighs and calves was deep.

Suddenly feeling dizzy, she took a deep breath. The dizziness passed; the physical pain she was experiencing notwithstanding, she dared to think that she was perhaps not as seriously injured as she could have been, considering how violent O'Connor's attack had seemed, and sighed aloud in some relief.

Walking tentatively, as if she were balancing on stones whilst crossing a stream, she went into the dressing room. She lifted the half-filled basin of now cold water, held her head back and poured it over her face and body, gasping as it touched her breasts and stomach, streamed down her body and puddled at her feet. Its shock quickly past, the cold water felt cleansing to her;

she stood in the mere for a moment, moving her hands slowly across her face, her breasts, her shoulders and arms, her stomach, all of her muscles screaming with each movement.

Feeling if not cleansed at least less violated, she experienced a sudden desperate urge to dress, and used a thick French body towel to dry herself slowly, even though it hurt her arms and shoulders, her wrists, to do so. Her skin tingling, she returned to the armoire; she retrieved a cotton shift and, struggling, gasping at the pain, she pulled it over her head, then selected a heavy dark blue wool, long-sleeved dress with peaked shoulders and a full skirt, and, with yet again a significant degree of painful effort, dressed—not even considering a corset or hip-pads, she painfully wriggled a light stomacher over her breasts and into the robe.

Sitting uncomfortably on the chair on which she'd slept, she decided against hose and slipped her bare feet into black leather French slippers.

She stood once again in front of the armoire, just looking at herself. Her mind had generally cleared; it seemed it was functioning again. She knew the time had come, and she was certain she did indeed have the courage. *The bloody bastard, he tried to kill me!* Recalling her final conversation with her mother, just prior to departing Derrynane, she nodded to her image. *I know precisely what I must do.*

She smoothed her hair as best she could and, taking a deep breath and a few tentative steps, leaning heavily on the mattress, she knelt unsteadily on the floor by the top of the bed. Letting out a low moan of pain, she stretched her arm beneath the bed, retrieving her leather pistol case.

She knelt alongside the bed and slid the gleaming gun out of its velvet sack, then double-checked the powder, charge and ball. She slowly made her way back to the armoire that held her dresses; reaching it, she yet again rested heavily against it, then first slipped the leather case itself deep into its recesses, behind her dresses, and then slowly withdrew a long, heavy, green wool mantle. Maurice had had it made for her in Paris the year before. It was full-length and elegant, the large hood lined with padded velvet, her initials woven into it in gold thread. She had worn it that rainy, misty evening she had learnt of her betrothal.

Setting the gun down on the bed, Eileen awkwardly managed to draw the cloak over her shoulders. She would normally have then lifted the flowing hem and swept out of the room; *like Queen Maeve; like her, I, too, am prepared to take a life, though I shall do it by my own hand*, she thought, though this morning her exit into the hall was slow and unsteady, each movement excruciating.

The house was eerily silent. Despite that, she stepped lightly; even her delicate slippers sounded on the uncarpeted part of the floor, the corridor itself dim, illuminated only by the light filtering up the stairs and from the fully open door of her own room.

Certain she could hear her heart thudding, she held the cocked pistol in her right hand, beneath the folds of the mantle, as she extended her left to open O'Connor's double doors, she was surprised to see the right one ever so slightly ajar. Gently nudging it open a bit more with the tip of her left slipper, she peered, and then stepped inside. The bedclothes were in great disarray, his clothing from the previous day and the black suit, hose and buckled shoes he'd worn for the wedding scattered on the floor, along with his dressing gown and nightshirt, several dresser drawers partially open, the door to his armoire even more so.

She stood breathlessly, listening for even the slightest of sounds from what she correctly surmised was the dressing room, but heard none at all. She called out softly, "John?"—silence the sole response. Her pistol at the ready, she moved achingly across the thick, vividly coloured Indian carpet, thrusting the barrel in front of her into the dressing room—which, as she entered, she saw was empty.

Sighing audibly, she leaned heavily against the doorjamb, whispering barely aloud, "You craven, cowardly bastard," and added, with a bitter, ironic smile, "now I shall have to hunt you."

She shook her head in disgust; *a brute . . . and a coward.*

Eileen left the rooms as they were. Stepping into the hall, she silently uncocked the gun and slid it into a deep pocket of her dress, beneath the mantle. She turned and calmly, painfully, leaned her back against the wall; standing quietly, a profound sense of anticlimax seemed to wash over her.

Her eyes closed, she disavowed any false bravado: *I did not charge him as Daniel did his make-believe foes with his wooden sword when a wee one.* Opening her eyes, she sighed. *Firm I am, in my heart, in my mind, in my very soul, that had O'Connor been in that room, I would have calmly approached him, perhaps even smiling, pulled the trigger, as I know well how to, and by now, I would have taken his life. . . . And by now have been done with it . . . and him. But now . . .* She sighed audibly yet again.

She looked around and shook her head. After a moment, she walked slowly towards the stairs. Looking down, she began to deliberately descend the same staircase up which she'd been carried by her husband less than twelve hours earlier, now leaning heavily on the banister, each step painful in so many ways. She winced but remained silent.

In the great hall, the clock indicated it was a bit before eight. The damaged harp lay where it had fallen. Eileen stopped and looked at it. She knew from the harps she had played at Derrynane that this one was at least a hundred years old. *Turlough O'Carolan himself might have cradled it,* she thought, saddened that several strings had broken, though the harp itself did not appear to be damaged.

Mama would have said right away, "'Tis a sign," and she would have been correct, she thought as she started to open the front door.

She heard light, hastening footsteps from another direction and turned just as Mary opened what apparently was the door in from the kitchen building. The woman gasped as she saw Eileen, who quickly said, "I *do* need to find my way about this place better," an immediate question halter.

"I was just coming to see to mistress's morning needs. Cook shall prepare tea or coffee, and . . ." the woman managed.

"Oh, how kind, but not just now, thank you. I was actually seeking out the squire."

"The squire, Mistress? I am told he rode out very early this morning, though I am unaware of his destination," she finished quickly.

Eileen turned slowly, stiffly, back towards the woman. "The use of 'Madame' is also acceptable . . . and, if I may, where precisely *is* my husband?"

"I do not know, Madame. I . . ."

Eileen took several painful steps closer, so close to Mary that the much shorter woman was compelled to crane her neck in order to look up at her battered face.

"*Where . . . is . . . my . . . husband, woman?*" Eileen demanded, her tone icy, chilling, indeed frightening, Mary felt.

"He has gone to Moyvane Castle, Madame, and is due back in a day, perhaps two," the older woman stammered.

Glaring at her, Eileen stood for a long moment. "How lovely for him." Stepping back, she looked down at the much shorter woman. "I require some air. I am going to walk briefly outside." Partially lifting her hood over her hair, Eileen added without turning around, "Whilst I am outside, certainly no longer than thirty minutes, you shall personally see to it that someone strips my bed, replacing all the linens and coverlets and providing new pillows and slips."

She then turned, again looking down at the older woman and speaking very slowly, "I am obviously injured and I am fairly certain you know how, perhaps even why and, I believe, by whom."

Mary's face flamed red.

"I *thought* so," Eileen purred cruelly. "I expect all to be in readiness for me. Once I return to my rooms, no one is to enter until I say so. You are to say nothing to anyone about this conversation, or about anything else that has happened here in the last twelve hours. You have obviously seen my face. When first I simply spoke to you nonsense, you appeared sufficiently intelligent to say no more. For your sake, I trust you are."

Eileen turned as imperiously as she could and was pleased to see Mary in a deep curtsey, which she did not acknowledge.

Her pain such that she regretted her decision to do so, nevertheless having made her way painfully downstairs, Eileen stepped out into the chill morning air, took a deep breath and walked gingerly, haltingly across the dew-covered, rough-cut grass.

Walking just a bit farther, the muscles in her thighs already spasming, her back began to throb. "Bastard," she hissed and turned back towards the house.

With no distractions other than her pain and, despite it, her head finally beginning to clear even a bit more, she was able to begin thinking, rationally, methodically, albeit slowly, just as Donal Mór would have had her do. As she gradually approached the now-fittingly grim-looking house that was Ballyhar, she was formulating at least the genesis of a plan—a plan of which, she felt, Donal Mór would have approved—and whilst thinking of this, and nodding to herself, she managed what was an evil-looking smile.

Though I may yet simply kill the man and be done with it . . . she thought dismissively; and then, after a few moments, she reflected more calmly, *or perhaps not . . . but whichever of the two—or any other course—I decide shall be that which is ultimately the best for me . . .* "For *me!*" she said sharply aloud into the silence of the Kerry morning.

With not inconsiderable difficulty, bending, her palms holding her thighs, Eileen climbed the rail-less stairs to the front door and made her way down the hall, in the direction from which she'd seen Mary come. Opening the door at the end of the hall, she saw a covered slate footpath—blessedly level— that led to the kitchen.

Seeing only the chatty Kate through the open kitchen door, Eileen was relieved. She entered and closed the door.

Approaching Eileen with her eyes lowered slightly, as was her habit, Kate said a cheery, *"Dia dhuit,"* "Good morning, God be with you."

Eileen responded in Irish, and as Kate looked up, she pushed back her hood.

"Holymotherofgodandthesaints. . ." the girl gasped, again in Irish, crossing herself, her eyes round, her expression a mixture of shock, fear and revulsion.

Drawing her hood partially open, Eileen stepped forward and softly pressed her finger to the girl's lips. "'Tis all right, girl, or at least I believe 'tisn't as horrid as it looks." She smiled wanly, slurring some of the Irish words.

"But Mistress . . ."

"'Tisn't . . . I fear it could have been far, far worse, but for now . . ."

The quiet Kate appeared from a side door, a basket of eggs on her arm. Seeing Eileen, she smiled broadly as she set the pannier on a table. As she walked towards them, the chatty Kate turned and sounded, "Shusssssh, girl.

Say nothing!" As the quieter Kate reached them, she stood silent, her mouth agape, crossing herself . . . she then began to cry very softly.

Eileen quickly stepped forward, gently touched the tip of one finger to the girl's lips and with the thumb of her other hand wiped her tears. She kissed the quiet girl's forehead and stepped back.

"'Tis not the time for tears, though I must admit I do not know what all precisely it is the time for." Two thoughts came suddenly to her mind: *I have not cried* . . . and then . . . hopefully, she asked the girls, "Padraig, *an buichaill* . . ."

"Ah, Patrick the boy, he left before dawn, Mistress," said Chatty Kate. "Mister David, he brought him a small sack of coins from the master last evening as we ate." Seeing Eileen's expression, her own face grew sombre. "He has gone, Mistress. I'm sorry."

Eileen sighed. "Then perhaps . . . 'tis time for some tea, please?" she said as she seated herself as comfortably as she could manage on a rough stool next to the large cutting table, itself set in the middle of the comfortingly warm room.

The quiet Kate handed her a rough goblet of steaming black tea. Wrapping her hands gratefully around its warmth, Eileen said softly, *"Go raibh mille maith agat,"* "thank you very much," and sipped. She finished her cup, saying little to the girls. Standing to leave, she began, "Say nothing to the others."

She turned to the door, stopped, thought and turned back. "I am going to need your help, Kate," she smiled wanly, "and Kate."

The girls leaned back on the worktable. Eileen began to speak softly in hushed tones.

Accompanied by both girls, one on either side supporting her, Eileen climbed painfully to her rooms, where it was apparent that her instructions had been followed by Mary, who was nowhere to be found. The bed had been stripped, the linens replaced and the room cleaned.

For the next three days, cared for by the girls, Eileen remained largely in bed, resting and preparing for what she knew would be O'Connor's eventual

return. Though her injuries were painful and, to a degree, temporarily disfig-
uring, she was satisfied that she would recover.

Her principal thoughts, as she rested and began to heal, were how she
would deal with her husband. For the moment, shooting him to death had
again become paramount in her mind, as, sedated by Cook's largely alcohol-
based remedies, she drifted in and out of a blessedly dreamless sleep.

As Eileen had discovered, O'Connor had left the house within hours of his
attack on her; he had attempted to sleep but without success, growing certain
only that he needed to be away for a time.

He had made his way to the barn, saddled his horse and ridden out into
a moonless night, having taken neither clothes nor any provisions with him.
He covered the rough ground between his home and Moyvane Castle slowly;
as he had attempted to mount the animal, he found that, in thrashing Eileen,
he had apparently injured himself as well, seeming to have strained several
muscles in his arms and legs, thus making the trip a plodding and uncomfortable one. O'Connor arrived near the dull grey pile that was Lord Moyvane's
castle shortly after sunrise, though he delayed his actual appearance at the
bridge for at least an hour before seeking admittance.

As he sat, he seethed with rage, now primarily directed at himself, at
his indiscreet, perhaps champagne-fuelled ramblings in bed, even more so at
his aggressive, indeed violent reaction to Eileen's theatrics. As he sat astride,
his hands loosely holding the reins, resting on the pommel of his saddle and
reflecting, he was_shocked as he replayed the confrontation and his own
actions, finally shaking his head. *I could have killed the girl. . . .*

As much as anything, at that moment he was deeply regretting the
entire transaction with Denis O'Connell. *What was it I was thinking? Toss
some gold, some pounds, and some perhaps worthless land in America I shall
never see at a greedy_bastard in return for a child bride, who would . . . who
would what? Provide me with consort, with happiness . . . Bah!* He spat on
the ground.

Though he valued the nobleman's counsel, O'Connor was suddenly lamenting coming to Moyvane Castle, recalling his friend's reaction to the O'Connell transaction as being largely negative. *O'Connor, you are sixty years and more of age, you are wealthy_beyond all reason, educated far beyond your standing and station*—though he had only spoken to Eileen of his time at Trinity College, Dublin, O'Connor had also sat classics at Magdelen College, Oxford—*well-read, relatively well-travelled. . . . Why in God's holy name do you require a wife, man?*

Gently booting his horse and muttering aloud, "Why indeed?" O'Connor finally crossed the bridge to the courtyard of Moyvane Castle, where he spent a generally uncomfortable three days.

When he did see Lord Moyvane, the noble seemed not at all pleased to have him there. "I suggest you rest, O'Connor, sleep even, and we shall speak this evening," Moyvane had said when first they met in the morning, as he learnt the reason for O'Connor's appearance, and adding somewhat dismissively, "I myself have a rather full day." Which, in fact, he did, the fullness consisting of, at least in part, time set aside to spend with a pleasantly soft, red-haired girl of perhaps fifteen named Nancy, who dwelt with her mother, two sisters and six brothers in a cabin on the extensive Moyvane estate. Her father dead one year now, she and her sisters had agreed to provide the landlord with what he had characterised as "occasional amusement," so as to assure that the family would retain its home.

"Ah, taken by the drink he was, as he often is," Nancy had related to her sisters after her most recent visit to the castle, "and hardly any effort it took to make him *happy*." She giggled cruelly. "Only a wee bit o'bouncin' and done he was, asleep soon he was." She indicated that whilst Moyvane had slept, she had enjoyed a hearty meal, including some porter provided by and shared with a girl who worked in the kitchens. And, after the kitchen girl had departed, Nancy had, as one of her older sisters advised that she do whenever possible, rifled through the lord's clothing and furniture, happily finding a hefty pouch of coins from which she withdrew a small handful.

Today, however, Nancy found that Moyvane was quite sober, for some reason unhappy and, perhaps as a result, unusually demanding. "*Twice* the old bugger did it to me, he did, smacking me, he was, *both times*, and, done with me, the fat old sod gets off me and throws me clothes at me. Then, 'Get out, bitch!' he says, and no food and no coins," she reported to her disappointed sisters.

Lord Moyvane was displeased because John O'Connor's sudden presence not only meant demands on his time and his hospitality but that he would inevitably be presented with problems to be solved, and, as often proved the case in dealing with those neighbours he generally referred to as "the local gentry—hah!" possibly a demand on his not insignificant wealth. "They never seem to have any money," he often would say in Dublin or London, though, as he reflected on his visitor this day, of money John O'Connor possessed a great deal. *So, a problem it is—business, politics . . . again, something I am looked to solve*, he groused to himself as he dressed following Nancy's departure.

Finally, as dusk was settling over North Kerry, both of them now sitting in the nobleman's book-lined study, a fire bright and ample whiskey at hand, O'Connor had briefly summarised the events of the previous night. Moyvane, already smitten in so many ways by and with Eileen O'Connell, listened intently, initially enthralled, his grey mood seeming to improve.

After describing the sex in detail and responding to the lord's increasingly salacious questions and asides, O'Connor pronounced, "It was if she'd been fucking for years."

"From what you say, oh my yes, my good man . . . yes, indeed it seems!"

Both men sipped their whiskeys. Lowering his crystal glass, Moyvane said, "I assume you told her 'well done, girl' or something like that. I mean, you did not just get off her and leave the room, did you? You at least patted her bottom, did you not?" He laughed.

O'Connor answered, again in some detail. After a pause, he continued, "So you see, I *did* tell her 'well done.' It might have been a bit colourful. I suspect the girl may not have been used to being spoken to that way."

Lord Moyvane raised both palms. "Perhaps not, but what can she say? She'd obviously pleased you, she said beforehand she understood what was expected of her and she did that apparently better than well."

O'Connor then set out what Eileen had said, including, much to the noble's obvious pleasure, the dramatic, almost theatrical manner in which she'd done it, striding about the room, her mane gleaming in the firelight, her body barely covered by the quilt, her shoulders and breasts bared.

"Spirited girl, that O'Connell girl, yes!" Moyvane exclaimed. "I think you should have simply thrown her back on the bed and remounted, as it sounds as if she actually likes being ridden!"

"Yes, yes. Perhaps I should have. As I told you, she said she desired more, but . . ."

O'Connor proceeded to recount, as best as he said he could remember, what next had happened, qualifying it as he began, "You must know, sir, I was enraged. *I* am not used to being addressed in such a way, certainly not by a just-fucked, naked girl."

"Certainly not," Moyvane observed quickly, though he became increasingly and obviously uncomfortable as O'Connor spoke of the blows and the kicks, and he visibly winced and gasped audibly as O'Connor described using Eileen's hair to violently propel her into the wall.

As O'Connor finished speaking, waiting until the silence in the room was profound, only then leaning forward, his hands resting on his knees, the nobleman looked closely at his friend. "I must ask, O'Connor, are you certain the girl . . . that she was alive when you left her?"

O'Connor indicated he'd slipped back into the room during the night. "Her breasts were rising and falling. I was satisfied she was then alive, and I assume she remains so this evening."

Moyvane had started to speak and then abruptly stopped. A now-thick, uncomfortable silence settled over the room, the fire becoming a bit smoky. Moyvane poked at the mix of burning turf and wood, opened a window and resumed his seat. "O'Connor, this is most awkward. I am your friend, yes, but I am also the king's justice of the peace. I am the one who enforces the king's writ here; perhaps you have forgotten."

O'Connor sat silently, his face ashen.

"You have described what some might say was a brutal attack; yes indeed, an attack that could have killed her, some might say. . . ."

The nobleman's mind, working quickly now, was putting the event into some perspective, some context, nodding as he finally again said, "*Some* might say . . ." Still not looking at O'Connor at all, he picked up a long clay pipe, already filled, and took some moments lighting it with a taper from the fire whilst O'Connor sat discomfited, in silence, the atmosphere in the room thickening even further.

Drawing deeply on his pipe and exhaling what became a spicy blue haze in the small room, Moyvane finally continued, his tone now somewhat lighter. "All of this being said, my good man, she *is* your wife, just a mere girl at that, and emotional, hysterical even, certainly not fully appreciative of your compliments, silly girl . . ." suddenly pausing, reflecting further.

O'Connor said nothing.

After long moments, Moyvane took a deep breath. "Upon reflection, I do not believe that the king's justice is seriously offended. *Truly*, if fine, loyal gentlemen such as your good self were to be charged for each time they find themselves compelled to administer a well-deserved beating to some hysterical woman, the gaols would have no room for the common scum they are supposed to hold."

O'Connor breathed a bit easier.

"This being the case, the king's justice is one thing, my good man," Moyvane said slowly, now very carefully choosing his words. "Dealing with the O'Connells of Derrynane . . . *this* is something else entirely."

O'Connor began to speak. "The eldest brother . . ."

Lord Moyvane raised his palms. "Hear me, O'Connor," he said firmly. "I understand your arrangement with the brother. He is known to be a greedy, grasping man. That he is one is clear by that he sold that girl to you."

"He did no such thing; 'twas business, pure and . . ."

The same palms were raised once again. "He sold her like a fine horse!" Moyvane snapped. Lowering his hands and leaning forward, he continued, calmer, though no less urgently, "Let me tell you something. I did not know him well, but I *do* know that Donal Mór Ó Conaill is restless in his grave this night over what has happened to that girl, both at the brother's hands and at yours. I truly believe if he could, he would kill his son for doing what he did, and he would kill you twice.

"From all I know of them, these . . . the O'Connells, they are unusual people. They are frighteningly intelligent; one is able to see and hear this in the girl herself. From merely a few moments spent with and near her last evening, I am able to say that her Latin puts the damned priest's to shame, her French is near flawless and—though she is still a mere girl, a child, and only just beginning to grasp the reality of who and what she is—even at this juncture she is as poised as a woman twice her age, and more regal than most I have ever encountered in Dublin, indeed in London as well.

"These O'Connells are arrogant and prideful, yes . . . they see themselves as somehow benighted, even though they are mere graziers and smugglers and thieves and cattle-rustlers, and God knows what else in addition.

"They live down there at the very end of Kerry, protected by their mountains and their own cunning and by what appears to be a strange combination of fear and awe that they have somehow managed to instil in their good Protestant neighbours, so as to keep them in thrall. They lie hidden in their glens, nourished in many ways by the ocean that they treat as their own; they journey to Spain the way we may go to London. . . . They are singular, indeed, like it or not, and many, many in Ireland do not!

"Despite the fact that the O'Connells may be disliked by many—indeed hated by some—*your* problem is that they do not appear to care what *anyone* thinks. They take care of themselves; they take care of their own. . . ."

"But . . ."

"But nothing, man. If that girl could today get a message to her mother – a 'dark woman of the glen,' said to possess a variety of mystical, magical skills, I have always heard, which, if 'tis true, would present an entirely different set of problems for you—or to even one of her hot-headed brothers, you would be dead. I have no qualm in telling you. *Dead*. And what you must understand is that, either because they have already told her or by some other means, she *knows* they would kill you for what you did . . . or, and hear me well, O'Connor, for *this* is much more immediately serious to you, *she may* very well yet *kill you herself*."

Such colour as had returned immediately left O'Connor's face.

"From what I know of the O'Connells—and as a loyal Irish subject and officer of His Majesty in this kingdom, I have made it my business to learn a great deal about these types of families—I have no doubt that this girl is armed as she sleeps in your house, and that she knows how to use any weapon. And lest you become comfortable, in the event that the instant situation somehow passes without incident," he gestured broadly with his hands, "*all* of this would be true if anything even remotely similar to the events you have here described to me were ever to recur; *ever*, do you understand?"

O'Connor sat, silent, numb, ashen. "I do not dislike the girl," he began hesitatingly. "So . . ."

"So remain here a while longer and then return home, O'Connor. Perhaps she *is* just a silly girl and will not kill you when you get there. If she does not then, she probably will not . . . though she may yet still leave it up to her family, so do not become complacent. In any case, remember what I have said: Do not trust her. Watch her. Have her watched. If you can, prevent her communicating with anyone, but I doubt that you can. Perhaps in time . . . it may resolve itself. In the meantime, you need be careful, *very* careful."

Moyvane himself departed for Dublin the following morning but left O'Connor with ample food, whiskies and wine. He had even considered offering him Nancy's services but decided against it. *I do not want that one hurt.*

O'Connor spent the three ensuing days at Moyvane Castle and, despite his consumption of significant amounts of Lord Moyvane's whiskey each evening prior to retiring, a series of most restless nights as well. Finally heading home, departing late midmorning on the fourth day after his arrival, O'Connor covered the rough ground slowly, his mind racing, seriously wondering whether he would face the barrel of a gun in the hands of his beautiful young wife.

Late that afternoon, racing about to where each of them were, one of the stable boys alerted the chattier Kate and Michael, a young groom, to O'Connor's imminent arrival, and Michael hastened to join her at the steps of the main entrance. Eileen and Kate had planned in advance, and both Kates having previously cleared the house, advising the servants that the master was returning, that he and the mistress wished the house entirely to themselves, without exception, Kate and Michael now perfunctorily greeted O'Connor, the groom taking his horse. Kate addressed him in, the squire noticed, an unusually sharp tone. "Mistress O'Connor, sir, she has asked me to advise you that she wishes your honour to join her in the sitting room, sir."

O'Connor eyed the girl first blankly, then curiously, saying nothing.

"The mistress, sir, she was injured and has been abed," Kate continued, her tone seeming to O'Connor to be approaching impertinence, "but would see your honour at a time convenient for you, sir."

O'Connor drew a breath. "Very well, then, girl. You may advise Mistress O'Connor that at the top of the coming hour I shall await her, as and where she wishes."

Kate nodded; she did not half-curtsey.

Seeing Kate watching him warily, O'Connor turned and slowly climbed the stairs, his riding boots thudding on the gleaming, smoothly worn steps.

By a message conveyed from Kate, by the time O'Connor had stepped into the house, Eileen was quickly made aware of his return and was waiting quietly on her bed for both Kates to assist her in dressing. Though she hadn't heard O'Connor ride up, her door purposely left ajar, she had heard muffled words echo in the hall below, and then his heavy boots in the hall and as he trudged up the stairs. *Not as lightly as the other night*, she mused bitterly.

She had then heard the delicate bare footsteps of Kate, and moments later of Kate, padding up the stairs. The sound of two doors being opened and closed by O'Connor echoed in the hall, one very quickly, and then the girls together stepped into Eileen's room.

With their help, she had been out of bed and had walked cautiously about her rooms beginning the day just prior, and, again, last evening and this morning. This afternoon she found herself feeling a bit stronger, her pain ever so slightly lessening.

Now, to confront her husband, her attacker, Eileen, with the girls' gentle assistance, over her chemise slowly donned a simple dark green cotton dress, without a corset but with hip pads, and a crisp white apron with a deep wide pocket, which the quiet Kate had brought up from the servants' pantry.

Despite her mother's parting caution against telling anyone of its existence, Eileen had concluded that the situation compelled her to take both girls into her confidence. Now it was the quiet Kate who, after slipping it from beneath the bedcovers where her mistress had lay, gently handed Eileen her gleaming pistol and watched in obvious awe as the taller girl, checking its readiness, slid it into her pocket.

"Mistress, are you meaning to . . . ?" she began, her voice trembling.

Gently taking the quiet girl's visibly shaking hand, Eileen said softly, "I shall do what I believe is necessary. . . ." She then eyed the chattier Kate, the girl's expression ashen.

"The two wee bottles, Mistress, they be in your apron, Madame, as you said," she responded softly, automatically, emphasising her respect.

Eileen, in turn, nodded. Her preparations nearly complete, she could hear the heavy sound of a man's boots descending the stairs.

"The squire, Mistress," the quieter girl volunteered.

Eileen nodded. *The squire, yes.* She waited until she heard the boots thudding across the entrance hall, heading into the side corridor that led towards the parlour. "Shall we, my darlings?" Eileen said, her throaty voice still weary.

The girls flanked her as they walked slightly sideways through the gleaming dark oak door, which Eileen herself nudged open with her slippered foot. Leaning heavily on the banister and supported by the chattier Kate, the quiet one leading the way, Eileen made her way slowly down the stairs. Reaching the hall, she gestured gently to the girls to step aside. "Alone I must now be."

They stood staring, their unease, their uncertainty patent. "I shall see you shortly, my loves, worry not," Eileen reassured them softly and, as erect as possible, she slowly, delicately made her way to the small sitting room in which she and O'Connor had taken tea the day of her arrival. As she leaned agonizingly forward to push the partially open door, Eileen's right hand rested in the same-side pocket of her dress.

She looked into the comfortable room, a potent silence now hanging heavily in the air. Though he was coatless, she saw that O'Connor was otherwise in dusty travelling clothes; as he began to rise as she entered, she pointedly noted he was holding a riding crop. Without taking her eyes off her husband, in a single, fluid movement, Eileen withdrew her right hand from the dress pocket and, with painful effort, fully cocked and aimed the striking weapon at his chest.

Instantly seeing, immediately comprehending, O'Connor abruptly froze at the point at which he had risen, motionless, an expression of horror contorting his face, his right hand now forming a pointless fist, his left still gripping the crop, visibly trembling. He sensed himself unable to speak, to cry out.

Impassively, Eileen squeezed the trigger, the hammer snapping forward into the frizzen, the hammer's flint scraping the frizzen's face, causing a shower of sparks to be thrown into the flash pan; igniting the black powder in the pan, it in turn lit the main powder charge.

A cloud of fire and smoke filled the room as the end of the barrel exploded in terrifyingly brilliant flame whilst a powerful blast shattered the prior stillness, the air instantly heavy with acrid smoke and the bitter odour of burnt black powder.

O'Connor fell heavily to his knees and crumpled to the floor, the crop falling from his fingers.

In the doorway, delicately veiled by the smoke, Eileen loomed silently, impassively watching—until suddenly she burst into laughter, a cruel, viciously triumphant laughter, her mirth incongruous to the dazed man, partially kneeling, his eyes wide, his chest heaving, his heart feeling as if it were about to explode.

Eileen remained still, leaning heavily against the doorjamb, looking towards him now. "Oh, dear," she feigned, as loudly as she could manage, whilst very slowly rolling a lead pistol ball between the thumb and forefinger of her left hand, on which her recently received wedding band now shone, and she laughed again caustically.

As she disdainfully observed O'Connor scrambling to collect himself and rise from a semi kneeling position, still pointing the gun in his general direction, Eileen moved slowly to the chair in which he had not been seated. As he himself stood unsteadily, she very slowly, tentatively, sat, her pain now profound, a moan of sorts finally escaping her still visibly split lips.

She purposely lay the pistol on her right thigh, the tip of the still delicately smoking barrel on her knee, pointed mockingly at the chair in which O'Connor would sit.

"Why, *please* be seated, husband," she purred, smiling condescendingly, gesturing a now weakly standing O'Connor to take his customary seat. "Since it appears your life remains your own . . . at least for now," she added, her voice knife sharp.

Visibly shaken, his face bathed in sweat, O'Connor sat heavily in the same chair he had occupied the day Eileen had arrived at Firies, his expression vacant. He said nothing, his eyes on the gun barrel.

"I should tell you, *John*," Eileen began, her husky voice icy, her tone cutting, "the other morning when early I came to your rooms only to find you gone . . ." She paused, pointedly appearing to be thinking deeply, whilst he stared numbly at her.

"I was just pondering, *John*," she finally resumed, lifting her head, gesturing at him with her left forefinger. "Did you depart—*flee,* actually—in the night out of shame for what you had done to me . . ." She paused, now permitting the fingers of her left hand to gently touch her battered face, her purple-ringed left eye, her bruised jaw. "Or 'twas it out of fear—no, actually, I *should* have said *cowardice*, yes, *yes* . . . now *that* would be the more proper word, would it not? Out of *cowardice* at what *I* might *do* to *you*?"

O'Connor said nothing; she noted his breathing had slowed, that some colour had returned to his sweat-sheened face.

"Ah, no matter, really . . . as I was saying, when I came to your rooms," she lifted the no longer smoking weapon, pointing it directly at him, "this dear object was both cocked *and* loaded, unlike now." She laughed again. "Have no doubt, sir, that had you not fled this house, you would now be dead. I came fully prepared to shoot and to kill you, sir. So . . . whether 'twas by your shame or your cowardice or both, you saved your life, at least for a bit longer."

O'Connor continued to stare at her in silence, his skin tone again ashen.

"Now then . . . the other evening . . ." she began.

Inexplicably, he put his hand up, a look of disgust now on what she now noticed was his unshaven face, looking blankly at her.

Eileen stopped, looking searingly into O'Connor's suddenly weary eyes, and leaned slightly forward.

"Let *that* be the *last time* you expect to silence me," she said sharply, re-aiming the pistol at his chest. "I am not one of your servants. As I was saying, the other evening was most unfortunate. I think you would agree."

Other than a noncommittal grunt, wordlessly O'Connor now gazed out the window, affecting, or at least attempting, a diffident air.

She continued, "I truly did not expect it to be thus, but I found the first part of our time together the other evening quite extraordinary. Unfamiliar with it all, as I knew nothing of *it*, but I do now understand some of the *wonders of it all.* 'Tis really quite something, is *it* not?" She paused, appearing now guileless, wide-eyed.

"*Fucking*, that is," she said, her expression suddenly arch, leering as she dramatically elevated her voice, its tone viciously cold. She paused. He remained silent, though at the instant he heard the word his eyes snapped towards her, and he was now looking at her, his expression one of sudden shock.

She continued, "Upon reflection, though, one thing I did conclude was even how much more extraordinary it must be for a young girl to *fuck* with a . . . *young* man." She smiled sweetly, viciously. "Nevertheless, I so enjoyed it and you so *obviously* enjoyed me," she pressed her fingertips to her breasts, "and what is *so* exciting to me is that I am apparently so *extraordinarily talented* at *fucking,* as you yourself so colourfully put it." She laughed wickedly, and though the pain in her neck and head was exquisite, she forced herself to toss her head back in disdain, moaning involuntarily as she finished the motion. "Can you believe that, John? *Me? Fucking?*" Her laugh was now bitter.

He began to speak, perhaps in response, at the same time, unconsciously perhaps, but nevertheless tapping the whip edge of the crop he had retrieved from where he had dropped it on his left boot toe.

"Just several things, *my dear*, if you would permit me," Eileen continued.

O'Connor sniffed and looked up at the ceiling, seemingly endeavouring to appear bored and disinterested. "Now . . ." he began to speak.

This time it was Eileen who held up her hand and continued. *"Now . . .* I am not unreasonable. I can appreciate a man's needs when widowed, although your degree of knowledge of the art of love as practiced by and, as you pointed out, *with* many women for pay, would indicate that, sadly, Mistress O'Connor did not satisfy you, and I suspect that most likely none of these *women* have, either." She paused. "So, henceforth it is I, and *I alone*, who shall satisfy your every need, your every desire, my dear."

O'Connor's mouth fell open at the remark. Thus distracted, he did not notice that Eileen, looking neither at the weapon nor at what she was doing, had begun to slowly, skilfully reload her pistol. Nor had he, perhaps more significantly, noticed the flash of a smile on his wife's cracked, still-bloody lips, for *she* had noticed *his* stunned, shocked reactions to her choice of words, and to her commitment to satisfy his sexual needs and desires. Eileen had unexpectedly added a weapon to her arsenal, and she knew she had.

"I do have requirements, however. . . ." She half-cocked the pistol. "You will provide me with the full details of the arrangements you have entered into with my brother. I want to know *everything*."

O'Connor grunted.

Eileen smiled. "I shall take that as an affirmative. Excellent!"

Continuing to look directly at him, as he now stared vacantly at her, she dribbled a small amount of black powder from the brass vial she had slid out of her apron pocket into the barrel and then let the round ball with which she'd toyed earlier slide into the barrel as well. She slowly removed an almost delicate gunmetal ramrod from beneath the barrel, her eyes remaining fixed on O'Connor, and effortlessly continued the loading process.

"Secondly, if you so much as attempt to repeat any part of either the use of the foul, demeaning language or even a suggestion of the violence you displayed the other evening . . ."

Perhaps unthinkingly, he continued to tap the crop on his boot, a bit harder, the sound of whip against leather audible in the quiet room.

She abruptly stopped speaking, stopped loading and glared at him until he at least appeared to look at her, the tapping now halted.

Resting the pistol carefully, horizontally on the broad arm of her chair and with obvious difficulty, she stood, placing her body between O'Connor and where the weapon lay, stepped towards him and, wincing, reached over and painfully managed to grab the riding crop from his hand. Standing as straight as she could, her eyes still fixed on him, she appeared to effortlessly snap it in two. *Her hands are stronger than a sixteen-year-old girl's usually are,* he thought.

Though she gasped in pain at the motion, she tossed the pieces into the low fire and slowly, agonizingly, sat back down heavily; leaning her head against the high back of the chair, she first winced and then moaned involuntarily.

O'Connor sat slumped, his expression blank, his breathing more laboured now.

Altering neither her expression nor her gaze, she now replaced the gun upright on her knee, shook a small amount of very finely ground gunpowder from the second, smaller brass vial, taken as was the larger one from her apron, into the pistol's flash pan and rested the weapon, now primed and loaded, on her knee, her right thumb resting on the jaw screw, her right forefinger on the side of the trigger.

Though he appeared to be watching Eileen now, O'Connor's eyes seemed glazed, his expression vacant.

"As I was saying, even a *suggestion* . . . which would include attempting to intimidate me by sitting here, slapping your boot with a riding crop . . . in the event that I do not then immediately kill you, you will very shortly be dead."

O'Connor's eyes narrowed. He was looking directly at her now.

Very deliberately, she paused before continuing, "And just one last thing, so you may understand how cautious you henceforth need be, I fully assure you that, despite my wee little performance, I still may well yet kill you for what you did to me the other evening, though I am just not sure when it may be. Now, before I depart this room? Today? Perhaps next week? Perhaps tomorrow?" Not thinking, she shrugged her shoulders, the pain searing across her upper back, neck and shoulders.

She paused, waiting to see if he had anything further to say. "Very well, then, husband, but you are cautioned: Threaten me, harm me, offend me and

I assure you, by my hand or another's, you will quickly be dead, and this foul deed to which you and Denis O'Connell are agreed will be undone with equal dispatch."

Holding the gleaming pistol at her side, the barrel facing floorward, her finger on the trigger, relying on the arm of the chair, leaning heavily on her left hand and arm, she began to rise, slowly, painfully, finally standing upright.

"In the meantime, I shall require rest and, unless I feel improved shortly, medical attention—I assume you have a physician up here somewhere—the medical attention being, of course, for the injuries I suffered whilst attempting to ride my horse too fast in a country unfamiliar to both my animal and myself. Do we understand each other, *my dear?*"

He looked up at her and barely nodded once, saying nothing as she began to walk away.

She stepped into the hall, but then abruptly stopped and slowly turned again, the simple *click* of her fully cocking the pistol shattering the returned silence. Wordlessly, battling, by sheer force of will alone, masking the now intense pain in her right shoulder, arm and wrist, nevertheless succeeding in holding it level, steady, she aimed the weapon at him, her jaw set, her expression again one of contempt, disdain.

Eileen stood for what seemed to O'Connor a very, very long time, until, with an effort the difficulty of which he could not discern, she managed to extend her arm rigidly, in full firing position, her hand equally steady, staring at her husband as he sat unmoving, his expression again blank, vacant.

Finally . . . in a deep, almost sultry tone, she purred "*Bannnggg!*" Standing for another long moment, lifting the gun as she uncocked it and, finally, very slowly did she then slide the pistol into her pocket. Eileen smiled, again dazzlingly. "Good day, then, *husband.*"

O'Connor remained in his chair, mute, not even looking up as Eileen, still facing him, closed the door with a soft click. His hands gripping the armrests of the chair were shaking; his forehead and face bathed in, his shirtfront and collar wet with sweat. He sat for some time, the all-too-prophetic words of Lord Moyvane—*I have no doubt that this girl is armed as she sleeps in your house, and that she knows how to use any weapon. . . . She may very well yet kill you herself*—echoing in his mind, ultimately finding but a small measure of comfort in Moyvane's conclusion that *Perhaps she is just a silly girl and will not kill you when you get there. If she does not then, she probably will not. . . .* For this O'Connor could only hope.

By the end of the third week following what she had come to refer to simply as *that night,* Eileen was visibly improving.

The servants appeared to understand, or at least behaved as if they did, that she'd injured herself whilst riding. She concluded and announced that she did not require medical attention, beyond that being provided her by the girls and Cook.

By the end of the week following that, she had cautiously mounted Bull; maintaining him at a gentle, easy gait, she had begun tentatively to explore her new home, mostly alone but once with chatty Kate and another time with David O'Connor, who proved to be good and pleasant company. He was expressively disdainful of both his father and elder brother, solicitous of his younger brother and sensitive to Eileen's position, though he displayed no indication of any awareness of the events of the wedding night.

Eileen had not seen O'Connor alone since the afternoon when he had returned from Moyvane Castle; indeed, O'Connor was to be seen little about the place in the coming weeks. Eileen would learn that he had gone to Dublin, and perhaps on to London following that. She thought nothing of it, and little of him. She had weightier matters on her mind.

Having given the matter solitary thought, she had dismissed Mary outright and had her summarily removed from the estate, cautioning her that were she to fail to remain silent, she would be permanently silenced, causing the woman to audibly gasp as Eileen pointed her pistol at her bosom. Some months later, the neighbourhood would learn that the woman had sailed to Canada, the reason for her somewhat unusual choice of destination never to be known.

St. Patrick's Day 1760 arrived, to be marked only by a quiet family dinner, the first time Eileen had appeared unannounced at table. At her place alone sat a small crystal bowl of brilliantly green shamrocks. As she sat, still rather stiffly, she looked at the bowl, gently touched it ever so slightly and nodded, equally so, to her husband, who had just the day prior returned from Dublin—only the length of the gleaming mahogany table separating them.

Ballyhar—April–May 1760

As the days became weeks and the passage of days and weeks carried her into her second and then third month at Firies, as Eileen's tall, striking figure and distinctive stride became a familiar and welcome sight about the massive house and grounds, she would have seemed to anyone who had previously known her to be healthy and sound, though it would also be readily apparent that she had changed, and profoundly so. She was maturing rapidly, acting independently, decisively, in ways she never had before, and proving to be a kind and sensitive mistress, especially to the tenant families, noting that, particularly in comparison to the Derrynane tenants, some of their lives were most desperate. She had ordered more seed potatoes for them and doubled the size of their garden plots without discussing it with O'Connor.

She had exchanged lengthy initial letters with her mother, Abby and Morgan, and much shorter notes with Hugh, who sent her a pencil sketch of himself and Madramór that made her cry. Her letters were chatty, optimistic and devoid of even a suggestion of there being any discord between her new husband and herself, much less of the events of her wedding night.

After all, she had concluded, *what is it that they could have done for me? Were Morgan here, he himself would of course have slain O'Connor that night or immediately afterwards. But now 'tis passed . . . and rather than summon aid from Derrynane, 'tis far better that this*—she tapped her left breast gently— *O'Connell care for herself, protect herself, as I have, and so I shall!*

When she was with O'Connor, which only occurred when she felt it was to her advantage to be in his presence, she maintained an at-first silent, then uneasy and, as yet more time passed, a merely awkward truce.

From a distance, and especially when he found himself in his wife's company, he eyed her warily, seeming very guarded in his behaviour, spending much time at his desk and more away from the place. Beginning the week following St. Patrick's Day, Eileen finally decided she should begin to appear regularly at meals. They proved to be uncomfortable occasions, until—as if by design, though that was not the case—an interplay developed between and amongst David, Eileen and, with chatty Kate's help, Peter, that largely silenced O'Connor, the younger John and his equerry, a quiet, handsome boy of perhaps nineteen named Matthew. As a result, the table became a more enjoyable time and place, at least for some of them.

The family, the servants and the visitors—of whom there were, at least initially, not many, though Lord Moyvane was a regular dinner guest—all took note of what was an obvious transfer of overall influence from the master's to the mistress's end of the table. Eileen clearly presided, dominating by her sheer presence, her bearing, her intellect and her wit—and her seeming ability to speak on virtually any topic, at length, if it suited her purposes.

For reasons virtually all of which she was unaware, Lord Moyvane was clearly enthralled with her; knowing what he did of her wedding night and witnessing how she had conducted herself since then, especially the measure of control she had already taken, he had come to sincerely admire her. At table he would invariably sit to her right, initiating brief side conversations in French—she found the quality of his uneven—and occasionally sharing private jokes.

As they had walked on the lawn one cool evening in early April, Lord Moyvane had taken Eileen's arm and looked up—he was several inches shorter—at her. "The first time I met you, at your wedding, as I walked away you may recall that I uttered a simple 'extrord'nry.' I repeat myself: you are, young woman, quite so. I have never seen a mere child—you are sixteen, yes, girl?—so young a woman so completely assume a role that is often beyond those much older and more experienced in the ways of the world. Well done, Mistress O'Connor, well done, indeed!" He smiled broadly.

To Moyvane, as the weeks went by, O'Connor seemed weary and somehow complicit in his own diminished role. With this apparently in mind, on another occasion, approximately a week later, as they were walking back towards the house, he again took Eileen's arm very gently, this time stopping and facing her. "My dear, if I may ask, is your husband perhaps unwell? At a time when he—with a new and, if I may be so bold as to say so, quite beautiful young wife just come into his home—after years of loneliness . . . he should be joyful, should he not?"

"I do not know, my lord. I shall have to be more solicitous of the squire's feelings."

Though she did give some thought to Moyvane's remarks, she remained very guarded in her relationship with her husband. Her actual time with him was limited, and she did not dwell on the topic.

Having continued—whilst walking or riding about the estate, prior to going to bed or sometimes on awakening—to seriously consider, to weigh the possibility more than once, since she had found O'Connor's bedroom empty the morning following *that night*, by mid-April Eileen had made a conscious—though, she told herself, not irrevocable—decision not to kill her husband. This being the case, and though she had come to feel relatively safe in her own person, she nevertheless continued to carry her loaded pistol in her dress, cloak or saddlebag, and she also continued to reflect on and occasionally reconsider her decision.

It should properly have happened that morning. Had he been here, had he not fled as a coward, I would have killed him then and been done with it, my obvious injuries being my defence. Yet by his return I sensed 'twas not then the moment to slay him, though my little play was designed to instil fear in him, as I believe it has, though—now she shook her head and sighed aloud—*not shooting him after I had reloaded and had him then at bay,* that *might have been an error. Were I to shoot him now, how t'woud be seen? As being unprovoked? Even as murder, perhaps? Certainly as a scandal. . . .*

The questions remained sufficiently nagging so that an ever-curious Eileen found herself poking amongst the shelf of dusty legal tomes she had come across on her numerous visits to the O'Connor library, which itself whilst not large was, for an Irish country squire, unexpectedly impressive.

Locating a hefty volume whose leather spine bore, in gold lettering, the simple title *CRIMES (Ireland, 1756)*, she slid it off the shelf and, standing behind and resting the book on the high back of a brown leather winged chair she quietly flipped the pages, eventually reaching a section headed "Killing," in which she ultimately came upon portions of "The Treason Act of 1351," wondering why it was so long, feeling herself puzzled as to why it did not solely address the murder of a monarch. *Such as poor King Charles; Cromwell killed him, or his men did.*

She learnt from the marginal commentary that, whilst the Act had been enacted during the long-ago reign of Edward III, it had only been extended to Ireland in 1495. Reading further, she came upon a section about something she had never heard of, "petty treason." Her deep blue eyes moved quickly to the bottom of the page, where she read that this particular type of treason was the murder of one's lawful superior, specifically including, she noted with surprise, those instances where a wife killed her husband, the tip of her right forefinger moving over the words as she read them a second, and then a third time.

Looking at the words, her finger resting on the line, she sighed. *Now . . . this is something I certainly did not know.* Turning the page, she quickly learnt something else she did not know, gasping aloud at the stated penalty for a woman convicted under the Act of killing her husband was to be burnt at the stake. *Oh, my dear God . . .* Her mind raced. She took little comfort in that the woman was no longer drawn on a trestle to the place of execution—as well as that successfully pleading the common law defence of "provocation" could result in a conviction of manslaughter.

Perched now on the arm of the comfortably worn chair, her bare feet resting on the seat cushion, the book on her lap, she slowly reread the last section. *Treason? Petty or not, I do not think killing the squire would be worth death in the flames.* Standing, she replaced the book and, easing her feet back into her soft leather French slippers, strolled back out into the fading sunshine, eying a mass of dark clouds moving quickly towards her, initially feeling merely perplexed, though as she walked and reflected on her readings, and her situation, she came to feel uneasy.

In any event, the result t'woud definitely be most untidy . . . and John the Younger would become the squire; och! . . . and, she sighed, *Mistress Eileen would be mistress no longer.* Here she physically paused in what was becoming a dull, suddenly damp afternoon and began to ponder.

It was on this particular reality that she dwelt and would continue to dwell upon for some time thereafter. Being honest with herself, she conceded that, indeed, this—her loss of position and all that came with it—might actually prove to be the ultimate determining factor in her *not* killing John O'Connor.

Accepting this as her reality, in the meantime, her loosely conceived plan was unfolding slowly. It involved her possessing what she came to understand was power, as much power as she could and, with such power, then exercising an increasing level of control over the people and events around her. Virtually everything she did now was accomplished with a striking degree of calculation on her part, something else virtually unknown to her before. Though authority, and the control that flowed from having it, was something Eileen O'Connell had possessed none of in her own life, she had witnessed enough of its practice by her parents and, of course, in her own case had experienced its use by Denis O'Connell. She understood there was strength in having power and, perhaps more importantly, in understanding how to wield it most effectively, and for one's own benefit.

By May it was quite apparent to those who took note that she was indeed exercising a not insignificant degree of power and slowly but most definitely assuming control: over O'Connor, over the estate, over his sons. Whilst at first it seemed quite remarkable to Eileen that this came as naturally as it did to her, increasingly she came to understand and embrace the still unfolding reality that at least part of being an O'Connell apparently meant that one was actually comfortable with possessing and exercising power, whether it was ceded by others or taken by oneself. In either case, she had no intention of relinquishing any of it.

Thus situated, Eileen was also growing both secure in and quite comfortable with her position as mistress of the house and the estate. Though still finding herself occasionally bemused when she was addressed as Madame or even Mistress, she was also coming to accept that she was fully due these genteel tokens of respect. One warm May afternoon, following her rounds of the cabins, stopping at the stables to see to an injured pony, having a conversation with Cook about purchasing provisions for the kitchen, followed by a brief visit with both Kates, she found herself smiling as she was strolling back to the house. *"Yes, Mistress." "Why . . . of course, Madame." "Whatever is Madame's pleasure . . . Certainly, Mistress!" "Yes, Madame" indeed!* She laughed, loudly enough to cause Thomas, a new groom who was walking a handsome young colt, to look up and smile at her. She smiled in reply and waved.

She was also, by this time, genuinely enjoying her role as caretaker, caregiver, teacher, nurse and companion, especially to the children and the elderly amongst the tenants. As her mother had long done at Derrynane, Eileen was insistent on "her people" maintaining cleanliness. "Cottages"—Maire disdained the more commonly employed term *cabin* save to refer to only the meanest of hovels—"are for people alone, my loves," her mother would repeatedly tell the Derrynane tenants. Standing next to a reeking manure pile set right at a cabin's entrance, Maire would ask one of the children, "Do you like this smell?" and she and the child would wrinkle their noses and shake their heads, *nooo.* "So away it shall go then," Maire would bristle and, grabbing any handy tool, she would herself trundle a small load off and away from the cottage. The adults came to understand.

At the same time, Eileen had begun slowly advancing her efforts to promote literacy amongst the children, much as her mother had at Derrynane.

"Whilst you cannot kidnap the wee ones and force them to learn to read and write, you may be able to gently help the parents understand the value of their children being able to," Maire had told her before she left for Firies, adding almost as an afterthought, "You may also allay their fears of running afoul of His Majesty's authorities. Simply tell them it is *you* whom the king's men will prosecute for educating naughty Catholic children!" her mother had laughed.

Eileen was now confident that she would shortly be seeking a master for a new hedge school at the O'Connor estate. *Then I, too, shall be violating the penal laws. Will not Mama and Papa be proud!* By July, she located and engaged a bright young man with vivid yellow hair whose Latin was as good as hers, who also was competent in Greek and who arrived bearing a harp, the last fact helping Eileen to easily decide to select him.

She now understood both why Maire loved being mistress of Derrynane and why she was often weary at the end of a long day.

Eileen had also come to understand the significant degree of freedom that her position, buttressed by the power she held, not to mention O'Connor's vast wealth, provided to her. She now had ready access to what in a brief letter to Abby she had called "nice things": new dresses and hats, cases of books of her own choosing, as well as other reading materials, periodicals from Dublin and London, all of which she eagerly awaited and read avidly. She felt it liberating not to have to seek her parents' or Denis O'Connell's permission—or, she reflected, even John O'Connor's, for that matter—to do what she wanted to do, to have what she wanted to have. She found she simply had to ask and whatever it might be would be done, ordered, procured and delivered.

So, too, had she come to enjoy gatherings at what she now regarded as being her home, particularly presiding at table, and especially when there were new guests, as it seemed there were, more and more frequently.

"People wish to meet you, my dear," the recently arrived Lady Elizabeth, Countess of Moyvane, a striking, full-figured blonde, blue-eyed Anglo-Irish woman of perhaps forty, who stood at least inches taller than her husband—*I see not why his lordship would ever stray, ever frolic with girls from the cabins; she is a comely woman, saucy and even naughty, I believe she could be!*—who herself appeared to have returned to Ireland this time with some degree of permanence in mind, told Eileen one evening.

Her voice soft, her tone elegant and precise—Eileen thinking, *more English than Irish, but Irish enough, and becoming more so*—Lady Elizabeth continued, "They are hearing you are an attractive, bright and charming young woman and they wish to see for themselves, and they return, and tell their friends, because you are all of these and more! Also, you honour your new husband by the grace with which you have adjusted to and are performing your role here. He is a very fortunate man." Eileen lowered her eyes respectfully and said nothing, though she had instantly come to like the woman.

As she was undressing late that evening, she continued to hear Lady Moyvane's elegantly spoken words . . . *you honour your new husband by the grace with which you have adjusted to and are performing your role here. He is a very fortunate man. . . .*

"He *is* a very fortunate man indeed," Eileen repeated aloud softly as she tugged a sharp brush through the ends of her thick hair. *In addition to what her ladyship says, I am permitting him to continue to remain amongst the living!* She laughed, perhaps just a bit cruelly, though less caustically than she would have only weeks prior.

She was daily growing more confident of her strength, her power in this place. *I believe Papa would be proud*, she smiled, *and most likely very surprised*, she chuckled . . . *indeed, the mistress I am, and the mistress I shall remain,* she added firmly, resolutely.

During the first week of May, the very beginning of the third month of her residence at Firies, Eileen was returning on Bull from what had become her daily visits to the tenants' *cottages*, as she now spoke of them, and urged others to, as well. She made a certain number of stops each day so that in every eight- to ten-day cycle she had been to every cottage. She had made it her business to check on the conditions and cleanliness of the dwellings and their occupants, especially of the children, as well as of the availability of food.

This particular round of visits had gone well; the little houses were swept, the dirt floors well packed, most of the manure piles now consistently remained well away from the door and, most importantly, the children appeared happy, clean and well fed. Eileen had made a point of visiting with each woman, sitting on a bench or on the grass in the warm sun, chatting casually; amongst other things, she was continuing to get the sense that the vast majority of the tenants very much wanted their children to begin to learn to read and write.

She was also pleasantly surprised to be hearing that more than a few of the adults were themselves interested. "I, too, Mistress . . . I would *so* like to read," Mary Healey, a pretty, redheaded, pregnant-again twenty-year-old mother of four had just this afternoon told Eileen, "and I would not be the only one." The girl smiled broadly. "Patrick, my husband . . . he says if I do, he *must!*" She laughed warmly ". . . and so he will!"

As Eileen and Bull slowly approached the house, she was surprised to see O'Connor riding in her direction. She understood he had been yet again in Dublin but was unaware that he'd returned. She reined Bull in, as with a raised right arm waved, and waited for him. Summoning her most cheerful, even comely manner, shielding her eyes from the bright May sunshine, Eileen had smilingly called out, "Mister O'Connor, good afternoon and welcome home, sir!"

O'Connor pulled up his gleaming black stallion—Eileen felt him to be a truly magnificent horse, appropriately named Champion—so he was but a few feet from his wife.

"Thank you, Mistress O'Connor." He paused, pleasantly surprised by her greeting. "You are well? The people in the cabins are well?"

"Yes as to both, thank you, sir."

Looking intently at his wife, O'Connor sat back in his saddle. "Might we ride a bit? I should be most grateful were I able to speak awhile with you, Madame," he said in a flat voice.

Wary but secure in knowing her loaded pistol was inches from her right knee in one of the saddlebags draped across Bull's neck, Eileen smiled and gestured to O'Connor to lead on. She deliberately kept a few feet back, so that they were not riding shoulder to shoulder. Certain that he was not looking, she undid the brass catch of the right saddlebag.

Reaching a thin grove of wispy saplings, planted recently next to a gently running brook, O'Connor drew up and turned his horse to her. "Is this . . . ?"

"'Tis fine," Eileen said. "I should prefer however to remain mounted."

O'Connor appeared puzzled.

With a flick of her right hand Eileen indicated the two stallions. "Ah, 'tis spring, sir; there are mares afield." She gestured and he nodded in agreement and settled back in his saddle.

O'Connor looked carefully at his young wife. She had obviously recovered from the beating she had suffered at his hands. On more than one occasion recently, he had quietly listened unseen as he heard her playing both hauntingly beautiful laments as well as playfully joyous reels on the centuries-old harp that had—as it turned out ominously—inexplicably crashed to the floor on their wedding night. He had also watched from afar as she moved gracefully and with ease, afoot or astride her massive horse. By all accounts she seemed to have developed a fine rapport with his people—the tenantry, he was told, had grown most fond of her, one of the younger women shyly advising, in response to his questions, "She visits our homes, sir, and she tells the wee ones tales of ancient Ireland, sir, ones I have never before heard!"—and even with his sons.

O'Connor was obviously well aware that—by virtue of a near-steady parade of them to his dinner table—through the efforts of Lord and Lady Moyvane, Eileen was being quickly introduced to the not insignificant in number, largely Protestant aristocracy of the neighbourhood, most of whom found themselves unexpectedly embracing the tall young woman from, as one clearly besotted elderly gentleman put it during the course of one such dinner, an "infamous native Irish, not to say Papist, clan of smugglers, thieves and pirates . . . yet is not she lovely?"

Each time O'Connor had seen her, no matter what the circumstance, his first thought was virtually always the same: Eileen was indeed a beautiful girl.

Though it was a conclusion reached in significant part at some distance, he had also concluded that she was a brilliant one, both from what insights a clearly smitten Lord Moyvane continued to relate, as well as seeing for himself her grasp of languages, learning of her knowledge of Ireland and of places well beyond, watching the ease with which she conducted herself, at the age of a mere sixteen years, in society. O'Connor also admitted to himself, reluctantly, that she made him smile, laugh even, something he had not done with any regularity for some years. He had even begun to hope, indeed to dare to daydream, in recent weeks that with Eileen he might yet achieve some measure of happiness.

Accepting even these simple realities had, at the same time, instilled in him a strong, continuing sense of unease, an emotion with which no woman had ever affected him. Connecting the realities to the sum of her armed entry to his empty rooms, her actually firing at him albeit with an unloaded pistol and her almost immediately afterwards pointing it, fully and effortlessly loaded, at him upon his return from Moyvane Castle, all coupled with her unretracted though never again repeated statement—*"please be fully assured . . . I may yet kill you for what you did to me . . ."*—had made him, to a not insignificant degree, apprehensive, even fearful. Indeed, fearful enough, at least in part, to do something he rarely did.

O'Connor took a breath and began, "I have for some time felt the need to speak with you . . . about . . . t'woud be . . ."

Eileen nodded but sat quietly, her toes still in her stirrups, her right hand resting on her thigh, looking at him.

". . . concerning the 'unfortunate events,' as I believe you characterised it, of the night of our wedding."

Eileen's expression remained impassive, her silence continuing, though O'Connor's own pause clearly indicated he wished she would say something, which she had no intention of doing.

"In any event, I deeply regret . . . in actuality, I sincerely wish . . ." He coughed and stroked his chin. "I am most . . . I most deeply regret my actions. I am truly sorry both for speaking to you in the vulgar manner I did and . . . even more so . . . *much* more so, for harming you. I truly apologise."

Eileen nodded very slightly, her expression unchanged.

O'Connor cleared his throat and continued. "I have given this matter much thought. I do want you to know that it has been so long, I cannot remember when, since I have maintained feelings of genuine affection for anyone, that I fear I had forgotten how . . . how to properly conduct myself, even how to appropriately speak to one such as you, especially in a setting such as we were on that night. I say this not proffering it as any excuse for my actions in February; there is no excuse, not even an acceptable explanation."

Eileen finally spoke. "You speak the truth, sir; there is neither in this instance."

O'Connor smiled weakly. "It is my hope that we might resume . . . at some point at least some measure of cordiality, if . . ."

Eileen nudged Bull up a foot or so closer. "You must understand, Mr. O'Connor, that everything I said to you—*all of it, without exception*—upon your return from Moyvane Castle remains true. If anything, I am more strongly resolved to maintain my dignity and my security."

"I understand, yes," O'Connor said softly.

The couple sat quietly for a long moment, simply looking at each other, until a random breeze blew a stray bit of Eileen's hair over her eyes, and she gently cocked her head ever slightly, the tip of her left forefinger pushing the locks back. O'Connor felt it a tantalizing, graceful gesture.

"All of this said, sir," Eileen's husky voice was strong, "as you have been candid, I feel it not inappropriate for me to acknowledge that some of my actions, some of what I said, particularly the manner in which I expressed myself . . . they were quite . . . *provocative* even, given the circumstances."

O'Connor thought for a moment and then decided to say nothing.

"I accept your words of apology, sir," Eileen said firmly. "As far as any cordiality, I am not necessarily averse . . . we shall see." At which point she smiled quickly but warmly and gently booted Bull.

O'Connor sat and watched her ride off; he did not notice that she had clicked her right saddlebag shut.

Whilst, primarily in furtherance of her plan, Eileen remained, as she had advised O'Connor, both fully committed and totally willing to satisfy her husband's sexual needs, those needs had so far proven to be nonexistent. One evening, however, shortly after their chat on horseback by the brook, when the couple had dined alone, the wine had flowed a bit more freely than usual and their conversation had grown relaxed. Almost an hour after they had gone upstairs to their separate quarters, Eileen padded barefoot down the hall to O'Connor's rooms, clad only in a long, deep purple satin dressing gown.

Not bothering to knock, she quietly opened the door and stepped in, immediately closing it. Propped up in bed, reading, O'Connor lifted his surprised eyes from his book.

Without a word but with a dazzling smile, Eileen playfully sauntered across the room, allowing her gown to fall open, and climbed up onto the foot of the bed, kneeling and then sitting back on her heels, her loose hair flowing over her shoulders and down her back, the front of the gown open, revealing her bare breasts. She smiled wickedly, watching her husband.

Though he'd obviously taken notice, O'Connor smiled wearily, nodding uncertainly.

Eileen rested her hands on her quite obviously now bare thighs and affected a mischievous, pouty look.

O'Connor shook his head gently—neither affirmatively nor negatively—his eyes fixed on the beautiful young woman.

Seemingly unfazed, Eileen, who, in the recesses of the squire's library shelves, had discovered and been reading at night in bed, with increasing interest, what she called "bawdy works"—a number of them being graphically, indeed she felt *titillatingly* illustrated—including John Cleland's book, *Memoirs of a Woman of Pleasure*, a work that would become better known and commonly referred to as *Fanny Hill*, now slowly wriggled on her knees, closer to her husband.

Stopping, she playfully parted the folds of his own dressing gown, exposing a healthy, now fully erect penis. Pushing all of her hair behind her head, her shoulders now bare as the gown slipped slightly, she affected an expression of surprise. An errant lock of hair falling over her left eye, now smiling saucily at O'Connor, she whispered, "What have we here?" as she boldly wrapped her long fingers around his shaft and, with her eyes seductively half-closed and lifted up to him, was lowering her mouth to . . .

O'Connor appeared genuinely pained to do so, but just at that moment he leaned forward and gently drew his robe closed, saying, "You are lovely, as always, and being . . . kind, shall we say, but I fear I do not share your exuberance in the moment."

Eileen removed her hand, sitting back on her heels. "John, I actually was . . ." she began, pulling her gown back over her shoulders.

"I am certain you were, and I am thus quite surprised by your attention, very pleasantly so, I must admit . . . but . . . I think not, *Eileen*," he said very softly, "not this evening."

She silently noted that it was the very first time he had ever spoken her name. She smiled and similarly softly said, "Very well, sir," primly closing her own gown; she then gently scrambled off the high bed.

Standing, she impulsively turned back, stretched and wordlessly kissed O'Connor lightly on the cheek.

"Good night, Eileen," he whispered, looking directly at her.

She nodded, her facial expression appearing gentle to O'Connor, as, with a delicate nod, she said softly, "And to you as well, sir."

When she turned and smiled saucily at him, this time from the doorway, he slowly nodded, his expression seeming to Eileen to be one of genuine regret, perhaps mixed with a degree of—could it be?—fondness. Stepping out into the hall after she had gently closed his door, she bent down and lifted her pistol from where it rested against the door moulding. She uncocked the weapon soundlessly and, holding it at her side, padded slowly back down the hall to her own room, her gown flowing open again, the chill of the night air feeling good against her bare skin. Eileen blew out her candle and, shedding her robe, she climbed up in her own bed and lay back in the dark, and in the dark she smiled.

As she did, O'Connor, too, having blown out his candles, lay back in the dark— though rather than smiling he gazed into the heavy silence of the night, his thoughts many.

Never have I declined the advances of any woman with more reluctance than I have just done this night.

Almost immediately, he shook his head, smiling sardonically, then chuckling softly, mockingly, perhaps even bitterly, to himself. *You old fool, O'Connor. Never has any woman ever made advances to you the like of which Eileen just did. . . . Hah, or is it that perhaps never has there ever been a woman, or girl the likes of* Eibhlin Ni Chonaill; *surely none as comely as she. . . .*

Finally, sliding down beneath his covers, his head cradled in a mound of down-filled pillows, O'Connor ultimately acknowledged that he had unenthusiastically spurned his young wife's advances for the simple reason that he was startled, indeed *shocked*, that she was even aware of the practice and, as he lay in the dark, the faint ticking of his small mantel clock the only sound, that he felt . . . intimidated or daunted, or even threatened; those were the words that came readily to mind.

Whilst unable to admit which, if any, of those properly described his emotions, O'Connor knew that it had always been he who had been in control in any bedroom, indeed in any encounter of a sexual nature wherever the location, with any girl, any woman since his early adolescence, and now—and of this reality he was certain—this would no longer be the case.

O'Connor spent a very restless night.

Ballyhar—June 1760

Whilst April and May at Ballyhar, and over most of Ireland, had proven largely rainy and dreary, June had exploded on its third day, St. Kevin's Day—*Thank you, St. Kevin!* Eileen had exclaimed to herself, her arms reaching for the sun as she stepped out of the house that morning—in all the glory of the best kind of Irish summer: brilliantly sunny, breezy and blue-skied days—stretching well into the late evening hours and, when night's darkness finally, reluctantly fell, absent any moon, it was overwhelmingly black, punctuated by a dazzling sweep of stars.

Eileen spent as much time as possible outside, whether striding about the property in a light-coloured cotton dress or riding distances astride Bull, she gloried in and embraced the warmth of the previously absent sun, even enjoying the bristling sensation of her forearms, and her cheeks and forehead becoming sunburnt, her large hats notwithstanding.

She continued her daily rounds about the estate, her visits with the women in the cottages having over the months become generally more informal and less like ones between landlady and tenant. She had developed her special favourites and at those homes she would linger, relaxing in the sun, sharing tea and chatter, often dandling a small child on her knee or, at one place particularly, permitting a wide-eyed little blond girl named Lucy, whom she found to be especially endearing, to stand behind her as she sat and rake her fingers through her hair.

Eileen had begun happily planning for the celebration of the summer solstice, which she referred to as Litha or Midsummer's Eve, the third week of the month. There would be a bonfire, a huge feast with abundant food and drink for family, servants, tenants and guests, and music and dance on the longest day of 1760. When she had first advised her husband of her plans, during dinner on the evening of her unsuccessful attempt to seduce him, his response had been a smiling "Fine," and when she inquired of him more than once thereafter as to whether he had any wishes or any desire to participate in the preparations, his reply was also a monosyllable, "No," but accompanied by a smile as he added, "I am certain it will be lovely."

By early June, Squire O'Connor and Mistress O'Connor were spending what appeared to be nothing more than unplanned, informal time together. What was not apparent was that, beginning with her initial unsubtle attempt at seduction, Eileen had been acting upon her conscious decision to take carefully measured steps towards a rapprochement between herself and O'Connor.

Providing he continues to conduct himself properly, he shall live, thus assuring that Mistress Eileen shall remain mistress of this house, this estate . . . and that is what is best for me!

Thus, whilst not daily, at least two or three times a week, Eileen would slip into his study or the library, in whichever he was, in the morning or the evening. O'Connor would invariably stand and greet her warmly, if not affectionately, and they would tell each other of what one was going to do during the day just beginning, or what one had done during the day then ending. More frequently, laughter had begun to be heard.

Almost from the beginning of these visits, Eileen had deliberately begun to flirt and tease. Wary and guarded at first, O'Connor had gradually become more relaxed, at times even sparring lightly with her. Referring to her nearly nude visit to his room, he had said, "Of it I have thought frequently, and more and more I find it to be most distracting from my business then at hand."

Eileen had then smiled playfully, her head cocked slightly, her eyes twinkling mischievously. O'Connor sensed that she was attempting to convey a message: *Perhaps, then, sir, you had best do something about the distraction.*

One quiet evening, after initial pleasantries had been exchanged, Eileen had walked to where O'Connor sat at his desk and begun to rub the man's shoulders and neck with her strong fingers, causing her husband to *mmm* very softly. Bending to his ear, she whispered, "I remain intent on achieving success at my next attempt to seduce you, good sir," causing O'Connor to turn, his cheeks a bright red, in silent, amazed response.

"I am a determined young woman, husband: Once I set a goal, I am not one to be deterred." She ran her fingers down his muscular arms and forearms, allowing them to play across his chest.

As June continued its slow, gentle stroll to midsummer, Eileen had, without giving it any thought, taken to occasionally joining O'Connor for part of what had for him been a solitary evening walk to Margaret O'Connor's grave. Taking his arm, they strolled in silence and, on reaching the top of the gentle knoll, she released it and walked back to the house alone whilst O'Connor continued on to the small graveyard, where he would remain for a brief time.

One morning she had playfully undone the neat, carefully tied ribbon about his queue and ruffled his thick, greying hair. She then stepped away, smiling mischievously; as O'Connor was picking the ribbon up off the floor, she plucked it from his fingers, gently gathering his hair and retying it into a neat queue, after patting the ribbon, pronouncing it "Finished!" she unexpectedly kissed his neck and then pranced off, humming.

Early one evening several days later, a gentle, warm one, O'Connor entered his study after his visit with Margaret, a walk on which Eileen had not joined him, only to find his wife seated in his chair, quietly reading. His surprise obvious, Eileen rose with a flourish and stepped to greet him, taking his arm and conducting her husband to his chair and, as soon as he had taken his seat, so too had Eileen sat—on the surprised man's lap, draping her hands about his neck.

She leaned to O'Connor's ear, whispering, "Determined I am, John," and, lightly pecking his cheek, she laughingly flounced out of the room, like the young girl she still was, calling back over her shoulder, "When you may least expect it, sir, when you may least expect it!"

In these weeks, after her first attempt to do so had failed, Eileen had, as she promised she would, again tried to initiate what she laughingly—writing to Abby afterwards—had called a romp with O'Connor, the second effort proving to be more than moderately successful.

She had come to his rooms, unbidden as before, but this time, as she entered, after gently closing and pointedly locking the door, she again sauntered slowly across the thick Chinese carpet, in the process letting the gown slide off her shoulders, and hopped onto O'Connor's bed nude, most of her hair streaming over her shoulders and down her back, though she purposely draped some so that it fell about her breasts, resting seductively at the top of her thighs.

She kept her eyes fixed on him, climbed between his nightshirt-draped legs and, kneeling, placed her hands behind his neck and firmly pressed his mouth to her right breast. His lips instinctively, softly licked, sucked—Eileen moaning softly. As O'Connor's mouth shortly then found her left breast, his fingers gently playing in her hair, moving over her neck and bare shoulders, when they reached her hips, her lower back, Eileen slowly turned seductively, falling on her back, her arms open.

What followed, which had been physical, passionate and lengthy, had proven enjoyable for them both. Most certainly for her, to the extent that she spent the remainder of the night in his bed and, considering how she felt when she awoke on yet another flawless morning, would surely have attempted to initiate further activity but for the fact that he had gone, in this instance to Tralee. He had left an unsigned note—*Thank you for a lovely evening*—which caused her to smile.

On his departure, rather than ordering that Champion be brought to the house as he typically did, O'Connor instead had strolled easily to the barns, and as he did was heard both by the women in the kitchen and by the stable boys to be whistling, something he never did, causing them to smile. The older of the two boys mischievously suggested in blush-producing graphic terms to the younger what was perhaps the cause of the squire's unusual behaviour.

As she slowly awakened to his note, holding it gently in her fingers, Eileen rested back against her pillows and smiled.

It was that morning and during the days following her success that she began to seriously consider, indeed deeply ponder and thoughtfully reflect upon the nature of her relationship with and her feelings for this complex, still distant but obviously passionate man to whom she was wed. *I no longer dwell on killing the man. Whilst I cannot forget* that night, *yet here I lie naked and in his bed and feel*—she stretched—*well; quite well, actually,* she laughed, *and . . . certainly without meaning to, I am come to enjoy his company, especially here*, she laughed again and, shaking her head, closed her eyes, smiling.

Astride Bull or whilst going about her business on foot, her thoughts, her reflections continued, and try as she might, she could not dismiss them. *Is it somehow* fond *that I am becoming of this man?* She shook her head. *No! That cannot be . . . can it?* "Can it?" she inquired of Bull as she leaned to his head.

More than once she had pictured Donal Mór and Maire strolling about after the evening meal on a gentle summer's evening at Derrynane. Arm in arm they had walked, and laughed and whispered and laughed even more. She remembered hearing her mother say in the weeks after Donal Mór's sudden death, "I have buried a huge part of my heart, a huge part of my soul," and Eileen had never forgotten that.

'Tis definitely not how I feel about John O'Connor . . . yet no longer do I wish him dead . . . or do I even think ill of him. . . . Yet neither part of my heart, certainly not of my soul does he possess . . . or . . . perhaps of my heart? Perhaps a tiny . . . just a wee bit . . . but how can that come to be?

O'Connor returned after more than a week's absence; she had been pleased to see him; she greeted him warmly, and he her. They spent that night together, again, more awake than asleep.

June 1760 was proving to be fecund in a number of ways as by midmonth, Eileen had birthed two foals, referring to both as being "pretty little girls." Both foals arrived in what Eileen had come to call the "borning room," a clean, sweet-smelling corner of the stable, thickly carpeted with fresh hay. Several lanterns, with fresh candles, were carefully hung at intervals on the stone wall, and the light thrown was yellow and soft.

In each instance, Eileen had carefully wrapped the mare's tail as the birthing process began. Whilst the first occurred without event, the second of the arrivals, on a still, black night, proved to be a hard and difficult one. By the time it was over, it left Eileen's arm and shoulder muscles ablaze, throbbing, her face, arms and clothing soaked in sweat and blood and her hair thickly speckled with hay from lying down with the mare, a sweet-dispositioned, dappled grey named Princess. She stroked her, talking to her in the softest tones of Irish and English, calming her, easing her stress as she struggled to give birth.

One of the boys, Michael, had come to fetch Eileen as soon as Princess's water had broken; she was already on her side by the time Eileen reached the barn, groaning audibly as she pushed to expel her seventy-to ninety-pound foal. Just as Eileen had knelt next to her on the barn floor, the edge of a smooth, clear white sac appeared, within which Eileen knew rested the foal. Within a few moments, however, Eileen recognised that Princess was straining longer than she should have been, quickly noting that only one of the infant horse's front hoofs had appeared. Michael now having been joined by Thomas, with both boys' help, Eileen succeeded in getting the mare to stand and take a few uncertain steps, her hope being that this would help the foal slide back into its mother's womb and make what Eileen felt would be her attempt to reposition the "little wee horse," as she called the foal, somewhat easier.

As the lads assisted the mare to lay back down, Eileen's heart pounding now, her face shining with sweat in the gentle candlelight, she, who had plunged her right hand and arm almost to her shoulder into a barrel of water, purposely leaving it wet, gently slid it into the horse's birth canal, following the foal's protruding leg, leading her to its heaving chest, which permitted her to locate the infant's other leg.

With Princess now again instinctively albeit weakly pushing, Eileen resumed assisting her efforts, softly murmuring, *"a bheith síochánta,"* and then, she would relate later, to be certain the horse understood, "easy, be peaceful." By that time, the stable boys, as well as others who had wandered in and remained as others left, could only watch and marvel. "Never have I seen anything like it, no, I haven't," young Michael would exclaim later after witnessing Eileen, who had been lying prone with the mare and now, on her knees, gently but firmly, holding both of the by then almost-born foal's front hooves.

Calling out to Princess, "Now, my sweet girl, *NOW!*" Eileen tugged each time Princess pushed.

Within moments, however, Eileen ascertained that, most likely exhausted, despite her—and Eileen's—efforts, the mare was experiencing difficulty in delivering the foal's head and shoulders. From her position on the barn floor, Eileen, again firmly gripping the baby's front hooves, this time pulled them down towards the mare's hind hooves, thereby helping to rotate the foal's head through the birth canal. To the obvious relief of all those gathered, the head and shoulders of what appeared would be a typically gooey, spindly-legged, seemingly healthy dark grey foal slowly appeared.

Eileen sat back momentarily on her heels, breathing heavily and exchanging affirmative, hopeful glances with her helpers and onlookers alike.

"The rear hoofs, Mistress," Michael called softly, and Eileen nodded, both aware that they would remain within Princess a while yet, as mare and foal rested from what had proven to be an unusually exertive ordeal.

"The mama and the wee one, they shall settle a wee bit," Eileen added, and all heads nodded in the gentle yellow light, chatty Kate leaning to Michael and asking "why?" Eileen carefully watched the pulsating umbilical cord as it continued to transfer what she had learnt at Derrynane was a significant, critical amount of blood from Princess to her foal.

Finally, wearily but naturally and with Thomas and Michael's assistance, whilst Eileen gently cradled the little filly, an exhausted Princess slowly began to stand somewhat unsteadily. Instinctively sensing that the now fully-born foal was anxious for her mother, Eileen's hands skilled and gentle beneath the newborn's belly, the suddenly alert filly joined its dam upright.

During the ensuing hour, the filly succeeded in beginning to nurse and Eileen successfully delivered the placenta, which she first saw as a large mass of red and white tissue protruding, as it was supposed to, from Princess's vulva. Finally, at long last, Eileen knelt and sat back on her heels, bursting into tears as she watched dam and foal nuzzle bathed in the gentle yellow light.

That, with barely a word other than to thank the boys who had helped, she had immediately hurried through the heavy silence of the humid night, literally running from the stables to the house and up the stairs to his rooms, to share news of this event with him, was profoundly indicative to Eileen that her overall relationship with O'Connor, already in a positive flux, was perhaps already fundamentally altered.

O'Connor was just dozing off when he heard the thud of what were Eileen's boots, racing up the stairs. Quickly awake, he had turned towards the door just as she burst into his room, a flickering lantern in her left hand, its light softly illuminating both of them. Sitting up in bed, he stared in amazement at his wife's appearance as she stood close to his bedside, her perspiration-soaked clothing stained with what were obviously fluids and blood, her hair streaked with hay and dust, her sunburnt face gleaming with sweat and her eyes aglow.

"John!" she began breathlessly, "such an extraordinary arrival we have just had in the barns, sir!" Eileen stopped to catch her breath, her breasts heaving gently beneath the damp bodice of her once-crisp dress.

O'Connor leaned to light his pair of tall bedside candles, then turned back to pat his bed. "Sit, wife!" he said with a smile. "Tell me everything! You birthed this miracle, I take it, yes?"

Setting her lantern down on the floor and nodding happily, Eileen clambered up onto her husband's high bed; kicking off her dirty boots and hose, she dangled her legs and bare feet over the side and, sitting like the adolescent girl she, at least in some ways, remained, proceeded to tell in breathless detail a rapt O'Connor the story of the birth of this "pretty little girl."

When she had finished, and after she had fully responded to several pointed questions, indicating her husband's significant experience at foaling, just as Eileen began to slip off the high bed, in a faux harsh voice, his eyes twinkling, O'Connor abruptly commanded, "Doff your clothing, girl; you are a sight!"

Surprised and then bemused as O'Connor slipped off the opposite side of the bed and into his dressing room, Eileen tugged off her soiled dress and her sweat-soaked, stained chemise, leaving them a small grubby mound of cotton on the floor. As her husband reappeared, she was leaning, her hands behind her back, against the high left post at the foot of the bed, the flame of the tall bedside candles now casting iridescently seductive shadows against the curves of her naked body, catching the sheen of sweat on her face, neck and breasts.

O'Connor had returned with a basin of tepid water and several cloths; his eyes on hers, he slowly, sensually drew the refreshing wetness first over her face and throat, her neck, her shoulders and upper back. Picking up, wetting a fresh cloth, O'Connor slowly circled, then delicately cupped her breasts, moving the cloth over her stomach. Kneeling, his eyes looking up into hers, he drew fresh wet cloths slowly across her lower back and bottom, massaging the muscles with his strong fingers, then drawing the cloth down her legs in the back, around to her insteps, up her calves and bruised knees, to her thighs in the front. Abruptly dropping the cloths, without looking at Eileen, his smooth hands gripped her bottom as his lips grazed her mound. Her fingers now reflexively in his thick, tousled hair, as his rigid tongue arched and then brushed teasingly . . . and again, and yet again, by then no longer teasingly but ardently, flicking repeatedly until Eileen finally cried out, her fingers gripping, her smooth nails digging into her husband's broad shoulders.

At that moment, looking up, seeing Eileen's eyes wide, her breasts heaving, O'Connor immediately stood and clambered onto the bed, doffing his nightclothes as he did, and Eileen immediately fell on him with a lusty whoop.

Both having slept soundly in O'Connor's bed, early in the morning, holding hands as they walked towards the stables, the couple went to visit Princess, and her spindly, wide-eyed little foal, which they immediately decided to name Míorúilt (*miracle* in Irish).

When he was at home, O'Connor continued to spend part of each week with lawyers and men who seemed to be some type of advisors, primarily strangers, who journeyed from Dublin and London. Eileen would meet them only at table, presiding elegantly as had become her custom, engaging in pleasant though what she felt to be largely meaningless conversation with, she concluded dismissively, a steady stream of dullards, whose company she did not enjoy.

Sensing that these suppers had become similarly obligatory for O'Connor, as each meal mercifully drew near to a close, she would nod to her husband, at which point he would rise, as would she, and bidding the men a perfunctory time of day, the wife's arm in her husband's, the Master and Mistress O'Connor would leave their guests. Whether there were guests or not, on pleasant evenings they would stroll outside for a bit; following a walk or on inclement ones, they would sit in the library, which, though a large, indeed imposing room, provided a comfortable, natural setting where they would visit, facing each other, in a pair of comfortably elegant high-backed leather chairs before the fireplace.

Some nights O'Connor would stop at her rooms to bid his wife a good evening; others she would do the same at his. The servants took notice that not long after they had begun, these visits had become near nightly events, some lasting only a few minutes, others as long as an hour or more—the lengthier ones sometimes being punctuated by laughter or other sounds—which caused the servants to smile, to exchange knowing nods.

O'Connor was by now showing himself to possess something of a very subtle, somewhat dry but funny, at times even mischievous sense of humour. He made light of the vast difference in their ages—"nearly a half-century," he would chortle playfully—but he seemed secure, as she felt he had every right to be, in terms of his sexual prowess and performance.

He joked about that as well, jesting of himself as the teacher and Eileen the student, to which she had quickly reposted, "and a talented and quick-learning student I am at that!"

Surprisingly, for Eileen, he had also begun displaying a gentle, even affectionate side; the first time he brought a bunch of wildflowers he had collected for her on his evening walk, she almost cried as he handed them to her, demonstrating the wonderfully awkward unease of a very young man. He began to reach for her hand on their walks, and she occasionally noticed him simply looking at her, saying nothing, exhibiting almost a sense of wonderment.

Additionally, he had begun to inquire as to her childhood and her family—especially her parents—asking one evening, "Is Derrynane as extraordinary a place as I have been told it is?" a question to which Eileen delighted in providing a detailed, animated and, he felt, quite magical response. O'Connor enjoyed watching her tell her story as much as he did hearing his actual question answered; she made it and the O'Connells' lives there come alive in her vivid, colourfully flowing prose.

Midsummer's Eve 1760 fell on 21 June, yet another nearly flawless day in North Kerry. Eileen had been up since dawn, seeing to it that the erection of dozens of trestle tables on the rough grass—made smooth by their deliberately grazing the sheep there over the last weeks—in front of the house had been completed, and that Cook and her crew's preparations of huge amounts of food and drink were already well underway.

Eileen's continuing reference to the day as Litha was warmly received in the cabins and amongst the servants, their ties to Gaelic Ireland being, like Eileen's and most of the O'Connells', much closer and far deeper than the largely Anglicized O'Connor household, though O'Connor, too, had begun to speak of the occasion as such.

They began to gather late in the afternoon, the sun warm and the breeze gentle, the family led by the squire and Mistress Eileen, who continued to enjoy David O'Connor's company—who appeared to have largely succeeded in avoiding excessive drink—and was sweet and friendly with Peter, as always accompanied by the chatty Kate, to whom, along with the quiet Kate, Eileen had provided her own pair of shoes and boots, and was equally pleasant to both John the Younger and his companion, Matthew, whom no one referred to any longer as being an equerry, and whom Eileen actually had come to like.

There were numerous guests, including Lord and Lady Moyvane, herself seemingly happy and well settled into Irish country life; so settled, in fact, that by summer's end, and after more than a few years of marriage, the neighbourhood would learn that she was joyously pregnant with the couple's first child. Eileen had already spent some pleasant time, at tea and in the saddle, with the effusively sociable noblewoman. As part of a select group of guests, they would spend the night at Ballyhar.

The serving tables groaned with meats, potatoes and turnips, as well as other garden vegetables. Eileen had gotten the receipt for French bread from

Derrynane, and one of the cooks had mastered it to the extent that dozens of loaves emerged from the kitchen house's ovens to be torn apart and devoured.

Similarly, there were seemingly endless barrels of imported porter and casks of wine. Eileen perhaps shocked her family and some of her guests but clearly delighted her people by admitting her recently acquired special fondness for the tangy ale begun to be brewed at St. James Gate in Dublin by a man named Arthur Guinness just in the last year, and quaffing more than just a token flagon during the evening.

As the evening continued, and remaining mindful of Abby's wise caution about stopping when one became giddy, Eileen's laughter and playfulness would continue to delight the massive extended family of the O'Connor estates, friends and guests as well. O'Connor himself, whose own festive mood was by most correctly attributed to Eileen's buoyant presence in his life rather than to his consumption of porter or ale, mingled freely amongst the tenantry, something he rarely had done in the past, joking with the men, teasing the pretty women and even playing with the children.

The vast majority of the huge group consisted of the household servants, the farmers, graziers, grooms and their spouses, the tenant families and the countless children of all of them, all scrubbed and brushed and sporting clean, carefully patched and mended clothing. All of the children and many of the adults were barefoot, and indeed, as the evening progressed and the dancing began, a number of the household staff, and also Eileen, had shed their shoes as well.

The collection of harmonious sounds that merrily echoed in the soft night air emerged from an artfully combined profusion of fiddles and bodhráns, flutes, several sets of uilleann pipes and more than a few tin whistles, all producing music for a variety of reels and jigs in which virtually everyone participated, even Peter and chatty Kate, John the Younger and Matthew joining in group dancing, even the normally-reserved David taking steps with several pretty girls.

Eileen was pleased that her husband required no urging; together they danced a number of reels, the couple's eyes on each other and the crowd's on them. When not dancing, the squire clapped his hands and tapped his foot with much of the music, and appeared to be genuinely enjoying the occasion—as it seemed so did everyone else.

The high point of the evening—at least to the point when it had occurred—was when, with little effort, a group of the younger tenant wives coaxed Eileen into joining them—"We'll show the lads some dancing, we will, Mistress!" several of them called to her—as they spontaneously began what proved to be an extended combined set of reels and jigs. Most of the musicians played for them, which resulted in almost everyone circled about, clapping, many dancing amongst themselves on the fringe, the many children joyously jumping and bouncing amidst the adults.

Watching them dance, O'Connor, in the company of Lord and Lady Moyvane, at that point casually leaning, relaxed, against a tree, his arms crossed, his head nodding with the music, his eyes seemed fixed solely on his tall young wife as, with the other women, all barefoot, she swayed and twisted, turned, jumped and laughed, clapping her hands, her hair streaming down her back, her face glowing with sweat and her smile dazzling in the torchlight.

When the musicians finally stopped and the women spontaneously collapsed onto the grass, the crowd roared with delight.

After they had clambered to their feet and embraced each other, Eileen raced across the lawn to where the O'Connors were grouped and flung her arms around her husband's neck, kissing him hard and saying, "'Tis a wonderful evening, a glorious Midsummer's Eve, is it not, Squire?"

Surprised, O'Connor nevertheless reared his head back, let out a loud "It is indeed, Mistress O'Connor!" and effortlessly picking her up by her waist and twirled her around, smiling broadly as he gently set her down.

As the lengthy twilight slowly deepened, the boisterous gathering itself began to quiet, some of the more distant neighbourhood guests, along with families having very young children, starting to depart. Whilst one each of the porter and stout barrels remained tapped, pastries and tea had begun to be laid out on the serving tables. The music, too, softened, the thumping bodhráns mostly silent, the reels now replaced by gentle airs.

As Eileen stood chatting with Lady Moyvane and several of the younger neighbour ladies, an elderly man known simply as The O'Toole, he being the beloved patriarch of a large tenant family, quietly approached her. Believed to be at least a hundred years—he spoke vividly, virtually firsthand of the horrors of the Cromwellian invasion and its aftermath—he was also one of a group of treasured elderly men reverently referred to on the estate as the Ancients.

The man humbly stepped up towards Eileen, his head lowered, his eyes looking up at her. He was holding a gleaming harp, perhaps as old as he.

Lady Moyvane, who saw him first and instantly recognised him, gestured for Eileen to turn to the man. As she did, he bowed as deeply as he could, given his age and the fact that he cradled a harp; seeing this, Eileen immediately executed a flawless curtsey to him, rising very slowly out of respect.

"Mistress, please, if you would," he began in Irish, his voice a tremulous whisper, "please honour us, please honour *me*, by playing. . . ." He offered her his harp.

Eileen, who was at least six inches taller than The O'Toole, bent and touched his arm lightly, "Oh, dear gentle man, 'tis *you* who will honour all of us and the land on which we live if you would play for us."

As The O'Toole softly protested, and seeing disappointment in his eyes, Eileen leaned to him again and whispered, ". . . and the greatest honour I could *ever* have, sir, would be if you would permit me to join you."

He smiled broadly, his delicately blue eyes suddenly twinkling, his deeply tanned, heavily seamed face now aglow. He spoke as loudly as he could: "Ah, Madame, so 'tis together then that we shall indeed play!"

Deeply moved, Eileen bent yet again to the stooped gentleman, saying softly, "My honour, my pleasure, good sir," and, as the people closest to them, who had heard the exchange, began to clap and cheer, at Eileen's request, the quiet Kate hurried into the house, scurrying back with the ancient harp, now intact, its strings repaired since the night it had fallen from its pedestal in the great front hall.

Two stools had been produced and the elderly harpist and the young girl sat side by side, their knees touching, smiling at each other—he a survivor of the very destruction of Gaelic Ireland, who, though largely illiterate, spoke Latin and Greek and recited Shakespeare's verses, and she a privileged daughter of one of the relatively few families of Gaelic Ireland to have survived that cataclysm and its aftermath reasonably intact. Now looking into his still-bright eyes, aware from several fascinating prior chats with him, that he had sat at the feet of the legendary blind harpist Turlough O'Carolan himself, Eileen considered herself indeed blessed to be in his presence, sitting in true awe, her mouth slightly open, her eyes wide with wonder.

Suddenly, silencing the gathered with a delicate gesture of his right hand, The O'Toole's fingers began their magic, the first notes of a relatively new air, "Mailí San Seóirse," floating into the otherwise soundless night. He nodded at Eileen, and she began the harmony, and what proved to be the true enchantment of the night commenced.

For the next hour, reflective airs such as "True Love Is a Tormenting Pain," this having come down from the Bardic period, mixed with reels and jigs the like of "A Ghardai Gould Mo Shláinte Uaim," which dated from 1724. Occasionally, one or more of the fiddlers or pipers would softly join in. Together, though Eileen primarily played in harmony, or, as was oft-times said, "behind him," they played perhaps a total of twenty pieces, before a hushed crowd.

It was only when The O'Toole reluctantly leaned towards Eileen and whispered, "I tire so, Mistress" that Eileen called out, *"Ní mór dúinn deireadh anois,"* and then "We must end now," and they finished one quick last air with a flourish.

The silence of the by now quickly gathering night was shattered by thunderous applause and cheering. Unknown arms lifted his right elbow and her left and gently stood the unlikely pair, both beaming. As if on cue, a hand taking her harp from her arms, Eileen turned and slowly curtseyed to the beaming man, as one of his many great-granddaughters gently took his harp from him, and he bowed back to her as the applause continued. After handshakes with the squire and his sons and acknowledging the continuing applause with delicate waves of both of his hands, surrounded by his large family, the old gentleman began to slowly make his way towards his home, Eileen standing quietly next to her husband, clapping still, tears streaming down her sunburnt cheeks.

Ballyhar—Summer–early Autumn 1760

Midsummer's Eve was the season's high point, and Eileen's first summer at Firies was passing quietly, uneventfully. June had inevitably eased softly into July, and July itself gently into August; though interrupted frequently by foggy mornings, late afternoon showers and some grey wet days, much of the glorious weather of June had replicated itself as the weeks continued to pass.

Eileen progressed ever more in her role as mistress of the estate, continuing to be involved in the lives of all of those whom she had come to think of as *her* tenant families. Now she was also seeing that her classically trained, yellow-haired schoolmaster had all the necessary supplies for the hedge school, for which use, in actuality, O'Connor and Eileen had together overseen the conversion of a small barn building. O'Connor himself declared, "If it is indeed," he laughed heartily at the thought, "the *Laws in Ireland for the Suppression of Popery* we are to violate, we shall see to it that the children have a decent academy building!"

Additionally, at and under O'Connor's direction, the loft in the former barn was converted into comfortable living quarters for young "Master Ó Sé of the Yellow Hair," as Eileen had come to refer to the schoolteacher, and with whom additional compensation had been agreed upon for his teaching of many of the children's parents.

As summer continued, what had begun quite informally, with Eileen asking offhanded questions in an effort to show an interest in her husband's commercial dealings, had quickly progressed to the couple sharing, to at least some significant degree, management of what Eileen was quickly learning were the vast O'Connor holdings.

At one point, early on in the process, as she sat across from him in his study, Eileen had posed a highly detailed and what O'Connor immediately saw as being an extremely well-thought-out question about the logistics of trade in the Chesapeake Bay region of America, between the Colony of Maryland, where she knew O'Connor owned lands, and that of Virginia. Smiling, O'Connor leaned back in his chair, beginning, "A fine and wise question that is, and answer it, at least as to what I know of the subject, I surely shall in a moment, but first, my dear girl, if I may, would you please tell me the source of your interest in such matters of business and commerce."

Eileen smiled back, without even having to ponder the question, matter-of-factly indicating that "Even as a wee child, listening to my papa talking to his men, his captains and the like, concerning things which at first I knew not what they even meant, 'movement of goods' and 'trade routes,' I found the words fascinating. I being just a silly little girl, they paid me no mind as I sat with my dolls or a book, listening, just listening, and *that* was how I began to learn of the O'Connells' 'commercial interests,' though 'twas some time before I came to more fully understand what *that* meant!" She laughed, knowing that O'Connor, of course, fully understood what *that* meant.

"And interested I became and interested I am now in what *we* do here and how 'tis all accomplished."

As promised, O'Connor did answer her question quite thoroughly, at one point jumping up to retrieve a colourful, surprisingly detailed map of the region, indicating with his long fingers the approximate locations of their tracts, and of the O'Connor lands' distances from the various Virginia settlements. "There are few if any roads on this eastern shore of Maryland," he told Eileen.

She smiled. "So 'tis much like Iveragh, then!"

O'Connor nodded in reply, qualifying slightly, "Indeed it is, but sandy and wet, I am told, and beastly hot in the summertime."

It was only later that he came to ponder, *How does the child know what the Chesapeake Bay region is, not to mention where, and where in it lie the colonies of Virginia and Maryland? And why any of this might be important?*

Quite taken by her continuing queries, O'Connor in a number of instances provided detailed and what he felt might have been overly complex responses to her questions, only to be pleasantly surprised to see how quickly she grasped concepts and details involving the O'Connors' extensive commercial activities in Ireland, England and even the New World, where O'Connor had acquired lands, in addition to the Colony of Maryland, in the West Indies and Barbados, as well as those properties in Jamaica ceded to the O'Connells in the arrangement that had originally brought Eileen to Ballyhar.

Part of each day now, husband and wife would sit—inside or out, depending on the weather—with books and papers, at times with a lawyer or advisors but never with John the Younger, though occasionally and then more frequently with David, working on and resolving commercial matters, reviewing, planning and together now managing the range of largely successful business activities that had made, Eileen had come to learn from her husband, the O'Connors amongst the wealthiest of Irish families.

Eileen continued to ask probing, often multipart questions and appeared to her husband to have an extraordinary memory, an incredible ability to seize the complexities of the myriad businesses. Daily, it seemed, she grew more confident and hesitated very little in analysing and offering solutions, some creative, others as even she would laughingly agree, saying, "You must remember, sir, I am thinking as I am talking!" being wholly unworkable, to issues as she and O'Connor grappled with them.

"I find it easy to forget how young she is when she discusses and even at times speedily solves problems whether involving the strengths of a particular horse or the disposition of lands in Maryland—in America of all places!" O'Connor confided to Lord Moyvane as they rode one afternoon.

"Ah, O'Connor, though very young she may be, given who she is and from whence she has come, wise beyond her years, you know long have *I* felt the girl to be."

Moyvane would later discover that Eileen had a surprising understanding of world geography and, as he questioned her, she indicated how she had, for example, become interested in Maryland. "'Tis said the province, the Colony of Maryland, is named in honour of the Blessed Mother herself!" she had exclaimed, still wide-eyed with wonder at the thought—though she had known for some time that the colony had been originally founded as a place where Catholics could freely practice their religion.

"I doubt, O'Connor, that there is a child in Ireland who knows what your young wife does about America," Lord Moyvane would advise his friend, "and . . . few men, fewer woman."

As the weeks passed, the still in many ways dissimilar pair discovered these shared interests in business problem solving and decision making was yet another significant aspect of life that continued to draw them closer still.

Though Eileen had previously been the primary initiator of their bedroom romps, it was more frequent now that O'Connor came to her rooms, including late one breezy evening several nights after her triumph of the Midsummer's Eve gathering. Though visibly surprised, she had enthusiastically invited him into her bed, laughingly pushing back the covers to reveal her naked body. The disparate couple experienced yet another vigorous, powerfully physical and, for both of them, adventuresome, athletic and intensely erotic night. Waking shortly before dawn, she was not unpleasantly surprised to see that her husband had spent the rest of the night in her bed. Kissing and touching him awake, she had tried light-heartedly, and was most pleased that it had proven successful, to resume their nocturnal activities, as she had come to happily acknowledge to herself that she had developed a lusty, even bawdy enjoyment of sex.

By this time she had also come to admit that as she more frequently awoke in bed with him, and on occasions such as when she had spontaneously raced to tell him of the filly's birth, in addition to a certain though still varying degree of fondness, she had come to feel a sense of . . . could it be peace, perhaps, in addition, perhaps more correctly a sense of security being in proximity to this man, her husband. . . .

She had come to understand that Donal Mór had been the ultimate source of her peace, her sense of security; he had been larger than life. When he was taken from her, she had felt she could look to no man for a similar feeling of sanctuary. Denis, though by custom the head of the family, she dismissed as wholly unsuitable for his role, being a dull, thick, unimaginative and uncaring being, and though she was fond of her other older brothers and dearly loved Morgan, she regarded them still as boys, *and*, she thought, *one cannot take boys seriously.*

But by this time also, she found she had arrived at a place at which she felt if not the powerful safety of Derrynane, nevertheless secure; this in addition to what she had already achieved, had built for herself in terms of amassing power, assuming control, none of which she had ceded back to O'Connor, or to the situation, nor did she ever intend to do so.

As unimaginably horrendous and difficult as their beginning had been, Eileen found herself becoming quite well accustomed to being the wife of a prominent, powerful, obviously extremely wealthy man, a man with whom she was gradually growing in a marriage, within which they were coming to seem a couple, forming a unit, as unthinkable as that could have been to her—to either of them—but a very few months prior.

As they were riding one day, O'Connor had even advised Lord Moyvane of the positive state of their marriage.

"Happy you must feel that the initial *situation*, shall we say, between you and Mistress O'Connor has, it would appear, been wholly resolved, yes?"

"Indeed, yes, my lord; resolved it is, to an extent unimaginable!" O'Connor had smiled and gently booted his stallion.

That O'Connor's more intimate feelings had progressed, as well, became clear very late one hot, still night in mid-July, as the couple lay sprawled in his high, massive bed, after engaging in what Eileen had coyly termed "teasing and playing," but, at that point, not actual intercourse.

"I was wondering, Mistress O'Connor . . ." he began gently in his slightly grainy voice.

Eileen, who was lying cater-corner to her husband on her stomach, covered principally by her hair, an open book to one side, looked up somewhat sleepily. "Yesss?" she drawled in a half-hearted attempt to sound seductive . . . or, she thought, perhaps merely to sound silly . . . in either case, she lay still, her eyes half-closed.

"Were you to possibly find yourself in the position of . . . ah, knowing that you might be . . . or have become . . ." He cleared his throat, and Eileen lifted her head up, pushing some of her hair away from her eyes with a delicate flick of a fingertip, looking intently at her husband, who now took a deep breath and continued, finally managing to say, "Should you find yourself with child as a result of . . ." He gestured about the bed. "How would that cause you to feel, Eileen?"

Eileen's eyes opened wide, her mouth fell open and she rolled onto her back, speechless, for once, O'Connor thought affectionately; drawing up one knee, she whistled aloud, as O'Connor smiled warmly at the sight of her thus, and at her reaction.

"Why . . . John, as we are only so recently wed, and, indeed, sir, have even more recently still been regularly abed . . . I had not even considered . . . *that* . . . but, if 't'woud prove to be the case, I should think that I would be proud . . . yes, *proud* I *would* be, I know I would be proud . . . and *happy.*" She sat up suddenly, smiling, shamelessly nude, her palms flat on the bed behind her, some of her hair falling over her breasts and onto her thighs as she beamed at her husband. "Very happy indeed, sir!"

O'Connor's smile was affectionate, almost paternal. "Good; that is good. I am happy to hear that, for 'tis how I would feel as well, very proud and very happy . . ." and he pulled his naked young wife down next to him.

The following morning, as she was washing and dressing in her own rooms, Eileen reflected on the conversation, watching a long time out of her windows as the filly whose arrival she had announced to O'Connor in such detail gambolled back and forth and about the partially fenced pasture closest to the house with her mother. Studying them, her eyes moist, she whispered softly, "Mother."

Though it had begun quite cool, what turned out to be an uncharacteristically sultry Kerry August progressed unhurriedly, the typical bustle about the estate slowing as well. Meals became smaller, lighter and less formal; the O'Connor men were rarely seen in coats or even waistcoats, O'Connor himself taking to rolling up his sleeves as he made his rounds on horseback, such that, as was his face already, his forearms had become sunburnt and then tan. Eileen was often barefoot from dawn to dusk and had occasionally taken to riding Bull bareback, leading O'Connor to refer to her as "my Gaelic maiden."

Eileen had jokingly whispered more than once to her husband that "the hot weather . . . it seems to ignite one's passions, does it not, sir?" as between them it already had, and would on more than a few occasions.

As they lay abed very early one morning in late August, O'Connor half-sitting, resting against a mound of pillows, appeared wan, ashen even; indeed, Eileen noted, his colour was sadly comparable to the grey, misty light of the dawn itself just breaking. She heard him say softly, "I fear I am quite weary this morning, Mistress O'Connor," though, after pausing for a breath, he smiled broadly, adding, "The night was quite remarkable, was it not then?" His breathing was light, somewhat laboured.

Eileen had been lying languidly on her stomach, her head resting on her hands, and she turned, looking at him with sleepy eyes, the covers drawn up to her hips, her back and shoulders bare beneath her tousled hair. She smiled and laughed softly, affectionately. "Remarkable *indeed*, old man!"

"Ah, an old man I fear I am become, Eileen. Daily I seem to grow more so. . . ." His voice trailed off, as, without thinking and as naturally as if she had done it many times, Eileen snuggled up to him, resting her head on his chest, over his heart, and fell back asleep.

In early September, O'Connor and David set off for Dublin and were absent some eight days. They returned quietly early one Friday evening. Hearing the horses, Eileen came out of the house to greet father and son, though O'Connor, again pleading weariness, excused himself almost immediately, making his way up the steps and into the house slowly, his boots heavy on the great staircase, which he ascended even slower yet.

As Eileen turned, David unexpectedly touched her elbow. "Eileen, if I may, you must know that the squire is not well; indeed, not well at all. He was felled in Dublin by severe pains of the chest, so serious that the doctors expressed that they were fearful for his life. He remained abed two days and more actually, and has been as you see him, quite diminished in strength. Our journey was slow and difficult."

Though Eileen's facial expression and voice had both evidenced obvious concern, David thought later, she did not display any great surprise. "He has recently spoken to me of being an 'old man,' of 'growing more so' each day," she had advised him not unfeelingly. "We shall all just have to be aware and vigilant," she added and, gathering up her skirts, returned inside whilst David and the grooms dealt with the luggage and the horses.

She knocked gently on her husband's door, waiting for what, when she heard it, seemed a somewhat distant voice: "Enter." Doing so, she saw O'Connor seated on the padded bench at the foot of the bed, the heel of his left boot in a bootjack as he tugged at it.

"Husband, please allow me." She turned her back to him and, bending forward, lifted and pulled his still-booted foot between her legs, it disappearing amidst the folds of her skirts before she drew it through her knees and looked around, smiling both at her husband and at how she knew she must look with her dress bunched up. She nodded and laughed as she felt the toe of O'Connor's right boot on her backside. As he pushed, she tugged, and the left boot slid off easily. They repeated the process, and Eileen stood the dusty boots side by side next to his armoire, bustling back to where he sat, immediately laying the coat he had removed to one side and gently beginning to untie the ruff at his neck.

"So you propose to undress me, Mistress O'Connor?" he inquired playfully.

"I do, sir! And perhaps to have my way with you, Squire O'Connor," she responded in her best saucy manner, and then immediately, gently, nodded her head, *No, not this night*, she smiled softly.

"Comfortable I want you to be and to rest," she continued, removing his damp shirt and then matter-of-factly helped him remove his breeches and hose, finally slipping a cotton nightshirt over his head and untying his queue. She fluffed his pillows and sat quietly for a few moments whilst he settled himself, just watching. His head resting against them now, he smiled, and Eileen stretched and gently kissed his lips. "Good night, my husband," she whispered.

"And to you as well, my good wife," he said even more softly. Blowing out the candle on his nightstand and carrying a smaller lit one, she backed out of the room, just watching him watching her.

After she climbed up into her own bed that evening, she rested her head against what she had only just recently come to think of as perhaps being *his* pillows and sighed in the dark. *Aware and vigilant . . . very much so indeed.*

And she remained so.

A week had passed uneventfully, the rhythm of the estate continuing, the second round of sheep shearing now completed and preparations for the early harvest begun.

The following Tuesday evening, Eileen had returned from her rounds and walked Bull to the barn. She chatted briefly with James, a very tall—it was their joke; he was one of few people on the estate taller than she—painfully thin young man and, carrying her gloves, still wearing her broad-brimmed straw hat, strode back to the house. Stepping lightly into the great entry hall, two of the rich, resonant *bonnnnnnngs* she had come to love sounded and she noted the time on the gleaming clock being half seven. At almost the same moment she observed a narrow halo of candlelight on the highly polished dark wood floor of a side hall, the glow emanating through the partially open door of O'Connor's study, and walked to the door and saw her husband seated at his deck, she stepped into the smallish, book-filled room.

"Why, good evening, good sir!" she said merrily, sweeping off her big hat with a flourish, anticipating that O'Connor would immediately look up and smile, perhaps even laugh.

O'Connor did neither; instead he scratched a few more words on the paper spread before him and, putting down his pen, only then looked up at his wife, his face fixed now in a quizzical expression. He partially opened his mouth and raised his right hand, as if he were about to speak.

His eyes still fixed on Eileen, his expression now placid, even serene . . . wordlessly, virtually without a sound, he gently toppled to his left, out of the chair and onto the worn but still thick carpet.

Crying out "John!" her voice shrill, as it never had been heard in the house, Eileen dropped to her knees on the floor, her hair falling about them until she pushed it all back over her shoulders and called even louder, "Anyone! Come! The squire . . . !"

As hurrying footsteps echoed in the house, she bent forward and gently eased O'Connor onto his back, immediately noting his stillness, his pallor. As she had seen her mother do with people, and as she had learnt to do with horses, Eileen instinctively felt for the pulse in O'Connor's neck, as well as his chest and wrist, with her fingertips, and placed her palm gently above his nose and mouth. Looking up at Cook, who had just come in, her expression was calm. Sitting back on her heels, her knees touching O'Connor's left arm, Eileen crossed herself, closed her eyes and folded her hands in her lap for a seemingly endless several minutes. Opening her eyes, she looked once again at O'Connor's now placid features, gently pressed his eyelids, softly touched his left cheek and, after a moment, leaned over and kissed his forehead, only then rising.

"Master O'Connor has died," she said calmly, her husky voice even, and she walked out of the room, leaving Cook and the others in mute, stunned silence.

Eileen had been correct; at the age of sixty-two years, eight months and several days, John O'Connor was dead. The doctors, for whom Eileen had immediately sent, would advise her that her husband had suffered an apoplexy, what would later become known as a massive stroke, which had killed him instantly.

The ensuing days were a blur to her.

John the Younger dramatically announced that he was "prostrate with grief," and that he would "take to his bed" until the funeral, which he promptly, for the most part, did. Though chatty Kate had several times gently tried to explain what was going on, Peter O'Connor was unable to grasp the concept of death, much less that it had happened to his father. David O'Connor, quiet, grave, sober, thus stepped in and up, seeing to his father's remains, ordering that a coffin be made, sending men with messages to Father MacCarthy, Lord Moyvane, the countryside, Tralee, Dublin and London.

Eileen quietly requested of David an additional man, to go to Derrynane.

Whilst the young man waited, Eileen sat to write for the first time at John O'Connor's cluttered secretary. Unconcerned with their subject or contents, gently pushing aside the papers on which he was working at his death, she drew a clean sheet from a small side drawer of the desk; once satisfied that there was ink in the well and that the point of the quill was adequate, she dipped the pen, withdrew it and began, in her broad, careful hand:

Ballyhar,
Firies, Co. Kerry
14 September 1760

My dearest Mama:
I trust you and all are well. I realise I have continued to be remiss in not being a better correspondent, but my life has likewise continued to become more demanding and fuller with the passage of each week.

The news of note and the purpose of my writing are the same: My husband, Squire O'Connor, has died, at yesterday. I had just entered the room from which I now write and he turned and looked up to me, seeming to prepare to speak, when . . .

Finishing, Eileen sat back and read her description of O'Connor's final moments.

Then, doing and touching and feeling and listening as I had seen you do, I correctly identified that Master O'Connor had indeed died. David, the leader amongst the sons though not the eldest, saw no need to summon the doctor.

She went on to briefly summarise the funeral plans, mentioning that Father MacCarthy would "shortly arrive, and I have urged upon David that a proper wake be held. . . ."

Deeming it finished, she read the letter, signing it, for the first time, "I remain then, your loving and most devoted daughter, *Eibhlin Ni Chonaill Ó Conchobhair.*

Once she had dispatched the messenger, she called for Bull to be saddled and rode off aimlessly, returning late in the evening, just as dusk was falling.

She rode in silence, not even speaking to her beloved horse, as she typically would. Her mind replayed the death scene—again and again, over and over—yet she did not weep.

Whilst Eileen had been riding, one of the household ladies who doubled as resident seamstress had taken a dress from Eileen's wardrobe and, retrieving a bolt of black woollen cloth from a cupboard somewhere in the vast house, had worked feverishly so as to create the first of what she planned would be at least three black dresses for the new widow. Completing it, she simply laid it on Eileen's bed. When she came in from her lengthy ride, Eileen had first noticed the dress as she sat on the edge of the chaise, removing her boots. Walking to her bed, she picked it up, looked at it carefully, front and back, and emotionlessly laid it smoothly on the chaise. She doffed her dress, slipped off her chemise and, completing her toilette in her dressing room, made her way across the still bedroom and climbed naked under the summer coverlet. She slept well that night.

The following morning, for the first time thinking of herself as being the Widow O'Connor, she emerged in her widow's weeds; Eileen was some six months short of her seventeenth birthday.

Eileen moved quietly, though both Lord and Lady Moyvane observed "quite regally," through the subsequent days, the raucous wake—she did not dance, she did drink ale and porter in some volume and she did join in singing, badly. some of the laments—the simple Mass and, on David O'Connor's arm, led the way from the gloomy house into the brilliant sunlight and a slight uphill trudge to the O'Connor graveyard. They were followed by the small O'Connor family and the very large estate family, Lord and Lady Moyvane leading a goodly number of neighbours, virtually all of the gentry, officials from the county and from Dublin, including the deputy lord lieutenant, representing the Crown.

Eileen had initially been there, not long after *that night*, to have, as she thought of it, a brief conversation with the first Mistress O'Connor: *Did he ever strike you? Or were you wiser than I, remaining silent as I did not? I am now thinking that perhaps his rage came on him only after your passing, even because of your passing. . . . Did you think him a good man? Did you care for him? Did he care for you? Did you love him?*

Today, as she stood next to David, awaiting the completion of the prayers, to which she was not listening, her eyes briefly moved from the freshly dug grave, itself awaiting John O'Connor, to the well-tended one alongside, and spoke silently to its occupant: *Ah, Margaret, is he there with you? Or has he not yet arrived? I am sure he will shortly arrive, for I do not believe him to be evil . . . though 'tis for God alone to judge, is it not, Margaret? Even so, God is merciful. You shan't long be alone.* She paused, sighing. *It is now rather for I to be alone.* She shook her head.

Father MacCarthy shortly finished.

Though the very young widow's thoughts had been and remained many, her words were few and her tears none, as all who were there would witness and as many in Kerry would hear in the days and weeks and months ahead, and as the story would be told and retold again and again, until it would be remembered always. It was at the graveside that she had unexpectedly stepped forward.

The very earth seemed to quiet as Eileen, after first lifting her eyes to heaven, looked briefly at the small assemblage, her eyes a frightening depth of blue, as if daring, challenging *anyone* to move or speak or *judge*, only then spreading her arms, her eyes focused now on the grave, she began to speak in Irish, her husky voice resonant, a distant expression on her face:

Ah, Seán Ó Conchobhair,
Your life I shared but briefly, though at its final
end, by the very Hand of God Itself,
'Twas I the last one, the only one with you.
Your voice already then stilled, and in your eyes: Myself alone.
Some will wonder, some may ask: What was
it, who was it that you saw, then,
Seán Ó Conchobhair,
In those, your final moments on this, God's green earth? Or
Was it your sins or past glories, or only the road that lay before you?
But, true it is, Seán Ó Conchobhair, you saw only the girl who
became a woman beneath you, with you, because of you—
Who, at your hands, by your very self and in your bed, learnt passion
And felt pain and ecstasy and joy

And who you leave now, Alone, draped in the cloth of mourning.

Still unknowing so much of you, Seán Ó Conchobhair,
'Tis I who grieve for you, and
I who mourn your passing,
And 'tis also I alone who must lament you And 'tis
only fitting and just that I do so, and so I do:

May those who have loved you and who you have loved mourn you truly,
May they shed their tears and speak only softly of you at their firesides.
May those you have hated and harmed, and those who
have hated you: Many of both, I fear there be—
May all seek, and if it be His Will, find peace.

Eileen's voice then rose, her arms spread wider, her eyes raised to the blue Kerry sky, speaking now, in part, also to God Himself:

*May God Himself and alone, in His holy wisdom, reward you, for
the good you have done, and, with His holy justice, chastise you,
for what evil you have done, both truly known only to Him.
And when all 'tis, at His Hand, and to you
in His Eye, finally be done to you,
May you then be at peace, Seán Ó Conchobhair.
But now, even as you await God's justice and His peace –
I say to you,
Farewell, my Husband, Godspeed!*

At that moment, Eileen gradually, dramatically lowered her arms to her sides and walked slowly forward until she was looking directly down into the open grave itself, at O'Connor's plain coffin resting on the rocky soil at the bottom. She stood still, just looking down, for what seemed a long time. She then smiled softly, nodded and, her eyes now straight ahead, her head high, her carriage proud, walked alone down the little hill, the eyes of all on her, a profound and utter silence upon all of them, the only sound the crunching of her steps on the broken rocks of the rough footpath.

Later, during the gathering of those in attendance, held in the normally glittering, now crepe-draped ballroom in which she had been wed, to those who looked closely, Eileen appeared to take on a distant, otherworldly appearance. Whilst she formally received condolences standing with David, atypically she did not mingle freely amongst the guests and excused herself before any had departed.

Slipping quietly out the door to the kitchen, she walked slowly in the early evening stillness back to the small graveyard. *I must go back. I need to . . .* Stepping to the newly covered grave, she knelt for several minutes in the dirt, her hands folded, her eyes alternating between the darkening heavens and her husband's grave, her mind at once whirling with snippets of prayers yet empty, numb. The evening's damp had come on quickly as she knelt; it felt heavy, dank even, heightening the deep silence that enveloped the young widow.

Crossing herself after a few moments, she began to stand then suddenly, as if pushed by a powerful unseen hand, Eileen knelt back down - hard - her knees this time thudding in the soft soil. Her arms hugging herself, her shoulders gently shaking, she swiftly, mindlessly dissolved in tears.

Eileen wept bitterly, her shoulders now heaving, her tears streaming down her face and, at first, wetting the bodice of her dress. Her sobs becoming more profound, heaving, then more wrenching still, she bent near to the grave, her palms, then her arms resting in the dirt on either side of the mound beneath which lay John O'Connor, her hair tumbling down about both of them, and from her lowered face, just inches from the mound of dirt, her tears fell onto the stony soil of the small knoll itself.

Suddenly, she began to wail in the screeching, heartrending voice of the "mourning women" as she had heard them in the scattered cottages and deep in the glens around Derrynane, her own pitiable moans broken by an occasional *Seán* or *mo chara* or *brón* and, just once, *mo ghrá*. Now only half-bent to the ground, kneeling in the freshly turned dirt, the young widow rocked her body from side to side for some moments until the paroxysm of grief—if indeed it was grief she was expressing, and, if so, was it at that moment for John O'Connor alone?—eased, the volume and intensity of her wails gradually subsiding.

Exhausted, drained, breathing heavily, her face wet with sweat and tears, she slowly knelt up, in silence—totally still, her dirty hands folded, her tears stanched—until she once again crossed herself, stood somewhat unsteadily and, casting more than one backwards glance at the grave, walked gradually back down the little hill to her home.

Succeeding in re-entering the house and climbing up to her room, noticed but undisturbed, she removed her clothing, washed her dirty hands, her face and eyes and slipped her still-moist body under the protection of the smooth sheets and light summertime coverlet. Burrowing into her pillows, resting on her side, she lay quietly staring into the dark for what seemed a long time. Finally, clenching her right fist, she whispered, "You bastard. How could you?" Both aloud and in her mind silently, again and yet again, she hissed *You bastard! How could . . . you?* sobbing softly until her tears finally exhausted, she was then quickly, blessedly asleep.

She awakened feeling physically rested, yet in continuing emotional tur-moil, as during that day and the days after, other than in her eventide vis-its to his grave, Eileen's still largely unexpressed (Lady Moyvane had asked her husband, *Had you any idea of the depth of her affection for him?*) feelings about O'Connor, her relationship with—or perhaps *to*—him, his death and her own life, remained complex, contradictory and extremely complicated; indeed she repeatedly now thought, 'twas barely six months earlier that he had severely beaten her.

Whilst anything significantly beyond the basic level of mutual affection she accepted that she and O'Connor had reached remained incomprehensible to her, beginning the morning after the funeral, especially in light of her spontaneous behaviour at the grave the previous evening, Eileen neverthe-less returned to yet again silently attempt to assess, as she had been doing for months, what she now accepted was the not insignificant degree of fondness she had come to hold for this complex, still-distant man, a man, who in many ways remained unknown to her, in death as he had in life, yet to whom she had been joined, to the extent of her now feeling she had lost both something and, more importantly, *someone,* that something and *someone* had been taken away from her.

During the week after the burial, she spent much of her time alone. She would take herself early to the kitchen, where her two cherished Kates would nourish her with steaming cups of strong Kerry tea, specially-baked French bread and porridge, and would then ride out on Bull. She journeyed vary-ing distances in random directions on the vast estate, but at some point dis-mounted and, gently holding the reins, would walk slowly, aimlessly, finally letting them drop as her massive friend simply plodded along at her side, his heavy hooves thudding gently. She would sometimes stop and nuzzle his head.

On the Thursday following O'Connor's internment, she was sitting on a large flat rock, her back up against another one, the late morning sun warm on her. Looking up into Bull's lustrous brown eyes, she smiled and began to ramble aloud: *Haven't we had quite the time, my dear, haven't we so? I wrote to Maire, though I am sure it is Denis who will reply, and I am not sure what it is he will be saying to us. So what do you think will happen to us? I am no longer the mistress, you know. Such was not in my plan . . . this was not to have happened, the mistress I was to have remained. I should think that Matthew is in actuality "the mistress."* She laughed aloud, and the horse looked quizzically at her, before resuming his grass and weed nibbling. *'T'woud be so much better were it David who'd be the heir, the new squire.*

She sat quietly then, the breeze picking up, looking at the patterns of the clouds as they raced across North Kerry, seeing nothing in them, as she usually did—a jumping horse, a puppy at play—instead now just cloud patterns.

She closed her eyes a bit, resting her head back against the rock as Bull moved slowly about, his hoofs gently thudding, seeking more shoots of tasty green grass.

Opening her eyes, she wondered if she'd dozed off. Not seeing him, she whistled, a piercingly-shrill sound, and the horse came plodding around the other side of the rock, appearing, she thought, sheepish. She smiled at him.

I can tell you, and no one else but perhaps Abby, and I know not when it will be that I may see her, so to you I must admit: I have come to like "The Business," indeed I have, my love, yes! Even that night, *before . . . well, whilst we were still prone,* that night, *'twas a marvellous thing; like hearing cannons, it is . . . and the feelings, the sensations, the . . . explosions within. . . .* She found herself smiling.

The horse had stopped nibbling and was looking at Eileen, his huge eyes soft and deep, as if he were trying to understand her.

The other times, too, I have so enjoyed it. I so enjoy . . . and her voice trailed off, as the reality of the fact that her access to this new wonder, as well as to so many other new things, had suddenly been wrenched from her.

Eileen sighed deeply and, picking up her broad-brimmed straw hat, about the crown of which she had dutifully wound a black ribbon *to match my new dresses,* she placed it atop her head, pushing it down over her thick hair. Bull, hearing her quick whistle, stepped in front of her and turned his left side to her, and she effortlessly mounted. She clicked twice to the horse, his ears pricked and, sensing her feet in the stirrups, he set off.

She remained largely alone until Father MacCarthy came for Mass on Sunday, when she decided to re-enter life. Even as she slowly emerged from her self-induced, emotionless fog, when anyone had inquired of her, she had simply said, "'Tis a sad time, indeed it is."

And in so many ways it was.

Life for Eileen continued to drift as aimlessly as her wanderings on Bull, though she was slowly accepting that the new realities of this life needed to be addressed.

She approached David O'Connor one still, warm evening after the meal, as he was working quietly in the squire's study, collarless, his sleeves rolled up. She knocked gently and he immediately stood, his tan face shiny with sweat, his shirt damp.

"'Tis warm," Eileen correctly observed as David gestured for her to sit.

Aware that she had not been in the room since she had written her mother on O'Connor's death, David softly asked, "Is this an uncomfortable setting for you?"

Eileen shook her head gently, *no*.

The pair sat, facing each other.

"I am aware of topics that need to be discussed," Eileen said softly. David nodded but said nothing. "I sense that, amidst all else in this sad time, you are dealing with difficulties involving your brothers and your respective positions, and . . ."

"Eileen, not to be rude, but if you would please permit me," David said slowly in a soft tone. It was Eileen's turn to nod and say nothing. "Some things had been addressed prior to Father's death, perhaps anticipating it in light of the situation here. I did not feel it appropriate to speak directly to you whilst he was alive, as it was for him as your husband to do so."

Eileen nodded, a bit of a questioning expression on her face.

"But now, assuming he did not have the opportunity to speak of these to you, 'tis appropriate for me to do so, as there are things of which you must become aware. The primary circumstance amongst these being that, by written agreement amongst our father, John and myself, John has formally ceded heirship of The O'Connor to me." He stopped and took a breath.

Though she didn't realise it, and certainly did not intend it, Eileen's expression changed to one of relief.

Seeing this, David nodded and continued. "Thus I shall assume—actually in effect I already *have* assumed—my father's role and status, whilst John, and, yes, Matthew—" he smiled, but not in a mean way—"and, of course, Peter, will continue to live here, their lives virtually unchanged."

Eileen smiled, just barely, "'Tis a good thing you are saying, David."

A gentle silence fell over the room, the sounds and aromas of the warm night floating in through the open windows.

Eileen cleared her throat, "Now, in terms of my own 'role' and 'status' and continuing to live here, I fully understand that I have ceased to be Mistress O'Connor and . . ."

David leaned back. "Your role and status are, in my mind, quite secure. You certainly may . . ."

Eileen gently raised a finger. "For *your mind* I am most grateful, sir, but I understand the reality of this life, and I know that you shall soon wed, as you certainly must as you are now the Squire O'Connor of Ballyhar, and at the point when you do take a wife, in fact and in law, there will be a new Mistress O'Connor, as sure as it is that it is the Squire O'Connor himself who sits across from me."

"You are a wise young woman indeed," David nodded, attempting, very much hoping, not to patronise Eileen, "as my father more than once told me."

"Thank you, kind sir, but this 'wise young woman' is also now a widow, and 'tis *this* that is *my* reality."

David O'Connor sighed deeply. "Please listen carefully, as were it Margaret O'Connor seated across from me here and now, I would say these very same words: You were the wife and are now the widow of the Squire John O'Connor of Firies; this is your home and we are your family. This is a fact that any wife of mine must and therefore shall accept."

Now it was Eileen who sighed, albeit very softly. "As it is I and not your dear mother who is seated here, there is one difference, and 'tis indeed a most significant one. 'Tis far easier for a young wife to accept an older woman as her mother-in-law, as it is both in fact and indeed *in law* that I would then be, but indeed . . ." She paused and shook her head ironically. "'Tis indeed highly probable that I would be younger than the new Mistress O'Connor."

She sighed. "What I am attempting to say is that 't'woud be an impossible situation for you, David. . . ." She caught herself and stopped. "I meant to say for you, *sir*."

"Eileen, I remain *David*, and what is it that you are proposing?"

Eileen sighed yet again, this time more deeply, smiled and continued, shaking her head. "Oh, *David* . . . I am quite honestly not wholly certain. . . . I need to reflect and consider; perhaps I may return to Derrynane, at least for a time. . . ."

David's expression changed. "*Derrynane*! I totally forgot, absorbed as I was before you entered. Messages have just today arrived from Derrynane. I am terribly sorry for being remiss . . . I meant to . . ." and he retrieved two thick parchment envelopes from the floor next to the secretary desk. "One is for you," he said, handing it to her, "whilst the second is addressed to me." He sat back, immediately breaking the wax seal of the one with his name on it.

Eileen shifted in her chair, recognising the handwriting as belonging to Denis O'Connell—*Just as I told Bull!*—and, taking note of the strutting stag on the O'Connell crest, broke the wax as well.

They read their respective letters from Denis. Whilst the salutations and introductory paragraphs of condolence and regret differed, the substance of both letters that followed was nearly identical, as Eileen read:

All of this being said, my dear sister, as you shall see from the enclosed document, the sad and regrettable eventuality that has now occurred had been anticipated by the late Squire O'Connor and myself. . . .

Eileen set down her brother's letter and scanned the second sheet, written in a scrivener's precise hand, which indicated it was a copy of an agreement between Denis and the late squire, their initials confirming the fact, apparently entered into at the same time as the original transaction that had brought her to Ballyhar. Her eyes widened as she absorbed certain words and phrases: *Given the significant disparity in their ages . . . In order to avoid, or at least minimise to the extent possible, the disruptions which shall certainly result from the inevitable death of . . . Upon the marriage*—her eyes went wide—*of Eibhlin Maire Ni Chonaill*—her jaw dropped—*and Donal Seán Ó Conchobhair*—she gasped audibly—*the same to occur after an acceptable interval of time has passed following the death of . . .*

The sum of £500 shall be lodged upon each of the said individually. . . .Whilst the additional sum of £2500 shall be paid to Denis Ó Conaill, acting on behalf of that Ó Conaill sept long, presently and foreseeably resident at Derrynane, Co. Kerry, along with the transfer of those lands more particularly described below, and located on the island of Barbados, in that area of the world known as the West Indies, as well as in the Colony of Maryland, in America. . . .

Her eyes still wide, her mouth half-open and a look of disbelief on her now gleaming face, Eileen laid the second page in her lap, looking across at David O'Connor, whose facial expression mirrored her own.

"They appear to have thought of everything, those two," David struggled to say.

Nearly speechless, Eileen began, "I am so sorry; my brother is . . ."

"A man most similar to my father, it would seem, a father who now seeks to control me, my life, from the grave."

"I can only assume that you were as unaware as I of this additional . . ." began Eileen.

"Absolutely! Nothing was said, nothing done beyond the agreement involving my father, my brother and myself. Nothing at all!"

The pair sat in an uncomfortable silence, both looking down again at their respective letters.

Finally, gathering the papers and the envelope, clutching them in her right hand, Eileen stood. "If you would so kindly excuse me, sir, I . . ."

David stood, almost formally. "Of course . . ." and he gestured her to the door and then followed her. "We should perhaps further discuss . . ."

Eileen turned to him, her face a mask of pain and sadness. Saying nothing, she turned, walked slowly through the large hall and climbed the stairs to her room, looking back once . . . and then once again . . . at David O'Connor.

The days that followed were an awkward mix of reality, fantasy, pathos and humour as Eileen and David O'Connor attempted to deal with the aftermath of the communications received from Derrynane revealing the plans, directly involving them, made months earlier by Denis O'Connell and the late John O'Connor.

Finally, on Friday evening, David asked Eileen to stroll with him from the house and they walked.

Turning to face her, David took Eileen's hand. "Eileen, you cannot imagine how difficult this is, but . . ."

"Yes, I can, David," she gently interrupted, looking directly at him.

He took a deep breath. "I have given it a great deal of thought, and . . ." he began to speak faster, "would you even *consider* a proposal of marriage from me?" He took a second deep breath.

Not releasing his hand, Eileen looked softly at the not unattractive man some eight years her senior though in many ways far less sophisticated than her. "I am sure that was most difficult, and I appreciate both the thought you have given and the . . . shall we say courage you displayed just now."

She paused, still holding his hand.

"As you spoke, I was preparing to decline . . ." she took his hands in both of hers, "but in my heart I feel I must give your true proposal true consideration, so whilst I am not accepting, neither shall I immediately decline." She sighed deeply.

David's face burst into a beaming smile, Eileen's much less so, but she linked her left arm in his right and they walked very slowly—like a courting couple—back towards the massive, silent house, saying virtually nothing.

The following morning, Eileen was up and out so early the grooms and stable boys were not yet in the barn, sweet smelling with the fresh hay laid down yesterday. Bull whinnied as she surprised him and happily chomped his oats after Eileen filled his breakfast bucket.

As soon as he finished, Eileen quickly saddled him, and they were leaving the barn just as tall, thin James was arriving. "Mistress, oh, Mistress, I am *so sorry*, please . . ."

Smiling down from Bull's back, Eileen told the boy that she'd come in early. "You cannot be expected to read my mind, so no apologies."

The boy nodded and bobbed his head respectfully as Eileen turned Bull and they cantered off.

That they rode for hours was all Eileen knew, that and the fact that twice she'd been lost, not recognising at all where she was and not knowing how she'd gotten them there. The second time, late in the afternoon, she stood in the stirrups and draped herself onto Bull's neck, whispering in his ears, "I thought 'twas *you* who was paying attention, my love!" and she laughed at herself. Sighting with the sun and following a brook, she was able to reorient them, and they began the long ride home, accomplished alternately between a gentle canter and a walk.

As she rode the final miles, Eileen expressed to herself, half-aloud, the still disordered conclusions—but conclusions nevertheless—at which she was in the process of arriving: *Well now . . . it all comes down to remaining the mistress or not, does it not, girl? You have grown to like it, to relish it; within weeks of your coming here, barely recovered from your bad beginning, you were already then glorying in it, were you not, girl?* "Mistress Eileen," "Mistress O'Connor," "yes, Madame, certainly, Madame." She laughed with bitter irony. *And then he died . . . and with him died "Mistress Eileen."*

She shook her head. "He died," she repeated softly aloud. "He died . . ." and her eyes grew cloudy, moist, and she lifted them briefly to the sky. *In an instant, you have lost it all: Power. Position. Standing. And now . . . now there appears a way for "Mistress Eileen" to return to life . . . on the gracious— or is it the pitiable? or perhaps even the romantic?—terms of David O'Connor. Ah, tempting it is; admit it, girl, tempting! Some time will pass. You will say the words you have already said once . . . and "Mistress O'Connor" you shall again be . . . and forever!*

. . . and yet this I cannot, I shall not do! 'T'woud be unfair; no, 't'woud be both unjust and unfair to him and to me, and for me . . . 't'woud be an utter disaster! And the very idea of it, it makes me uneasy, though this I cannot say to David. Indeed, 'tis uneasy I am at the whole thought of . . . to be wed to the father, and then the son?   That this reality seems to have concerned neither the squire nor Denis O'Connell is reason enough for me to reject the notion! 'Tis my life; I must try to lead it as I feel it should be led. To do otherwise in this instance 't'woud render me a trollop of sorts, would it not? Being passed from man to man as decided and then decreed . . . by men!

Suddenly standing in her stirrups, her right hand forming a tight fist, she screamed passionately into the hot, empty Kerry late afternoon, "*No . . . No! I shall not do this! I shall not have it done to me*—never, never, *never* again!"

Whether it was the unusual volume of her voice or the fact that he was hungry, Bull tugged at his reins, and she reined the stallion in—hard!—so hard his head snapped up short. Realising what she had done, she bent and hugged his neck. "I am so sorry, my darling, my dear friend." She let him walk slowly ahead, the reins loose, and his pace began to quicken almost immediately.

"Easy, please," Eileen said softly. "I am in no haste." Though the horse was; he was thinking of his evening bucket of oats. She gathered the reins and did not give him his head, but they still approached a long boreen that ultimately led to the house at a canter.

As they were within sight of Ballyhar, which somehow seemed even drearier and more massive in the gathering late summer dusk, and with her mind now loosely made up, Eileen finally gave Bull his head and he pounded to the stables and his dinner. Thomas, the young groom, awaited, and he smiled broadly as Eileen came into view, pulled up Bull and slid off the animal's back, landing with a thud on the packed-earth floor.

"He has had a most full day," Eileen said, stroking the horse's left flank. "I feel I should do it, but might I trouble you to rub him down well after his dinner? And to give a good helping of warm bran in addition to his oats? He has earned all of it."

She turned and then turned back "Thank you ever so much. . . ." Carrying her hat and gloves, she ambled out of the barn, the young man's eyes following her, as all the young men's did.

She entered a quiet house, the soft sounds of the beautiful clock's brass pendulum being all she heard as she closed the night sounds out on shutting the massive door. She stopped to notice the hour—almost half-nine—and turned for the stairs when she caught the gentle sound of a quill point scratching on parchment coming from the study.

Her fingers on the just ajar door, she scratched the nails of her other hand on the wood, and David O'Connor's soft voice responded, "Enter, of course enter, Eileen."

Leaving her hat and gloves on a chair just outside the door, Eileen stepped inside a room darkened, darker even than the hall save for the light thrown by three candles, set on and by the secretary desk at which David had been writing.

Her eyes adjusting, Eileen squinted slightly and offered a soft "Good evening to you, sir."

David smiled, stood and gestured her to sit.

She dropped back into a side armchair, rested her head back and sighed deeply.

As he remained standing awkwardly, Eileen looked gently at the man, who appeared stricken. "David, sit, please." She gestured to the desk chair. "Please."

He sat heavily, leaning his elbows on the desk; his forehead in his hand, he shook his head slowly.

"David," Eileen began, and he looked up, sat back in the chair, turned and faced her. "This has been a difficult and tumultuous time for all of us, for me very much so. That you care, it means . . ."

"Eileen, Eileen—I *do* care, I care so very much. Ever since you first arrived . . ."

Eileen's expression instantly became serious, her hands folded in the lap of her black dress, dusty now from her day in the saddle. "I have sensed that, and for that I am grateful as well, but I fear I am not in a position to return your feelings, David."

As he began to speak, Eileen gently raised her hand. "*Please . . .* if I do not say this now, I shan't be able . . ." and David nodded.

"In barely half a year I have gone from a girl, a child amongst many, to being a wedded woman, to a man of great position, mistress of a grand house, of a great estate . . . and, in an instant, am thrust into widowhood, all before my seventeenth birthday. My relationship with the squire . . . 'twas . . . complex, and my feelings, of him, for him, in many ways the same, so difficult, so . . ." Her voice trailed off. "At the same time, I hold you truly in high regard and I understand and remain most grateful for the sincerity of your feelings and of your proposal. I have been weighing it—most carefully, I assure you—against a number of things, about some of which I remain unable to be fully candid. I shall never be able to tell you everything; please trust me that I cannot!"

David's face was pale and he nodded his head gently: *I understand.*

Eileen sighed deeply. "It is difficult for me to say the words that I know will not be those you wish to hear." She took a deep breath. "I am unable to accept your kind and gracious proposal of marriage, as to do so would result in my being at the centre of another's life rather than acting as what I keep thinking of as a compass for my own. Perhaps at some time in the future I shall find myself able and willing to be the centre of someone's life, but now is not that time."

Eileen paused, looked up at the ceiling, stood and folded her arms. She began to walk in the small room, as much in frustration at herself as anything. "I fear I may not be adequately conveying my feelings. I am sorry. . . . I have since a little girl done—though certainly not always willingly, not immediately obediently—those things that I have been told to do, and most recently this has proven to me to be a great sadness, for reasons of which you are aware, as well as some that, as I have said, I am unable to tell you, from all of which, in all truth, I feel I may never fully recover. I believe I have grown beyond being the child I was when I came here, perhaps even beyond being Mistress O'Connor, as I was not given a choice in originally assuming that role.

"I feel you, dear and gentle man, have given me a choice—and the choice I have made, after much thought, is the only correct one, for to do otherwise would be unfair, especially to you, but also to myself. You have provided me with an opportunity to lead *my* life, a life that, for good or for ill, David, will be my own."

She sat again, looking across the desk at an ashen, disappointed man. She fought thoughts of pity. David said nothing, his eyes on the papers on the desktop. Eileen continued to sit for what seemed to be hours, saying nothing else.

She finally stood and very softly said, "Good night, sir." David looked up but said nothing. She went quietly to her rooms; she did not sleep well.

Eileen rose before dawn, washed her face and pulled on yet another black dress. Carrying her slippers, she padded quietly downstairs and across the gleaming floors of the entrance hall, gently easing open the massive front door. She dropped her slippers onto the stones at the bottom of the stairs and stepped into them and thence into the slowly awakening day.

She noticed just the aura of the sun on a distant horizon, thinking, as her face and hands felt moist from the mantle of dankness that rested over North Kerry at dawn that the warmth it promised would be welcome. As she began to walk, the final night sounds clashed with those of the early birds' and a distantly barking dog. The smoky sweet aroma of the revived or freshly-lit turf fires reminded her that she was not the only one awake at this early hour.

She strolled neither slowly nor quickly across the rough lawn and to the broken stone path leading up the gentle knoll where now John O'Connor slept. She had not been there since learning of O'Connor and Denis O'Connell's agreement.

Reaching the gravesite, she nodded, as she always had, at the stone marking Margaret O'Connor's place and, folding her hands beneath her waist, she turned her attention to the mound of dirt upon which rested fresh flowers but as yet still no stone.

Well now, good morning, husband. She stood quietly for a time, just looking at the grave. *You are not perhaps aware of the fact, husband, but irate at you it is that I am, sir. Very angry I am that you have died, that you have gone and left me, left me more alone than I have ever felt in my life. I know we do not choose the moment, the time of our deaths, 'tis to God alone that this belongs . . . yet I sense that you somehow knew, and that you somehow settled with God. . . . Was it just another business dealing? Or was it that you were ready to depart?*

She smiled bitterly and shook her head gently. Her eyes filling, she looked about, briefly lifting them to the brightening sky above.

She then gazed again upon his grave.

A lovely day it appears it will be here, husband. She paused, abruptly glaring at O'Connor, as if before her he stood. "How could you have left me, John?" she suddenly cried out, her fists clenched at her side.

Was it not a good thing, this marriage we were building? This marriage that began so horribly now 'tis ended horribly! Horribly at least for me—she tapped her breasts with her fingertips—*perhaps not for you, but certainly for me, sir! You have taken everything from me! Everything, do you understand? By your leaving! My home, our home! My status . . . and, yes, oh yes, I shall miss, I already miss being abed with you, sir! You wonderfully wanton old man! Though abed only with you have ever I been, I feel—no, I fear!—no younger man could be more so than you, could take me to the heights, the depths I have been with you, old man!*

Again she paused; again she shook her head as her hands clenched into fists. . . . *And already I miss you. . . .* Tears streamed down her cheeks. *'Tis no wonder I called you "bastard" on the very night you were interred! Did you know that, sir? And what of this "arrangement"? Am I to now wed your son, sir? And thus to retain, or perhaps regain that which by your departing you have taken from me? What you do not know, husband, is that he cannot replace you—*she touched her left breast, her heart—*and no matter how benign your intentions may have been, I cannot, I shall not submit to Denis O'Connell, not now . . . not ever again!*

She stood quietly, her arms folded beneath her bosom, looking, just looking at her husband's grave, silent tears yet again streaming down her cheeks. Finally, she stepped closer to the mound of dirt, out of which tiny sprouts of thin green grass had begun to appear.

We shall speak yet again, husband. A good day to you then, sir. . . . She walked slowly away, down the crushed-rock footpath, her steps lightly crunching.

Late in the afternoon, Eileen sat at the simple, petite desk set between her bedroom's two large windows. She quickly assembled paper, pen and ink and once again began a message to her mother:

> *Ballyhar*
> *Firies, Co. Kerry*
> *4 October 1760*

My dearest Mama:
As always, I trust you and all at home remain well. 'Tis a difficult and sad time for me here.

I have received a message and enclosure from Denis, written further to my letter to you as to my husband's passing. Master David O'Connor has received a similar communication. I do not believe you are aware of the contents of these letters. I find I am unable to fully express myself, so much having happened to me and in my life in the barely half year that has passed since I came here from Derrynane. I continue to experience a tumult of powerful and barely appreciated thoughts, feelings and emotions. Denis's message contained words neither of comfort nor condolence.

She sighed aloud, only briefly considering whether her next words would contain a request or a declaratory statement. She nodded firmly as she dipped the quill, as she returned the freshly-inked tip to the paper.

Rather than dwell on these matters further, I am making preparations to return to Derrynane, anticipating departing here after my husband's month's mind, to be celebrated 14 Oct, inst. Whilst I am at the moment uncertain as to how I shall get there, my plan is to engage our good ship's master Dennehy at Kenmare, to transport Bull, myself and my belongings down the River to Derrynane. I have written him to this end, and I shall attempt to send word ahead to you prior to my departure from Kenmare, though I may be unable to do so.
I so long to see you, very much do I need to be, once again and always—
Your loving, though not always obedient daughter, Eibhlin

Eileen quickly folded the sheets and slipped them into a thick envelope. Lighting the candle on the desktop, she drew out a stick of red sealing wax and her own seal, with what she called the swaggering or strutting O'Connell stag, and dribbling the wax onto the envelope flap, pressed the seal into it. She suddenly, unthinkingly, smiled; he *is* strutting.

Ballyhar to Derrynane—October 1760

John O'Connor's month's mind was indeed commemorated on 14 October 1760, in the same room where he had married Eileen barely eight months prior and where he himself had been waked and his funeral Mass held. Father MacCarthy said again the simple requiem, attended as before by the family, led by Eileen, as the widow, and David, as the new squire, and the entire household. Once again, Lord and Lady Moyvane and several other local nobles, as well as the high sheriff of Kerry—Protestants all—were in sombre attendance.

As was the custom of month's mind, a light meal and refreshments were served afterwards. In a freshly laundered and pressed black dress, Eileen circulated quietly amidst the attendees, thanking them and saying her formal good-byes.

"You are due to depart when exactly, my dear?" Lady Moyvane asked gently.

"By the end of next week, my lady," Eileen responded softly. "David has kindly arranged for . . ." she smiled, gesturing in her direction, "Kate"— the quieter one—"and her fine new husband"—who was Michael, one of the grooms—"to accompany me to Kenmare."

"Well, then, I suspect that this evening will be one for *our* farewells, will it not?"

Eileen lowered her eyes for a long moment. "It will be, my lady. I doubt that I shall be returning. . . . The situation here . . . 'tis a complex one."

The noblewoman stepped closer, nodded and lowered her voice. "I understand; indeed I am certain it is. There can be but one mistress, and she is the one to whom the master, the squire, the lord, whoever he may be, is wed . . . though I am sure that should you wish . . ."

Eileen gently touched Lady Moyvane's arm and indeed then took her hand in her own, looking gently at the older woman. "To be sure, I have spoken with the new squire at some length, and he has advised that I am most welcome to remain, that this is my home, for which I am most grateful. But I have shared with him the reality of what would transpire once he made a woman the new Mistress O'Connor, and he now understands that the chances of the widowed mother-in-law actually being younger than his wife are quite excellent, thereby creating an untenable situation, as much for him as anything. 'T'woud be no way to begin a marriage."

Lady Moyvane looked carefully at Eileen. *Is she aware of the details of how my own marriage began?* Eileen wondered.

"As my husband has more than once said of you, Eileen, you are a very wise young woman. I admire you more than you shall ever know, and I shall miss you . . . very much."

The women spontaneously embraced.

Eileen's emotional preparations in the days following were complex. Some days she actually toyed with the thought of perhaps ultimately accepting what she now viewed as David O'Connor's gallant proposal, thus permitting her to remain the mistress. Before the end of any day in which she did, she nevertheless knew in her heart she could not, would not do so, that were she to return to Ballyhar she would be doing the bidding of Denis O'Connell, and she felt she had come too far, had struggled too hard for independence and control, and had survived and matured too much, to live her life according to the plans of anyone other than herself.

In a gentle and in many ways sad conversation, she had advised David that her decision was final, and candidly told him why. Looking at Eileen, David had nodded. "You are indeed a brave and strong woman. I respect you, and I respect your decision."

Unable to sleep on the night prior to her departure, her mind again drifted and wandered. *I never did shoot to kill*, she mused, lying in the darkness, her mind racing on this as it had on more than one night, *and I wonder . . . what if I had?* Unspoken questions unanswered, she finally drifted to sleep.

The day set for her departure was cool and dreary. Kate and Michael and the packhorses were ready early. Eileen had begged and then, in perhaps her last order as mistress, virtually decreed that there would be no farewell. "I could not bear it," she told David and a group of the tenant wives, who'd approached her about a "proper, fitting farewell for ye, Madame."

So, after a light breakfast and a solitary stroll to John—and Margaret—O'Connor's gravesite and a hug to John the Younger—and, yes, his Matthew—and to a grim David, into whose eyes she looked for what seemed a very long time, a not quite comprehending Peter and chatty Kate, Eileen, her widow's black dress freshly laundered and crisply pressed and a broad straw hat on her head, with a nod, a lip-quivering smile and her eyes deep with tears, swung up onto Bull's back. Seated, she looked down from that great height at the O'Connor family, nodded, gently turned Bull's head and even more gently touched his sides with her boots. Without looking back, and after touching her right saddlebag, she led Kate and Michael and the horses away towards Kenmare, the River Kenmare . . . and herself to Derrynane.

The journey was uneventful and, at least superficially, unemotional. The three young people spoke freely amongst themselves as they rode. They shared reminiscences, joyous and not, funny and not. They talked of their own childhoods, of the stories they knew, and Kate told Michael repeatedly of the wonders she'd seen at Derrynane. "All the people, so many, and the house so beautiful," she would go on.

During the course of those four days, whilst the three were drawn closer, they inevitably began to grow more distant as well. As the result of both, the person who was still "Mistress Eileen" and "Madame" on departing Ballyhar had faded a bit more into each of the evenings' mists, so that by the time they reached the village of Kenmare, she had become simply Eileen.

As they guided the horses slowly towards the quays at Kenmare, though she was still relatively distant from Derrynane, Eileen experienced a small sense of homecoming. She knew where she was. People took notice of the striking young woman astride the massive stallion, some nodding in recognition, two men touching their hats: *The O'Connell girl, the one they call Dark Eileen, that's who she is.*

Though Kenmare was not a large place, it was frequently a busy one; given the virtual nonexistence of roads on Iveragh, the River Kenmare played a critical role in commerce, amongst other things transporting Kerry butter cross-river to market in Cork and beyond. Even then, the farmers took days crossing rough country just to reach the oft-times bustling quays at Kenmare.

Finally, seeing Master Dennehy in conversation with friends on one of the quays, she stood in the stirrups and waved and called, "Good Master Dennehy!" At that, the huge man's ruddy face exploded in an incandescent smile as he waved back.

Within moments the packhorses had been unloaded of Eileen's battered satchels, Bull unsaddled and horse and baggage trundled onto one of the O'Connells' compact river ships, as Master Dennehy himself oversaw every move; only at the last moment would he gesture to the eager young man who would help take Eileen on the last leg of her journey to cast off.

In striking contrast to the enthusiasm at the boat, Eileen stepped back towards Kate and Michael and embraced them individually; then, her left hand resting gently on Kate's right shoulder, her right on Michael's left shoulder as the couple stood facing her, their eyes upraised, tears finally streamed down her sunburnt cheeks, and Eileen struggled to speak. Finally, her tears unwiped, she began, "Thank you, thank you. I am more grateful to you, and Kate, to your 'sister' Kate—you will tell her, yes?—more than I can express. I do not know when or if I shall see you again, but I expect a message . . ."

Kate began to speak, to remind Eileen that their literacy, the lessons for which Eileen had begun and overseen, was still in its formative stage, and Eileen—perhaps for the last time, she knew—raised her hand gently and Kate instinctively, immediately silenced herself. "And if the event is sooner than I think it will be, Master David will see to it that it is written for you, in which I am told that your wee one has arrived safe and well, and if 'tis a he or a she."

The couple looked amazed, shocked, and Eileen was able to laugh. "I have learnt much in these six months. 'Tis a baby you shall be having! You wait, you shall see!"

Eileen and her dear, quiet Kate embraced once again and then, as she had at Ballyhar, Eileen stepped back, turned and walked towards the boat, not looking back. She did stand, however, at the low rail and wave at the young couple, and they at her, as the sturdy little craft slipped away from the quay and a suddenly brisk early morning breeze caught and filled its sails. Eileen turned from Kate and Michael and Kenmare and the people on the quays and looked downriver, in the direction of the place where the river would, willingly or not, give itself to the wild Atlantic, the place where Derrynane waited for her.

During the gentle, not quite day-long journey, Eileen alternated amongst chatting with Master Dennehy, of whom she was most fond, standing with an obviously nervously tethered, partially hobbled Bull, who whinnied his gratitude for her attention and the turnip bits she produced from her pocket and quietly walking up and down the small, open deck, casting an eye on Kerry to her right, and then, inexplicably at one point, in the direction of County Cork, a place she had never been despite its relative closeness, which lay beyond her sight and to her left (the lands on that bank part of Kerry, as well). She imagined both Kerry and Cork as being dazzlingly green, wondering if both were as peaceful as Kerry appeared.

Eileen gloried in the warmth of the sun on her face and, as they came ever closer to Derrynane, the increasingly brackish, even salty, smells of the air. Mingling with the tang of damp turf and gorse, moist, fresh and drying seaweed, wet sand and dead fish on the shore, it combined to smell like *home*, something for which she was now very, very grateful.

She was leaning against the mast when she saw the horizon open wider, and felt a sharp change in the wind in her face. She pointed, laughing with joy. "'Tis the Atlantic!" she cried out spontaneously, and good Master Dennehy nodded vigorously.

"Close we are getting now, m'lady!" he called back through the suddenly cooler wind, and soon it was that the islands, Scariff and Deenish, as well as the large rocks, named and nameless, resting in the gentle arc of Derrynane Bay came into view . . . and, in the distance, its presence already patent to Eileen, the dark outline of Derrynane House itself. She held her arm across her forehead, keeping her hair back, her hand shading her eyes from the reflection of the brilliant late-afternoon sun on the water until she could make out the details of the house and, though she was unable to determine who they were, the people gathering in response to the small ship's clanging bell.

She was home.

Derrynane—October 1760

The sun, nearing the end of its steady, inevitable passage across the brilliantly blue sky of Kerry, was far closer to its setting than its rising as Eileen finally stopped speaking and, weary now, rested her head against Abby's shoulder.

And so the sisters sat—silent, lost in the immensity of what had been said in the hours now past—until Abigail's eyes filled and she began to cry. Slowly at first, she dissolved into what quickly became heaving, sobbing, weeping, the depths of which she had never experienced before, and which Eileen had never witnessed in her frequently laughing, invariably sunshine-filled sister.

Eileen draped an arm around her sister and gently rocked them, saying nothing and crying not at all, reflecting silently, *I have shed my tears, shed enough tears; as Mama said with her eyes to me last night, "No more. Enough."*

As Abigail's own tears slowed and finally stopped and after, the girls sat quietly, speaking of nothing important, it was Eileen who stood first and extended a hand to her older sister.

Abby stood and the sisters embraced, and with Eileen's arm again draped over the shorter woman's shoulder, they walked slowly to the ever-patient horses and, with them, began the gentle descent from their rocky heights to the sanctuary of Derrynane below. They rode carefully now, as the particular angle of the declining sun over Derrynane Bay was casting subtle shadows on the rocks and the gorse, the distant sounds of gentle waves and circling falcons providing a chorus for their slow downward journey home. As they descended, the cooling air became markedly damp against their skin, the pungent odour of low tide slowly capturing the early evening.

Handing the animals over to William and, a bit more abruptly than usual, bidding him the time of day, the girls had begun to walk directly towards the house when Abby took Eileen's right hand in her own left one and tugged her sister away from and around the far side of it. Her eyes red from weeping and still visibly upset, Abigail held her younger sister's hand as they continued walking, now directing them towards the strand.

"Something must be done! 'Tis a crime, is it not?" she cried with unusual passion.

Eileen, obviously drained for so many reasons, could only shake her head. "What is it that is a crime, my darling?" she asked, her expression genuinely quizzical. "That our brother sold me away? That the man who was my husband beat me senseless the very night of our wedding—or that, after I had some-how recovered from such a thing and began to feel . . . *something*—I know not precisely what, nor certainly not why—that he was stricken and died on the very floor, as I knelt next to him? That less than a year ago I was a girl . . . here"—she opened her arms in gesture—"and, after all that I have told you has happened, I am yet again, here"—she opened her arms again—"but now . . . a widow and not yet seventeen! Yet I honestly do not ken where a 'crime' might be said to lay amidst this . . . this *wreckage*.

"I love you, Abigail, and I cannot tell you how many times during these tumultuous months I wished I could have spoken to you, with you, as I have this day, but, my darling sister, my dear, dear friend, I do not see that anything that has happened to me, though perhaps unfair—yes, unfair indeed!—could be viewed as criminal, except perhaps by God, who will judge the men involved, as I believe He perhaps already has begun doing, in His own time and manner."

Abby's eyes flashed. "So what is it that you are saying, my sweet girl? That *no one* is to be held accountable in this world for the evil, the tragedy that has befallen you; indeed, child, that has befallen this house and family," she cried.

Eileen ran her long, thin fingers through her tangled hair, pushing it back from her forehead, a look of genuine pain on her face.

"True it may be that there is nothing *I* can do to undo the events of these months." She paused and took a step away, then turned back, facing her sister directly and taking both of Abby's hands in her own. "But what *I* can do— and indeed as I have related to you, what I *have done*," she emphasised in her again strong, husky voice, "is to assure as best I can that I am *never again* a pawn in any man's, in *anyone's* chess game, whether it is Denis O'Connell or John or David O'Connor, or . . . anyone."

She leaned closer to Abby, whispering, "I cannot, I *shall not* permit *anyone* to control me, my life, though my hopes, my dreams even . . . have been dashed, I have *survived* . . . and I shall hope and dream again, of this I am certain."

The house was strangely quiet as the sisters entered it. Her mind now set, wordlessly, Abigail took Eileen's hand and led her onto the grand staircase. Suddenly docile, almost trancelike, Eileen permitted her sister to do so and, still holding her hand, followed Abby upstairs. Only at the last moment, as they approached them, did she seem to understand that their destination was their mother's rooms. As she tried to pull back, Abby silently turned and looked firmly up into her eyes. This proving sufficient, her momentary resolve collapsed and Eileen followed her.

Beyond the heavy door, Maire sat engulfed by a large leather wing chair in front of a low fire. She turned her head at Abby's knock and responded with her customary *"Cuir isteach, teacht i,"* "come in," and, standing, smiled broadly at her daughters. Opening her arms wide, she approached the girls, hugging them together. "So, my loves, you were on the mountains today," she said softly.

Eileen began to speak, and then Abby, and Maire, holding up her hands, laughingly interrupted them both. "Surely you cannot believe that *anything* of note occurs here without my knowing it, do you? Brigid was to my rooms with my breakfast most likely before you left sweet William's barn," she continued, laughing as she resumed her seat and directed the girls to the pair of smaller high-backed leather chairs flanking the hearth at angles and facing hers, indicating they should pull the chairs closer.

"Mama, if I may," Abby began in an unusually sombre tone, which their mother perceived immediately, her facial expression becoming almost grave.

"Yes, Abigail?" Maire nodded, as serious now as Abby.

"Eileen and I have spent the day together and she has related . . ."

"Nil!" Eileen, whose mind had been wandering, now fully comprehended the enormity of what was about to occur, suddenly rose from her chair, exclaiming sharply, "'Tis not the time, not the place, sister!"

Abby was on her feet equally fast, leaning forwards and, in a way she never before had done, glaring angrily up at her younger sister, who, visibly shocked, sank immediately, almost meekly, back into her chair. Standing, though in a much softer voice, albeit still in a commanding manner, Abby continued, "Sufficient time has passed, *child*, and it is *not* for *you* to set limits, to decree borders."

The younger girl, her eyes wide, her lips barely parted, nodded gently, her tenacity broken.

Maire's gaze shifted from girl to girl, until Abigail, again seated, smoothing her skirts, her hands folded in her lap, leaning ever so slightly toward her mother, began in a firm, "Things involving our child here have transpired, things about which we have had no knowledge, but which you must know . . . now."

Maire sat silently and gestured for her to continue.

For the ensuing hour, without interruption, Abigail repeated, in a calm, steady voice, an abbreviated, though still highly detailed version of the tale Eileen had related to her during the course of the day now ending.

Maire sat in total silence, her reactions, however, clearly apparent from the quickening of her breaths as well as by the steady clenching and unclenching of her fists, the occasional tapping of her right foot and the tears that periodically streamed silently down her tanned cheeks, through much of the rendering. Eileen herself appeared numb, occasionally nodding, joining her mother's soundless tears solely when the events of *that night* and those surrounding John O'Connor's death and its aftermath were revealed. Only at the mention of Eileen's *caoineadh* did Maire display the faintest suggestion of a smile.

Coming to her conclusion, Abigail drew a deep breath. "And *that* is what has happened to our child, and *that* is the tragedy that this family has suffered by the actions of and at the hands of another, and indeed of one of our own!"

The only sounds in the room came from the fireplace—a gentle hiss from the burning turf—and an equally soft ticking of the small blue and white Chinese porcelain mantel clock. Maire sat for what seemed a very long while, her hands folded beneath her chin, as if in prayer.

Abruptly, the small, compact woman stood. "Abigail, my darling, you may leave us; we appear to have spoken through tea, but Brigid and Annie will have something for you in the kitchen."

Understanding, Abby rose and kissed her mother's forehead; by the time her skirt had swished and her boots softly thudded across the thick Indian carpet and the door had clicked behind her, Maire was sitting on the rug at Eileen's feet.

Her hands on her daughter's knees beneath the rough wool skirt, the older woman looked up silently at this beautiful, wounded girl she had borne and raised, and who— Maire was now feeling—she had sent off to a horrid and wholly undeserved fate.

Finally, looking plaintively at her daughter, she said, "Eileen, my darling, my beloved child, before anything else is said or done, I must—and I *do*—first beg your forgiveness for what has happened to you. I should have stopped it, tried to stop it; the lads, Morgan especially, begged me to do so, and," she sighed deeply, "I did not. I was a weak woman and I," she swallowed her next thought, tears streaming down her cheeks, "and *we all* failed to come to your aid, as I promised you we would, as well we should have, as . . ."

Eileen leaned forward, her hair dull and dusty from her journey and yet another day in the saddle and in the countryside, and took Maire's hand. "Mama, first of all, you did not know. . . . I myself was not honest. . . . And secondly, 'twas I who decided that in the situation, I was the O'Connell who would best protect myself, and I did . . . and I believe I did very well indeed!

"As difficult as it is for me to say the words now, I was indeed fully prepared to and would have killed John O'Connor that morning, but 'twas not to be . . . neither at that moment nor afterwards. During this time, I thought often of you and Papa and the things you both taught me, and relying on that wisdom, I maintained myself safe. To have summoned aid from Derrynane, from the O'Connells . . ." Her voice trailed off as she gently shook her head, her hands resting on her mother's.

"And lastly, our laws and customs—not the king's but *ours*—made Denis *príomhfheidhmeannach ár clan*, head of our family. I accept that, as we must. If anyone bears responsibility for any part of what I have called the 'wreckage,' 'tis Denis alone, and, as I have said just this evening to Abigail, I am not sure if even he . . ."

"Oh . . . *he does!*" Maire interrupted loudly. "Responsible he is and fully accountable he shall be held!" She cast an eye at the small clock, gently ticking on the mantel. "'Tis half-eight, my darling. Are you hungry, weary?"

Eileen glanced at the clock and back at her mother and nodded, softly saying, "*Níl, ní.*"

Maire stood, gesturing for the girl to remain seated, and bustled in her customary fashion out of the room and, closing the door, into the hall, from whence the single, deep *clannnnggg* of an iron bell carried through much of but not the entire rambling house. Little Hugh, in a too-big nightshirt, immediately poked his tousled head out of his own door, and Maire gestured for him to go back in and close the door, which he did.

Within moments, Annie came hastening up the stairs, so rare was it that Maire's single ring was heard. "Yes, Mistress?"

Though she was invariably gentler with Annie, whom she regarded and treated as one of her daughters, just as she regarded and treated Brigid as a sister, Maire was at this moment abrupt. "Please have Master Denis come to my rooms now, immediately," and she turned and went back inside, closing the door sharply.

Eileen was standing in front of the hearth, her hands folded in front of her, gazing into the flames.

"I have sent for your eldest brother. We shall begin to address this now, tonight. Abby is correct; too much has happened, too much time, too much hurt, too . . ."

There was a sharp, brittle knock at the door. Maire sat and gestured Eileen to do so as well, then said "Enter" in an icy tone.

Denis O'Connell, in dusky brown breeches, smudged hose, dusty shoes and a worn-more-than-one-day white shirt, entered silently, his jaw set, his hair untidy, untended, the queue ribbon askew.

Maire gestured coldly. "Sit. Now."

His demeanour markedly different from that of the prior evening, now casting quick, uneasy glances both at his mother and sister, the man did as he was told, tentatively setting his elbows on the armrests, his fingers seeming to shake ever so slightly, as Maire began, her voice dry, icy. "Well now . . . Abigail has related certain things to me this evening, things about which I . . . and I presume *we* have previously had no knowledge, being events that transpired during Eileen's tenure at O'Connor's, at Ballyhar."

Denis sat silently, his eyes looking into his mother's.

"Am I correct in assuming that . . ." she began.

Denis took a deep, pained breath. "I have just seen Abigail in the house, and all she said to me was that *I* am 'to consider myself fortunate that the Dark One is alive and here.' *I* know nothing about which she speaks, nor why

I should feel thus as she says." His tone was now the superior one he usually affected.

"Very well," Maire said, and she immediately proceeded to relate to an apparently shocked Denis O'Connell the events only of Eileen's wedding night.

"Whilst there is much more, amongst the principal 'more' being the little arrangement you and the now late Squire O'Connor entered into that allows you and indeed permits him to attempt to rule people's lives from his grave, I shall not discuss it, at least not now."

Looking at the grave expression on Eileen's normally glowing face, he sighed and began, "Sister, I did not know, I could not have known, I am only . . ."

"Only what?" the girl snapped, standing suddenly to her full height. "Sorry? Regretful? Displeased? What do I care what you are, Denis O'Connell! Actually, I know *exactly* what you are." She pointed her finger directly at him. "You are evil! *You are malign*! By your very being, you defame the name of Donal Mór Ó Conaill! By your very existence and the position you hold, a position for which you have proven yourself utterly unworthy, for which you are totally unfit, you sully every Ó Conaill . . . alive and dead! And, yes, Abby was correct; you are lucky indeed that I am alive and . . ."

She stopped abruptly, making a dismissive gesture with her right hand, and shaking her head at her mother, she sat back down, her brother's face ashen, his expression fixed in shock, his eyes following her as she sat.

"'Tis not worth the exertion . . ." she said, only half aloud and to no one in particular, and rested her head wearily against the high back of her chair.

Silence filled the room for several very long moments as Denis's mind processed all he had heard, as a result of which his expression eased, his composure regained, so that when he finally began to speak, after clearing his throat, his tone was crisp. "All of this said, I do indeed of course regret—sincerely regret—what befell you at the hands of O'Connor, but the fact of the matter is that we all have our roles in and duties to this family."

Maire's eyes grew wide. Eileen, noticing it, tentatively held up her fingers, as if to say *'Tis all right, let him continue.* With difficulty, their mother sat silent.

By now, having succeeded in fully absolving himself of any responsibility and therefore of any need for remorse, Denis continued coldly. "What *does* remain to be addressed sooner rather than later is the matter of your marriage to David O'Connor. I feel this is far from being settled, far from resolved."

"What possible care could I have for how *you* feel about *anything*, brother?" Eileen snapped. Maire continued to sit in silence.

Unfazed, he went on. "Not only are you the Widow O'Connor, you also have an obligation to do what is best for this family, to do your duty."

Eileen rose and very slowly circled the chairs in silence, returning to the hearth and, standing regally straight whilst leaning back against the mantel, her arms folded beneath her bosom, glared down at her brother. "Denis," she began, her husky voice cold and very calm, "I fully understand what my obligations are as an O'Connell, and I feel it in my heart, in my very soul, and I believe any reasonable man would agree that I *have . . . done . . . my . . . duty.*"

She stepped forward and leaned over to her brother, so close that her hair fell about both of them. "And it nearly cost me my life, you rotten, foul bastard!" She straightened up abruptly and dropped back into her chair.

Looking at Denis, deliberately not looking at her mother, she continued. "Assuming you did not know any of this sordid tale until now, something else you do not know is how very close you came to at least in part having the blood of Squire John O'Connor on your hands, *brother.*" She paused for a long moment. "The morning after I was attacked, I entered his room, my pistol drawn. . . ."

Noting her brother's mouth was now agape, her voice rose slightly. "Had he not cowardly fled in the night, I would have then and there shot and killed the man for what he had done to me. Have no doubt, *brother,* I would indeed have killed him."

"And where did you . . ." Denis began.

"*I* gave it to her, with ample ammunition and powder, the day before she departed here," snapped Maire, "and I have no doubt Eileen indeed would have killed the man . . . as *I wish she had!*"

On hearing her mother's final four words albeit unnoticed, Eileen had winced visibly.

Maire stood slowly, as regally as her short stature permitted. "We are finished here this night." Then, looking at her still-seated son, her voice emotionless and direct, she added, "It is my decision that Eileen is free to remain here or to return to the O'Connors; it, and the timing, is and shall remain her decision and her decision alone. My hope and prayer is that she stays on at Derrynane, that she will, in our midst, recover from all she has been through, ready then to resume life as *she* wishes to lead it. In terms of . . . other matters, they remain for your brothers and me to address."

Eileen sat quietly whilst Denis began to speak. Maire held up her right hand. "As I have just said, *sir* . . . we are finished here this night," and she turned away from her daughter and son and fixed her gaze through her window into the blackness of the Kerry night.

The siblings stood. Without looking at him, Eileen waited for her brother to leave, then followed him out of the open door, which she closed with a gentle click.

Standing where she was, Maire crossed herself and, folding her hands, closed her eyes; finished praying, she raised her eyes to the window and nodded affirmatively to God.

Derrynane—late Autumn 1760

The weeks that followed witnessed Eileen slowly emerging from the shell of an oft-times distant, diffident girl who was a stranger to her own siblings into someone more like the sister they had known and were now beginning to see again. *And yet there is a difference, is there not?* the siblings had inquired of one another, with no one able to adequately explain precisely what it was.

In actuality, though she in many ways had indeed changed forever, Eileen additionally was experiencing a lingering wistfulness, indeed at times a significant degree of discontent, unhappiness even. She knew she could not, in good faith to herself, return to Ballyhar; yet, as grateful as she was for her family and for the strong sense of place she felt, she did not necessarily want to be back at Derrynane, at least not indefinitely. When she appeared to be deep in thought or perhaps moody, it was these realities upon which she was reflecting. *I cannot tell Mama or even Abigail how I am feeling, though, can I?*

True to her word, the three black dresses had been quietly burnt, and she alternated amongst classic blue, grey, brown or green full-skirted heavy woollen dresses; or heavy tweed skirts and jackets, especially on the days she would spend most of her time with the horses. As the weather grew increasingly chill, she resumed wearing a heavy, rough woollen Scottish-made arisaid, woven in a simple grey and black plaid, which, as she skilfully folded it several times, she was able to draw about her broad shoulders as a long, roomy cloak, the fabric gathered by a substantial pewter brooch bearing the O'Connell stag. She quietly continued to wear her simple gold wedding band. *After all, I am a widow, am I not?*

With Abby much more than their mother hovering about, Eileen slowly reintegrated herself into the daily life of the large, active household. She resumed her chores, doing her share of cooking, cleaning, light washing and her special tasks, which she enjoyed most, working with the stable boys and grooms, caring for and training the ever-changing covey of Derrynane horses. She once again spent part of each afternoon with Elizabeth and Anne, now ages ten and eleven, going over their lessons and sitting on the floor to play dollies with them, in addition to which Eileen used the latter to work on improving the little girls' French; Anne's rag doll named Betsy and Elizabeth's, named Annie, magically spoke only French in a familiar husky voice, and for the younger girls to be able to join in the conversation between the dolls and their sister so, too, must they.

With the exception of Denis, whom she purposely avoided and who avoided her entirely, her other brothers as a group seemed to view her as being fragile and were extremely gentle with her; even Morgan, with whom she had shared an openly rugged relationship to the extent of, until very recently, wrestling and playing at hurling, spoke softly to her and behaved accordingly. Of her more contemporary brothers, it was Morgan with whom Eileen was closest, perhaps because he was the one most like their father, both in appearance—massively built, with a head of tumultuous blond hair, and handsome—as well as personality—bluff and gregarious, given to definite opinions and equally strong passions. He was, by choice, becoming the local face of the O'Connells, despite his relative youth, cultivating personal and commercial relationships throughout Ireland, especially in Kerry and Cork, beginning to oversee the estate's tenants and serving as the family's eyes and ears in terms of Irish matters.

It was not until her second week at Derrynane that, though they had chatted at table and in passing several times, Eileen had purposely sought out her quiet, oft-times distant twin, Mary, the two visiting for a time in Mary's rooms. If anything, Eileen's absence had made the already-significant emotional chasm between the two yawn even wider. To Eileen's gently-posed questions as to her well-being, interests and activities, the shorter, quieter blond sister's replies had seemed perfunctory, almost curt. Eileen, in turn, felt that Mary's inquiry, "Despite all that has happened, you remain well, yes, sister?"—as she continued knitting—was insensitive, responding, ". . . if by *all* you mean that I have been taken from my home and returned, wed and widowed in but three seasons, I would say, yes, sister, I am as well as possible. . . ." Gathering her skirts, she rose, half-curtseyed in response to which Mary had smiled genuinely and walked out of her sister's room, Mary resuming her knitting.

It was with Hugh, however, that Eileen's most unique relationship lay. Now just three months past his fifth birthday, he was usually seen wearing a too-big, cast-off linen shirt, inevitably blousy in any wind, rough wool knee britches, bare legs and feet—though, as the weather continued to cool, he ultimately yielded to the realities of a shapeless tweed coat, rough wool hose, heavy shoes—his long blond hair regularly held back by a barely still-tied piece of ribbon, Madramór, his huge, shaggy grey wolfhound, as tall as the boy trotting at his side.

Hugh was perhaps best known outside the family because he was the youngest of the vast brood; as his mother, who was well into her fifties when he was born, would laughingly say, he was *"An-seo caite, go deimhin!"* – "the very, very last indeed!". Shortly after he was born, Eileen had instinctively taken on much of his care, even to "changing his linen," as she said with a smile, and feeding him. It was as if she knew that for Maire the joys of motherhood had dimmed; Maire loved Hugh, as she did all her many children, but there was no novelty in caring for an infant and, in fact, she believed that she had much more critical matters with which to be concerned, both in terms of the operation of the vast, complex Derrynane estate as well as the O'Connells' commercial interests.

Clearly enjoying her maternal role, Eileen, it was observed early on, had quickly begun to impart her own interests and indeed in many ways her personality, onto the child, who quickly became known as "Eileen's wee lad."

This being the case, the little boy already loved to read and was frequently with a book in hand, quickly as well as quite amazingly acquiring a working knowledge of spoken Irish, English and Latin simultaneously. "He appears rather bright," Morgan pronounced to no one in particular at the family meal one night shortly after Eileen returned from Firies. Hugh simply smiled and bobbed his head, whispering to himself, "I am indeed that!" He was a happy, open little boy, obviously quite advanced for his years, though, at least Eileen felt, not precociously so. Under her daily tutelage, he was also becoming a good, largely fearless rider, bobbing about on one of the family's sturdy little "Kerry Bog" ponies in the vast, rough place that was Derrynane.

With her return from Ballyhar, Eileen resumed spending much of her time with Hugh, though she was surprised, and not wholly pleasantly so, that, in her nearly eight-month absence, the little boy had shown that he had taken on yet another part of Eileen's complex makeup: He appeared to her to have become, especially for a five-year-old, quite amazingly independent, and significantly less in need of her maternal care. More and more, she saw that he made his own way in the somewhat curious setting that was Derrynane. In the months she had been gone, a new young Jesuit priest had begun teaching him and several of his younger cousins for part of each day, the priest fostering what he saw as a healthy degree of competition by placing the boys on one side of wherever they were, the girls on another, being either in a quiet corner of the rambling house or outside. The rest of the time, Hugh was free to read by the fire or play with his small armies of lead soldiers if it was rainy, as it often was, or to just wander the Derrynane lands, usually with Madramór.

All of this being the case, as the weeks progressed it was more close companions and good friends Eileen and Hugh appeared to have become, and it was this relationship that the two would always retain.

Abigail continued as Eileen's self-appointed guardian. She *did* hover; and, shamelessly so, she asked the questions no one else in the family—including Maire— could or would. She delved deeply into what had gone on the previous months, and was able to develop a sense that, whilst wounded and profoundly saddened, Eileen was by no means fundamentally altered. She was still a brilliant, fun-loving, brave—to the point, Abby had always felt, of being foolhardy—and caring girl.

It was Abby, too, who, after but a few weeks, first sensed that, inevitably, it was more properly, as she told her mother, "a young woman rather than a girl that Eileen is now." Though she did not disclose any of their more intimate conversations to Maire, it had become clear to Abigail, despite that she had none of her younger sister's experience, that Eileen had developed a lusty, perhaps even bawdy enjoyment of sex, and that she had matured far more than was apparent from simply observing her as she moved through her day's activities, especially her reading and doll-playing and riding with the younger children.

Abigail sat, enthralled, whilst the two of them were alone one evening before the library fire with the door closed and sharing a fine French brandy, Eileen had spoken, softly, conspiratorially about what she called "the wonder of it all."

After describing in vivid, colourful—indeed, Abby thought, wonderfully naughty—detail, the varied forms of athletic eroticism she had most come to enjoy, Eileen exclaimed, her face glowing, "Oh, my darling girl, you cannot imagine. 'Tis like the explosions of a hundred cannons going off in your head and," gently touching herself, "*here*." Eileen smiled wickedly and laughed heartily for the first time since she had returned, tilting her head back, as

Abby, who had kissed just two boys in her twenty years, gasped and then giggled and stifled a scream.

Eileen confessed—though not truthfully—that "even though 'twas perhaps not all that many times, and you know the aftermath of the first one . . . but I unashamedly admit I revelled in it." Pausing, she sighed softly . . . then blushing, she said no more.

Additionally, Abby noticed changes evidencing maturation in terms of what she told Maire was Eileen's "regal" bearing and demeanour, in the manner in which she carried herself, how she interacted with the servants, the tradesmen and others who stopped at Derrynane, including the inevitable guests.

"I can see it," Abby confided in her mother. "If you look and listen you will see it as well . . . 'tis *Mistress Eileen* she remains," and, lowering her voice, "whilst she was conversing with the new Spanish captain who was delivering the shipment of wines and brandies from France the other afternoon, when he addressed her as *Madame* 'twas as natural as can be that she accepted the title and said nothing that would indicate he should otherwise speak to her."

What both Eileen's mother and her favourite sister also began to notice was the emergence of an at first subtle and, as the days passed, a quite obvious bristle by Eileen at the frequent times when she was referenced as again being amongst "the O'Connell girls," as the five sisters at Derrynane often were grouped.

"This may prove to be a very difficult adjustment for our Dark Eileen to make, Abby," Maire said as the two walked arm-in-arm after the Sunday Mass Father Francis said for the usual large, highly disparate congregation of family, household staff, tenants, guests and neighbours in what the younger O'Connells called the ballroom several weeks after Eileen's return. "I see, as have you, that she is no longer the girl who left us. Whilst 'tis difficult for a mother to accept, 'tis not difficult at all for me to see it. The horrid situation she faced, at least at first, aside, she was nevertheless, as she has said, indeed the 'mistress of a great estate and a grand house,' and the wife of, no matter what else of him is now known to us, a prominent and apparently extremely wealthy gentleman. To return to her family's home from a position such as that out in the world, and to resume playing dollies with one's little sisters, 'tis more than a simple adjustment to make. It may be that she will have to seek some other role, or that some other role will have to be identified for her beyond the ones to which she has returned. If this is indeed the case, it very well may not be easy, and it very well may not be here." She gestured at Derrynane.

A sharp breeze blowing up from the bay, Maire wrapped her long, heavy shawl about her.

"Ah, 'tis winter that's coming on," she mused, and quickened her step.

The Hofburg, Vienna—November 1760

The morning sky above Vienna was near cobalt, the sun brilliant and the wind rolling down from the mountains sharp but not yet severely cold. There was an expectant air about the Hofburg, the Imperial family's sprawling principal palace, in the centre of the crowded, vibrant city. The summer and autumn over, they had returned to Vienna from Schönbrunn, and the Imperial court was preparing for Christmas and the whirl of the winter's social season.

The precincts about the palace were but slowly coming awake at this hour, so the clattering of hoofs of a large animal on cobbled stone, and their pounding on packed dirt, sang through the air as a single horse and rider drew nearer the looming gateway of the ancient Schweizerhof, the Swiss Wing, its existence first documented in 1275, at the centre of the palatial complex that was the Hofburg.

A cordon of dismounted Austrian dragoons stood immediately to rigid attention at the approach of the tall, heavily built and magnificently uniformed officer, the white stallion on which he was mounted seemingly aware of the soldiers' respectful attitude as he pranced and tossed his extraordinary mane and tail.

General the Baron Moritz O'Connell had just turned forty-eight within the last month; he was still technically a counsellor to the Empress Maria Theresa, though he was at present the general officer commanding a regiment of infantry, foot and mounted. He could barely suppress his laughter at the horse's exuberant behaviour.

"I suspect we look quite the sight, do we not?" he whispered over the horse's head, in his mind picturing the dusty, bedraggled pair—soldier and horse—who had only two days prior arrived in Vienna from the army encampment of his regiment on the Styrian frontier. "Not too bad for a Kerry lad and a horse from Cork, eh?" The officer grew yet again solemn as, drawing nearer to his destination, he eyed the imposing, hand-carved rendition of the Habsburg crest that dominated the space above the ornate gateway.

Though what would be known as the Seven Years War lumbered heavily on, it had been not quite twelve months since General O'Connell's last major engagement, the Battle of Maxen in Saxony. There, serving under Field Marshal Count Daun, the baron had led his men in what became a rout of a Prussian corps of 14,000 men, commanded by Friedrich August von Finck, which had been sent to threaten lines of communication between the Austrian army at Dresden and Bohemia. Count Daun attacked and defeated Finck's isolated corps on 20 November.

Since then, General O'Connell and his troops had experienced a series of desultory engagements, most of them successful, others inconclusive, none defeats, though their overall contribution to the ultimate outcome, if any, of the continuing war remained unclear. Off the battlefield, much of O'Connell's time had been spent overseeing training and strategizing with his fellow officers.

A bluff, hale Kerryman, O'Connell, who spoke his German with, despite a deep rumbling voice, a musical Kerry lilt, into which he regularly mixed and mingled a dizzying array of French, English, some Irish and, as he laughed, "a wee bit of Italian and some Latin, just for spice." Count Daun often joked in a surprisingly gentle voice that softened the sharper, harsher edges of the German language, "I often know not exactly what it is that you are saying, but your men must. They do what you say and they win battles for the empress!" The baron was grateful for his more linguistically accomplished junior officers, to whom he could speak French and Irish, to others, Irish and English, all of whose German, he felt, was superior to his own.

Born near Tarmons, County Kerry, and originally christened Muircheartach, which had become, amongst the family, Morty, he had adopted the use of Moritz as being better suited to both written and spoken German and French than the nearly unpronounceable Muircheartach. In his early teens, with the thought that he might become a physician, he had been sent to Louvain and then on to Vienna for schooling. It was in the Habsburg capital, however, that, having met him at several equestrian competitions, O'Connell had fallen under the watchful eye of the ascetically tall, dauntingly brave, colourfully ribald, Count Otto von Riemenschneider, who, recognising early on O'Connell's extraordinary skill as a horseman, had enticed the tall young Irishman into the Riemenschneider Regiment of the Imperial Austrian Dragoons as a subaltern. There he remained for a markedly successful several years, advancing to a captaincy. It was, however, after O'Connell's unexpected transfer to the command of a new, primarily-Irish unit of ground forces that he came to be recognised as a natural large-scale battlefield tactician and military strategist. In that role, he enjoyed steady advancement, achieving a degree of fame and catching the eye of the empress herself, with whom he had unintentionally developed a singular relationship and, his military abilities aside, under whose patronage he had become a baron at thirty-five and a full general at forty.

Reining in the high-spirited animal, the baron dismounted stiffly and landed heavily on the cobblestones of the *Schweizerhof*'s courtyard. Handing the reins to a waiting groomsman, he returned a phalanx of salutes and, sweeping that side of his flowing dark blue cloak back over his right shoulder, removing his tricorn hat and sliding it under his left arm, he stepped to the pair of massive, gleaming oak doors.

Though two liveried footmen immediately swung them open, the baron stopped short of stepping inside. He smiled mischievously at the young corporal, standing stiff and straight on the top step, his eyes, according to protocol, averted from the baron's. "Are you not going to greet me, young Master Sheehy? My sensitive feelings are sore wounded by . . ." and O'Connell broke into a roar of laughter, clapping the serious young man on his left shoulder, causing him to turn and his face to break into a sunny smile.

"Ah, Your Grace," he stammered. "I . . . oh, welcome home, sir, welcome home indeed!"

"That's better now, lad," the baron said with a laugh. "You are well, I trust, and the latest news from Kerry, if any there be: is it of any note?"

Though still wide-eyed, as he held the general in some degree of awe, young John Sheehy was more comfortable now. He had grown up within sight of the O'Connell home at Tarmons, and being of a huge albeit a tenant family himself knew and was known by many of the O'Connells, both in Austria and at Derrynane. General the Baron O'Connell had himself recruited him for the Imperial Army more than four years earlier in Kerry, and he had served under the general until he had been wounded at Maxen and was personally returned to Vienna by the baron's aide-de-camp, with specific orders to return him to duty at the palace, not the front.

John Sheehy had gloried in the panoply, the colour, the exhilaration of battle, but he had experienced terror, had taken life and had feared for his own. He treasured his service with the general's polyglot troops—Austrian, Hungarian, Saxon, Irish, Swedes even—in the field and adored Morty O'Connell, all six feet six of him, but he was now enjoying Vienna: the beautiful buildings, the magnificent court dress, the music—how he was coming to love the music and the magnificent opera house!—oh, and the women, the girls . . . he blushed just to think of them!

Looking directly at O'Connell now, young Sheehy's expression remaining one of deep respect, he spoke softly. "Captain O'Sullivan, he has only just returned from Kerry, sir. He stopped three days past and kindly spoke with me as you are now doing, Your Grace, and of the news he had, the most interesting," the boy lowered his voice and leaned slightly towards his superior, "being that your good niece, the Lady Eileen at Derrynane, has been wed and now widowed, both in the space of half a year, and I know not . . ."

"Indeed?" O'Connell responded, and then quickly slipped through the open door, having feigned, he thought successfully, a degree of diffidence, though as he heard the boy's words his immediate thought was not at all diffident. *What is occurring there now?*

The soles and heels of his gleaming high black boots sounding heavily in the quiet morning air, O'Connell strode knowledgably down one long corridor, up a magnificent staircase and then the length of a second corridor. Of the young soldiers posted and snapping to attention at various junctures he knew only one Irish boy—*from Clare*, he thought—and not by name.

In 1529, some forty years prior to the outbreak of the first of the pair of Desmond Rebellions, in return for Spanish assistance in his own efforts to contain English penetration into Ireland, limiting the invaders to "the Pale," the four counties surrounding Dublin, the eleventh earl of Desmond, James FitzGerald, entered into the Treaty of Dingle with the plenipotentiary for the Holy Roman emperor, King Charles V of Spain, who was at the time also king of Germany. The Treaty provided the Irish, notably those of Desmond and his successors' male subjects, whether they be brave or bored or merely foolish, in search of adventure or, perhaps most frequently, an opportunity to stand tall and earn a good wage, with the chance to serve in the Imperial armies, and to be granted citizenship in Austria, Spain or the Austrian Netherlands. Perhaps even more significantly, it provided a formal legal basis for the rights of citizenship and other privileges that civilian, as well as military, Irish exiles and émigrés would enjoy in those countries.

A significant number, such as General O'Connell, were able to achieve status, honours, titles and security, as well as, in many cases—albeit not O'Connell's, though he was indeed quite satisfied—a considerable degree of wealth.

In remote Kerry, despite the complex patchwork scheme of protections the O'Connells had successfully created and maintained for themselves, Morty O'Connell would still be subject to the worst of the Penal Laws. He was barred from service as an officer in the English king's armies, whilst here he was a general. In Ireland he could still be compelled to sell his magnificent horse to any Protestant who might demand it for five pounds, whilst here he had four fabled warhorses. In Austria, he was free to educate his children, if any he were to have, and his family to practice their cherished Catholic religion. General the Baron Moritz O'Connell thanked God every day for his many gifts and for what he saw as the privilege to serve Her Imperial Majesty, Maria Theresa, who now awaited him at the end of this very long corridor.

A twelve-foot-high, seven-foot-wide door loomed before him, flanked by two more soldiers—solid, sombre Austrian lads—in front of which waited an ancient little man, his wig and livery perfect, his posture equally so. With aplomb, he bowed at the imposing Irishman and with ease he cast open the massive portal: "His Grace, General the Baron Moritz O'Connell, Your Majesty."

O'Connell stepped inside and knelt on his left knee, his head bowed before a woman he had come to respect far more than any man he had ever known.

A soft German voice spoke a gentle, "Rise. Approach, my faithful General O'Connell."

Only then did he stand, and he approached slowly, his gait elegant rather than swaggering.

As Maria Theresa rose from her desk and approached him, O'Connell lowered his head, his lips brushing ever so gently at the proffered right hand of the forty-three-year-old monarch, who gently drew him up and, standing back, looked up at the ruddy, rugged man, smiling broadly.

"Well, well, my dear baron, my Irish warrior, welcome!" she said in French.

O'Connell smiled down at the small woman. *"Ich danke Ihnen sehr, Majestät,"* he said softly, as opposed to his usual booming tone. "I am most grateful to be back in Vienna."

"Sit, please, good sir," said Maria Theresa as she resumed her chair, pleased that the baron had indicated his desire to speak German and happy to do so herself.

The pleasantries, whilst sincerely exchanged, were quickly concluded as, in her customary direct manner and firm tone, the empress looked serious and continued, "My wish, my dear general, is that you will remain with us now in Vienna."

An ever-so-slight expression of surprise appeared on the baron's sunburnt, windburnt face.

The empress sighed. "This war, it moves slowly, *ja*, progresses not at all. I was gravely disappointed by last year's supposed peace negotiations at The Hague. I know not where this all will end for us . . . perhaps we shall yet regain Silesia, perhaps not." O'Connell noted more than a suggestion of wearied frustration in her voice.

The general sat quietly, listening intently. Due to his absence, these moments with her had been of late rare, though—he now knew—remained singular, having only recently come to learn, to fully appreciate, that she apparently spoke far more candidly to him than to most of her varied entourage of ministers, advisors and counsellors. More than once she had said to him, as she would again this morning, "The emperor does not know this, but . . ." or "You will please keep this confidential between us, *ja?*"

"I have called you from the field to ask that you resume a place at court. 'Counsellor' is a broad, all-encompassing title; should you prefer a different one, perhaps we can together *create* one! Whatever it is, dear Baron, it is immaterial: I require your wisdom, your common sense, your humour and, *ja*, your laughter. How I have longed to hear it in these halls. These are uncertain times. I need honest men, candid men, possessing the wisdom of the Irish scholars, if not the total sanctity of your Irish saints." She laughed.

O'Connell smiled. He was aware that she knew he had a ribald, colourful sense of humour, enjoyed a glass and, selectively, the favours of the more attractive young women of her court.

"Whether you return as counsellor or under some other title is immaterial then, good sir. Howsoever it is done, it shall provide me with the access to you that having you directing troop movements and ducking and dodging ball and shell, whilst all valuable to me, to the empire, yes, these things have prevented. So . . . we are agreed then, *ja?*" she finished in her usual direct manner.

O'Connell, whose head had been resting, more casually than he meant, against the back of the high chair in which he sat, straightened himself and leaned ever so slightly forward.

"Madame, I am at your service, wholly, totally and proudly. *Ja, ja* indeed! I shall of course remain at court, as you say," and, being unable to contain it, he smiled broadly.

Noticing the empress beginning to stand, O'Connell was immediately on his feet, just beginning to kneel, when she stood on her toes, stretching her arms so as to permit her hands to reach behind his neck. She firmly pulled him down and placed a sincere though business-like kiss on each of his cheeks.

After releasing the shocked soldier, Maria Theresa, looking up at his full height, said, "Thank you, General, my baron. I am most grateful . . . obviously so!" and she laughed heartily, as she did only infrequently.

Amused at the sight of the usually vocal O'Connell standing dumb before her, seemingly incapable of speech, she waved her hand in a mock dismissive manner and, as he began to kneel, softly said, *"Nein, ist es nicht notwendig"* – "**No**, it is not necessary"and turned her back to him.

Picking up his hat and cloak, O'Connell began to back out, but the small woman at the large desk said, half aloud again, *"Ist es nicht notwendig!"* and he turned and strode to the massive door that, as if by magic, opened at his approach.

At her desk, the empress of Austria, Hungary and the Holy Roman Empire was humming part of an Irish air she had heard one of the regimental bands play at Schönbrunn during the previous summer.

News of O'Connell's transfer from active service quickly spread throughout the civilian and military bureaucracy in Vienna, and, in the following weeks, out into the field as well, reverberating particularly in the armies, where he was highly regarded by his superiors, respected by his confreres and idolized by many soldiers, officers and other ranks, especially by the younger troops and not only the Irish.

Count Daun, for example, was far from pleased. "A military genius O'Connell is not, except on the days and at the times when he is!" he groused, and then laughed good-naturedly. "I am not, however, going to joust with Her Imperial Majesty for his good services," he said, and left it at that.

All of his baggage, the contents of the baron's field tent, as well as, inexplicably, the tent itself, arrived at the small villa he occupied on the edge of Vienna just as he was settling back into court life, which he now recalled could, in its own way, frequently be as stressful as the field of battle. "Though the principal weapons here," he gestured broadly to Captain Denis O'Sullivan, the officer just recently returned from Kerry, "appear to be the pen and the tongue!"

Over a simple, hearty meal of steaming Hungarian goulash in the baron's dining room, the two Irish officers traded news and gossip from both the field and the Imperial court. O'Connell, however, waited to inquire as to any specific news from Ireland until they had retired to a pair of massive high-backed leather chairs, facing a blazing fire and separated by a small mahogany field table upon which rested a fresh bottle of fine French cognac and a pair of intricately cut Irish crystal brandy glasses.

As the men relaxed, now informally in waistcoats, the general poured his junior officer (and second cousin) a second snifter, the distance between the two being principally one of military rank —though both (as the general's mother was herself an O'Sullivan) were fully aware of the fact that, in Gaelic Ireland, the O'Sullivans of County Kerry far outranked the O'Connells—in a place given to formality, even amongst the Irish officer corps, lessening, O'Connell, resting his head back against the high chair back and not looking directly at O'Sullivan, asked, "Upon my arrival, en route to see the empress, I was greeted by young Sheehy, and he indicated he had spoken with you recently."

"Aye, so we did speak; a lovely lad, is he not? The Sheehys, his people: they are your neighbours," O'Sullivan began cautiously, exhibiting his intense dislike for the term *tenants*, "or is he at Derrynane?" He believed he knew immediately the point of the general's indirect question.

"His people's home is at Tarmons, but many of them—the boy included—have spent time and are otherwise well known at the home of Donal Mór and Maire," O'Connell answered and then drew a deep breath. "Sheehy indicated that Eibhlin Dubh . . . that the girl had been both wed and widowed in not half a year's time; is that indeed what you have learnt?"

O'Sullivan drained his glass and, leaning forward on his knees, turned to face the general. "'Tis true, General," he said softly, "though not known by many people, 'twas much spoken about by those with whom I was. I know only that she was wed to an O'Connor of Ballyhar, near Firies, said to be an extremely wealthy and prominent gentleman, though also said to be not at all a young man, in February, and that he suffered an apoplectic attack and died in August or September, both in this year."

O'Connell, having yet again refilled his guest's glass as well as his own, sat back in his chair, stretching out his long legs, his boots resting on a hassock.

Waiting to raise his glass yet again, O'Sullivan continued. "The last I was told and had heard, 'twas that Eileen had returned to Derrynane sometime in October. I had hoped to pay a visit on the Lady Abigail there, but most unfortunately 'twas necessary for me to depart for Vienna without doing so."

Grateful for a brief diversion, O'Connell smiled. "The Lady Abigail, you say? Have you an interest in her, lad?"

O'Sullivan blushed. "I have taken a distinct fancy to her, yes, sir. I find her quite delightful; amongst the three of them, Eileen and her twin, Mary, and her good self, she seems . . ." he paused, "the least *complex*."

"You are a wise young man, Denis O'Sullivan, and insightful. Young Mary and Eileen are the most disparate of twins possible." He shook his head. "Mary is gentle but bookish and, I think, overly shy, though very pretty. Eileen is the personality of Donal Mór and Maire ní Dhuibh combined, in all of their positive and not so positive traits, and," he laughed, "in her all of the traits are magnified! She is indeed a striking girl, though I fear too bright for her own good—and all about her! She has a mind of her own, perhaps too much of one, and she expresses herself too often and on virtually everything. 'Tis perhaps cruel to suggest, but if anyone could have driven the poor man— an O'Connor, you say?—to his death, 't'would be Dark Eileen." He began to laugh again but instantaneously swallowed it when he noticed that O'Sullivan was not amused.

Clearing his throat, the general continued, "The Lady Abigail I find totally and completely delightful. She is truly a joy; of all of them at Derrynane, she seems to be the happiest, the most joyful and, as you correctly have said, 'the least complex.' Were I you and interested, I should not delay."

"I know not when I shall next return to Ireland, so perhaps 'tis just wishful thinking then, sir. I have never even written anything of . . . substance to her."

O'Connell reached over and squeezed the young officer's leg above his knee. O'Sullivan jumped. "I need to write to Madame Maire. I shall attempt to open a line of correspondence for you and Abigail." He poured them each yet another cognac and tossed a huge log on the already blazing fire. The officers talked of many things, long into the chilly Viennese night.

Very early the following morning, still in his heavy dressing gown, a silver coffee service along with a warmed porcelain cup at his elbow, the general wrote:

> *Vienna*
> *18 November 1760*
>
> *My dear Sister:*
> *A dinner visit with young Captain O'Sullivan of Carhen earlier this week reminded me that I have failed to write you as promised. Indeed as my last letter to you was from the field, upon reflection, I fear it perhaps never left Germany, much less arrived in Derrynane.*
> *Whatever the case, I trust you are well. Since the death of your beloved husband, whenever I have had occasion to communicate in writing with you, as now, I seem uncertain as to how to address you, dear lady. So close was I to your beloved Donal Mór, and he to me, that despite being cousins 'twas natural for us to be seen as and think and act to each other as brothers and for myself to be uncle to your children and you a sister to me. I trust this is not inappropriate.*
> *I have learnt from O'Sullivan of our dear Eibhlin Dubh's marriage and untimely widowhood; such a burden for so young a girl! Though I am sure her good and gentle mother is helping her to bear the same. Would that I could be of some assistance as I have always been fond of the child; perhaps it is that we share the same view of the world: from great heights!*

The general chuckled at his attempt at humour and then continued writing, advising Maire of his return to court, and of the intrigues and crosscurrents inevitable in such a setting.

I have no single clear role here. I am at the empress's beck and call, she consults me as much about matters of government and politics, court protocol even—I remain a counsellor, after all!—as about matters of state and things military in nature, and we often discuss all of these topics at the same time, so I am rarely bored!

He continued in the same vein, whilst attempting to delicately suggest a liaise between O'Sullivan and Abigail; subtlety in such matters escaped him, and he decided in favour of directness; *as the empress is direct,* he laughed to himself.

He explained O'Sullivan's interest in Abby and thought as he wrote, *Would the young people but have an opportunity to meet soon again, Abby having been made aware in advance of young O'Sullivan's interest, I should think 't'would result in a most pleasant outcome for both of them.*

I have always been especially fond of Abby, thinking of her as the daughter I have not yet had –

The general cast his eyes towards the blazing fire across the room, watching the flames dance and the shadows they cast about the high-ceilinged room and toying with thoughts and phrases as he did, and as he took a sip of now cold coffee, which, being alone, he spat back into the delicate French-made porcelain cup. Finally, he dipped his pen:

Dear Sister, and good Mother, would you ever think that Abby might consider a time here in Vienna?

He almost scratched out the thought, but, as was his practice in difficult combat situations, in which he felt strongly his military objective was correct though not fully certain of his tactics, he lowered his intellectual shoulder and charged on:

There are significant opportunities for lovely, talented and accomplished young women of good family, and I assure you I could both secure such a position for her and serve in your stead as a loving guardian and protector.

He sat back and read, immensely pleased with himself. *No need to attempt to open a stilted correspondence; I shall bring the girl to O'Sullivan!*

Satisfied with his tactics, the baron completed his letter with warm Christmas and New Year's wishes and, folding it, slipped it into an envelope, addressed it to Maire at *Derrynane House, Co. Kerry, Ireland* and dribbled his red sealing wax on the thick envelope. As he pressed his seal into the wax, he smiled: *The stag this morning is prancing!*

Derrynane—December 1760–February 1761

Autumn quietly passed into winter on Iveragh, and, as always seemingly aware of the passage, the Atlantic commenced its annual multifaceted assault on Derrynane. The westerly winds shrieked and moaned, first heralding the arrival of thick grey sheets of rain and then joining with them in an often numbing chorus of, on an especially grim day, what the O'Connells had come to refer to as "black noise," whilst on a gentler one, "grey noise," but a constant howling nonetheless.

Many days, the Atlantic unleashed its own unique fury on Derrynane, a rage it had contained during the gentle months, as it now propelled a limitless procession of mighty, towering grey walls of angry water into the bay and onto the strand.

Never was the O'Connells' choice of stone and slate in the construction of the massive, outwardly dark house better understood and more appreciated than during what the family had come to call "the dark months."

As distressing as it might be beyond the house's seemingly impenetrable walls, thick, iron-banded doors and locked and sealed windows, the fires, constantly tended and fed as the living things they were—a mix of turf, cut locally and stored, as well as coal and wood, brought in from wherever the ships that entered Derrynane Bay and harbour in the pleasant months had come—provided a comforting level of warmth. Though the men's waistcoats and long coats and the women's thick shawls, and the heavy woollen clothing and hose for all, were oft-times necessary indoor wear, the O'Connells complained not often of winter's discomforts but remained grateful to Donal Mór and Maire and the earlier O'Connells who had begun the house.

On Christmas Eve afternoon the sheets of rain lessened and by evening had ceased altogether, whilst the Atlantic winds, though remaining constant and bitter, had also swept the Kerry sky clear and permitted the heavens to glimmer with a myriad of Christmas stars. Wrapped up in greatcoats and scarves, Eileen and the younger ones braved the cold to seek out and—at least the wee ones believed—had actually seen the Christmas star from the Gospel stories.

Late in the evening, Hugh, as the youngest child, led his mother, brothers and sisters, as well as Brigid, Annie and the house and stable staff, in procession through the house and into the ballroom to the large crèche, which had been brought from Italy some years before, the figures of the Holy Family and the angels, the shepherds, sheep and cattle, as well as the sturdy little donkey that had carried Mary to Bethlehem, all delicately hand-carved and painted now set in a detailed wooden stable, which Hugh and Eileen had earlier filled with fresh hay from the Derrynane stables. All was in readiness for the Baby Jesus, gathered gently in Hugh's arms.

Maire smiled, watching as her fast-growing littlest boy solemnly knelt before the crèche and gently laid the figure of the Baby Jesus in the manger. She noted that, as befitting his role, Eileen had helped Hugh into a black suit, ruffled shirt, clean white hose and an apparently new pair of black buckled shoes, his unruly hair gathered into a neat queue and tied up in a fresh black ribbon.

Afterwards all of them, as well as the many tenants and neighbours who successfully found their way through the bitter cold, attended Father Francis's Mass at midnight and partook of steaming punch and buns afterwards.

St. Stephen's Day, the arrival of the year 1761 and Twelfth Night closed the Christmas festivities, Eileen's seventeenth birthday was celebrated in late January and the torrents of rain and the Atlantic's shrieking winds persisted in their collective full fury as the dark months continued uneventfully . . . at least until a thick, heavy envelope—slightly dirty, battered and evidencing having been at least moist, more likely wet one or more times—arrived. The handwriting addressed it simply to *Mme Maire Ó Conaill, Derrynane, Co. Kerry, Ireland*, broad, heavy and, though slightly smudged, readable, as was the notation on the flap, above the O'Connell stag, his prancing frozen in red wax: *Gen. M. O'Connell, Vienna.*

The messenger who brought it, along with other letters, circulars and months-old papers delivered all to Brigid's kitchen, where, flipping cursorily through the bundle, as was her custom, her eyes suddenly grew wide at the handwriting and immediately understood its import.

Gathering her skirts, Brigid slipped the envelope into the deep pocket of her crisp white apron and, clutching her heavy black wool shawl about her, hustled through the bitter wind into the main house in search of Maire, whom she found in an animated conversation with Eileen and Abigail, the topic of which she could not determine, nor did she particularly care to.

Abby, who was speaking, her hands aflutter, as Brigid entered the dining room, stopped and smiled at Brigid, as did the other women.

"My darling, come in," Maire said, seemingly relieved. Noticing the small parcel clutched in Brigid's hands, she immediately sensed it was not unimportant.

"My dearest girls, please leave us," she said, with more formality than she had intended, but Abby and Eileen rose and, their skirts rustling, swept out of the room.

Brigid had been standing apart and now stepped forward, offering the envelope to Maire. "'Tis from the general, Mistress, in Vienna," she said, a touch of awe in her voice as Maire received the envelope and set it on the table in front of her, looking down at it as if she expected the inert paper to do something.

Smiling, she stood and kissed Brigid on the forehead. "Thank you, my darling sister. I believe I shall settle myself before my own fire to read what dear Morty has to say . . . and," seeing Brigid's expression and knowing its meaning, "yes, I should be most grateful for tea, my love. Thank you."

When Brigid arrived some minutes later with a steaming pot of strong tea and a plate of freshly-baked French bread, Maire was settled in her massive chair, the fire burning brightly and the missive from Vienna resting in her lap, unopened.

She nodded as Brigid set the tray on a low mahogany table and said a soft "thank you." The other woman smiled broadly but left wordlessly. Brigid readily distinguished between those times when Maire was her mistress and those when she was her "sister," and always knew when her mistress wished to be left alone.

Pouring her tea into a delicate porcelain cup not dissimilar to the ones the letter's author used in Vienna, Maire took a deep draught of the scalding liquid and, seemingly thus fortified, her thin, rough fingers tore purposefully at the envelope's flap. Sliding the many pages out of the envelope, Maire rested her head back and read . . . . smiling, chuckling and—ultimately—her light blue eyes wide and sparkling. *Oh, my darling Morty, yes, oh yes, you may call me sister; with thoughts like these you have written, you may call me virtually anything!* Maire laughed aloud, as she read General the Baron O'Connell's broad, looping handwriting, especially parts of three sentences again and again:

Would that I could be of some assistance as I have always been fond of the child, he had written, referring to Eileen; *perhaps this is true as we share the same view of the world: from great heights!* And *[W]ould you ever think that Abby might consider a time here in Vienna?* And *There are significant opportunities for lovely, talented and accomplished young women of good family . . .*

Clutching the letter to her compact bosom, Maire stepped to the window and stood silently, her mind far beyond the frosted panes and the dismal, grey and white and dusky brown scene beyond. *I actually may have* two *lovely, talented and accomplished young women for you . . . and they come from an extremely good family.* She smiled, momentarily resting her forehead against the icy chill of the glass.

That evening, as the family gathered for a light supper of thick chicken and vegetable or beef soups, loaves of their favoured French bread and, except for the younger girls and Hugh, an array of wines and porters, they all noticed Maire seemed distant, distracted, though not unpleasantly so.

"'Tis as if you are having a pleasant dream whilst wide awake, Mama!" the ebullient Abby finally said, laughing warmly; as was frequently the case, she had yet again spoken for all of them, even for Eileen, who this evening seemed far away as well, though not in the same pleasant location as their mother.

Maire smiled. "I have just this day received a lovely letter from your Uncle Morty; all the way from Vienna he has written, and it has taken nearly six weeks for it to reach me," she said, her expression wide-eyed, and *perhaps a wee bit mischievous,* thought Abby.

Maire suddenly stood. Wrapping her long, heavy, naturally coloured sheep's wool shawl about her trim shoulders, she said, "A lovely evening to all of you, my darlings, and a good night." To the calls of various similar sentiments and expressions, in deep voices and soft, in Irish and English, as well as little Elizabeth's *"Bon nuit, Mama!"* the petite woman left the room, an obvious lightness in her step. Stopping Annie in the hall, she said, "I shan't have need of anything else this evening, my dear. I have some correspondence to work on and I shall retire afterwards." Kissing the younger woman gently on the forehead, Maire ascended the stairs, her step as buoyant as when she had left the dining room.

Once in her rooms, Maire quickly changed into her softest, heaviest nightdress, pulled on a thick dressing gown and drew a writing table and chair close by the fire

Derrynane
Co. Kerry
18 February 1761

My dearest Brother:
I was overjoyed to receive your gracious letter of November last. Whilst by its envelope's appearance, it had experienced a most difficult journey from the glittering court of Vienna to Iveragh, heavily veiled in the darkest of the dark months, its arrival nonetheless was a warm and bright event for me, and I have read and reread it several times again, sensing the warmth and affection of your good self and verily hearing your laughter above the Atlantic gales!
Please, please!! Please allow me to once and forever disabuse you of any discomfort on my part on account of your reference to me as "sister." I glory in the appellation; do not ever think it or of me otherwise. Many, many years ago whilst a new bride from seemingly far distant Glenflesk, I have never forgotten that 'twas your good and gentle self amongst the very first of the fearsome O'Connells of Iveragh to greet me, welcome me so warmly and embrace me with the familial love I had feared I had lost by leaving Glenflesk.
For lo these many years, my dearest Brother, I have always and shall always think of you thus.

Maire rested and read over what she had written: *a bit effusive perhaps, but 'tis all true; I do so adore the old lad.* She wrote several pages of news and, yes, she admitted, local gossip, though much less there was of both, especially the latter, in the depths of a Kerry winter.

You were so kind to speak so thoughtfully of Eileen's sad year of 1760. For one so very young, she is a strong girl, and she has come through the tumult of the year far better than most women I know. It is a gift to have her now amongst us, and I see strengths and a degree of maturity that I never have before. I do feel her return here—after all, she was for half a year mistress of a great house, a grand estate and the wife of a prominent gentleman—is difficult for her, in ways that I feel your insights would help you to understand.

Brother, does your thoughtfulness know no bounds? Your gentle comments about Abigail were so gracious and so appreciated! I have met young Captain O'Sullivan on at least two occasions and I found and believe him to be both handsome and quite charming, and at the risk of violating her confidence or seeming the over-weening mother, I believe that Abby too has a "fond interest" in the fellow!

I shall take the liberty of sharing, via your letter, the captain's thoughts—and, if I may— yours with Abigail. I believe she would be quite pleased to both hear from the good captain and to see him—ah, but how the latter?

Maire lifted her pen, flicking the stiff quill against her cheek, thinking, *'Tis now the difficult part: to respond to his mention of the "significant opportunities for lovely, talented and accomplished young women of good family . . ." at the Habsburg court, without seeming . . . oh, seeming what?* Though she had no knowledge of military tactics and battlefield objectives, Maire was well known for her "ways," one of which was being totally honest and direct without seeming to be overreaching. So now she, too, lowered her intellectual shoulder and dipped her quill:

Your letter, dear man, was a gift to me in so many ways, unknown to you, but two in particular:

By sharing the "realities" of Captain O'Sullivan's apparent feelings for Abigail, you gifted me with the opportunity to perhaps make this dear child, who brings so much happiness to all of us here and many others, truly happy for herself, and her future. I shall speak with her immediately—perhaps even before I dispatch this letter to you.

Secondly is Eileen, my dear, wounded child. I shan't go into all of the events of those nearly eight months she was away in any detail save to say that they were trying times for her. This notwithstanding, for those same months her role as she described it vividly to me was not unlike mine has been and remains in this house and on these lands, she has now returned to life at Derrynane, which I observe she is finding to be difficult—for perhaps no more reason than she is longer addressed only as "Madame" or "Mistress Eileen."

All of this being said, 'twoud seem that some dramatic departure from her situation may be the answer to the quandary in which I believe she may feel herself to be.

She muttered quietly, thoughtfully for a moment, smiling ironically, "Damn subtlety," and dipped her pen:

Ah, there is no way to address this other than directly: May I have your permission, dear Brother, to raise the possibility of the extraordinary opportunities at Court with both Abigail and Eileen? The idea may come to naught with Eileen, though not with Abigail, whom I believe would be thrilled. I shall perhaps succeed in restraining myself until I hear from you further—or perhaps not!

She laughed as she wrote those last words.

I shall arrange for this to be carried to you directly by the fastest means possible. My hope is that it will reach you in no more than four weeks and, should your response be positive, please permit that before year's end I may then send off both girls on what I know would be a grand adventure for them! One for which they would be eternally grateful to their beloved Uncle!

Anxiously awaiting your response, and wishing you health and God's daily love and care, I am yours as ever, your grateful Sister, Maire

Exhausted, Maire left the pages under a book on the writing table, climbed up into her bed and was quickly—and peacefully—asleep.

Upon awakening and after briefly considering at least mentioning the news of O'Sullivan's interest in her to Abigail, Maire decided instead in favour of hastening the letter on its journey across Europe.

She immediately sought out her second-oldest son, Maurice, who, junior to Denis, was primarily responsible for scheduling the movements of the family's ships, finally locating him as he entered Brigid's kitchen. She nodded to Annie, who, immediately upon setting two mugs of steaming tea before mother and son, withdrew from the room.

"When have we next a ship going to Europe, my love?"

"Thursday next. Why, Mother?"

"I have correspondence for Uncle, General the Baron." She smiled mischievously at her serious second-born son.

"Is your correspondence—or his—in any way treasonable?" Maurice inquired, shaking his head gently.

"Ah, not at all, dearest son, not at all; just news and notes between two old ones, it is."

Maurice smiled, as broadly as he ever did. "Thursday next, quite early actually; you may stroll down to the wee cove at Iskeroon with me and place your note to the old lad in the captain's hands yourself, then."

As of course she did. After she and Maurice had trundled a while along the rough path, over and in some places through the rocks, and reaching the hidden cove from which the ship was to depart, Maire had placed her letter in the rough, scarred hands of the good Master O'Mahony himself, moments before the ship would head out, its destination being an undisclosed spot, a little-known, barely-used cove such as this one, on the French coast. There the Irish captain would place it in the hands of a trusted acquaintance, who, slipping it in his saddlebags, would take it with him to Paris, where he, in turn, would place it in the hands of a young Austrian diplomat whom he had been, correctly, advised would shortly be departing Versailles to return to Vienna.

Barely three weeks after Maire had placed the letter in the trusted mariner's hands, it was safely packed in the youthful Austrian's baggage and almost through the Black Forest, well en route to Fribourg and from thence to Vienna. Just short of a month after it left Derrynane, a breathless messenger handed it to a young page in General O'Connell's ornate official rooms, a short distance from those of Her Imperial Majesty within the Hofburg.

The Hofburg, Vienna—late Winter 1761

When the general returned from a draining series of meetings with the empress and various of her ministers and counsellors, the serious young man immediately advised him the letter awaited him on his desk, and O'Connell clearly shocked the seemingly always solemn lad by laughing loudly.

"Ah, Mistress O'Connell of Derrynane; she is nothing if not prompt," he boomed in English to no one in particular. Ripping open the slightly battered envelope, he dropped heavily back in his oversized chair, resting the heel of his left boot on a low stool and leaning his powdered hair against the high back of his chair began to read.

His greyish-blue eyes quickly scanned Maire's sentiments—*Such a sweet little woman*—and the limited news of Kerry, much of which he'd heard from O'Sullivan and other young Irish officers, as a striking number regularly seemed to traverse Europe to and from Ireland.

He finally reached the portion of the lengthy missive he was seeking: "*Both of them? Abigail and* Eileen?!" he laughingly roared aloud, standing now and thumping about his room, until, addressing a portrait of the empress's husband, Francis Stephen, he enquired of the Holy Roman emperor, "What is the woman thinking?"

No Imperial response being forthcoming, he paused where he stood, reread the page and smiled broadly, nodding, and tapped the page of rough writing paper. *She knows precisely what she is thinking* and *doing; 'tis brilliant she is, for one so tiny. She will see that Abigail is well matched with handsome young O'Sullivan, and as for Eileen . . .* he paused, reflected for a moment and sighed thoughtfully, *'tis indeed most likely true that only by coming to Vienna, or taking some such other measure, can she have any chance at beginning her life again . . . and, verily, here she will be my responsibility, not my dear "sister's." Brilliant she is!*

He resumed his chair and rested his head back again, closing his eyes and picturing the beautiful, ebullient Abigail and the indescribably striking Eileen, both in elegant court dress, gracefully moving about the halls of the Hofburg. *Ah, yes, I can hear it now: "They are the nieces of His Grace, General the Baron O'Connell; are not they lovely?*

He immediately called for a fresh pen, a full inkwell and paper.

The Hofburg, Vienna
19 March 1761

My dearest Sister,
Yours of last month was received here in fine fashion this day. Thank you for all of the news, major and not; 'tis always good to hear familiar names and places.

I originally believed I had much to write in reply, though, having considered the same, I have concluded to the contrary. As to your proposal that both *Eileen and Abigail, being, as you—brilliantly, I must say!—repeated my very own words to me, "lovely, talented and accomplished young women of good family . . ." and, my being in full accord with such characterisation, I agree to your proposal: They would* both *prove to be charming, and also valuable each in her own unique ways, additions to this Court.*

The only cautionary, which I would urge you to make clear to them, is that these positions—not unlike my own, you may tell them!—invariably involve assuming multiple roles and responsibilities, some of them clearly domestic in nature. Whilst the young women wash neither clothing nor cutlery—indeed all of their needs, clothing (some quite magnificent, I might add), sustenance, living quarters, entertainments, including attendance at balls and the like, as well as at the opera and such venues, are very well addressed and provided for—they may, for example, be attached to a young archduchess or other member of the Imperial royal family, for purposes of, pas example, *tutoring or companionship.*

If our girls understand and agree as to these requirements, there is no need for further communication between us, dear Sister, about this matter. Send them to me! I shall make the necessary arrangements here; your duty shall be to see that they are safely delivered to the care of Major John MacCarthy, who is an aide-de-camp attached to the Austrian mission at Versailles. I shall notify him post-haste to expect the arrival of the Ladies Eileen and Abigail at some to be determined time within the coming months. Your good Master Dennehy will see to it that they are placed on one of your own ships, by which they shall thus be properly transported to a safe harbour on the northern coast of France and from thence to the location in Paris that is employed for such travel, where Major MacCarthy shall be awaiting them. Please be assured that they will thus be spared having to appear at the court of Louis XV, a sordid and squalid, morally and otherwise, place indeed! At this juncture and forward, they will be, in effect, already in my care, as they shall journey by coach, safely and in as much comfort as possible, accompanied by a detachment of young Imperial Austrian Dragoons, traversing the breadth of France and thence on to Vienna, where I shall welcome both with all my love and affection.

All details of their housing, wardrobe, etc., will be addressed before they arrive here, and their positions identified and prepared for their arrival.

The general reread his relatively brief letter, signed it with his usual flourish, addressed it, sealed it and handed it off. It would arrive at Derrynane as yet another harbinger of a warming, hope-filled spring of 1761.

Derrynane—late March–early April 1761

Barely a week after she had dispatched her glowing response to General O'Connell, Maire awoke in the predawn calm of her massive bed. Rather than linger and luxuriate in the warmth of her puffy, down-filled Austrian coverlets, as she frequently did, she tossed them off and slipped on an equally puffy dressing gown.

Stopping only to splash some freezing water on her face, she hurried barefoot down the long corridor to Abigail's rooms, knocking once gently and immediately admitting herself, closing the door behind herself with a gentle tug.

Justly famous in the family for being both a sound sleeper and a usually reluctant riser, Abby was buried in her own down quilts and barely stirred as her mother quietly entered, the light in the room a murky grey.

"Abigail, my darling girl . . ." Maire said, softly—just loud enough to be heard—as she approached her daughter's bed.

"Hmm? What? Who? *Mama?*" was the sum of Abby's response, though, after speaking, her head popped up from beneath her covers and she smiled sweetly at her mother, her untied hair wildly tousled, her eyes sleepy.

Maire climbed up the small set of highly polished wooden steps and dropped onto the high bed as Abigail sat up and rubbed her eyes.

"I must speak with you, darling," Maire began excitedly.

Stretching, Abby softly replied, "Very well, of course, but . . ." Her voice was soft and clearly not excited, especially as she saw now that it was barely light.

"I have had an exchange of correspondence with Uncle Morty, my darling."

"Mama, how lovely." Despite a yawn, Abby tried to at least appear interested. "And how *are* things at court?" she managed to add, again rubbing her eyes, stretching again, but then flopping back against a mound of pillows, her eyes beginning to close.

"Things are lovely indeed, dear, his letter mostly simple chitchat, although he did mention dining with a Captain O'Sullivan, and . . ."

Abby's eyes were no longer closing and she sat straight up. "*Denis?*" She cleared her throat. "I mean . . . yes, Captain Denis O'Sullivan, of the Hungarian Hussars, you remember him . . . he . . ."

Maire was laughing warmly as she squeezed her daughter's leg and made her jump as the baron had done to O'Sullivan in Vienna.

"Yes, dear, I do indeed remember him; he is a Kerry lad. He is quite dashing, is he not?"

Abby smiled primly, attempting a diffident, "He is quite nice, yes." Immediately recognising her failure at diffidence, her smile broadened as she exclaimed, "Oh, yes, he *is* positively dashing *indeed!*"

Her mother grew briefly solemn. "His scar . . . " she said very gently, brushing her right forefinger in a line from the upper left side of her forehead to just above, beyond her right eye, continuing down her right cheek to beneath her ear. "It does not concern you, cause you any unease, my darling? It is a frightful gash, is it not?"

Abby's expression was serious as she took a breath. "*Unease*, you say? Not at all, Mama. For me, if anything, 'tis the mark of a grievous wound suffered by a brave horseman in battle, and indeed 'tis in large part why I say he is positively *dashing*," she added firmly, her eyes aglow.

She would later learn that, whilst still mounted—incredibly, he had not been unhorsed in the furious fray—O'Sullivan had killed two men that day: the one who had inflicted the nasty slash he now bore and a second one who had tried to rescue the attacker from O'Sullivan's sabre. There would come a time when Abby would not even notice the scar.

Brightening again, Maire could contain herself no longer. "Might you then have some interest in this young man, this brave warrior, my dear daughter?"

Sitting up now, her arms outside of the covers and hugging her knees, Abby sighed softly. "Yes, Mama, but . . . he is so far away and whilst he was last here so briefly, though more than friendly in both tenor and substance, our talk, it did not go much beyond the pleasantness of the day we were enjoying together, but . . ."

Maire knew when to remain silent, though doing so required a great effort, and now she only nodded, listening.

"But," Abby's voice softened almost to a whisper, "I do believe that Captain O'Sullivan, he . . ."

"He-may-well-have-an-interest-in-you, is *that* what you are saying, daughter?" The combined statement-cum-question streamed out of Maire's mouth practically as a single word.

Abigail smiled and nodded emphatically, her ruffled hair shaking on her shoulders. "Yes, Mama, I *do* believe he may." She smiled, and the sun appeared in her room before it did over Derrynane. "Just from the way he behaved and smiled and looked at me . . . and"—she lowered both her voice and eyes—"he even held my hand . . . though *of course* he asked if he could before he did so. . . ."

Relaxing now, Maire slid up so she was facing her daughter. "My darling daughter, at least according to General the Baron." Maire laughed; she found all titles so pretentious. "Your belief is quite correct, and . . ." She began to relate in detail the contents of her correspondence, both as to O'Sullivan and to the possibility of Abby going to Vienna, as Abby sat wide-eyed, listening intently. She purposefully said nothing about Eileen.

Abby collapsed back against her pillows. "Vienna? The court of Maria Theresa? You are certain that is what Morty was saying? *Me? I?*" she asked.

Maire nodded, and, as Abby's eyes grew wider still, she continued to relate a scattering of information: the details of possible travel, the multiple roles she might expect to play there, the dresses, the balls . . . and, of course and more than once, she mentioned Captain Denis O'Sullivan of the Hungarian Hussars—and then sat quietly again.

Abby drew her knees up under the covers and again rested her arms on them. "Mama, 'tis so exciting sounding, is it not? But I fear I might find such a journey lonely and stressful, not to mention being virtually alone in a foreign land."

Maire instantaneously thought—and immediately dismissed—the notion.

"We should speak more of this, darling, when you are fully awake. I should be pleased to relate excerpts of your uncle's letters to you." *And,* she thought quickly, *better this be done in small portions. . . .*

Mother and daughter breakfasted alone in Maire's rooms and thence proceeded to stroll, arm in arm, away from the house.

Fluttering selected pages from the general's letter before her eyes but not giving any to Abby, Maire quoted from some, parsed others and connected it all as she deemed necessary, with what she felt was appropriately clever surmise on her part, so it all—facts, partial facts and, from what she viewed as being just a wee bit of obligatory make-believe—came together quite nicely in Maire's mind.

As they came to the tenth-century ruins of Ahamore Abbey, after briefly, silently stopping at Donal Mór's grave, they seated themselves on a warm flat rock, the breeze off Derrynane Bay gently warm. Abigail sat quietly for what seemed a long time, a gentle, faraway expression on her face.

"I believe I should like to do this, Mama, to have a grand adventure . . . perhaps even . . ."

Maire smiled softly. "Yes, my darling, perhaps even . . . if you go with a willing heart."

The women smiled, and each said her own silent prayer.

During the ensuing days, Maire and Abigail exchanged only passing, cursory thoughts about Vienna and all its many facets.

To her siblings, Abby seemed almost withdrawn as she went through her days—chores, reading, music, meals—and even Eileen, still frequently lost in her own thoughts, even she sensed . . . something.

During a quiet afternoon of the Wednesday following her mother's predawn visit, as Abby was strolling back from the kitchen house, sipping a mug of tea, Eileen crossed her path, her clothing liberally smeared with mud, drying dung and hay, grass and gorse, her loose hair heavily flecked with even more hay, grass and perhaps, it appeared, other substances as well.

Abby's face was immediately lit by her typically brilliant smile. "Sister, forgive me, my darling, but aren't you quite the sight."

Eileen smiled and shook her head, tugging off her also muddied gloves. "The new mare, the one that remains nameless," she pushed her hair back over her shoulders, stripping some hay out of it, "she also remains unbroken." She laughed, adding, "Please forgive me if I step no closer to you."

Abby leant against a pillar and sipped her tea. "Thank you for *not* doing so," she said with her familiar, honest laugh, playfully wrinkling her nose. *Eeeeewwwwwwwww.*

Eileen smiled. "Might I join you in some tea? I shall ask them to hand it out to me so I do not enter the kitchen and 't'would ask of you that we take it outside, so . . ."

Receiving a rough-bottomed, salt-glazed mug, similar to the one Abby was cupping in her hands, through an open window from a smiling Annie, who playfully pinched her nose, Eileen joined her sister on a randomly placed stone bench as the mid-afternoon sunshine flooded the green-turning grass.

Eileen took a deep draught and looked at her elder sister. "My darling, you seem . . . is there perhaps something . . . ?"

Immediately, setting her mug down on the grass, seemingly without taking a breath, Abby proceeded to flood the still air and Eileen's mind with the full Baron-General-Captain-O'Sullivan-possible-position-at-court-in-Vienna-beautiful-dresses-and-gowns adventure. As she listened, Eileen's eyes grew wide, her lips slightly open, sitting silently, her own mug resting on her right knee, until her sister ultimately wound down and said breathlessly, "And *that* is why I have seemed perhaps a wee bit . . . *distracted*!"

"My goodness, my darling, how truly extraordinary!" Eileen smiled broadly. "When shall you be departing?" she asked matter-of-factly.

Abby's mouth dropped open. "Are you not shocked at the suddenness of it all? Shall you not miss me terribly? Would you not be wanting to ask questions, to discuss any of the details?"

"Abigail, 'tis an extraordinary opportunity it appears you are being given. 'Tis not simply a journey as on one of Papa's ships to the sun in Spain as when we were little girls; this is indeed a true *adventure*." Stopping in midthought, Eileen grew suddenly silent, her eyes misty, her expression abruptly becoming distant.

Abby's hand reached for and rested on her sister's leg and squeezed it very gently. "Are you not happy for me, sister?"

Eileen smiled albeit weakly. "'Tis so very happy indeed I am for you, Abby, my love, even though, truth be told, my heart shall have a huge empty place for you. I believe we all are given different opportunities, adventures, chances. . . . 'Tis what life is. My recent 'adventure,' it . . ." She sighed, paused and, slightly altering her direction, observed, "Life is a series of them, some grand, some not . . . much like the mosaic of the ancient city of Jerusalem— the one we have in the upstairs hall, from the Holy Land—it has some different colours and kinds of marble, other stones that appear like precious gems and some just dull, very unpretty rocks. But then, all together, they make quite a beautiful picture, do they not?"

Gently setting her half-drunk cup on the lawn, she began to stand, but Abigail tugged her back down by her sleeve and she resumed her seat.

"Darling, would it not be possible . . . might you consider . . . could you perhaps desire *another* adventure; I mean . . . so soon after . . ."

Eileen smiled broadly and laughed heartily, genuinely, shaking her head. "Oh, my beloved, you are so sweet, my dearest girl, but could *anyone* envision *me* at the court of Empress Maria Theresa?" She continued laughing as she spread the arms of her mud-and-dung-spattered jacket and displayed her similarly-conditioned skirts, lifting her feet off the grass and gently kicking her boots together as small clumps of the dried mud and dung scattered on the newly-growing grass.

Abby did not laugh; rather she was quiet, soft now, her voice barely above a whisper. "They give you clothing, pretty dresses . . . and gowns even, Uncle says . . ." and burst into tears, sobbing and leaning on the rough woollen shoulder of Eileen's short coat, the taller, younger girl stroking her hair as her tears ebbed.

Still holding her, rocking her gently, Eileen whispered, "Abby, Abby, *Abigail*, what is it, my darling?"

Abby sniffed, her voice still small. "'Tisn't fair, it *isn't* . . . for me to go and you . . ."

Eileen continued to rock her sister gently. "No, no, my love, 'tis *your* time, *your* adventure. I have had one," she laughed ironically, "and certain I am indeed that I shall have others."

She released her older sister and began yet again to stand, and yet again Abby tugged at her sleeve. "Would you go if you could?" she asked, her voice soft, small, like a little girl's, her eyes wide, looking up at Eileen as a little girl would.

"Abby, 'tis *you* Morty has asked for," Eileen answered softly, looking down at her. "Could you see me in—what is it they call it—'court dress'?" She shook her head. "Could *anyone*? I think not!"

Abigail sat up straight now, her voice firm. "Well . . . *I* think so! Yes, I could see you thus . . . and, and . . . I believe I shall now . . . indeed, I must. . . ." Saying nothing further that Eileen could understand, she was quickly on her feet, stalking away, leaving Eileen alone, her eyes following her sister's determined steps.

Eileen sat quietly after Abby's abrupt departure, her eyes looking at the familiar scenery about her, seeing nothing.

I am indeed most diminished in stature here . . . never did I believe 't'woud be of issue for me, yet it has become so, has it not? I had perhaps grown more accustomed to being Mistress Eileen than I had thought. Whilst I would certainly never want Brigid or Annie to address me as "Madame," save in jest, as Annie does, I perhaps would again like someone to . . .

I fear each day I grow more and more dreadfully bored, as much as I love this place. . . . Even my "little boy" in these seven—aye, nearly eight months of my absence—has grown so independent; he appears no longer to require me so much. . . . Her eyes quickly, unexpectedly filled with tears, which she promptly brushed away, shaking her head slightly.

My . . . choices as to the future are not many. I have enjoyed visiting with, amongst others, young Squire Ó More. He is quite handsome, is he not? But I fear him to be not terribly bright, our only shared interest seeming to be in horses. I am not certain if he is even fully literate. . . . She sighed.

Grateful now to be in conversation with herself alone, she continued, *I also do not believe I should particularly enjoy mounting or, even of lesser interest, being mounted by Squire Ó More. Am I terrible to consider such things? No! 'Tis quite relevant: Whilst I surely do not desire to forever remain a widow, though 'tis a widow at least I am, not a spinster! The fact that Mr. Ó More may be the best of the lot, 'tis not at all a pleasant thought.*

John O'Connor has perhaps spoilt it all for me, so graceful, so facile . . . so wanton, she could not help but laugh at the irony, *a lover he proved himself to be. After what I have been through these months, it could be no worse, could it? . . . The court of the Empress Maria Theresa of Austria, Hungary and the entire bloody Holy Roman Empire?* she laughed aloud again, smiling now, though immediately growing thoughtful again. *And what did Abby say? They give you "pretty dresses". . . "gowns even"? I like pretty things. People do not believe that I do, but I do!*

I believe I could adjust to court life . . . "Yes, I most certainly could!" she harrumphed aloud, making her throaty voice even deeper, reflecting again, in silence, *I was, after all, as I have said and others have agreed, "mistress of a grand house, of a great estate," was I not? Wed to a man . . .* she paused . . . *wed to a man whom at first I loathed . . . and then whom I . . .* she paused abruptly, shook her head and sighed . . . *did not loathe . . . and, after I finally came to care for him, who then bloody well died, leaving me a widow! Now living once again in my parents' house . . . playing dollies.* She caught herself, her eyes again full, and sniffled, several tears nevertheless sliding down her cheeks.

I have indeed been out in the world. Abby is in this way, and in many others, the "younger sister." 'Twould be unfair of me to have her go off all alone, across Europe, to a strange place . . . would it not now? She nodded her head firmly in agreement. She would speak with her mother; perhaps tonight even.

In the coming weeks, acting on what had proven to be a pair of highly animated and not wholly coherent exchanges with both Abby and Eileen, Maire would skilfully structure a series of conversation between herself and each of her two daughters separately, as well as amongst the three of them together, which led to several late-at-night conversations on each girl's bed. All of which resulted in Eileen believing that she had been specifically requested by their concerned mother to accompany her older, though largely innocent-in-the-ways-of-the-world sister, whilst Abigail believed she had convinced her younger sister to join her on a "grand adventure."

Derrynane to Vienna—Summer and Autumn 1761

In the not quite four weeks that were required for a thick packet containing three letters —one being of gratitude, containing, in addition, neighbourhood news and gossip from Maire; the others from Abby and Eileen, also expressing gratitude, as well as conveying excitement and posing an extraordinary array of questions—in separate envelopes to be dispatched from Derrynane and received in Vienna by General O'Connell, the planning and, at least in part, execution of the arrangements that would result in Abigail and Eileen making a similar journey were already well underway and continued apace through the summer of 1761.

Maire's announcement at table one evening was gently delivered and calmly received. Eileen had spoken with her twin, Mary, and of course with Hugh, and whilst saddened, neither seemed terribly upset at the prospect either of their leaving or their probable lengthy absence. Mary appeared perfectly content with her seemingly blossoming relationship with young Dr. James Baldwin of Macroom, County Cork. The younger girls, Elizabeth and Anne, both said they would miss Eileen's company—"Our dollies, they shall have to acquire new voices, will they not?"—but seemed more enthralled with the romantic storybook words they heard, such as *archduchess* and *empress*, whilst after some surprisingly brief initial tears, Hugh only sought assurance that Eileen would write him letters and perhaps send him small things, as he so formally phrased it, "military in nature," both of which she smilingly promised to do.

"If anything, 'tis I who am just a wee bit saddened," Eileen mentioned to Abby as they walked to outdoor Mass one hot Sunday in July. "I so treasure Hugh, but it appears he is already growing so independent, he . . ."

"Mightn't it be easier to leave knowing that he *is* independent and will not be devastated by your absence? I should think so," Abby said gently.

The other brothers had all nodded their approval. They loved their sisters, but they were a busy group of young men. Denis, who frequently absented himself from Derrynane and remained largely isolated from the family, Maurice and Morgan were about the family business, and Conaill had his mind and eyes solely on the sea, whilst Daniel seemed firmly intent on following his own dream of a military career.

"It is to Vienna itself I believe I should like to go as well. My hope is that it will not be long," he had said firmly and frequently.

"I have no doubt that you will, my love." Eileen had on the most recent occasion smiled, adding, "Perhaps the Habsburgs should fear the coming of another *empire* in their midst, given our good selves, not to mention Uncle General the Baron." She laughed.

Nodding apologetically to her younger brother, patting him on his knee, Abby quickly interjected, a bit archly, "*You* must now begin taking the whole matter of titles and honours and ranks quite seriously, sister."

Eileen, realising the truth and the reality of what she had said, nodded. "I understand. I must and I shall. I am actually trying to learn some Austrian, Hungarian—'tis a confusing mix of countries, speaking different languages, all together in one kingdom, is it not?—history," and also indicated that she had requested a German-language grammar and vocabulary book from Dublin.

Hearing that, Abby sighed. "You are indeed fortunate. Languages come so easily to you, my love. I am only grateful that Uncle says French is the language of the court at Vienna, though he indicates his German has gotten quite good."

As the weeks passed, Eileen did become much more aware of titles, honours and ranks at the Habsburg court and elsewhere in Europe, such that, amongst other minutiae, she was able to explain to a bemused Abigail the distinction between a count and a baron, as well as that the Austrian archduchesses, of whom there presently appeared to be a rather great number, were similar to princesses in England. "*Archduchess* sounds much more regal, though, does it not?" She smiled to Abby as they had begun final preparations for departure, the summer now racing to its conclusion.

In the meantime, the girls spent part of each day speaking only French to each other, and both—Eileen's facility with other languages not seeming to have extended to German—struggled, albeit together, with Vienna's local vernacular. "Harsh it sounds, does it not?" wondered Abby aloud, "or is it just my unskilled ear?"

Eileen nodded. "No, my darling, harsh it sounds and harsh I fear it is."

Detailed correspondence with General O'Connell and, increasingly, with a Countess von Graffenreit, one of the apparently numerous officials of the Imperial houschold, albeit a seemingly senior one, who, from her letters, seemed a bright and sensitive woman of some significant experience, served to substantially simplify the sisters' preparations. The countess carefully indicated what they were to bring—which seemed to be little more than travelling clothes, personal items and perhaps some favourite books—as well as what would be awaiting them upon arrival: She provided a detailed inventory of wardrobes consisting of splendid-sounding afternoon dresses, ceremonial court dresses and an array of ball and opera gowns, all complemented by matching shoes, boots, hose, gloves, cloaks and more. Lastly, she emphasised they would each need to be fitted for heavy, fur-lined and -trimmed winter cloaks for sledging. "Whatever *that* may be!" laughed Abigail as she reread the note.

"One large and perhaps one smaller trunk each, sister, 'tis all we shall need . . . between us!" Abby added one afternoon.

Her eyes scanning the countess's latest letter, Eileen shook her head and smiled. "With that I cannot, I do not, disagree, my love. I had been jesting prior when I suggested the same, but now 'tis the actual case: virtually all we may materially require appears to await us."

One night, alone in her rooms, Eileen reflected on the small list of possessions she had written out prior to her departure from Ballyhar; aside from her favourite books, her pistol, in its velvet sleeve and leather case, and her long green mantle remained at the top of the list. She repeatedly deferred broaching the subject of her most precious possession, reflecting that Bull was far more than something she owned. "He is my friend, my dear friend," she finally sniffled softly to her mother the following evening.

Maire nodded. "Then with you he should go, should he not?" As Eileen pondered what she believed would be the inevitable "*but*," her mother continued, "So 'tis with this in mind that I have spoken to several men knowledgeable on the subject and have also mentioned it to your dear uncle. From reading his most recent letter, your large fellow, I am able to say, will be most welcome at Uncle General the Baron's barns," she said affectionately.

Eileen brightened; smiling broadly, as her mother leaned forward, tapping one rough palm with a fingertip: "You shall have to ride him whilst you travel by land from wherever you are landed on the coast of Normandy to Paris. The ship will accommodate him; though we shall try to utilise one that is best suited for his transport, it is possible that neither you nor he shall necessarily approve of his quarters." Eileen nodded, then frowned.

"Once you arrive in Paris and are safely in the care of the Austrian military, on your journey from there to Vienna, you will have the choice of riding him at times, whilst, at other times, he shall be able to travel in what I am told is called a *van*. The Austrians use these large wagons, drawn by far-less-favoured horses, to transport certain animals, seemingly ones acquired for royalty, the nobility, but Uncle Morty said . . . ah, suffice it to say that neither Bull nor you will have to walk from Paris to Vienna."

Relieved, Eileen smiled a broad, genuine smile and, leaning back, briefly closed her eyes and said softly, "Mama, how do you suppose I shall appear in 'court dress'?"

Maire smiled and envisioned aloud, "I imagine a very tall, very beautiful young woman in an ornate, embroidered robe, upon whom every eye shall rest."

Eileen's eyes came open and she smiled brilliantly. "Mama, I believe we may be ready to depart."

And so they were and so they did, on a brilliant early October morning, roughly two weeks after Maire had, following the general's directions, written to inform Major MacCarthy in Paris of the girls' approximate arrival.

Just prior to going downstairs, Eileen stood quietly alone for a few moments in her room; she looked about the high-ceilinged, crown-moulded chamber, largely emptied now of her belongings. *'Tis yet another ending, another beginning*, she reflected, and she very slowly removed the simple gold band from her left hand, the remaining tangible of her being the Widow O'Connor. She kissed it softly and slipped it into her pocket. She would quietly give it to her mother before walking to the ship.

All of the family—even, surprisingly, Denis O'Connell, standing sullenly alone, by choice, on the periphery of the group—the household and stable staff, a huge array of the lesser O'Connells, entire tenant families, neighbours and the ever-present guests, had gathered on the sunny lawn as William brought around a dramatically prancing Bull, as well as a cart drawn by a pair of packhorses to carry the girls' relatively small amount of baggage to the Derrynane beach, where awaited one of the O'Connells' smaller though sturdy cargo vessels.

The young women had been told that their trip would take them straight out into the Atlantic off Derrynane and, depending on wind and weather—as well as any detectable indication of the presence of the Royal Navy—either in a south-easterly direction around Dursey Island off the Beara Peninsula of County Cork or instead on a straight westerly tack, farther out into the Atlantic and ultimately due south and yet again west to the coast of Normandy, where the O'Connells' captains had a number of favoured remote inlets and harbours, each of which would possess the capability of providing the women with transport to Paris.

The principal logistical and security concerns arose out of the fact that, as Great Britain and her ally Prussia continued to war against the French and Austrians, the Royal Navy had largely succeeded in blockading key French ports.

This notwithstanding, both Maurice and Master Dennehy had assured a suddenly concerned Maire that, as Maurice pointed out, "We have moved freely in and out of France since the war's beginning; we are well prepared for . . ."

At that point the fleet's master had smilingly interrupted, as if on cue: ". . . just about anything, Madame. We even fly the English ensign and the flags of Portugal and . . . oh yes, my own favourite: Sweden!"

Eileen took hold of Bull's bridle, and she and Abby joined hands as they led the suddenly quiet, almost sombre group across the lawn, down to and thence over the dunes to the broad sandy beach, the waters of Derrynane Bay gently lapping at its fringe, the boat anchored, its long gangplanks lowered.

Though their good-byes had been said over and over again during recent weeks, each girl's eyes were misty, their facial expressions somewhat uncertain as they hugged Maire yet again and finally stepped onto the plank. Standing on the deck as Bull and the baggage were loaded, Eileen's eyes went to her mother and to little Hugh, now leaning against her, Maire's arm close about his shoulders. As the planks and the anchor were raised and the snug ship's sails caught the gentle morning breeze, both mother and son smiled bravely and waved, whilst silent tears streamed down their faces.

Standing alone next to Bull, Eileen raised a gloved right hand, just to them. As the vessel finally turned and began to sail in a slight south-easterly direction, she rejoined a vigorously waving Abby at the rail, the two sisters again holding hands, waving and now sobbing shamelessly, their eyes scanning their immediate family, relatives, friends and neighbours, many of whom continued to wave, and to call out words of farewell.

"Where be they off to now, the O'Connells, lad?" a well-dressed squire, just down from Limerick to meet with Morgan later on that day, inquired of William as they stood in the small crowd on the beach. The boy half-smiled and shook his tousled yellow-blond head. "'Tis to Vienna they be headed, to be princesses or some such, sir. I know not precisely where it may be, nor why they would leave Ireland to go there."

Holding his tricorn hat, the gentleman gently clapped William on the shoulder. "Ah, my boy, only the O'Connells appear to understand why they do what they do, though as a rule they do appear to have their reasons." He lifted his hat in the direction of the snug little ship and waved it gently, the silhouettes of a very tall woman, a shorter one and an extraordinarily large horse now framed against the horizon.

Tightly holding each other's hand, Abby and Eileen stood, neither saying a word, simply watching Derrynane Bay slip farther and farther away.

"Well, my love, 'tis on our way we are," Abby, now smiling, stated the obvious.

Wiping a final tear from her right eye, Eileen turned to her dearest sister, her closest friend, and whispered, "Thank you."

Abby looked puzzled but said nothing.

"'Tis *you* who have given me this opportunity," Eileen said. "Were it up to myself alone, 'twould be mothering Hugh until he needed such no longer and caring for obstinate horses I would be doing, or marrying kind David O'Connor and living and dying at Ballyhar, or wedding dull handsome Master Ó'More and . . ." She shook her head and bent and kissed Abigail softly on both cheeks.

"As they do in Vienna," she said with a smile. "I am thanking you for allowing me to dream, sister. I know not where this . . ." Eileen gestured at the open ocean with spread arms ". . . may lead, but for this opportunity I shall be ever and forever grateful to you, my darling sister."

Of the ensuing journey, Maire had been correct both in terms of Bull's accommodations, as well as in her observation that the voyage out into the Atlantic and across the English Channel would be an insignificant event to her daughters, who had travelled several times to Portugal and Spain whilst younger with Donal Mór. They were thus perfectly happy, both that the voyage was relatively brief and uneventful, and that the ship's captain had apparently arranged for a young gentleman with a strange-looking vehicle, neither as comfortable as a carriage nor as rough as a wagon, to transport them and their baggage on to Paris. It was a three-day journey that was itself without incident, almost to the extent of being boring, during which Eileen and Abby agreed that the scenery of France was quite lovely but not inspiring, save for the striking chateaux that occasionally appeared, usually in the distance.

It was only when the conveyance carrying Abigail and their belongings—with Eileen and Bull trotting alongside—arrived in Paris that the O'Connells both grew silent and more than a bit amazed at what they saw, heard—and, both would later agree, *smelt*—with Abby alternating leaning out one side and then the other, her eyes wide. She and Eileen were both quickly in a state of nearly numb amazement, calling and pointing out to the other the next source of such astonishment, ranging from glittering coaches carrying jewel-bedecked nobility to sad groups of ill-clad, barefoot, hardscrabble children, as pitiable as any seen in Ireland, whilst the O'Connells passed magnificent buildings not far removed from dingy warrens of dank hovels.

They moved eastward into the somewhat more bucolic location of the Austrian mission, in the developing area along and above Rue St Honoré. Proceeding much slower now, after first stopping at a high, starkly unadorned gate and being admitted to the space beyond, they drew up in a paved courtyard before a large, recently constructed sandstone-and-granite building flying the striking black-and-yellow civil flag or *Landesfarben* of the Habsburg monarchy, the impressive Habsburg arms flanking the large double-doored entrance.

"*Nous sommes ici,*" the young driver called out as he reined in his team. Eileen and a wide-eyed Bull clattered to a halt alongside, the massive Irish horse apparently having experienced an equine reaction towards Paris similar to that of the Irish girls'.

As Eileen dismounted, a compact young man in uniform suddenly appeared, with a broad smile on his face and a gloved hand extended to Bull's bridle. "Welcome to Paris, ladies! I am Corporal Timothy O'Moriarty, at your service," he announced in English.

As she stood holding Bull's bridle, Eileen could only laugh, whilst Abby literally jumped out of the carriage, calling "Helloooooo, Irishman!" her face resuming its customary sunny expression. The young soldier appeared somewhat taken aback—whether by Bull's size, Abby's unexpectedly effusive greeting or, perhaps, judging by the vertical path of his eyes, by Eileen's height—but smiled again and said, "Welcome indeed, ladies!"

As she was standing closer, Eileen extended her own gloved hand to the soldier. "We are just now arrived from Kerry; we are the O'Connells. I am Eileen and—" she gestured with his still gloved left one, "my quite animated sister there is Abigail." Abby, who had by then released herself from the vehicle, was standing beaming at the young soldier.

"We have been expecting you, ladies; yes, we have, if . . ."

The right door at the head of the steps opened and a tall, strikingly handsome man of perhaps thirty-five, obviously an officer by the elegance of his uniform, stepped out and quickly cleared the stairs. As the young corporal snapped to attention, so, too, did the officer, greeting the O'Connells and returning the proffered salute in a single gesture. "*Tá mé* Seán MacCarthy," he began in Irish, then continued in soft English, "We have indeed been expecting you. I have exchanged several communications with your most delightful mother and General O'Connell, of course." As he spoke the general's name, he seemed to straighten just a bit, Eileen observed.

Three days passed quickly in a pleasant rush of luxuriously soft and warm beds, hot baths, laundered, pressed and repacked clothing, the consumption of large amounts of excellent food and wine and several carriage tours, with Austrian cavalry outriders clattering alongside, of some of Paris. Eileen was clearly in awe of the magnificent Les Invalides, learning that the striking gold prominence that gave the Église du Dôme its name was what dominated the open plain on the far side of the Seine, whilst Abigail was fascinated by the presence of an Irish College, in a bustling neighbourhood, referred to as the Latin Quarter, also on that side of the river. As they were being driven by the school, she and Eileen surprised—not at all unpleasantly, judging by their broad smiles—a pair of solemnly black soutaine-clad students as they greeted them effusively in Irish from their momentarily stopped carriage, chatting briefly with them. Both young women were enthralled by the cathedral called Notre Dame, set on an island in the middle of the Seine and by a smaller church, located close by the busy law courts, also near the Seine, called Sainte-Chapelle. Alighting at both places on a sunny, breezy afternoon and walking about inside for a time, they found themselves awestruck by the stained glass in each, though they were especially taken by the magical, jewel-like qualities of Sainte-Chapelle's.

The sisters enjoyed the near constant, wholly agreeable company of an excitingly varied—Austrian, German, Hungarian, Swiss and Venetian, as well as the Irish they had already met—group of, they agreed, quite handsome young officers. Gesturing at the bevy of beautifully uniformed men, a beaming Abigail observed, "Perhaps *this* is what Vienna shall be like, sister?" and Eileen's eyes quietly lit up at the prospect. Abigail was both surprised and gladdened to see her sister's lighthearted reaction.

On the morning of their fourth day in Paris, twice as many dragoons as had accompanied them about Paris, under the apparent command of two junior officers—a Captain Ó Néill and a Lieutenant O'Brien—and, to bid them adieu, Major MacCarthy, gathered in the forecourt, a light though comfortable-looking carriage at the ready. Abby and Eileen, both in long travel coats and hats, were escorted by the buoyant Corporal O'Moriarty, who had greeted them on their arrival and was carrying their small travel bags.

Major MacCarthy saluted. "All is in readiness, ladies." Laying a gloved hand on the black-painted—offset by a single yellow stripe—side of the vehicle, he continued, "This is a *britzka*; it was originally designed by an Austrian gentleman of that name and is now being manufactured in Vienna." The sisters noticed immediately that it was a spacious four-wheeled carriage, with a soft, folding top. A young, freckle-faced Irish soldier was already in the driver's seat, holding the reins of a pair of sturdy grey horses, who stomped and whinnied almost playfully.

The young officer explained that it was constructed so as to provide space for reclining at night when used on a long journey. "Though, unless you prefer to sleep in transit, the plan is to stop at some form of hostelry at the end of each day. Is that not correct, Captain?"

Captain Tomás Ó Néill, Donegal born, red-haired and ruddy, said, in a musically-rolling burr, "Aye, 'tis the plan, sir; yes, sir," and the O'Connells looked at each other in some relief.

Waiting outside of the courtyard in the street was a plain coach, principally a baggage, supply and mail carrier. Once outside the city walls, Captain O'Neill explained, they would be joined by two vans, the horse transport vehicles about which Maire had spoken to Eileen. "In the meantime," began Corporal O'Moriarty, "if I may?" He handed Bull's reins to Eileen.

Turning to Major MacCarthy, she smiled demurely, nodded and thanked him kindly. She mounted Bull with her customary ease, whilst the major handed Abby into the *britzka*. "Be off, then; Godspeed to you all," MacCarthy called out and, as his salute became a wave, the small cortege clattered off, Abby leaning out the side of the carriage and waving.

The women, well used to being around a diverse covey of young men at home, quickly put the handsomely uniformed horsemen at ease, Abby entertaining a corporal named Fritz with her still often-unintelligible use of the German language. Fritz's hearty laughter became a hallmark of the journey, causing the officers and other ranks to laugh aloud as well. The cavalrymen appeared relieved when, at the first midday stop, the O'Connells proved themselves to be experienced travellers by simply, and without comment, heading off into the nearest woods in a direction opposite that chosen by the men for a similar purpose. Afterwards, as they sat down to a simple meal, Abby smiled impishly at Captain Ó Néill. "We know how 'tis done on a journey, sir," she said, in response to which a blushing Ó Néill could only manage an "*Indeed!*"

What followed was, for the young women, an interesting but otherwise neither a dull nor terribly eventful two-and-a-half-week-long journey across a significant part of Europe.

They found the conditions under which much of the French peasantry appeared to live appalling and, not surprisingly, the dispositions of those they passed along the roadside understandably sullen at the sight of two young women being transported in obvious comfort by a cadre of mounted soldiers.

"One would think that, given the generally flat terrain and the seeming fertility of the land, the farms would be more prosperous, bursting at harvest time," Abby observed one afternoon after Eileen had joined her in the carriage.

Eileen nodded. "They have few obvious rocks, no gorse and appear to have ample water and yet 'tis a sad picture here," she gestured.

Many of the French villages were tidy and appeared more prosperous than the countryside. The larger towns, such as Nancy, were not unattractive, though neither were they remarkable.

Each day Eileen alternated between riding Bull—usually from an early-morning departure until midday—and then joining Abby in what proved to be a very comfortable vehicle in which to travel such a great distance. When not being ridden, Bull appeared to Eileen to be relatively content in the van, which he shared with one of three—the other two following in their own van—magnificent French yearlings, all three bound for the Imperial stables in Vienna, each of the four horses travelling in its own separate enclosure. The small procession usually stopped briefly at midmorning, midday and once in midafternoon. They continued to be amply provisioned with cold meats and cheeses and fresh breads, as well as wine and water. Nightly they were lodged in a variety of monastery guesthouses and convents.

Leaving Paris and heading east by south, the small cavalcade had passed through Château-sur-Marne, Sainte-Ménehould and Nancy, on to Strasbourg—the last place of note in France—then entering and beginning its passage through an array of German principalities and free cities at Freiburg, which Abigail pronounced as being "German with a French touch." They then proceeded directly east into the Habsburg states via the Black Forest, through Munich, Augsburg, Günsburg and Ulm.

Though they were there only overnight, from what they had seen of Munich, it appeared to be an advanced and prosperous city ". . . *und das bier, es ist ganz gut!*" said Abby as she sampled the local brew in a massive stein, which she raised with both hands —to Eileen's feigned shock and surprise and the soldiers' collective delight, especially as Eileen immediately accepted a foam-capped stein as well and smilingly agreed, ". . . *es ist ganz gut!*" laughingly adding, "indeed!"

The young women saw the smaller towns in the German principalities and those in the Habsburg states themselves as being generally tidy and prosperous, the people overall seeming happier, and certainly friendlier, than those of eastern France. Abby especially did her part for Habsburg diplomacy as she repeatedly engaged local women, at markets or on the streets of the towns in which they stopped, in her by now largely intelligible though frequently still convoluted version of German, causing much mirth.

"*Wir sind aus Irland. Wir fahren nach Wien,*" a smiling Abigail animatedly advised one large, jovial woman at a market, a gaggle of beautiful little blond girls tugging on her skirts, Abby immediately holding hands with two of them. Though her grammar and syntax correctly advised the bemused lady, who smiled broadly and nodded during their exchange, of the O'Connells' origin and destination, as she continued to chatter on, Abigail's Irish lilt confused her such that Abby called out for her friend, Corporal Fritz, who helpfully confirmed all of what had been said and went back to his mount with a hefty wurst for his efforts, which was shared all around at the evening meal.

For their last stop the evening prior to entering Vienna they stayed at the guest quarters of Melk Abbey, not quite forty miles west of the capital. Originally established by the Benedictines in the eleventh century, the abbey had nearly been destroyed by a fire in 1297 and withstood a Turkish invasion in the sixteenth century. Largely rebuilt in the Baroque manner by the early years of the current century, it was now a massive yellow structure, sprawling across, dominating a high bluff overlooking the Danube River. Captain Ó Néill advised that the monastery was said by many to be the most magnificent in Austria—a reputation that both O'Connells quickly felt was well-deserved.

Warmly received as honoured guests by one of the abbey's several lesser abbots, the young women were provided with a brief tour of the stunning building, during the course of which they were shown two crucifixes: The first, in the simple Romanesque style, was distinguished by its age, said to be from approximately 1200. The second was from the fourteenth century; it was before this one that both Abby and Eileen immediately knelt, venerating the object—as it contained a sliver of the cross of Christ. As they began to walk away, both found themselves gazing back in wonder at the object.

"This time tomorrow, I believe there shall be a very happy and I am to a degree certain quite relieved general in Vienna," Captain Ó Néill said to the O'Connell sisters over a simple, though—as had been the case throughout the journey—very hearty dinner of wurst, noodles, beer and wine.

Very early the next morning, with the help of the good sisters who cared for the guesthouse where female travellers stopped, bathed, freshly coiffed— the latter thanks to the giggling though wholly able efforts of a young novice whose mother was a coiffeuse—and in their finest travelling dresses, Eileen, having given Bull over to the soldiers for transport directly to General O'Connell's stables, and Abigail began the final day of their journey—a day that seemed to both women to pass both quickly and far too slowly.

As they made their entry into Vienna the carriage was open to the bright October afternoon sun, the event inevitably well noticed, whether because of the Habsburg yellow-striped vehicle or its impressive mounted escort of Imperial Austrian Dragoons, headed by two junior officers. The cacophony of street noises, smells and the crush of people aside, seeing many people stop and stare, some even pointing at them as they rode past, Abby wondered, "Should we not greet them, sister?" Eileen, only half in jest, raised a gloved hand in salute to their new home, whilst Abby, in earnest, waved effusively to a surprised group of nuns, several of whom smiled and waved back.

Captain Ó Néill drew his mount alongside Abby's seat in the carriage. "'Tis to the Hofburg itself we are headed, my lady. Whilst some of the court is still in residence at Schönbrunn, some five miles or so south, our orders are to deliver you to General the Baron O'Connell." Abby and Eileen both nodded and smiled.

Within moments the carriage and its outriders clattered to a halt in an expansive cobblestoned plaza, the massive complex of buildings that comprised the Hofburg itself seeming to both girls to be embracing it and them with an unusual sense of warmth and welcome. They had drawn up in front of that part of the palace that had been home to the Habsburgs since the thirteenth century.

On the top step of a grand-looking staircase loomed Uncle General the Baron himself, at attention and resplendent in a full-dress uniform, with young Corporal Sheehy, substantially similarly turned out, proudly standing one step below and to the side, holding General O'Connell's personal standard, which the young women noticed bore, in addition to the Habsburg double eagle, both an Irish harp and the O'Connell stag, fluttering gently in the breeze swirling about the broad courtyard. Though Abigail did not at first recognise him, at the bottom of the steps, his sword upheld, its blade glinting even in the dull sunlight, a tall young officer, elegant in his own dress uniform, briskly gave orders in German in a familiarly lilting Kerry brogue, causing the small detail of troops to snap to attention and present arms as the carriage drew to a halt.

"*Denis!*" screamed Abby as she began to stand in the still-moving carriage, Eileen gently tugging her back to her seat, noticing that the young man was biting his lip.

Their uncle cleared the steps quickly and nodded to Captain Denis O'Sullivan, who, scabbarding his gleaming blade, stepped to the general's side and extended a white-gloved hand to Abby's much smaller one. "Lady Abigail," he said as he handed her to the cobbles, Abby's face wreathed in her own sunshine, her eyes wide and joyful. She took virtually no notice of his scarred forehead and cheek; she would rarely do so ever again.

General O'Connell extended his own white-gloved hand to Eileen. *"Willkommen in der Hofburg, in Wien!"* he boomed, and Eileen tentatively replied, *"Danke, lieber Onkel."* They all laughed, as she smilingly whispered, "Ah, 'tis practicing we have both been!" All protocol aside, the general gathered his nieces into his arms, though Abby's eyes remained fixed on Denis O'Sullivan.

Within moments, and with effusive praise by and gratitude from the O'Connell women, duly noted by the general, the officers and men who had brought them from Paris were, along with the soldiers present for their arrival, including young Sheehy, dismissed, with the thanks of General O'Connell, who, one girl on each arm, he led into the palace, Captain O'Sullivan having fallen in behind.

Following tea in the general's compact though elegant audience hall— during which neither Abby nor the captain said more than a few words, their eyes resting largely, dreamily on each other—and O'Sullivan's reluctant leave-taking, the general announced, "Now, 'tis the Countess von Graffenreit to whom I must hand you over. I am told that she and her ladies have all in readiness for you, including temporary quarters whilst your own rooms are being finished." He reached behind his chair and tugged noiselessly on an embroidered belt, and within seconds an earnest young page appeared. The general nodded, and the boy withdrew without fully closing the massive door. In another moment an attractive ash-blond woman, of medium height and age, of fullish figure, elegantly attired in an arresting deep blue afternoon dress, entered the room, her train whispering. The general stood, the O'Connell girls instinctively curtseying.

They exchanged a simultaneously murmured "Your Grace . . ." — though Eileen was aware from her self-study that the countess outranked the baron—and Countess von Graffenreit extended a hand to each girl whilst they gently rose.

Maria von Graffenreit, whose name the young women had immediately recognised from their exchanges of correspondence, was several months shy of her forty-second birthday, the widow of, as Eileen and Abby would learn, a beloved, greatly admired and highly decorated colonel of a regiment of the Hungarian Hussars. She was very much as she had seemed from her letters, a bright and sensitive woman of quite some experience, long in service to the empress.

She took several steps back, still holding the girls' hands, looking very carefully at each of them. Without releasing them, she turned her head to the general and smiled, speaking in English. "My dearest general, you have not done your young ladies justice: They are more beautiful, more poised than you have allowed." Feigning an arch, haughty manner and tone, she advised, "I shall have to deal with you most harshly, sir," as, letting go of Abby's hand, she shook a delicate finger at him, laughing warmly.

Releasing Eileen's hand as well, she stepped back a bit farther, again studying the sisters, nodding as she did. "I must now remove you from the baron, so as to see that you are happily settled in as quickly as possible. You will, please then, come with me," she said softly, though with more than a suggestion of command, as she turned away.

General O'Connell quickly gathered the girls into his arms once again, kissing them each on the forehead, and stepped back, extending his open arms. "They are now yours, Your Grace." He smiled and turned towards the window as the three women swept out of the room, Eileen casting a glance up at the emperor's portrait as she did so.

As they stepped into the corridor, the countess extended an arm to each of the girls and thus joined—an attractive feminine phalanx of silks, satin and wool—they progressed down a series of corridors and up a magnificent staircase to an even more magnificent hallway. "We are coming to some of the Residences," the countess pointed out, now speaking French and continuing, "I must ask you to endure sharing a suite of rooms whilst each of yours are being completed," and both women nodded. "Your wardrobes are largely finished and have been delivered to your temporary quarters . . ." she continued as they arrived at a high, gleaming door with a magnificent knob that the countess turned and pushed, opening into an elegant sitting room.

"Your home for the moment, my dears," she said, now in German.

"*Das ist schön, Gräfin!*" exclaimed Abby as they stepped inside, her smile immediately matched by the countess's own as she heard the Irish girl's spoken German.

"Very good . . . very good indeed, Abby," the countess said, now in English, as she hugged her. "You will have ample opportunity to speak all of your languages here, though 'tis French that is most commonly used, and I understand both of yours is flawless, so . . .

"Now, let us sit, my dears," she continued, gesturing the women to a mauve satin-covered settee whilst she took an ornately crafted, elegantly upholstered deep-blue satin high-backed chair for herself.

After indicating that each girl would have her own bedroom, each with a small dressing alcove, sharing the sitting room, the countess proceeded to explain that, hopefully within the week, they would each be moved to their permanent apartments, "in the areas of your primary duties," adding that each would have a sitting room, a bedroom and a separate dressing room. "You will also have complete access to the suites in which you shall serve and live," which sounded more mysterious, at least to Abigail, than Countess von Graffenreit meant it to.

Correctly sensing more than a degree of interest, expectancy, perhaps even anxiety on the O'Connells' parts, the countess continued: "I am sure you should like to learn at least some of what it is that you shall henceforth be doing?" and, quickly exchanging glances, both girls nodded, smiling.

With a slow, single nod, the countess sagely looked first at Abby. "Abigail, my dear, you shall be entering the household of Her Imperial Majesty," she said lightly, almost matter-of-factly.

Abby's eyes went wide, her mouth opening, her hands shooting up. "But . . . but, Your Grace, the empress herself? I do not believe that I would be able to . . ." Eileen reflexively rested her hand gently on Abby's left knee, halting her in midsentence, as she'd hoped she would.

As she resumed, the countess's tone was gentle, but—as before—nevertheless subtly commanding. "You are now twenty years, yes . . ." she nodded firmly at Abigail, ". . . and from my numerous conversations with General the Baron O'Connell, I believe you will find this to be an excellent use of your talents. The empress is most pleased, I assure you. I expect that you shall there *thrive* and that you shall advance quickly . . . this, you must know, my dear, is my plan, yes . . . and that of the empress, and this plan we shall discuss at length.

"Now, *Mistress* Eileen." The countess nodded gracefully and smiled knowingly. Eileen lowered her eyes, thanking her. "Whilst yours will perhaps be an even greater challenge, it is one for which I am fully certain you are most uniquely qualified," the older woman paused dramatically, "for it is the household of the Archduchess Maria Carolina and the Archduchess Maria Antonia that you shall be entering, a setting in which I believe—*no*, more than that, I have *no doubt*—there you shall *flourish*."

Eileen could not contain herself: she smiled broadly. "Oh, Your Grace, 'tis wonderful indeed!" she exclaimed.

Having absorbed all of the information the countess had sent, along with what General O'Connell had provided in response to her numerous questions about the Imperial court, Eileen was aware that Maria Antonia, also known as Antoine, was almost exactly the same age as Hugh, and that Maria Carolina, called Charlotte, was perhaps two or three years older. Both little girls were already said to be eventually bound for European queens' thrones. She thus had reason to believe that her role would involve more than serving as a governess to two Imperial children; that it would permit her to assist in the preparation of both for their future roles, in which each would, with her respective spouse, play at least some role—depending on the country, perhaps even a significant one—in shaping and governing Europe for many years.

Seemingly emboldened, Abby began tentatively, "Your Grace, perhaps as there are *two* young archduchesses . . ."

Smiling, the countess quickly stood and immediately knelt gently at Abby's feet, her folded hands resting on the girl's right knee, her large green eyes looking into Abby's. "My darling Abigail, Her Imperial Majesty has herself made these selections: You both may rest assured that much thought has been given to the full use of your individual talents and experience . . . as well as to assuring the total happiness of each of you."

Her lips parted, her eyes little-girl wide now, Abigail could only nod, *yes.*

The countess rose gracefully, the younger women standing immediately as well. "Now, please . . ." She gestured to the partially open doors on either side of the room. "You will make yourselves comfortable and examine your new wardrobes and belongings, and I shall return in one hour, perhaps a bit longer . . . so that we might begin to make some preliminary introductions, during which time your trunks shall be delivered . . . and we shall see later to your evening meal."

Her hand on the knob of the parlour door, she turned and smiled. "I have taken the liberty of selecting your afternoon dresses and ensemble for today, only because I felt it would help, as will the girls I shall be sending to assist you in dressing." She added with a smile, "I understand you both have exquisite taste in clothing . . ."

She stepped outside, closing the door, though, as she immediately heard the girls' buoyant laughter from within, stopping, she could not help but hear Abigail merrily exclaim, "Oh my yes, Your Grace, we *both* have the most *absolutely exquisite* taste in clothing, provided 'tis made of heavy, rough Irish wool and coloured white or black!" and her sister laugh heartily in response, adding ". . . or Scottish wool in grey and brown plaids!"

As she strolled down the corridor, the Countess Maria von Graffenreit smiled knowingly. *Perfect this is going to be . . . absolutely perfect!*

Within moments of the countess's departure, Abby and Eileen had raced into their respective bedrooms and emerged wide-eyed and as excited as little girls:

Do you have . . . ?
Did they give you . . . ?
I have never seen so many . . . dresses . . . gowns . . . shoes . . . in my life!
No wonder the countess selected . . .

Regaining some measure of composure, Eileen proposed that they at least begin to change into the afternoon dresses Countess von Graffenreit had selected, now laid carefully on a chaise in the corner of each one's bedroom, adding, "I do not understand why assistance would be required for us to dress; we shall simply help each other, as we have done at home when the formal corsets are required."

Abby agreed, but both women quickly remarked on the relative complexity of the new garments when compared to their own simpler garb.

Typically, even today, each wore a light corset into which a trim woman could with relative ease cinch herself and a hip pad, which, when fastened about that part of one's body beneath a dress, provided the broad, free-flowing appearance of a woman's long, full-skirted garment, even one made of the densest, heaviest of Irish or Scottish wool, as the O'Connells had, at least until now, customarily worn.

In marked contrast, in addition to their afternoon dresses, there were arrayed what appeared to be a variety of undergarments and devices, including complex corsets that were cinched in the back.

Within the half hour, they were thus relieved when two pretty young girls arrived, curtseyed and with little conversation proceeded to assist the young women to don their preselected outfits, Eileen's being a sky blue whilst Abby's was a deep cream: substantially similar, full-skirted with flowing trains, narrow-waisted and long-sleeved, each displaying an ample amount of décolletage, to the extent that, to the amusement of their dressers, both were giggling and tugging at the fabric. "'Tis no use . . . *exposed* we are to be, my darling!" laughed Eileen as she stood before a full-length looking glass, noticing her own ample bosom and watching Abby still attempting, unsuccessfully, to push her full breasts down into the bodice of her dress.

Approximately at the time she indicated she would return, the countess knocked softly and Eileen stepped to open the door. Entering, the older woman smiled broadly. "Lovely, yes, very lovely, as I fully expected."

The door still open, she indicated that an individual still in the corridor should step in. "This is Lady Alexandra; you will please permit her to assist with your hair." A compact, slightly plump dark-haired woman of perhaps thirty entered, carrying a soft leather valise and smiling warmly.

She skilfully raked her fingers through each girl's hair, nodded, and then, smiling, stood in front of first one and then the other, framing their faces with their hair. She removed several brushes and some pins from her satchel.

Within moments Abby's thick curls had been brushed and swept up on all sides, gathered and pinned on top of her head, accentuated by a pair of simple pearl earrings, which the countess had brought.

Eileen's hair presented more of a challenge to the obviously talented coiffeuse, though in a relatively short time her flowing raven locks had been brushed, with some being gathered and pinned so that they framed her face and the remainder swept over her shoulders and well down her back. Her earrings were substantially similar to those now being worn by Abby.

"So now, we are off to introduce the court to you, and you to your new lives!" the countess exclaimed happily, gently nudging both women through the open door—and into a new world.

The Hofburg, Vienna—late October–November 1761

The weeks that followed their arrival at the Hofburg were, for both women, exciting, confusing, exhilarating, exhausting, humorous, enjoyable and terrifying— sometimes all in the same, incredibly long day.

What Countess von Graffenreit viewed as being an auspicious first several weeks—primarily involving meeting and being generally well received by a dizzying array of nobility, both major and minor, all levels of staff and various factotums—presaged a successful passage for both Abigail and Eileen from being the O'Connell girls from Ireland to becoming young ladies of position at the Imperial court in Vienna.

This notwithstanding, even prior to the O'Connells' arrival the countess, through her intricate web of connections, her multiple sources of information—or, as some referred to them, "spies and informers"—became aware of a not insignificant level of resentment by some lesser-titled individuals, primarily though not entirely on the periphery of the Imperial court, in reaction to the attractive Irishwomen's arrival.

She had learnt of the remark that originated from one minor Imperial cousin, characterising the O'Connells as being "overprivileged Irish peasants, nothing more than pretty girls with feathers for brains, here prowling for titled husbands who will rescue them from having to ever return to their soggy bogs." The countess was enraged when she discovered that several variants of the comment were being widely repeated, often embellished, by a small but vocal group of courtiers.

Given the circumstances, and despite the fact that she had long considered him to be an insignificant figure, the countess had had one outspoken man, whom she recognised as a troublesome, habitual agitator—a leader amongst those at court whom she unhesitatingly referred to as being of "the permanently disaffected"—unceremoniously brought to her office, which adjoined that of the empress.

The countess remained seated as the officious little man, a baron of slight consequence other than being a cousin to the empress, entered. Pointedly neither greeting nor requesting him to sit, she immediately inquired if he had shared his displeasure concerning the O'Connells with . . . and she pointed to the simple doorway that connected the suites. "Do you not wish to do so, Your Grace? As you have spoken so frequently of these young women, *who have been invited to court by Her Imperial Majesty herself*," she purred, "you and your nasty little coterie." His jaw dropped.

The man, who had responded shakily in the negative, a nervous smile on his pasty face, was wringing his hands as the countess stood unexpectedly, stepping around her elegant writing table, theatrically drawing her train towards the front, forcing the man to have to step back.

Standing regally before him, her tone was harsh, threatening. "Not only a worthless individual and nasty, malicious gossip but a *coward* you are! Should I learn of any further attempts of this type of disparagement, even the suggestion of a single such remark henceforth being made, whether by you or by any of your valueless little circle of valueless little people and . . ." she leaned even closer to him ". . . as quickly as *this*"—she snapped her long, elegant fingers within inches of the man's perspiration-streaked, wide-eyed face—"on my word alone, you shall finally and at long last be banished from court, once and for all!"

Moving as if to turn away, she spun herself sharply back, her skirts rustling, again confronting the now visibly trembling man. "You will know, in this event, payment of your stipend would of course immediately and permanently cease." She smiled cruelly as she gestured with an elegantly diffident flick of her right hand that he was to depart. The shaken man struggled to bow and stumbled as he attempted to withdraw, walking backwards. Shaking her head, the countess purposely laughed aloud at him, making sure he heard her final muttered word, "Worthless."

The undercurrent of gossip ceased almost immediately.

By virtue of their positions, both Abigail and Eileen were largely isolated from the day-to-day life of the extended Habsburg court and thus from the type of incessant rumour, gossip and backbiting attendant amongst a large group of mostly self-important individuals with too much unfilled time and too little to do. Both young women would nevertheless ultimately come to learn of the existence of such people and their conduct and to, each in her own way, successfully deflect and otherwise deal with the realities of the privileged, insular place in which they now resided.

Blissfully unaware of any of this at the time, Eileen's formal presentation to the young archduchesses was, by all accounts, a wholly successful and highly enjoyable experience, both for the Imperial daughters and their new governess.

On the brilliant morning of the fourth full day following her arrival, under the watchful eye of Countess von Graffenreit and with the assistance of a very pretty flaxen-haired girl of perhaps twelve named Anna Pfeffer, who, the countess advised, would henceforth be her maid, Eileen was fully attired for the first time in ultra-formal court dress. In this instance, she wore a beautifully and thickly embroidered, heavy, long-sleeved robe of deep blue and gold thread with a full train flowing from the waist and ample décolletage, made all the more impressive—and cumbersome—by the petticoat-covered pannier on each side (*basket* in French, which Eileen readily agreed was an appropriate name for the contraptions).

Once again the talents of Lady Alexandra, the countess's favourite coiffeuse, resulted in Eileen's hair being brushed to a blue-black sheen and draped elegantly over her shoulders, then permitted to flow down her back to her waist. Standing back, a brush in each hand, Lady Alexandra smiled at the countess. "The 'up-sweep,' the 'pouf' I believe is not for your Lady Eileen. Her raven locks, they are too stunning to be pinned, even as slightly as I did upon her arrival, and piled, and toyed with. Unless Your Grace should require it of me, I shall *never* want to do that again! Henceforth," she extended her hands, "my hope is that, contrary to general practise at court, she shall appear thus, and only thus, yes, Your Grace?"

The countess smiled, nodding firmly. "Yes, yes indeed! Save when such would be considered a 'mortal sin,' violative of etiquette, protocol!" and henceforth so it would be: Through her years in Vienna, save in the case of rare, protocol-dictated circumstances, Eileen's raven locks would remain a singular, eye-catching mane.

Thus attired and coiffed and on the arm of Countess von Graffenreit, Eileen entered for the first time the larger of the two formal audience rooms of the younger archduchesses' apartment at precisely eleven o'clock.

Standing in the centre of the strikingly formal room were the two little archduchesses, both wearing miniature versions of Eileen's court dress á pannier, save that Maria Carolina's was mauve and Maria Antonia's a robin's-egg blue. Except for the difference in their ages, the girls were also markedly similar in appearance: luminously blond with pink complexions, gentle blue eyes and the sweetest of little-girl expressions on their faces. Behind them stood the Countess Brandeiss, at present the governess to both girls and ranking lady of the household, in a less formal though no less arresting grey afternoon dress.

As she and the countess had practiced, walking the exact number of steps and stopping at a precise point, Eileen executed a flawless deep curtsey before the elegantly dressed little girls and the other countess, and, as she had been instructed, genuflected on one knee, her head bowed, remaining thus whilst she was formally introduced by Countess von Graffenreit, who spoke in French to the children and the woman who would be her direct superior in the household. "Your Imperial Highnesses, Your Grace: I am truly honoured to present to you the Lady Eileen Mary O'Connell, daughter of the late Squire Donal Mór O'Connell and Mistress Maire O'Connell of Derrynane, in the

County of Kerry, Province of Munster, Kingdom of Ireland. She willingly and gratefully places herself in Your Imperial Highnesses' service."

Only when Maria Carolina, who was nine, indicated in a soft yet firm voice that "You may rise, Lady Eileen," did she—and in doing so it became obvious, as it had not been on her entrance and immediate curtsey, that she towered over everyone else in the room. Expressions of spontaneous, almost playful amazement appeared on the little girls' faces as they looked up at her, Maria Antonia's mouth falling open.

"You are most welcome to our household, Lady Eileen," Maria Carolina nevertheless continued evenly. "Both my sister and I are most grateful to have you in our service." Waiting a moment, and then another, without redirecting her gaze, she cleared her throat, nudging her younger sister, who was still staring up at Eileen. Without lowering her own wide-eyed gaze and in a flat voice the little girl finished, "We are most happy to have you here, Lady Eileen."

Eileen suppressed a chortle but allowed herself a soft smile and an equally soft, "*Merci, Vos Altesses Impériales,*" as she nodded at the little girls, who, Countess von Graffenreit had advised, she might address unceremoniously as Charlotte and Antoine, "though never in public!" immediately and firmly cautioned Brandeiss.

Countess von Graffenreit, who, Eileen had correctly surmised, was senior to Brandeiss, suggested they sit, and they did for the next hour, a generally relaxed, genuinely informative —for Eileen as well as the little royals—occasion.

Under the countess's direction, Eileen, speaking in her lilting Kerry French, with which the little girls especially seemed instantly enthralled, provided a brief narrative of her life, where she had come from—"Our home, it is called Derrynane, 'tis in County Kerry, a remote place in the southwest of Ireland, where the River Kenmare meets the Atlantic"—where precisely Ireland itself was—"'Tis an island at the far-western edge of Europe"—a bit about her large family—which, she explained, was similar in size to the large Imperial family—and, in passing, touched on her marriage and widowhood, the girls' expressions turning briefly solemn. She told them she loved children, about her special relationship with Anne, Elizabeth and Hugh—noting that her brother was the same age as Antoine—and mentioning the French-speaking dollies—the girls smiled brilliantly—horses—adding that her "very big" horse had come to Vienna with her—and dogs, which caused little Antoine to clap her hands, exclaiming, "I love doggies!"

The countess added that General O'Connell was Eileen's *onkel* and the girls beamed. "He is sometimes funny!" Charlotte giggled.

So, the baron is known within the Imperial household, Eileen thought.

As the conversation wound down, as and almost precisely when it was designed to, Countess Brandeiss quietly dismissed the little archduchesses after they both gently kissed Eileen on her cheek, though Antoine also draped her small hands around Eileen's neck, and they scrambled down the hall. "To their commons," the countess advised Eileen.

With Countess von Graffenreit joining them, Brandeiss showed Eileen about the large apartment the little girls shared, making note that each had a separate audience room, parlour, bedroom and dressing room, as well as the large bright room, into which Eileen peeked, seeing the girls playing with dolls and a magnificent doll house in the shape and design of a castle. "It is there," Brandeiss pointed to a book-lined corner of the bright room, "where we have our lessons."

As they walked, the countess began to advise Eileen of some of her duties. "Whilst we shall discuss all of this in much detail, I believe it is sufficient now for you to understand that you will *assist me* as governess and teacher of both of their Imperial Highnesses. Is that understood, my dear?"

Eileen smiled her sweetest smile and nodded demurely. She did not notice that Maria von Graffenreit had sighed, deeply and audibly, thinking, *must the woman be so terribly officious?*

"Additionally, I understand you are an extraordinary equestrienne, yes?" Eileen again lowered her eyes. "I am aware of this from General O'Connell," she advised as she stopped walking.

Eileen similarly halted, then smiled and nodded. "He speaks well of my abilities . . . ?"

"He does *indeed*! Accordingly, then, you shall henceforth assume primary . . . no, more correctly, I should have said you shall henceforth have *sole* responsibility for seeing to their Imperial Highnesses' individual equestrian skills. I shall see to it that you are introduced to all the many amenities we have here, including the indoor facilities of the Winter Riding School . . . it is also, you may know, referred to as the Spanish Riding School, yes . . . so you may commence your work with the archduchesses immediately, and that you shall be provided with an excellent mount, as well as any and all equipment you might require."

"Your Grace, if I may?" Eileen had begun to smile tentatively once again. "I have been fortunate to be able to bring my own horse—and a rather large and extraordinary fellow he is—with me from Ireland, so, as gracious as your offer is, I shall have no need for an animal."

Countess Brandeiss, clearly surprised, paused, then continued. "Very well, then. Is this the new horse I understand is at General the Baron O'Connell's barns?" Eileen nodded. "I did not know he was yours, believing him an addition to the general's array of magnificent animals. We should be pleased to provide him lodging here, should you wish."

"Oh, thank you, Your Grace, that is so thoughtful of you! As Bull is also my dear friend, it will be lovely having him close by."

"His name is Bull, you say? Extraordinary! . . . Also, we are saying *he*. I am assuming *he* is gelded, yes?"

Eileen took a deep breath. "In truth, he is a stallion, Your Grace, a handsome, spirited and whole Frisian . . . albeit somewhat unique as he is chestnut rather than being all-black. I myself broke him to the saddle, and I know and assure you that he is gentle enough for either one or both of their Imperial Highnesses to be placed on his back this very day."

Von Graffenreit turned to a window and smiled to herself. *Beautifully done, Mistress Eileen. All that my dear general has told me is indeed true and accurate.*

Countess Brandeiss seemed surprised, even shocked, and she spoke sharply. "On a massive Frisian stallion? I think not! They have their own mounts, do you understand?"

"Yes, yes, Your Grace, certainly, fully," replied Eileen in a soft, fully deferential tone.

The brief moment of tension dispelled, they continued walking, the sounds of craftsmen and their implements growing closer.

"We are now almost finished, my dear. Please permit me to show you your new quarters, which I am certain you will find to be beautiful," said Brandeiss, now gently taking Eileen's hand and leading her to the end of a short hall. She opened the door on to what appeared to be still very much a construction and decoration project, with carpenters, painters and gilders still at work in the parlour and bedroom. Slightly wide-eyed, Eileen found the apartment to be truly remarkable, especially as she and Countess von Graffenreit stepped onto a small terrace from which the countess directed Eileen's eyes past the teeming streets of Vienna towards Schönbrunn, Laxenburg and in the direction of Hungary.

"Oh, Countess Brandeiss!" Eileen exclaimed. "It is already quite beautiful. Thank you so much."

"You shall be in residence before the end of the week, my dear," pronounced Brandeiss somewhat officiously. "*I* have seen to it."

Turning from both women, von Graffenreit rolled her eyes.

"You shall commence your duties tomorrow, then; first thing in the morning you will be in attendance at their Imperial Highnesses' breakfast, *ja?*"

Eileen smiled pleasantly, lowering her eyes, her voice barely a whisper. "*Oui*," she said. Realising her linguistic slip, Brandeiss smiled awkwardly and repeated the French affirmative.

Countess von Graffenreit smiled, and dazzlingly so, her thoughts of earlier in the week echoing in her mind: *Perfect this is going to be . . . absolutely perfect.* As they took their leave of the countess, placing her arm in the tall Irish girl's, she escorted her back to her temporary apartment, a noticeable spring in von Graffenreit's always graceful steps, certain now that Eileen's already deftly-displayed high degree of intelligence would more than offset the well-meaning but less than bright Brandeiss's lack thereof.

The following morning, whilst Eileen was beginning her service in the household of the little archduchesses, a very anxious Abigail was preparing to be formally introduced to Her Imperial Majesty, the Empress Maria Theresa.

Though she customarily would have requested one of the dressers to assist Abby into her own court dress, Countess von Graffenreit nevertheless came early, planning to awaken Abby herself, only to find her up, her toilette completed, sitting on her bed, reading, quietly awaiting her dresser's arrival.

As she entered the bedroom, Abby immediately hopped off the high bed. "Your Grace, I am *so* happy to see you!" she cried out spontaneously, quickly putting her hand to her mouth as she realised how loudly she had spoken. The countess smiled and kissed the young woman's forehead.

"You are enchanting, Lady Abigail, truly," she whispered, standing aside as a young girl cinched Abby into a complex corset and panniers. The countess herself then proceeded to assist a suddenly and atypically quiet Abby into a dress substantially similar to Eileen's of the previous day, save that it was primarily gold with deep blue threading.

This completed, von Graffenreit led Abby to a full-length looking glass. Seeing herself thus attired for the first time, her waist slight, her bosom full— her magnificent robe rendered even more imposing by the dramatic effect of the panniers, Abigail O'Connell audibly gasped and stood numbly, her arms at her side, just looking at herself, finally softly managing, "'Tis a very, *very* long way from Kerry I am . . . a long way indeed."

Noticing two silent tears on her lightly freckled cheeks, the countess stepped forward and enveloped the younger woman in her arms. "Abby, Abby, my darling girl, it is indeed a very long way from Ireland that you are . . . but you are here because you are very much wanted and very much *needed*, truly, dear." Abby sniffled, and the countess wiped her eyes with a linen handkerchief.

"Now, it is to the empress we shall go . . . she awaits you most expectantly."

As the women stepped into the corridor, several of the servants curtseyed deeply, and Abby nodded and smiled gently.

The countess held Abby's hand as they traversed the huge palace—their trains sighing softly. At one point she advised, "We have crossed into the Leopoldine Wing. Her Imperial Majesty's apartments are on the first floor." When they finally came to a simple door, *'Tis it now into a pantry that I am going?* wondered Abigail silently.

Smiling, von Graffenreit produced a small gold key from the pocket of her dress. She unlocked and opened the door, revealing a light-panelled, thickly carpeted stairway, a skylight high above it providing the only illumination. "This is a secret!" the countess teased girlishly, "so sssh." She laughed softly and gently nudged Abby's lower back, indicating she should descend first.

It was a quick two flights down to another simple door. Holding her finger to her lips, the countess once again unlocked and gently opened it, nodding for Abigail to proceed.

As Abby stepped first through the door, a short, robust-looking woman in a plain dark brown dress, long-sleeved and peaked at the shoulders, around which was draped a simple grey wool shawl, stood casually to one side, half-looking out the high windows in what appeared to be a very basic though comfortable antechamber. The woman smiled and turned back to the windows.

Abby nodded politely, murmured a perfunctory *"Guten morgen"* and, noticing an elaborate doorway at the end of the room, assumed that was where they were going and continued striding toward it.

It was only when she heard a soft laugh from across the room, and as the countess then gently caught her hand and began to curtsey deeply, that Abigail began to realise it was quite possibly the empress herself to whom she'd been mildly pleasant. She immediately joined von Graffenreit in her curtsey, an English, "Oh, my good God in heaven!" audibly escaping her lips.

Maria Theresa stepped forward, smiling broadly, her arms open, and softly said, "Please rise, my dear ladies."

Abby visibly trembled as she stood wide-eyed; the empress, sensing what she correctly felt was Abigail's near terror, took both of the attractive young woman's hands in her own, looked deeply into the Irish girl's soft blue eyes and gently kissed her on both cheeks. *"Willkommen in der Hofburg,"* she said gently and stepped back. Still holding Abby's trembling hands, speaking now in soft French, she continued, "My dear Lady Abigail, I so regret our little charade. It was my idea, mine alone; dear Countess von Graffenreit is wholly innocent. I believed it might be more comfortable, perhaps even a bit of fun, but I fear . . ."

"Oh, no, Your Majesty. . . Your Highness . . . Empress . . . Madame . . . 'tis my fault, mine alone," Abby began tremblingly in English, immediately realising both that she had suddenly forgotten both how to properly address the most powerful woman in the world as well as that her listener did not speak fluent English. It was only when Maria Theresa, mother of fifteen children, instinctively embraced her, drawing the young woman to herself, thereby silencing her, that Abby did not burst into tears.

The empress placed her left arm around Abigail's still shaking shoulders, speaking softly in French and gesturing with a gentle movement of her right hand. "We have coffee and pastries set. Let us all relax and begin again."

Abby nodded with relief, her dark-blond curls bouncing. As they crossed into the room Abby had indeed correctly assumed was their destination, their slippered feet cushioned by a deep Indian carpet, Maria Theresa sensed Abby was beginning to calm. Reaching a grouping of furniture next to a huge window, she drew her to a settee. "Come, darling, you sit with me," she said, and gestured to the countess to take a high-backed leather chair.

They sat quietly for a moment.

"Now," Maria Theresa began, continuing in French in a soft, motherly tone, "as I should properly have done: Welcome, Lady Abigail, to our home. I hope you will come to think of it, as well as Schönbrunn and Laxenburg, as yours as well, and that you will be very happy here."

Turning slightly, Abby smiled warmly and responded in French, spoken with what Maria Theresa sensed was the musical lilt of Ireland, "Thank you, Your Majesty. I fear 'tis still a bit in awe I am, still a girl from deep in Kerry that I am, as well."

The countess smiled softly as she spoke, and Maria Theresa smiled broadly and said, "Oh, I hear Ireland in your voice. Please, dear girl, never, *never* lose your . . ." She paused and softly, tentatively said, in English, ". . . your brogue, is that correct? *Brogue?*"

Abby's usually radiant expression instantly returned. "Brogue is correct, *ja!*" She laughed, as did the empress and the countess.

The ice broken and all formality set aside, for the following hour and a bit more the three women chatted and visited, almost as old friends. Perhaps most importantly—though Abigail did not, could not have realised—as von Graffenreit had planned, the time permitted Maria Theresa to care-fully observe, hear and to immediately fall in love with Abigail O'Connell, whom virtually everyone who had ever met had similarly, instantaneously adored.

Sipping cup after cup of strong Viennese coffee, and—albeit in a totally ladylike manner—devouring half of the tray of pastries, Abby was, as her mother would have said, "being Abby": warm, intelligent, humorous, thought-ful and genuine, posing even the most delicate questions in such a guileless way that Maria Theresa could only laugh and answer—"No, darling, there are those people amongst us whose tasks specifically include the removal of such 'pots'"—and laugh again, nodding at the countess as if to say, *She is precious! She is perfect! She is everything you have said, everything the general has said and more!*

The allotted time passed far more quickly than any of the women would have liked, and, as a simply gowned young girl knocked softly once and opened a door, the empress stood. "I fear, my dear ladies, that I must excuse myself and join the Lady Abigail in donning the most formal of court dress . . . as a new plenipotentiary from the Venetian republic is to be presented to us."

Standing, Abby was beaming warmly, her face wreathed in its customary sunshine.

"And, *Abby*, we shall visit like this at least once a week, and I shall see to it that we always have coffee and pastries." Maria Theresa said, tapping her on the right arm. Abby blushed and then flawlessly executed the deepest of curtseys, remaining thus until the empress raised her up. Her eyes shining, she gently kissed Abby's cheeks, whispering, "I am so very happy that you are here," and turned and walked away.

Derrynane—late Autumn 1761

In the weeks since Abigail and Eileen had departed for Vienna, Maire had become quiet and withdrawn in ways reminiscent of the dark period that fol-lowed Donal Mór's death.

"'Tis mourning I am, I fear, my loves," she said to Morgan and Maurice as they walked late one afternoon, this being the first time she had admitted the depth of her sense of loss to anyone.

"I believe 'tis natural, Mother," said Morgan. "'Tis departed from us they have, and far away indeed they are. We know not when, or dare I say, *whether*, we shall see either or both of them again."

As Maire began to weep softly, Morgan immediately regretted his remark. Maurice gently draped a long arm around her shoulder and they continued to walk in the gathering dusk, a misty fog drifting up from Derrynane Bay, settling about mother and sons like the sheerest of gossamer.

"Perhaps given that we are compelled to deal with difficult transitions, might it not be time to discuss again Denis . . . ? We have not arrived at any resolution and continue to drift," ventured Morgan.

Maire looked up at both of her tall sons, the trim Maurice and the bulky though solid Morgan, and she nodded silently, *'Tis time, aye.*

It had become evident to the brothers that Denis, by virtue of what Maurice had come to refer to as "the O'Connor matter," had lost his always tenuous hold on the authority that ostensibly had been his as the eldest son since their father's death.

Once the facts surrounding at least Eileen's initial time at Firies, as disclosed by Abby to their mother, became known to the young men, Morgan had very seriously considered killing his brother, as he very matter-of-factly told him, as well as their mother and brothers. Having been at least temporarily dissuaded by a mix of fraternal logic and maternal emotion, he had indicated that for him the only alternative to Denis being dead would be for Denis to be physically—and permanently—removed from Derrynane, and from the family. "I strongly urge you, sir, to make arrangements for yourself . . . away from here, away from Ireland, preferably away from Europe," Morgan had told an ashen-faced Denis finally, some two weeks prior to the conversation on the lawn with their mother.

"Tonight then, now even," said Maurice crisply and quite appropriately, for it was upon him that the mantle of *priomhfheidhmeannach ár clan*/head of family would rest.

"I shall gather the lads, including Hugh, yes, brother? . . . Mother?"

Maire looked pained but nodded.

"Quite right, Morgan," said Maurice. "Though he be still a wee lad, he is aware that something horrible has happened to Eileen, whom he adores, and that 'twas Denis who sent her to that place. He is properly present, aye."

Leaving his mother and sibling, Morgan strode to the house, his boots heavy on the rugs, on the floorboards. He walked to the library; without knocking, he opened the door, finding Denis pouring over a ledger at the writing desk.

"Ah, 'tis good you are here; you have thus saved me from having to scavenge for you, like the vermin you be. You will remain here, in this room, sir," he snapped and closed the door with a slam.

Having admitted Maurice and their mother to the library, Morgan was just ascending the grand staircase as he saw Hugh at the landing above.

Smiling weakly, he said, "Lad, I wish you to join all of us in the library, though would you please first gather Conaill and Daniel and bring them with you?"

Though puzzled, Hugh stood up a bit straighter, nodded a quiet "Yes, sir," and smoothed his hair back as he went to do as he had been requested.

Within a short while, all of the O'Connell brothers and their mother were assembled in the library. Though Maurice had seen to it that sufficient chairs had been brought in from the dining room, he smiled to see Hugh perched on Maire's lap, his mother's arms enveloping him. *'Tis good for them both at this time.*

Maurice stood in front of the fire, Denis having remained slouching diffidently in what had been their father's desk chair. An icy expression on his thin face, Maurice looked to him. "You shall stand, sir; 'tis a long time, if ever, that you have been worthy to sit as and where you do now."

Impassively, Denis stood very slowly.

Maurice then sat, leaving the eldest brother standing alone, awkwardly, bereft of any legitimacy, certainly of any power.

"This matter has been permitted by all of us, myself included, to linger much longer than it should have. I nevertheless felt—and I believe everyone agreed—that 'twas appropriate to wait until Abby and Eileen were off." His brothers, including Hugh, nodded. Maire spoke with her eyes.

Looking directly at Denis, he continued coldly, "This being said, 'tis the agreement of those who will remain the men of this house—*all* the men of this house, and this family, and concurred in by our mother—that you, sir, shall immediately remove yourself from Derrynane, never to return hence."

Maurice glanced at Maire, her face now a complex reflection of the pain, the sorrow any mother would feel, coupled nevertheless with a firm acceptance of the correctness of the decision. *Responsible he is and accountable he shall be held,* Maire had declared, had firmly committed to Eileen after learning what had happened at Firies.

"So heinous were the actions, taken in secret by you alone and prompted solely by your own greed and misplaced aspirations, with utter disregard for the life, safety and security of our innocent sister, and so horrific were certain things that befell her and have befallen us, we have agreed that as a direct result of those actions, you have relinquished any rights as a member of this family."

Denis began, "Rights I have by law!"

"By the king's law, perhaps," snapped Maurice, waving his left hand dismissively. "The King's Writ is given little authority in all of this County of Kerry, all of this Province of Munster and certainly none in this house, sir!" stormed Maurice. "'Tis largely Gaelic law, Brehon law, that *we* recognise in the conduct of the affairs of this family, and 'tis consistent with both that you are to be and shall be banished, do you hear me, sir?"

Denis stood white-faced, his fists clenched at his sides. "What is it precisely you are saying then, *brother?*" he asked, his voice tremulous.

Silence hung heavily in the room. Hugh looked up at his mother, who gently kissed the top of his head.

"If I may, sir?" Daniel said almost softly, addressing Maurice.

Though he had several alternate ideas, Maurice nevertheless nodded to his seated brothers, his mother. *He is a bright lad; I wish to hear what he is thinking.*

Daniel stood, addressing the room. "My understanding is that as part of Denis's *arrangement* with the late Squire O'Connor, we, the O'Connells, have acquired significant land holdings, all outside of Ireland." He looked coldly at his eldest brother, whom he had loathed long before this time. "Is that not correct, *sir*?"

Denis nodded affirmatively, and Maurice smiled, tightly but visibly. *A very bright lad he is.*

Daniel turned respectfully to Maurice. "I believe, brother, that 'tis to our holdings in Jamaica *he* should go, and go *soon*, and 'tis in Jamaica he should henceforth remain."

"Brilliant! Bloody brilliant!" shouted a beaming Morgan, half-rising and shaking a partially clenched fist at Denis. "You desired land in such godforsaken places, you bastard . . . *you* go and see what it is your avarice has gained for us. I understand that properly managed sugar plantations can prove to be valuable. Yes, you go . . . you manage it, you operate it; perhaps you will make us wealthy, for 'tis *money* I understand you have said we lack. Make us money and you shall be permitted to remain in Jamaica." He laughed caustically, with bitingly deliberate cruelty.

"Should you fail, you shall be dismissed, as would any *servant*." His words hung heavily in the still air.

Denis swayed visibly where he stood, his legs spread slightly.

Daniel spread his arms, thus inquiring of the brothers.

"Here, here!" called out Conaill. "'Tis brilliant indeed."

"What think ye, brother Hugh? You have a say, lad," said Maurice after nodding his own concurrence.

Still leaning closely against his mother, the little boy nevertheless straightened himself. He sat for a moment, looking wide-eyed up at Maire, and she nodded, encouraging him to speak.

"Juh . . . may . . . ca," his little boy voice spoke, "like Daniel said . . . to Jamaica." Leaning forward and turning his head to face Denis directly, speaking now with all the feelings that had welled up since his beloved and obviously wounded sister had returned. "You go now," Hugh said firmly, and leaned back against Maire's bosom. Saddened by the reality of what was happening, she nevertheless proudly enveloped her little boy.

"I agree as well; 'tis a sound proposal, Daniel. So then, 'tis decided," said Maurice crisply. He stood and walked to Denis, looking his brother directly in the eye as they were approximately the same height. "You shall begin to make immediate arrangements to depart. You know where Jamaica is, and I assume you will know how to get yourself there.

"We shall, amongst ourselves—the brothers, our mother—we shall agree upon a sum of money that we shall settle on you: sufficient for your transport and for your basic needs in Jamaica. I am assuming you know whether there is a dwelling already built there. If there is, you may occupy it. If there is not, you may sleep in the trees so far as I am concerned. You may contact us and request moneys for a dwelling, and we may agree to provide them. Immediately upon your arrival, you shall familiarise yourself with the place, the operations, planting and all. You know all about sugar-growing, I am sure, because you know all about everything, do you not? You shall thence prepare a written report of the same and send it to us—we, the people for whom you work—paying particular attention to and specifically projecting when we might expect to begin receiving proceeds from *our* sugar holdings in Jamaica. Have you any questions, sir?"

Denis impassively nodded *no*.

"If I may, brother?" spoke Morgan, with none of his usual passion. "Upon reflection, I fully agree with brother Hugh in his saying 'You go, now.' I, too, wish him gone forthwith: to a cabin in the mountains, to Dublin, to his fancy friends in London . . . just gone from here . . . *now!*"

An affirmative chorus sounded in the room: *Yes, now! Immediately! Tomorrow! No, tonight!* including the voice of the little boy, though a broken-hearted mother said nothing, the pain on Maire's face deep and inevitably heartrending, her strong agreement with her sons notwithstanding.

By the end of the week Denis O'Connell would sleep in his rooms for the last time. Early on Saturday morning, a significant sum of money in cash and drafts having been settled on him and without a word to his mother or his brothers, he saddled his own horse, affixed luggage to a packhorse and departed Derrynane, the only sounds accompanying him being those of the sea, the wind and the hooves of the horses on the morning-misted grass and the stones of the rough track beyond.

Vienna—early Winter 1761–62

Despite Countess von Graffenreit's good intentions and Countess Brandeiss's somewhat officious pronouncements to Eileen, it was Abigail who was first moved to her permanent apartments, whilst—accompanied by much of what Eileen called "creative noise" between painters and gilders—the completion of Eileen's was delayed a week or more.

"'Tis of no real concern, Madame, now that I have mastered the route between my rooms and the apartment of the archduchesses," Eileen advised Brandeiss, who pronounced herself "mortified" and promised "severe action" would be taken against the warring craftsmen.

"Ah, no . . . please, not on my account, Your Grace," Eileen gently protested, and Brandeiss relented—or promised she would.

Though incredible as it seemed to both of them, and though Eileen had not yet had an opportunity to visit her there, Abby was happily ensconced in a tastefully luxurious apartment of three rooms: a lovely parlour, a comfortable bedroom and a well-appointed dressing room. "I think 'tis only to hold all my clothes," Abby told the other young ladies of the empress's household, causing them all to laugh in unison. Her seemingly blasé attitude notwithstanding, Abigail was truly enthralled by her new home. The first evening she was there alone, in the sitting room, she moved from chair to chair, from sofa to chaise, sitting briefly on each as if in a lovely dream. Her bed was an extraordinary work of art in itself, beautifully carved, with vines and flowers and small woodland animals, a firm mattress and the smoothest of linen, the puffiest of down covers and down-filled pillows.

Lovely as her quarters were, it seemed to Abby that frequently she was there primarily to sleep, so busy and full were her days. She did, however, take unspoken note of the apartment's close proximity to those of both the empress and Maria von Graffenreit.

Early one Tuesday morning, in the third full week of November, as Eileen was dressing, with Anna's assistance, a young woman whom Eileen had only met once gently scratched on the door of her still-temporary quarters. "*Entrée,*" Eileen called softly, as she was in the process of being cinched into her dress by Anna, who was in midlacing.

"Good morning, Lady Eileen; a good day to you," said the woman, who reminded Eileen that her name was Christiana. "I am happy to tell you that your apartment is now ready, yes? As soon as you go to join their Imperial Highnesses, all of your belongings, your clothing, will be moved, yes? Oh, my lady, I am to ask: Is your bed satisfactory?" she inquired.

"Quite so, yes," Eileen said as Anna continued to lace and tug. "Very comfortable."

"Ah, is good then. I shall have the men move your mattress, pillows and coverlets, yes? Too much change can be difficult, I find."

Eileen nodded a very grateful thank-you. Stepping into her low-heeled shoes, she was ready for her day, so happily weary was she at the close of which, some thirteen hours later, that she had forgotten she had been moved and had begun to walk away from the archduchesses' quarters before she caught herself and turned around, her soft laugh echoing in the corridor.

When she reached her apartment, a smiling Anna greeted her at the door. "I have just now delivered to you your new winter cloak, and I thought perhaps you might not yet have been given the keys to your dressing room," she said, jiggling a ring holding two shining brass keys in the air.

"Anna, thank you! How kind of you, especially as, no, I have not." Plucking the ring out of the girl's proffering fingers, Eileen bid her a good night. As she turned to close the door, Anna held the door with her fingertips for a moment, saying softly, "Should you require *anything*, remember . . ." and as Eileen lightly stepped into her new home, Anna made a tugging motion in the air.

Having quietly closed the door behind her, Eileen leaned back against it. *My, my—how far have we come in so short a time, my good self,* she thought as she surveyed her new domain. A fire blazed merrily beneath a mantel upon which gently flickered a brace of new candles in a pair of double candelabra, their glow reflected in a large mirror hanging above. Though the heavy drapes were drawn against the cold of a Vienna December night, Eileen tugged one aside to peer into the darkness, broken below only by the occasional lantern and, in the sky, a dazzling display of stars and a perfectly full winter moon— larger, brighter, more brilliant than any she felt she had ever seen.

Closing the drapes, Eileen turned back to her sitting room; *my sitting room*, she thought. The sofas and chairs were obviously new and matched, with mahogany wood and gold-threaded white and light blue–striped upholstery, complemented by a predominantly blue rug with white striping. The tables and several small bookcases were gleaming mahogany as well, the shelves already partially stacked with the little library she had brought with her. The white paint was gleaming, the gilding on the chair rail, the crown moulding, the cornices, all flawless. *'Twas perhaps worth the war of words amongst the craftsmen after all.*

As she slowly circled the room, delicately touching the fabrics, rubbing the woods of her furnishings, she noticed for the first time—tucked quietly away in a corner of the parlour—a delicate, crème-coloured cylindrical object of some three feet in height, perhaps a wee bit more, with an understated design of vines and tree boughs crafted into what proved to be its ceramic bulk. As she drew near, she felt *warmth*; curious, she reached out to touch it with her fingertips, just barely doing so as the object was hot!

Slipping off her shoes, Eileen stepped onto a thick, dark blue woven rug and into her bedroom, already made comfortable by a less dramatic but still gently warming fire, the room dominated by a massive mahogany canopied bed, a single candle soothingly flickering on her nightstand, the bed already turned down and welcoming. Looking into the room's corners, she saw again the porcelain stove, smaller but appearing very much like the one in her parlour.

On a chaise with flower-and-vine upholstery lay the winter cloak Anna had delivered and of which she had spoken.

Lifting it, Eileen gasped. *'Tis truly magnificent!* And so it was: full-length, dazzlingly bright soft, heavy folds of red wool, trimmed literally from head to toe in a striking silver-grey fur—was it fox, perhaps? Eileen had never seen a fur garment before—with a large, similarly fur-trimmed and -lined hood; the clasps on the front were made of gold, inlaid with what appeared to be fine rubies, complementing the fabric. Draping it about her shoulders, Eileen stepped into her dressing room and stood before a full-length looking glass. She admired herself, drawing the hood up to just past the middle of her head and turning slightly. *My, my, my . . . even Mistress Eileen never had a cloak such as this.*

Looking about at her neatly displayed, carefully arranged—and, she continued to feel, vast—collection of dresses and gowns and everything millinery she could possibly desire, Eileen nevertheless yawned, and yawned yet again. Noticing the embroidered belt subtly hung by the door, she gently tugged it, as she had seen various people do—and as Anna had just indicated she also was now able to do—and within moments she heard a gentle knock at her front door.

Anna softly padded in and stood at the dressing room door, then raised her hands and wiggled her fingers smilingly at Eileen. "I untie you!" she offered, trying out her English, and whispered, "Your cloak, it is lovely, yes?"

"It is lovely, *yes!*" Eileen smiled broadly and yawned again as Anna slipped the garment from her shoulders.

As the disrobing progressed, it was Anna, responding to Eileen's questions, who advised her mistress that the stoves were the principal sources of heat in most of the vast palace's apartments, telling Eileen that they were fired by an army of virtually-invisible men known at court as "stove-stokers," from hidden, parallel "heating passages," thus avoiding soiling the rooms. Eileen would come to learn that the many fireplaces throughout the palace served primarily to augment the stolid, virtually-unnoticed ceramic heaters, and—unlike at Derrynane or any other place she had ever been—more than anything else, they served to provide a cosy ambiance and charm.

As Anna was brushing Eileen's hair—as she did, morning and night—she happily related that she, too, had been moved, her simple shared quarters being just on the other side of the building, " . . . and it, too, has a stove." She smiled happily.

Yawning several times as Anna handed her up into bed, Eileen was tucked in and asleep in less than a quarter hour.

The Hofburg—Winter 1762

The O'Connells' first Christmas in Vienna, during which the Imperial family made every effort to include the young women in as many events as possible, was a joyous round of festivities: concerts, balls, wonderful food and drink and extraordinary music. A small parcel of gifts, primarily books, had arrived from Derrynane, sent by Maurice and their mother not long after they had departed, the girls happy they had dispatched a large book of coloured drawings of Vienna to the family shortly after they had arrived in the autumn, as well as a set of toy soldiers for Hugh and two dolls, dressed as little archduchesses, for Anne and Elizabeth.

Not long after the beginning of the new year of 1762, Vienna began to be buffeted by a lengthy series of spectacular snowstorms, the likes of which Abby and Eileen had never experienced.

In the midst of an exceptionally dramatic one in February, Eileen found herself drawn repeatedly to the high windows of her apartment—indeed to any windows she was near, including those in the suite of the little archduchesses—and staring in wonder and, at times, disbelief, at the swirling, frequently wind-driven whiteness.

"Does it never stop?" she said half aloud in her soft French to no one in particular early one morning as the little girls were finishing their hot chocolate.

Antoine gently put down her cup at the gleaming little mahogany table at which she and Charlotte had been sitting, stepped to Eileen's side and took her hand between her two small ones. "Are you afraid, Lady Eileen?" she asked, her voice soft, evidencing a child's genuine concern.

Eileen smiled and quickly knelt; she had become sensitive to the fact that, though Hugh and her little sisters hadn't, both Charlotte and Antoine seemed to crane their necks whenever they spoke to her, save when at least Eileen or all three of them were seated. "Oh, no, my darling! 'Tis just that I have never seen snow like this before. Remember, I told you it hardly ever snows at Derrynane because the ocean there is magically warm."

In the months since Eileen had begun as part governess, part teacher—these roles under and clearly subject to Countess Brandeiss—as well as riding mistress, companion and friend to the two young archduchesses, they had spoken frequently of Ireland, Kerry and Derrynane itself, and the children were enchanted by her vivid descriptions of the unimaginably-green land, the looming grey mountains, the restless sea and the colourful array of people, as well as tales of her travels on Bull. As time passed, Eileen was pleasantly surprised to discover that she was also able to speak of the positive aspects and experiences of her time at Ballyhar, such as the grand Midsummer's Eve celebration. "You danced in your bare feet on the lawn? How exciting!" Charlotte had cried.

Eileen and the little girls were enjoying getting to know one another. As long as she in no way appeared to threaten her position or challenge her authority, Countess Brandeiss seemed to genuinely welcome her presence.

Eileen's days with the archduchesses began early: Anna would bring her a silver pot of dark black coffee, pastries and fresh fruit, which she sipped and nibbled whilst dressing, after which Eileen would briskly make her way to the little girls' bedrooms. If either one or both was still sleeping, she would gently awaken the child and have any number of young serving girls assist with their toilettes, whilst Eileen would oversee their dressing, see to it that their table was set properly and received their breakfast.

The little girls were then brought to table, where, after a brief prayer, Eileen would supervise and occasionally share in their breakfast. Sitting in her own small chair, she would invariably have a more relaxed cup or more of the strong Viennese coffee she had come to enjoy.

Countess Brandeiss supervised their studies; Eileen assisted, noticing that neither little girl appeared to be working as hard as she herself had been made to by the various tutors by whom she had been taught at Derrynane over the years.

"Perhaps that is the way it is with royalty, sister," Abby had opined on one of the rare evenings they had gotten to spend together.

Both Abby and Eileen happily agreed that it was solely Countess von Graffenreit's doing that they found themselves alone and free for an evening, during which they were served wine in Abby's parlour and then dinner in Eileen's, settling before her fireplace for a wee bit o' brandy and the type of conversation they had shared daily at Derrynane.

Slippers removed, bare feet daintily propped up before the fire, they were once again the O'Connell girls, and happy to be so.

"Ah, my love, how strange it is to say this—as we live, though vast it may be, under the same roof—but 'tis true: I have *so* missed you!" Abigail smiled as she poured both of them a wee bit more out of the Irish-made, cut-glass decanter into matching brandy snifters and handed Eileen's glass back to her.

"'*Tis* true, sister dear." Eileen smiled, toasting Abby as she leaned back. "So busy we both have been; though I am thoroughly enjoying everything, I did not think separated it was that we would become." She sipped, then feigned a pout, a slight flush on her full cheeks.

"I am loving it all . . . yes," replied Abigail, "but I must say: I both adore and am in utter awe of Her Imperial Majesty. Even though we begin each day at dawn. Can you imagine me? *Dawn*! Everything Uncle, everything the countess has said, pales in light of being with her, watching her, listening to her. I sometimes find myself just staring, listening to her. Then she smiles or nods and I know to be about my tasks, but 'tis difficult: This woman is ruling much of Europe and I am in her presence much of every day." Abigail shook her head and smiled ironically, then nodded to her sister: *and you?*

Eileen rested her head back, gazing into the flames and gently swishing the brandy in her glass. "Whilst my days are in no way like yours, I, too, am fascinated by it all, though it is the fact that both of my little girls will, in a few short years, be queens of some kingdom. Even now, the Countess Brandeiss tells me that my Charlotte is the subject of active conversations, perhaps even my sweet Antoine as well!"

Abby swirled her own brandy and nodded. "Your sweet Antoine, too, is indeed a topic. The empress has indicated to me when I should be still and listen and, afterwards, will say 'You have heard. You may quietly mention this to . . .' and she will indicate a very tall person. Though 'tis just now that I am having the chance to do so: The countries of which you hear are correct," she whispered circumspectly. "Though 'tis Archduchess Joanna who is of prime discussion of late, not one of your archduchesses." Abby paused. "These little girls are indeed like chess pawns, are they not?"

Eileen nodded. "'Tis, after all, consistent with the dynastic motto, is it not?"

Abby smiled quizzically. "Only *you*, my darling, would have learnt the 'dynastic motto.' And it is . . . ?"

Eileen smiled broadly, mischievously reciting, "Since you insist, 'tis . . . *'Bella gerant alii, tu, felix Austria, nube'*!"—which, after a playful pause, she laughingly translated, in a commanding, faux-pompous tone, "'Let others wage wars, but you, happy Austria, marry'!"

Abby shook her head and the sisters laughed.

"Is it not nevertheless difficult," Abby queried after a moment, "to think of these children as shortly being sovereign monarchs . . . even by virtue of marriage?"

"It is hard indeed," Eileen nodded, "especially as they seem so in need of affection. I cannot imagine having to share Maire with much of the world, yet they must so share their mother . . . and their papa."

As Eileen then told her sister, the little girls' lessons were interrupted most days by brief visits from the empress and the emperor, sometimes together, sometimes not. Eileen said she had come to find both of them delightful, though both she and Abigail recalled that they had been quietly advised by Countess von Graffenreit that Emperor Francis Stephen "is quite well-known for his roving eye and very active, shall we say, hands," and at that moment Eileen's eyes had opened just a bit wider. "It is a source of disconcertment, yes, that is the word," the countess explained. "He adores Her Imperial Majesty and the children, but . . ."

Eileen had nodded. ". . . but he is a *man!*" She had smiled archly, and both women understood each other completely.

Eileen related this to her sister, as well as the fact that she had eventually come to be introduced to the much-spoken-of Princess of Auersburg, a truly beautiful girl Eileen's own age with her gleaming dark brown hair tumbling over her trim shoulders, who, both O'Connells had learnt, was the emperor's current fascination.

"I was compelled to curtsey," Eileen said with a sigh, "her being a princess, but I truly believe she saw my thoughts in my eyes, my expression. As soon as I rose, I removed my hand from hers, smiled and withdrew. I also feel she was somewhat intimidated by General O'Connell," she added naughtily. "'Twas to him that I said, 'I do not see myself as a prig . . . but 'tis so untidy!' querying, 'Is it not, Uncle?'"

Eileen indicated to Abigail that the baron had shaken his head. "My darling, I have never heard it characterised as such, but you are quite correct, very *untidy* it is indeed, but *it* is also a reality of life here."

At that point Eileen had leaned closer to her tall uncle. "Does the empress not know? Does she not care?" In response O'Connell had sighed. "She knows and cares, deeply . . . and she is wounded deeply, for she adores him, as he does her, though not enough to be faithful. It is terribly complex, my dear girl. One of the very many things with which you are charged is to see that your little girls remain innocent of this type of behaviour. At all costs, yes?"

Eileen recalled nodding vigorously, and both O'Connells had gratefully accepted just then proffered glasses of champagne.

Cupping her snifter, she sighed and relaxed a bit, as, slipping unexpectedly into Irish, Abigail advised, "Ah, met the Princess of Auersburg I have as well, my darling, and 'twas not pleasant for me to do so either, the curtseying and all, though the look on her face, part shock, part fear, part arrogance when I was presented—when she heard 'the Lady Abigail O'Connell of the Kingdom of Ireland, secondary lady-in-waiting to Her Imperial Majesty, the Empress'—ah, now *that* was lovely, it was. I was civil, but I fear just barely so. I did not have Uncle at my elbow, but Denis O'Sullivan gently removed my good self from the 'danger,' he did." She laughed, more at her deliberately convoluted Irish sentence construction than at the recollection.

At the mention of the officer whom she had come to refer to as the "dashing Captain O'Sullivan," Eileen smiled warmly at her sister; she was genuinely happy for Abigail, though they had had little conversation regarding what the future might hold. Eileen purposely chose not to inquire. *Abby will tell me when there is something to tell.*

Though Eileen had begun to take notice, even selectively indicating her appreciation of the ever-increasing attention being paid to her by a myriad of young officers and Austrian nobles, at this moment in her life she was quite grateful that much of her time was spent with and amongst children. *'Tis far easier, less stressful and much tidier,* so she had thought frequently, and now so advised her elder sister.

Abigail said, "Noticing you they are, my love, I must tell you . . . and asking as well: 'Who is that? From whence has she come? Where does she spend her days?' and I simply smile and perhaps say, 'Oh, that tall girl? She is my younger sister . . .' and I say no more, so 'tis with intrigue that I am cloaking you, my darling." She laughed, and Eileen tossed a heavy linen napkin at her.

Always elegantly attired in a constantly changing series of afternoon dresses, as required by even the considerably relaxed court etiquette of Maria Theresa and Francis Stephen, and the flowing train of her dress notwithstanding, Eileen found herself quite comfortable sitting on the floor with the children whilst they played with their dolls and other toys, and both archduchesses seemed especially to enjoy cuddling up with her when she read to them.

Eileen carefully chose her—and the archduchesses'—reading material. She herself had long been fascinated by *Robinson Crusoe* but decided the topic was a bit frightening, so she relied heavily on *Mother Goose* and the more humorous excerpts from Jonathan Swift's *Gulliver's Travels.* She had mentioned the fact so frequently that every time Eileen sat down with *Gulliver,* one or both of the little archduchesses would say, in well-practised English, ". . . and Jonathan Swift was an *Irish*man!" and giggle. Eileen judiciously avoided mentioning that he had also been dean of St. Patrick's Cathedral, Dublin, Church of Ireland, and thus was a heretic, though he did write well.

At Derrynane, Eileen recalled, they had always taken the *Lilliputian Magazine*, begun in 1751 by John Newbery in London, and had acquired virtually all of what had proven to be the substantial number of children's books that company had published since the 1740s. Eileen was disappointed that there were not as many such non-English titles available, at least not in Vienna.

Besides reading to, and with, them from books, Eileen told the little girls many Irish stories of the "good" fairies—she taught them to call them *Sioga*—and other magical creatures and happenings, such as Oisin and his time—carefully avoiding what had happened when he ultimately departed—in *Tír na nÓg.* Early on, however, Eileen had become aware of Maria Theresa's concern that her children know very little fear—of ghosts, as well as things like fire—and, seeing it in some ways akin to her own upbringing and life-long awareness of brave Queen Maeve, less so of nasty leprechauns until she was older, she both agreed with and honoured the empress's wishes. "So no tales of the banshees," she laughingly revealed to General O'Connell one afternoon when she came upon him whilst on an errand for Countess Brandeiss in a distant area of the vast palace.

She also had a considerable repertoire of Kerry stories, such as *The King with Horse's Ears*, as well as Irish tales with a special Kerry connection, like *Fionn mac Cumhail and the Fianna of Ireland*. "Way up over the mountains from Derrynane," she would gesture towards the looming, rough grey, gorse-punctuated heights she still saw clearly in her mind's eye, "is the village of Cill ar Ne, and 'twas there that the Fianna came to hunt," she'd say, her eyes growing wide. "And not far from there is Lough Brin, the lake named for Fionn's magical dog, Bran, who was always there to warn Fionn and the Fianna of the coming of any danger," she'd say, a sense of wonder in her voice, to the archduchesses of Austria and Lorraine, sitting across from her on the floor by the fire, their own eyes wide, enthralled.

At their request, Eileen told and retold the tales; to the continuing delight of the girls, she would expand, alter or change them each time she told one, much as Donal Mór and Maire had done when she was a little girl.

In addition to caretaking and teaching, she was also developing strong relationships with the sisters, both individually and collectively, especially as they had grown even more comfortable with her. She found one day that playfully referring to the little girls as "moppets," as she and all the O'Connells had been affectionately called by their parents and virtually the entire household when they were small children, made them giggle. One afternoon, a week or so later, Antoine announced to a bemused empress, "*Mama, nous sommes 'moppets'!*" causing Maria Theresa to turn a puzzled expression to Eileen. "*Quels sont les moppets?*" the young governess explaining, as best she could, that it was a seventeenth-century English term of endearment for small children that appeared to have no equivalent in German. Repeating the playful-sounding word—"mop-pet"—the empress smiled in approval; the expression had instantly become an integral part of the lexicon of the archduchesses' household. After that, Eileen's distinctive husky voice would more than occasionally be heard in the august halls of the Hofburg and elsewhere, calling out "Moppets!" immediately followed by the sound of delicate little-girl French slippers as the young archduchesses would laughingly race to her.

Each day, whilst one girl was working on her individual lessons, Eileen would sit with the other, and they would discuss a seemingly wide range of topics, including, sometimes on the same day, horses, pets, dresses and dreams.

Eileen learnt that Antoine loved music and singing, and they began to practise the harp together at least twice a week. Charlotte seemed on some days quite mature and sure of herself, very conscious of being the older sister, and Eileen sensed that Antoine loved having her as thus, looking to Charlotte frequently in a variety of ways, even one as basic as the choice between dark and white bread: "I prefer the white, please," Charlotte would say to Eileen as they sat to breakfast one morning; and "I prefer the white, please, also," Antoine would add, though looking at her sister and appearing pleased at receiving the older girl's approval of her choice.

As the girls matured and the three of them grew together in their relationship, Eileen saw Charlotte as being naturally brighter, more assertive and much surer of herself. Antoine, on the other hand, had a softer, dreamy personality. She saw in the girls parallels between herself and Mary, and Eileen became more conscious of her own assertive, self-assured persona—and, in doing so, became more sensitive to the needs and increasingly more protective of Antoine.

"Charlotte is able even at this young age," Eileen had mentioned to Abby, "to care for—indeed even to protect herself—whilst my wee little Antoine is far more vulnerable." Abby understood and agreed with her sister.

Brandeiss had advised Eileen early on, "The archduchesses, they are so close, as were they twins, really," so Eileen took time one blustery March afternoon to discuss with both of them the pros and cons of twinship, reminding them that she was a twin herself.

"My sister Mary and I are so very different; you two, however, are very much alike, and that is a wonderful thing," she would say somewhat wistfully.

"How are you different?" Antoine queried, leaning back against a cushion, her soft, almost dreamy blue eyes on Eileen.

Sighing softly, giving herself a moment to craft her response, Eileen began, "To start, she is more than half a foot shorter than I," and the little girls laughed.

"Does she have long, long, *long* black hair?" asked Charlotte, and Eileen nodded no. "'Tis only to her shoulders, and 'tis a very light brown."

And so the conversation continued, until Antoine, her little face sombre, asked, "But are you and Mary *friends?*"

Eileen thought for a moment of her quiet, sometimes distant but often sweet twin and smiled softly. "Yes, yes, we are . . . but you must also understand that 'tis often the case that a twin may be closer to another sister. You have seen the lovely lady relatively new to your mama's service, yes? The one with the beautiful smile? She is my older sister, and 'tis with and to her—her name is Abigail—that I am closest in my whole family. So you see, my little ladies, one can be very close but very different and still be good sisters and good friends." She gathered both girls in her arms and they all hugged one another.

Brandeiss, who had been standing unseen in the archway, smiled and walked away, humming softly.

As Countess von Graffenreit had indicated they would, shortly after Christmas she and Abigail had indeed discussed at length Abby's immediate and longer-term future in the household of the empress.

In the midst of what was clearly intended to have been a glittering dinner party hosted by Maria Theresa and the Emperor Francis Stephen, for what appeared to Abby to be a group of very elderly, retired courtiers, men and women both, the progress of which—not for the least of reasons being the advanced ages of most of the guests—had slowed considerably, making the evening now seem interminable, Countess von Graffenreit stepped to her side as Abby stood behind the empress.

"Abby, darling, after our Mass tomorrow, please join me in my apartment. We shall eat excellent food, including superb pastries," she laughed warmly, "and drink excellent wine . . . and talk and visit."

Abby smiled brightly and whispered, "*Oui, merci, Comtesse.*"

When Abigail finally returned to her quarters, she was ecstatic to see that a steaming hot bath awaited her in a copper tub in her dressing room.

She smelt the sweetness of the perfumed soaps as soon as she stepped into her parlour and only peeked in the dressing room before she stepped out into the corridor to see a beaming Elena, her very young—perhaps thirteen or fourteen, Abby had estimated—very sweet maid, with whom Abby had become fast friends. "Thank you so much, my dear!" She smiled.

"My pleasure, my lady. You have had a very long day. Soak! Relax!" she replied, and Abby did precisely that, with Elena speeding her into the tub by assisting her in disrobing even more quickly than she typically did.

Consistent with her reputation as being the soundest sleeper and most reluctant riser at Derrynane, so soundly did Abby sleep this night that it was Elena who gently awakened her in the morning, with barely enough time to dress and hasten to the small chapel where Mass was celebrated for members of the empress's household. Elena assisted Abby in hastily donning a soft grey afternoon dress, quickly but elegantly pinned her tousled hair, provided a demitasse of thick black coffee and pointed her toward the fastest route to Mass.

At the rear of the chapel, Countess von Graffenreit was smilingly awaiting her. "Elena is an efficient dresser, yes?" She laughed softly. "I requested her to permit you to sleep as long as possible." Taking Abigail's arm through her own, the countess led the tall young Irishwoman down the aisle to a pair of first-row, high-backed chairs. After first genuflecting to the Blessed Sacrament, whilst the countess then did the same, Abby sank momentarily into a soft cushion before kneeling on an equally soft prie-dieu.

Abby found her first chapel Mass to be a simple, efficient, no-nonsense celebration. Even the sermon was brief. Immediately afterwards, von Graffenreit eased Abby and herself out of the chapel and away from the small congregation, and they walked quickly to the countess's apartment.

As promised, both the food and wines were excellent, as were the pastries, of which the countess had two, perhaps three whilst she gently watched Abby, in the most delicate way possible, daintily nibble her way through the rest of the small tray's offerings.

"We shall take a wee bit of brandy in the parlour," the countess advised, smiling at her Irish turn of phrase, and requested of the wine steward at the door, and she and Abby settled across from each other in a matching pair of seductively soft high-backed chairs. The warmth of the fire was on their faces, hands and feet as the countess daintily kicked off her slippers and indicated that Abby should do the same.

Abby smiled at the older woman, and von Graffenreit began, more directly than even she usually did, "And now, my dear, are you as happy and content as you appear each day?"

Abby's eyes widened slightly and she nodded vigorously, replying in an equally direct manner, "I am so very happy, much more than I thought I would be. Thank you so very much."

The countess rested her carefully coifed ash-blond head back against the chair and closed her eyes briefly. "That is very good. I am happy to hear. Now . . ."

Abby shifted slightly so she was facing the countess.

"As I indicated on your arrival we would, we shall now finally speak at some length."

Abby set down her brandy snifter and folded her hands in her lap.

"First of all, Her Imperial Majesty speaks highly of you, dear."

Abby smiled softly.

"Secondly, she does not often do that . . . though I believe not unreasonably so. She is a demanding woman who expects much of herself, her children and all of those who serve her."

Abby forced herself to sit and listen. *Say nothing, girl; keep quiet, listen and learn!*

"So, you have begun in a very positive fashion, for which, given my plans, I am most grateful," the countess said, at the same moment noticing a suggestion of puzzlement on Abby's part. Her green eyes twinkling, she continued, "You are curious about *my plans*, perhaps?"

Remaining silent, Abby nodded, though she did finally softly say *"Ja."*

"When His Grace, Baron O'Connell, first spoke to me of you, he spoke much: Many details of your personality, your interests, your abilities, your numerous strengths and . . ." she smiled broadly, "even your very, very few weaknesses, including—" and she laid her head aside on her hands and made gentle snoring sounds, then laughed affectionately—"which is why we have

Elena. Quite seriously, as I pondered all he said, including also your appearance, manner and personality, I began to think, for the very first time, of the future.

"You know I love Maria Theresa," she smiled at Abby's reaction at her use of the empress's name, "and each day in her service is a gift from God. No monarch could ever have been kinder than she at the time of the count's death . . ." she paused, "was to me. Without her, I could not have continued on. You are perhaps not aware of this, but I have two daughters: the younger one, also Maria, who is your age, and the older one, Elisabeth. Both—*both!*—are titled young women, wed to fine gentlemen of wealth and position, men who my girls adore and who adore them. The reason I say this is that . . . I believe the Irish use a term, *matchmaker*, is it? The matchmaker for these very happy marriages was the empress herself."

She paused, sipped her brandy, thought and paused, while a rapt Abigail, whose mind was whirling, also thought: *How sad her loss of the count must have been, him dying in battle; how wonderful for the empress to have been so kind; how lovely for her, having daughters; 'tis so glad I am that she has a family. . . .*

The countess went on. "All of this being said, I am not a young woman, and I feel quite responsible for providing Her Imperial Majesty with . . . shall we say . . . a *successor*, at such time as I choose to leave my post." She looked intently at Abby. "You are a bright young woman; you understand what I am saying, do you not?"

Abby's face flushed and her hands formed tight little fists in her lap.

"Do you not, Lady Abigail?" She feigned an arch expression, though it quickly dissolved into a warm smile.

Abby took a very deep breath. "Your Grace, I believe I may understand. . . . Though, to say I do, it would seem to me—were I you, though, of course I am not—that I was a terribly prideful and, yes, perhaps terribly arrogant young woman . . . barely here a matter of months, and . . ."

Maria von Graffenreit laughed—warmly, effusively—and laughed again.

"Oh, my darling!" she said. "You are further from being prideful and arrogant than any person I have ever known!"

Abby sat back and smiled, though her hands were perspiring.

Von Graffenreit poured herself—and Abby—another brandy and sipped hers deeply. Her lovely face ever so slightly flushed, she continued. "We both understand of what I speak, *ja?*" She smiled across at Abby, who was cradling her brandy snifter between her hands and nodded silently, *yes.*

"I am a titled woman, the widow of a beloved man, a *hero*, in truth. I have a small castle, of which few are aware. I have more resources than I require. I am blessed with my beautiful daughters, and," she leaned forward conspiratorially, "I am to be *twice* a grandmamma in the coming months." She laughed heartily. "My hope in bringing you here was that you would prove a *gift*; my thought was that if you even approached being the woman of whom your dear uncle told me so much, I could seriously consider that you might—should you wish it, of course—possibly succeed me here." She sat back and sighed, thinking, *There, I have said it. Will she consider me mad? Will she flee this room now?*

Abby took a deep sip of her own brandy and gently set the Irish crystal glass on a tiny table at her elbow. "Your Grace, I do not know all that General O'Connell has said of me to you, but I do know he is a man not given to elaborations or untruths. He knows me very well, as he does my sister, and if what he has said gave you reason to think and feel in the manner you have expressed, I am truly humbled. . . . I do not know what else I can say . . ."

"There is nothing for you to say, darling, save that you will not say *no,* absent further conversations between us."

The women sat quietly, the popping and crackling of a revived fire and the ticking of the mantel clock being the only sounds in the room, as a heavy Austrian dusk began to envelop the palace and Vienna itself.

There were a number of conversations between the older woman and the younger over the ensuing months. Before they separated that first evening, the countess did request that Abby, at least for the present, refrain from speaking of it with Eileen—or anyone else, including General O'Connell—to which she agreed.

In the weeks and months that followed, Abigail learnt much of what being the Lady-in-Waiting to Her Imperial Majesty would involve, and she found it all *fascinating, intriguing; yes, that it is, most intriguing . . . I believe I could do this!* she would think to herself in quiet moments or whilst walking from one place to another in the vast palace. She came to understand that, if she agreed, it would be she who would ultimately administer the empress's household—the people and their duties, her appointments and schedules. She would, in addition, be, as the countess emphasised, a "discreet friend" and, at times, Maria Theresa's "closest companion."

"The empress and I have shared the greatest of joys, the most devastating of defeats and the most profound sorrows over these years," Countess von Graffenreit told her, ticking off the births—and deaths—of the Imperial children, victories at war and defeats in peace time, the, frustration, distress and on-going though rarely displayed rage of the empress at the conduct of her beloved consort.

Relatively early on, the countess did broach what she had called a "delicate topic," and she did it whilst the women were walking, heavily cloaked, through a gentle snow shower one morning in late January: "Please forgive me for being so forward, my dear, but am I correct in believing that you and Captain O'Sullivan of the Hungarian Hussars—did you know that was my beloved husband's command?"

Abby did, and she lowered her eyes in respect.

". . . that you have a, shall we say, understanding of sorts?" She stopped as the flakes dusted her bright red cloak.

Abby blushed. "We have . . . we have spoken, yes, Madame. I believe 'tis safe to say that, yes, Your Grace, we do . . . we do have such an understanding, though no time has been discussed and I hasten to add that I have not breathed a word of our *discussions* to Denis—to Captain O'Sullivan, Your Grace."

The countess smiled. "And have you 'feelings'?"

Abigail's face glowed, a sudden burst of summer sunlight in the grey of a Viennese snowfall. "Oh, Your Grace, I *love* him; I do!"

Von Graffenreit smiled, a soft, maternal expression on her own face. "And, if I may ask, how it is that you know . . . it," she began.

Apologising for interrupting, Abby immediately related Maire's words, spoken of Donal Mór being "a huge part of my heart, a huge part of my soul."

"*That* is how I describe my feelings for the captain," Abby said, her voice a mix of sweet emotion and steely certain firmness. "*That* is what *I* believe 'love' is."

"I believe that is a perfect definition. I have never heard love expressed as being thus, but with it I can agree," the older woman responded softly, a suddenly faraway expression on her gentle face.

They walked a bit farther, the snow lessening, their boots crunching in what snow had fallen and the ice on the cobblestones beneath.

"The reason I so forwardly mentioned this is that the position of which we speak is a demanding one, requiring much effort to learn, at the inception, though it becomes less stressful as one goes along, as you shall see . . . very, very quickly, I believe. The point I make is that a new marriage might . . ." She sighed. "You might find it better to delay marriage for a time, several years actually. . . ."

Abby stopped and turned to face the countess. "I do not believe that marriage is in the immediate offing. The captain indicates that, even with this dreadful war ending, his place will be in the field, or with some foreign embassy. I understand this, and he knows I do. We are both relatively young. We have time, God willing. . . . Also, quite honestly, he wishes a major's chevron on his sleeves before a wife he takes."

After pointedly making a mental note of O'Sullivan's military aspirations, the countess nodded. "So . . . a marriage in, say, two or so years would not present any difficulty," she murmured.

"No, Your Grace, no difficulty at all," Abby said firmly in English, and both women smiled, the countess taking Abby's hand as they continued their walk. It had resumed snowing.

As winter progressed, at least twice a week, usually on Tuesdays and Thursdays, Eileen returned to her apartment at midday and there met Anna, who assisted her in—as quickly as possible—changing from her afternoon dress into what at court was referred to as a riding habit, an elegant—not rough Irish—fine black wool short jacket and matching long full skirt, silk shirt and what Eileen pronounced a "quite stylish" narrow-brimmed Tyrolean felt hat with a perky feather and gleaming black boots.

Thus attired, after drawing her brilliantly red winter cloak about her, Eileen strolled alone to a private entrance several floors below and there awaited the little archduchesses, dressed not all that differently than she; from there they were all three bundled into a sledge, tucked in with heavy robes and blankets, for a short, speedy journey in the bitter cold.

Though the Winter Riding School was physically a part of the vast collection of buildings and wings that made up the sprawlingly-massive palace that the Hofburg had over the centuries become, by having the archduchesses and their riding mistress transported by sledge—or, in warmer weather, a carriage, or having them stroll the distance—their riding lessons had become a more special occasion, far more pleasant for the trio than trudging by foot through the immensity of the palace's interior.

As they rode, the little girls and Eileen laughed and chattered and sometimes even sang, during the at most ten-minute sledge ride, their breath frosty in the cracklingly sharp air. The horses' bells gaily marked their progress to the huge, ornate white building that housed the renowned Winter Riding School, also known as the Spanish Riding School, as it had thus been named for the horses that originated from the Iberian Peninsula during the sixteenth century and were considered especially noble and spirited, as well as willing and suited for the art of classical horsemanship. Eileen learnt that, in 1729, the empress's father, Emperor Charles VI, had commissioned the magnificent structure in which they rode, and it finally had been completed in 1735. She had immediately fallen in love with the edifice, its history and all that went on within, to the extent that she had come to regularly smile at the massive portrait of the monarch, mounted on a magnificent white charger, which graced one end of the splendid riding hall.

By asking many questions, as well as being directed to books—the majority of which, being in German, she had to have parts read to her—Eileen had been fascinated to discover that the Spanish Riding School was the oldest riding academy in the world, and the only one at which what was called the

High School of Classical Horsemanship had been maintained, since at least the mid-sixteenth century.

Though the training and riding of the magnificent animals was done exclusively by men, Eileen nevertheless enjoyed occasionally watching the stallions in training and in what she accurately felt were performances, much like ballet.

She had early on attempted to determine if Bull could learn any of the intricate movements but laughingly gave up when one of the handsome equestrians gently explained the extent and complexity of the horses'—and riders'—rigorous, decades-long training.

The young man, a lithely compact, golden-blond athlete of perhaps twenty-five years named Horst Spiller, who spoke fine English, was instantly charmed by the attractive Irish equestrienne, impressed both by her riding skills as well as her choice of a large stallion as her own mount. For all of these reasons, on a number of occasions during Eileen's years in Vienna, especially when they found themselves alone in the rink, he had permitted her to take his own mount out into the arena, which she joyously did, always laughingly promising to "*noch nie davon sprechen!*"—never speak of this!—despite that their arrangement and activities were well-known about the institution. He similarly relished the opportunity these occasions provided him to ride the singular Irish chestnut.

On what was perhaps amongst the most memorable of any shared instance, one quiet late winter afternoon, perhaps two or three years after she'd arrived, Eileen delighted being aboard Spiller's solid little white stallion as the magnificently-schooled horse circled the ring several times and, with Eileen following Spiller's directions, remembering what they'd practised numerous times, successfully accomplished one of the Lippizans' most impressive manoeuvres, the demanding *capriole*, in which the horse made a vertical leap into the air from the *piaffe*—a cadenced, in-place trot—with all four legs kicking out, his hind legs such that his body became virtually horizontal. As with all of the jumps performed by the stallions, Eileen had to accomplish it without stirrups, finding it difficult not to let out a joyful *whoop* as the horse's hoofs again touched the rink's soft soil.

Today, as the sledge jingled to a halt outside the elaborate baroque entrance, they were greeted by a coterie of grooms and riding masters, who quickly unbundled the tall young woman and her small royal charges and hastened them into the relative warmth of the massive arena, their boots clumping over the polished flooring and thence padding onto the soft, almost silky, sawdust-laced soil of the riding rink itself.

From her first days in Vienna Eileen had found herself frequently employing the term *magnificent* to the buildings, rooms, churches, opera house—so much so that she'd inquired as to the appropriate German usage; advised that there were some thirteen—some tongue-twisting—ways of expressing the characterisation, she settled on *großartig*. It was as a result of her near-instantaneous feelings for the Riding School that she would quickly learn to say *wirklich großartig*, meaning truly magnificent. The phrase came to mind virtually every time she entered the riding hall itself: its galleries buttressed by, despite their size, almost delicate Corinthian columns, massive and dazzlingly white, the hall illuminated on gloomy winter afternoons by a series of extraordinary crystal chandeliers, their dozens of candles flickering, as if each flame danced to its own unique tune. The crowning intricately-fashioned vaulted ceiling above the lights was an extraordinary work of art in itself.

The breathtaking surroundings aside, it was the moment she and the archduchesses actually stepped onto the rink's soft soil that had quickly become one of Eileen's favourites. She would sound a familiar shrill whistle, so as to be heard by an as-yet-unseen listener, whose ears immediately perked and who was then immediately released by a stable boy into the rink.

"Bull!" Eileen would cry out and, as the little archduchesses invariably beamed, clapped and squealed with delight, the massive horse, his chestnut flanks gleaming as they never had before, even at Derrynane, his head high, tossing his black mane and flaring his long black tail, raced directly towards the three of them, only to pull himself up short, rear back on his hind legs and quickly circle the large rink.

Eileen could only smile, laugh and more than once shed a tear as she watched the magnificent animal who was also her dear friend, as he finally slowed, then walked towards them, stopping directly in front of Eileen, who rubbed his downy face with her soft leather glove and usually playfully planted a kiss on his nose, to the little girls' delight, their own small gloved hands gently stroking his flanks. Bull had also come to take notice of the sisters; his huge, soft eyes now gazed warmly on these little people, who seemed so fond of his beloved mistress, his own dear friend.

Though Eileen frequently rode alone, or with other adults, at other times during the week, these afternoon events had become special and joyous occasions shared only by her and her little charges and in which they revelled.

Whilst Eileen held Bull—and indeed frequently inspected him, even lifting his hoofs and checking his teeth—a groom, standing on a small ladder, set a thick padded saddle blanket and then her splendid Spanish saddle on Bull's back. Permitting the groom to complete the tacking, Eileen turned as the little girls clambered up onto their own mounts under her careful gaze. She watched and then walked towards them as each sat in her saddle. Wordlessly, using a crop as a pointer, Eileen would tap Antoine's booted toes—point them up—then, reaching under her long skirt, tap Charlotte's calves, encased in her high boots: straighten them. Handing off the crop to a stable boy, she would step between the horses, her gloved hand rubbing Charlotte's right and Antoine's left thigh, squeezing the muscles. "Tighten, squeeze, tighten, relax . . . Squeeze your horse now! Yes, like that!" Soon neither Eileen nor the archduchesses needed to say a word; she came to speak with her eyes, her facial expression, her smile, even an occasional frown.

Then Eileen would step back and look up at the girls, now astride their horses, with their shoulders straight and their heads held high, and as she watched, it seemed to her that they appeared to sit even straighter.

Clapping her hand, Eileen called out, *"Allez vous, maintenant!"* and the girls would turn their horses' heads and click to the animals, riding away from Eileen. *"Rapidement,"* Eileen called out, her husky voice clear in the otherwise quiet rink, the horses' hoofs muffled by the thick soil. On her command, the girls urged their horses into, at first, a fast trot, followed by a controlled gallop.

"Bien, très bien, mes enfants," Eileen called out as she swung effortlessly up onto Bull and had him quickly take them to where the children had, on her direction, stopped short, turned and now sat, awaiting her.

For the next two hours, the world in which Eileen and the little girls dwelt was one of soft, sawdust-scented soil and sweet-smelling hay, both mixing with the not wholly unpleasant odour of fresh dung and magnificent animals, following their riders' directions, trotting, cantering, galloping, walking and, on selected afternoons, jumping.

Some days the archduchesses would practise sidesaddle, others astride; on other days Eileen would choose to have only one of them mounted sidesaddle. At times she would walk, at others stand still in the middle of the rink; much of the time she spent astride her beloved horse. She and the girls would occasionally stop to chat; she would joke with them, they would all laugh, but always Eileen was teaching and they were learning, even if the children did not understand that they were.

As she watched her charges go through their paces in this setting, Eileen found it very easy to forget that both girls were destined to ascend European thrones in the coming years, though when she did consider that reality, she told herself that no matter the domain over which each would rule, the queen of that land would be an equestrienne with few equals. Their time on horseback together would continue virtually until both archduchesses departed for their adult lives.

One afternoon she called out, *"Regardez moi, et regardez Bull,"* and the archduchesses sat astride their horses, their gaze fixed on their young riding mistress and her horse. Their eyes grew wide as Eileen leaned back in her saddle, her hands resting on her thighs, Bull responding effortlessly as she guided his movements—walking forward, turning left, then right, stopping, circling, even bowing to the awed archduchesses—principally by using her knees, with only the lightest of tugs on his reins, an occasional gentle heel and, sometimes, a softly spoken word.

As she had Bull walk her to where the girls and their horses were, Eileen smiled. *"C'est dressage,"* she pointed out, very briefly explaining the theory, technique and practice of being able to direct and control the motions of a horse with the minimal use of a rein or bridle. "I shall teach you, and Bull and I shall help you teach your horses," she told the little archduchesses as they were being tucked back into their robes and blankets for the return trip.

On one particularly cold though brilliantly sunny afternoon, Eileen leaned towards the sledge driver and asked, "*Würden Sie bitte übernehmen Sie uns für eine kleine Fahrt?*" As he looked at the young Irish officer whose group of dragoons awaited the sledge's departure, Eileen smiled and said, "I have asked if we might have a wee bit of a sledge ride before we go home. Their Imperial Highnesses have worked very hard at their riding today."

"*Ja!*" the young man called out, smiling broadly, and the little caravan moved merrily off down a broad, snowy and—thanks to the cavalrymen who, in response to a silent order and a deft flick of the officer's wrist, and had galloped ahead—suddenly empty boulevard, the horses' bells gay in the frigid air, the laughter and singing of the young woman and her little charges sounding equally joyous.

With dusk falling quickly, the sledge jingled to a halt at what was sometimes referred to as the archduchesses' entrance. There a fur-wrapped Countess Brandeiss awaited, her cheeks ruddy in the cold air, her face breaking into a smile as the little girls tumbled out of their blankets and robes onto the snowy pavement, chattering and laughing as they told the countess of their riding lessons and the wonderful surprise ride they had just had. The older woman listened smilingly and then sent them off with a young girl to prepare for their baths and evening meal.

"It was lovely, yes?" the countess inquired, still smiling as Eileen stood before her.

"Very much so; thank you for permitting me to ask," Eileen answered, her throaty voice slightly hoarse from their time in the ring as well as in the sledge. Eileen was learning much, finding that by making gently-diplomatic requests of Brandeiss, her superior would be far more likely to grant them.

Abigail, too, had been learning, and, as Countess von Graffenreit had foreseen, advancing rapidly. Seemingly overnight, the sweet Irish girl whom the empress herself had proclaimed "my ray of sunshine," and who at first had simply made everyone, from the Imperial family, nobles and servants alike, laugh, had transformed herself into a poised, genteel young woman, secure in her being, embracing all of what she understood it meant to be an O'Connell and carrying this daily into an often dizzying array of tasks and situations, which she completed and dealt with, according to all who observed her, with an ease—indeed an élan—not thought possible by some of them, which most definitely did not include the Countess Maria von Graffenreit.

"Certain I was that she would bloom!" laughed the countess, joyfully affecting an Irish lilt and sentence structure as she shared coffee one morning with General O'Connell. "I understood she was a bit awed at first, but . . ." Her voice trailed off as she nodded firmly. "I knew, I just *knew* she would be perfect and she is!" she finished, her hand resting gently on that of the baron's, who took it into his own, smiling softly.

"Happy it is that I am then, for the Lady Abigail and for you, my dear countess."

As the winter gently eased into an early, most-welcome spring, periodically the countess would outline a series of tasks for Abby first thing in the morning, or, more typically, simply advise her of the day's issues and problems; in either instance, she would then mysteriously disappear for hours at a time.

With no alternative to do otherwise, Abby proceeded to do what needed to be done, to solve the problems that needed to be solved, precisely as Countess von Graffenreit had anticipated she would.

Ironically, Abigail found her daily interaction with the empress herself in many ways less stressful than those with minor courtiers with protocol-ruffled feathers or wounded pride. Abby had little patience for those individuals whom she came to characterise as small people, no matter how exalted their positions or lofty-sounding their titles. She could be brusquely efficient, albeit totally respectful, in disposing of matters involving such persons, whilst extremely patient and calm with an errant servant or a cook who had spoiled the empress's midday meal.

"Mend it, then, we shall, my love," Abby would exclaim softly, sounding, were she to reflect on it, exactly like her mother in a somewhat similar situation, even to bustling into a kitchen and helping in the preparation of a replacement, the meat now unburnt, the bread being from the freshest bin. "See, then, solved it is!" she would call out, nudging the cook into the empress's dining room, with the words of a quickly but carefully scripted apology that Abby knew would satisfy Maria Theresa.

Abigail had come to move with a striking degree of ease in and out of the empress's presence. Together they had decided, during one of their informal weekly pastries-and-coffee get-togethers, that, whilst they were completely alone, should she wish to do so, Abby would henceforth be free to address the world's most powerful woman as "Madame," and that, at such times, curtseying could be dispensed with. Abby nevertheless began and ended each day with a curtsey to the empress.

As easy as it would be for someone in the position she found herself in to do, Abby never once crossed that delicately invisible line into the area of untoward familiarity with the sovereign. She instinctively understands, Maria von Graffenreit thought the very first time the empress had advised her of how Abigail had been conducting herself.

It was late in the winter that the empress had drawn General O'Connell aside one dreary afternoon, following a lengthy, at times acrimonious, council meeting, during which she had felt the Irishman had been especially effective in devising on the spot a workable consensus to a myriad of complex, interconnected fiscal problems—and even more effective in leading the by then discordant group of men in adopting O'Connell's plan, surprisingly without any significant debate.

State Chancellor Wenzel Anton Kaunitz-Rietberg was, in addition to his formal role, the empress's long-serving foreign affairs advisor. It was he who had negotiated the treaty memorialising Austria's historic rapprochement with her now-ally France, which, through his efforts, now supported Maria Theresa's own efforts to protect Austrian territory from the grasping hands of Frederick II of Prussia. Though at first highly-sceptical of the physically-immense, at times bluff military man, Kaunitz had come to share the empress's oft-expressed opinion of O'Connell's strength in terms of governance, coming to believe, as did she, that, unlike most career officers, the Irish general's significant military experience served him well in the wars of the conference table. On a number of occasions, such as today, he would yield, as he would oft-times jest, "command of the field" to O'Connell, frequently with—again, as today—more than satisfactory results.

Afterwards, the empress had discussed the general's thinking and, with some fascination, questioned how he arrived at his strategy, O'Connell answering, not quite matter-of-factly, "When one leads men in battle, one's mind must be sharp and quick, Majesty. I am blessed that mine has, or so it would appear, remained both!"

After laughing with her Irish warrior, Maria Theresa had grown quiet for a moment, the pause, as was her custom, suggesting a change of topic, which O'Connell had come to understand, so he, too, sat quietly, awaiting what would next be discussed.

"So, I continue to benefit from your military training and practices, yes, my dear baron?" The empress smiled. "Indeed, I appear to be benefitting from your presence here much more than I ever could have anticipated."

The general continued his silence, a warm expression on his face, as Maria Theresa cleared her throat. "My dear general, the fact of the matter is that, as I and the Countess von Graffenreit had both hoped and anticipated, your nieces have proven themselves to be much more than mere ornaments to this court."

The baron permitted himself a broad smile. *Ah, 'tis good to hear that*, he thought. *Hoping I have been that it would be thus . . . and that the dear lady would at some point so advise me.*

"Though lovely they were said by your good self to be and indeed quite beautiful they both are, they have also brought intelligence and substance, contributing in many ways to the workings of this complex place. Both of the young women possess strong personalities, though their personalities are different indeed. That it appears there are no limits to their abilities in resolving small and sometimes not-so-small daily 'crises,' be they involving my young daughters or a suddenly discontent courtier. What is apparent to me, and to the many individuals with whom I have spoken, is that, untitled as they may be, they are set apart from the many other lovely young women—young women of noble birth, some bearing many titles—who come to court by the fact that they appear to possess an innate sense and their own unique variety of nobility, as if it were in their blood, in their very being, as I have come to believe it indeed is.

"I know little other than what I have learnt from you, my dear baron, of the place, the setting from which they—and you, good sir—have come to us, but I now must say that your Derrynane, your Kerry, must be extraordinary places, and the house, the family in which these girls were raised . . . quite extraordinary as well. As I have come to both adore and respect the Lady Abigail, I must tell you that my youngest daughters are positively enthralled with the Lady Eileen. They, especially Antoine, chatter on about her: her wonderful stories and her prowess in the saddle. Thank you, my dear general, for these gifts you and your family have given me," she said.

O'Connell nodded at the empress, who grew quiet, indicating the general might now speak. "Your Majesty, I do not believe that I have ever heard the term *nobility* used to refer to the girls, or to the O'Connells"—he smiled—"though, upon reflection, I would agree that, especially as to Abigail and Eileen, the designation is indeed a wholly fitting one. As their blood is in many ways mine, I cannot speak as fulsomely as I perhaps feel, as arrogating to my own self some degree of *nobility*," he laughed softly, "it could be said that I am doing, but, this aside, and as Your Imperial Majesty knows me well, I dare say, I would agree that there is, yes indeed a certain *nobility* that pervades much of the life lived by them, as Your Majesty is to a degree aware, in the some-would-say desolate place from whence we have come to you.

"So, Your Imperial Majesty, *noble* it is that both they be, and *proud* it is that I am . . . of them, indeed of our family."

The empress smiled. "And so should you be."

Derrynane—late Winter 1762

"Brother, might we speak . . . in private, sir?" Daniel Charles O'Connell had quietly asked of his eldest brother, Maurice, as he came upon him very early one morning. Nodding, Maurice wordlessly led his younger brother through the house, so that within moments the two of them sat at the rough dining table in the kitchen house at Derrynane. With her innate sense, shared with her mother, Brigid, of there being a "reason for everything," Annie Moriarty had set porridge, a loaf of freshly-baked French bread, butter and a pot of fresh, near black Kerry tea for the older and younger brothers and quietly left the kitchen to the men.

Maurice, tall, thin, fair and serious, perhaps having grown even more so after the ouster and banishment of Denis O'Connell, took a deep swallow of the scalding brew and leant back, draping a long arm over the back of the rough, rush-seated chair, identical to the one in which his brother sat. His fair blue eyes suddenly softened. "Does now suit you, lad? We are alone, and I assure you I shall honour your confidence."

Daniel O'Connell, now sixteen and similarly tall, trim and fair, with an unruly shock of what Maire called "dirty blond" hair and eyes almost as blue as Eileen's, sat up a bit straighter. "'Tis a matter of great . . . I wish . . . it is very important to me, sir." He sighed in frustration until Maurice leant forward and spread his fingers on either side of the boy's thigh, just above the knee, and squeezed. "Och!" Daniel cried out, and laughed, as did his brother.

"My boy, I am not Denis, not one to be feared. I continue to attempt to emulate Donal Mór in as many ways as possible, with perhaps just a wee bit less tumult, avoiding the near-constant uproar," he said. "Now, lad, what is it?"

Daniel cleared his throat, his hands resting on his knees and his back straightened again. "'Tis about my future, sir, that I should like to speak."

Maurice smiled affectionately and nodded, gesturing for him to go on.

"Ever since I was a wee lad, my hope has been to become a soldier." Having said it, Daniel sighed with some degree of relief.

"I am well aware, my boy, and I both honour and respect your aspirations. The profession of arms is a proud one. I believe it tests a man, and I esteem those men we know who have taken it up."

Daniel smiled. "'Tis those very men, such as our dear uncle . . . as well as Captain O'Sullivan, sir, I have long admired and looked up to."

Maurice chuckled. "Especially 'our dear uncle,' I should think." He craned his neck, looking straight up at the whitewashed ceiling, and both man and boy then laughed, any remaining tension for the younger one being broken.

"Indeed, yes!" said Daniel.

Maurice leaned back in his chair. "'Tis a very appropriate time to speak of this, lad. We have been through much these many months, beginning with Eileen's departure and unexpected return. We have dealt with Denis." His face grew cloudy and he paused for a moment. "Tragic that, what a man can bring on himself." He looked at his younger brother and Daniel nodded, to show he had learnt from that.

". . . and Abigail and Eileen are now safely, and apparently from what we have heard from them and from General, the Baron, happily, indeed joyously, settled in Vienna. And our dear mother appears to have come through it all. . . ." His voice trailed off.

Daniel sat quietly; he had learnt to do that as well.

"So, lad, it is of Vienna, of service to the Habsburgs of which you are thinking?"

Daniel nodded. "Yes, sir, indeed whilst he was briefly here last . . . to pay court, I believe to dear Abigail," he smiled ". . . 'twas to Captain O'Sullivan I took the liberty of speaking. He believes a fine Hungarian Hussar I might make," the boy said brightly, sitting up just a bit straighter yet.

Maurice nodded. "I have no doubt of that, but would you listen a moment to me, lad? I speak not to dissuade you from your aspirations, but to provide you perhaps with yet another route to follow, or at least an additional one to consider."

Slightly puzzled, Daniel nodded. "Certainly, sir. I respect anything you might say."

"I wish to speak to you as a man now, brother, and share with you things that a man would understand but a child would not even think of," Maurice began as Daniel sat, his eyes fixed on his brother, quietly flattered at what he had just been told. His lips parted ever so slightly—a gesture most of the O'Connells seemed to affect in such circumstances: one of concentration and just a bit of surprise.

Maurice continued, "There are obvious reasons for a bright Irishman to follow a military calling in Europe, all laudable: One needs to look no farther than Moritz O'Connell, a full general at arms, ennobled as a baron, now apparently daily at the very side of the empress herself, to understand the obvious. Advancement, ennoblement justly deserved, hard-won honours and privileges . . . and I do believe the old fellow is fully enjoying life in all ways," he added, laughing warmly.

"But 'tis of the not so obvious that I speak: A man like General O'Connell, a man of great position, in addition to that position, is also, in fact, a representative of our family, our ambassador, if you will, to the Imperial court at Vienna. Whilst he honourably and faithfully serves his empress and sovereign, he also serves *our* interests, and this role is fully known to and acquiesced in . . . Nay! In actuality, 'tis supported—*strongly* supported—by Her Imperial Majesty.

"The general is our eyes and ears in Austria, both upper and lower . . . and," he smiled, "Hungary, Bohemia, Moravia, the Austrian Netherlands and I could continue. . . . You see, lad, he is invaluable to us, in terms of information, of both good and bad tidings, opportunities, possibilities. We move freely about much of Europe because of the presence of General O'Connell in Vienna . . . indeed, the Imperial grace, a direct result of his presence, covers us like an unseen mantle, protects us, indeed it enhances us . . . though, except for the general and now our sisters, none of us have ever been there.

"The reality, lad—and I do not expect that you have ever heard it expressed thus—is that, as inept as they are, as tenuous as their rule beyond the Pale may be, the English have in at least some ways succeeded at what Cromwell and his hordes began in the last century: They have rendered Catholics largely landless and illiterate"—his expression tightened and he shook his head—"in this, our own land.

"For those of us who, through the grace of God and our own continuing labours, have avoided this cruel dual fate, there is only so much that can be accomplished by remaining in Ireland; both our own interests, and those of Ireland as a whole, are better served by placing some of us strategically throughout Catholic Europe. Thus, boy, Lord Clare and the Dillons in France, yes?"

Daniel Charles nodded.

". . . and, as I have been saying, Uncle General the Baron in Vienna, *ja?*"
He laughed, as did the boy, before continuing, "Indeed, speaking of Vienna,
I believe it is important also for you to understand that the roles of our sisters
are, in many ways, no less significant or critical than that of the general. The
little girls for whom Eileen cares, they shall both ascend European thrones in
not too many years."

Daniel's eyes visibly widened. "I was not aware of that."

Maurice smiled, nodded and went on. "Whilst Abigail, our laughing and
smiling, sunshine-filled Abigail, spends her days largely in the presence of the
empress. So you see, our girls are valuable as well."

The boy was now obviously enthralled with the new things he was learning, flattered that his elder brother had taken him into his confidence.

Sensing this, and also that the lad could use a moment to absorb what he
had heard, Maurice paused and refilled his brother's teacup and his own. "I
believe you understand what it is of which I am speaking, yes, lad?"

Daniel nodded thoughtfully; though he found the information more than
a bit overwhelming, he did indeed grasp its significance, as well as the importance of General O'Connell, Eileen and Abby being in Vienna.

"My thought . . . and before I continue, I assure you that this is something we can certainly discuss, whilst our interests are being well protected in
Vienna, this, however, is *not* the case in France, lad, and it is this that I would
be grateful if you would consider remedying."

Daniel's mind instantly began to whirl: *France? The glittering court
at Versailles? The famous national brigades in the French king's armies, Irish
particularly, it harkening back to the first of the "wild geese" following the
Williamite victories, which led to the Treaty of Limerick at the end of the previous century.*

The young man nodded. "I shall consider any opportunity, any one . . .
which . . ."

". . . which places you in a proud brigade, and which might prove to
be of assistance to our family, perhaps?" Maurice asked, his facial expression
indicating to his young brother that he sincerely hoped he was not being inappropriate in doing so.

Daniel nodded again emphatically. "Yes, *sir*! Very much so, sir," he said, deepening his voice.

His brother smiled. "I have taken a great liberty, my dear boy. Anticipating that we would be having this conversation sometime soon, I have already communicated with General Dillon at Versailles. Indeed, his young nephew Arthur is, I should think, a relatively near-contemporary of yours. I trust you are not offended? I should deeply regret were I to have offended you, sir."

Daniel smiled broadly. "Oh, not *at all*, sir. 'Tis a fact that a wee bit flattered I am, brother, I must admit."

Relaxed—or as relaxed as Maurice ever would permit himself to be during these trying times—again, he continued, "A letter I expect I shall receive from him in a matter of days now."

Versailles,
6 April 1762

My dear friend Maurice —
How very pleased I was to receive your letter! I so enjoyed hearing of all the goings-on at Derrynane and the news of the many O'Connells. I find it very difficult to believe that Abigail and Eileen are old enough to have journeyed off to Vienna, much less that Maire would permit them to do so. Had I known their aspirations, I might have attempted to lure them into the service of Louis XV himself, but . . . ah, in truth, 'tis perhaps best that they are where they have gone. The lines at the Hofburg are a bit sharper than those at Versailles, and—even were they not—your good General O'Connell is, I am sure, caring for and watching over both of your girls. 'Tis good to know that the baron is well. In terms of freedom of movement about Europe, despite our sovereigns' alliance, we have been separated by this loathsome war, but it seems to be nearly at an end, when I shall embrace your uncle and indeed my many fine friends in the empress's armies, not soon enough will that come! Forgive me, my dear boy, for my lengthy discourse. I am not ignoring the purpose of your kind missive.
Pleased it is I am to learn of young Daniel Charles's aspirations. I recall him only as a wee lad, which brings to mind that he had fashioned a fine wooden sword, which I never saw removed from his belt, save when he did so to very briefly

permit me to hold it. So he has always had and never abandoned his desire pour
la gloire!

*I am grateful for your candour in terms of the boy's strengths and the areas in
which he requires direction, correction, and honest and true with you shall I
likewise be:*

*This is a propitious time for a boy such as Daniel to come to us, the war being in its
final stages. The officer corps—old and young alike—are weary; the old shall take
their leave, and many of the younger nobles who have served out of a sense of duty
rather than aspiration shall similarly depart, all of them to be replaced by the next
ranks below, who shall, in turn, energise the corps, augment* esprit *which is most
badly required, and, in the process of their own advancement in rank, themselves
leave ample places at the lowest commissioned rungs, to be filled by young man
such as your Daniel, entering service now, training as cadets and being educated as
young gentlemen whilst in the uniform and under the flag of France.*

*Of one critical point I must make you aware: The Irish Brigade is an exception-
ally weary place at least at the moment as we have suffered gravely, and it shall
require time and effort to heal it, all of its regiments. Whilst I should nevertheless
be pleased to—and would happily—receive Daniel into Dillon's Regiment, as I
am sure Lord Clare would into Clare's, please permit me to ask that you will allow
me a most humble but strongly made suggestion:*

*Were I a young man such as the boy or a man in your position of sending him off
to service here, 'twould be to the Royal Swedish Regiment—*Royal Suédois—*that
I would urge that you send him: 'Tis a vibrant officer corps, though to date and by
custom virtually all Swedish, such that both Louis and Alfonsus desire it to become
more eclectic; on Lord Clare's and my own humble recommendations a bit of a
royal mandate exists that 'tis to the Irish that the* Suédois *look for suitable officer
candidates.*

*I hesitate not a moment in this: 'Tis there Daniel should go, and trusting my
instinct, which, in turn, dear boy, trusts the instinct of your good self, I shall make
preliminary inquiries and arrangements even as I am posting this letter to you.*

*Were Daniel Charles my own son, I would recommend this course. As an aside,
my dear nephew, Arthur will shortly join us as well; would that I could place him
amongst the Swedish, but—what shall I say? Appearances do not permit me this
latitude.*

All of this said, I would foresee our young men will, in good time, be comrades together in the Irish Brigade, but for now I shall anxiously await news from you. Should he indeed come, please so advise me and I shall have him safely brought from La Havre, perhaps to my own chateau, perhaps directly to Paris, where I shall there await his arrival. In any case, I assure you that I shall personally see to his arrangements and placement. Please convey my most respectful and warmest regards to your extraordinary mother, as well as to all the other O'Connells, whether at Derrynane or elsewhere. Please know, sir, that I am now and shall always remain,

Most faithfully, your friend—and
that of all O'Connells—

Theobold Dillon,
General Commanding,
Dillon's Regiment, Irish Brigade

Schönbrunn—Summer 1762

"Lady Abigail, *Lady Abigail!*"

Abby heard the soft German voice coming from a distance; a great distance it must have been, for her head rested on the elegantly uniformed knee of Captain Denis O'Sullivan of her Imperial Majesty's Hungarian Hussars, as the officer himself leant back against a huge oak tree somewhere in the countryside beyond Schönbrunn, the majestic Imperial summer palace some five miles south of Vienna.

"Lady Abigail—please!"

Abby heard the voice again, a bit closer now. It sounded perhaps like sweet Elena, but how could it be? *'Tis just Denis and myself sitting here, a picnic we have had, even wine . . . and 'tis so lovely . . . so . . .*

"Oh, Abby! Please, Abby, please awaken . . . *please.*"

The hearer's tousled head peered over the light downy summer quilt and she yawned and smiled at Elena. Sitting straight up, Abigail shook her head, shook her shoulders and, in a single motion, was standing as Elena was covering her naked body with a dressing gown.

"Oh, my!" Abby exclaimed. "We've no time for morning's niceties; so sorry, I am *so* sorry. . . . The dress, please, my love, *please . . . the dress!*" and she streaked into her dressing room and, without meaning to, slamming the door, only to emerge within minutes, her toilette completed and a sheepish expression on her always sweet face.

"Dreaming I was, my love." Abby smiled as Elena skilfully assisted her in wriggling into—despite their presence at Schönbrunn and despite it being late July—what was still a relatively formal afternoon dress with a full train, though of a much lighter fabric.

"I think so, my lady, dreaming, yes," Elena said softly as she fastened the back of Abby's light blue dress and draped the train. "And I know was so late when you returned last evening; was a lovely ball, yes?"

Abby smiled—how fond she had grown of this thoughtful girl—and how she so thoroughly enjoyed Elena's increasingly frequent forays into the English language.

"Yes, it was indeed lovely, especially dancing with Captain O'Sullivan."

"Was also why I come now *early* . . . I know you sleep . . . sound? Yes, *soundly*, and I know Her Imperial Majesty, she be-gins at four o'clock, yes. . . ."

Abby was still rubbing her eyes as she squinted and peered at the tiny porcelain clock on her bedroom mantel. "'Tis only half-three then, yes?" she cried out in joyous relief.

Elena smiled her most glowing smile "'Tis, yes, *ja!*" and they both laughed.

Abby leaned over to kiss the girl's slightly moist forehead, "God bless you, the saints preserve you, you sweet, you magnificent girl!"

Elena waited by the full-length looking glass for both of them to view Abigail, who nodded at her reflection and smiled. "Done it again, you have, my love . . . rescued me you have!" Laughing the infectious laugh by which virtually the entire Imperial household had come to know her, the Lady Abigail O'Connell swept out of her apartment and strode purposefully down now familiar corridors to the cluster of Imperial apartments.

As she approached, a familiar, stolid, smiling man, just closing the door behind himself, greeted her, "Lady Abigail, *bon jour!*" effusively, indeed loudly, called the resolutely non-German-speaking Emperor Francis Stephen I, as Abby eased into a graceful curtsey.

"Bon jour, bon jour, Majesté!"

The emperor and the ebullient young Irishwoman, whom he knew to be what he called his spouse's "lady-in-waiting, in-waiting" had developed what Eileen had concluded and earlier in the summer had told her older sister was a largely genial "relationship of compromise":

"He knows you are aware of his 'activities' and that you know that he knows you look on them with disfavour. Nevertheless, he is an endearing old cad and you have become tolerant of him and them, and, in the process, even perhaps somewhat fond of him—and that he knows as well. He also knows that Her Imperial Majesty adores you . . . oh, yes, she does! Lastly, he has come to similarly adore you."

Abby had stood listening, her eyes wide, her voice—unusually—stilled, save for a barely audible, *"So?"*

"So . . . 'tis very much like the manure pile that built up at the stables at Derrynane that summer, when William and the other lads were all so ill and no one would muck it fully away: We all stepped around it, going about our lives, smiling and talking and living . . . and paid it no mind, though we obviously knew it was there and it was not going to be removed."

Having at least in her own mind fully resolved the matter, Eileen had then gathered her skirts a bit, smoothed her train and, quickly determining who was or was not about the place, uncharacteristically casually ambled off, down the corridors of Schönbrunn, her laughter merrily echoing in the august surroundings, causing those who heard it to smile.

Once she had yet again successfully dispelled any image of the Derrynane barns from her mind's eye, Abby smiled sweetly at His Imperial Majesty, the Holy Roman Emperor Francis Stephen, wished him an equally-sweet *"Bon chasse,"* and stepped into the Imperial office suite at precisely four o'clock.

Maria Theresa was already at her document-strewn desk; though obviously deep in reflection, she immediately looked up and smiled warmly as Abigail quietly entered. Despite their agreement as to informality whilst alone, Abby invariably began their day together with a graceful curtsey and a warm "Good morning, Madame."

"Sit, darling, please," gestured the empress. "Today is not an especially busy one, or so it appears," she began as she ticked off items on her calendar, cross-referencing with Abigail those times when her presence was required and those when not. "I believe today might perhaps be an opportunity to invite Captain O'Sullivan to luncheon, yes? Would you enjoy that?"

Clearly surprised, Abby's face glowed and her eyes brightened.

"Ah, is good then, because I have already requested his presence at precisely noon. I trust that comports with my lady's own calendar," the empress continued.

Abby nodded vigorously, her curls bobbing. "Thank you, Your Majesty," she whispered softly.

"Is only what a good mother would do for her daughter," Maria Theresa responded equally softly. "As your dear mother is so far away, *someone* must . . ." and her voice trailed off. "Captain O'Sullivan will await you"—she gestured—"on my portico, a luncheon of my choice shall be set for you; I trust you will find it satisfactory."

Abby smiled brilliantly, her curls bouncing merrily. *It would be perfect!*

At approximately half eleven, Captain Denis O'Sullivan reined in his grey charger at the entrance to which he had been directed by the sentries. Tugging off his gloves and folding them over, he slipped them under the saddle before handing the handsome animal over to a waiting stable boy.

He stood for a moment, surveying the loveliness that was Schönbrunn in the summertime, and walked slowly outside for a bit. Though the palace was but a relatively short distance from the intense confines of Vienna, its bucolic setting provided O'Sullivan with a sense of being far removed from the capital, not to mention the all too frequently monotonous training duties he was currently performing.

The young officer strolled briefly about the periphery of the palace's magnificent gardens, ultimately reaching the zoo, which had been established by the emperor in 1750. Never having wandered this far, he stood in mute amazement at the exotic animals. A pair of lions, their coats gleaming gold in the now warm spring sunshine, eyed him warily; then he craned his neck at a giraffe, who himself stared down at the cavalryman's striking uniform. It was only when O'Sullivan heard a distant church bell striking the noon hour that he abruptly turned, quickly making his way back to the palace—its wings open in embrace to him, he felt—and to Abby.

As he strode purposefully towards his destination, a number of individuals took note of the handsome officer. Denis O'Sullivan, who had been twenty-six on his last birthday, stood six feet and some four inches in height, trim, ramrod straight, with wavy dirty blond hair, elegant in his heavily gold-braided red Hungarian Hussars uniform. He carried himself—naturally and without effort—as an aristocrat, most fittingly as, in Gaelic Ireland—before the Elizabethan bloodbath of the 1570s and 1580s—his family, the O'Sullivan Mór, had held sway over southwest Kerry, the O'Sullivan Beare holding the same position in west Cork, beyond the Kenmare.

In the late sixteenth century, however, violently, brutally, mercilessly, the English queen's armies had visited upon the O'Sullivans massacre and defeat, largely dispossessing them of their ancestral lands. These losses resulted in more than a few O'Sullivans giving, as it was said, "their hearts and their swords" to the monarchs of Catholic Europe. Amongst the more notable, Denis's much older second cousin, Sir John O'Sullivan, had joined the Wild Geese in the Irish Brigade of the armies of Louis XV, achieving distinction and notoriety—little of it positive—in the service of Prince Charles Edward Stuart, especially in connection with "Bonnie Prince Charlie's" failed efforts to regain the throne of England and Scotland for the Stuarts. It was O'Sullivan's role in what became the cataclysmic defeat of the Jacobite army at Culloden Moor in April 1746 that won him small praise and widespread opprobrium, despite that there continued to be significant debate as to whether the tragedy rested with him or with Lord George Murray—or, as many now felt, with the "Young Pretender" himself.

In either case, O'Sullivan was credited with spiriting the defeated prince out of Scotland and, ultimately, to safety in Rome—from whence he had come and where he would die—after which Sir John eventually resumed his duties in France. Denis had found himself fascinated with the entire history of the Jacobite risings, continued to read all he could on the subject—and remained uncertain as to whether his relative was being treated fairly or not.

Denis O'Sullivan had been born and raised near Carhen, on the western side of the Iveragh Peninsula, several hours' rough ride from Derrynane, on a not insignificant holding his grandfather and father had, despite their dispossession, quietly assembled and secretly secured. At fifteen he had been sent, first to the university in Salamanca in Spain and later to the Theresian Military Academy, founded by the empress herself in December 1750, there to complete his education and ultimately commence his military service. A bright lad, he had matured into a brilliant young man, fluent in Irish, English, French, Spanish and German, literate in Latin, a voracious reader of poetry, the classics and history as well as a variety of professional tomes, great and minor, covering such military tactics as strategic battlefield positioning and the effective use of cavalry in hilly terrain.

He had seen significant action and had been seriously wounded several times during the Seven Years War, now lumbering towards an inconclusive end, and had been heavily decorated. Those to whom he passed closest could not help but note that the otherwise handsome officer bore the deep scar of a nasty cat-a-corner gash across his forehead and right cheek with stoic grace; he was more sensitive to its possible effect on children than anyone else, and had concluded that an application of powder usually softened its impact. He was an able, firm—some said at times even harsh—commander, demanding much but giving as much of himself as he required of his troopers.

O'Sullivan was a serious young man, soulful many observed. Others would note that he seemed at times bitter; bitter, perhaps, it was said, at the reality that in Ireland he would be a step or two at most above being a peasant, the acceptance of which reality led him to come to hold and frequently express a profound sense of gratitude for the strength of Catholic Europe, particularly for the career he had been given the opportunity to build, to merit, and the life to live by the Habsburgs. Closely tied to this thinking, these emotions, was a deep, abiding commitment to the concept and institution of monarchy; to the preservation, the maintenance, the strengthening of the absolute monarchy he served and to the order—and in his mind the security—it provided at all costs, and with it a harsh disdain for those who would seek to "reform" any aspect of it. "If this be arrogance, so be it," he had declared to his fellow officers on more than one occasion. "I prefer to think of it as loyalty, pure and simple."

Since returning from the field, he had been engaged in training young, would-be hussars, utilising the magnificent equestrian facilities the Habsburgs had created, including, periodically, the Spanish Riding School, where he had several times stopped to watch as the Lady Eileen O'Connell put her small archduchesses and their horses through their paces. *She is most impressive, most impressive indeed as a horsewoman.*

But it was only of Abigail that he thought, indeed dreamt. *Beguiled is what I am,* he would admit to himself. As giddy as his own presence rendered Abby, she had a similarly intoxicating effect on the otherwise dignified young officer. Abby was the first woman he had felt any genuine affection towards, and he was glorying in the sensation.

Escorted by a chattering young corporal from Tipperary, whose patter, whilst pleasant, he largely ignored, O'Sullivan soon found himself on a sun-drenched balcony overlooking the fields and forests of Schönbrunn. His hat and sword having been taken, he leaned his arms forward over the nearly chest-high balustrades, feeling himself being absorbed again into the peaceful calm of the place, the sun warm on his face and hands, a slight sheen of per-spiration appearing on his tanned forehead, his cheeks glowing.

At the sound of a heavy glassed, wrought-iron door swinging open, imme-diately followed by a swish of fabrics and a gentle click of small shoes on the pavement, O'Sullivan straightened himself and turned, his face wreathed in a smile at Abigail's arrival, a smile brilliantly returned by the lithe young woman walking towards him.

He extended his hands to her, and she hers to him, and they stood at arm's length for a long moment until O'Sullivan firmly pulled Abby to himself, her face to his, their eyes fixed on each other, and delivered a tenderly passion-ate kiss that caused Abby to audibly, though very softly, moan and return it. Unlocking her hands from his, she reached around the back of his neck, beneath his neatly tied queue. Finally, as if by mutual agreement, they released each other and stepped back, ever so slightly, smiling almost sheepishly, both of their faces shining, their eyes aglow.

"And a good afternoon to you, then, Captain O'Sullivan," Abby said, and took his hands again, her eyes softly on his. "How lovely that was, good sir. . . . I believe it warrants a fine luncheon, it does," she observed as she removed a small silver bell from deep in her side pocket, and its high tinkle joined with the chorus of birds.

Abby had been released for the balance of the afternoon by the empress, and O'Sullivan's commanding officer having received a copy of the empress's invitation to him had done the same. The young couple idled their way through what was for both of them an unusually quiet, even gentle afternoon, nibbling on the cold meats and vegetables, the puffy rolls, both sipping the proffered wines and beers until Abby settled on a light chilled Riesling and O'Sullivan on steins of a Munich pilsner, both of which seemed to them to go equally as well with the platter of pastries as they did with the main course, all of which having begun to arrive with the magical sound of Abby's little bell.

They held hands and looked into each other's eyes, speaking, mostly in English, at times almost playfully in Irish, earnestly—as they had begun to do—of the future, though neither had ever spoken aloud the words *marriage* or *love*, or even any variant of the latter. O'Sullivan was aware that Abigail would become the primary lady-in-waiting to the empress, her closest confidante, a reality that daunted him not in the least. Similarly, Abby accepted that O'Sullivan was a career military officer. Though she secretly hoped that her increasing prominence at court could, as much as possible, eventually keep him out of harm's way, she maintained this hope with the full knowledge that Countess von Graffenreit's occupancy of the position to which she would eventually ascend obviously could not prevent her own beloved husband from dying in battle.

Both also understood that they were several years away from the altar. "The countess wishes the transition to be what she calls 'seamless,' so I shall be largely acting in her stead whilst she is nevertheless still present here," Abby explained, enjoying the sensation of the cold pewter wine cup in her hands as they sat in the warm afternoon sun. "In many ways, this has already begun. . . ."

"I have so noticed, and the court appears to have taken notice as well . . . and approving are the remarks I have heard." O'Sullivan smiled, casually leaning back in his cushioned, wrought-iron chair, an arm slung nonchalantly over its low back. He had shed his heavy red uniform coat, and Abby thought he looked handsome in his white ruffled shirt and buff-coloured waistcoat.

"*That* is good to hear . . . from you," Abby said, her hand reaching to pat one of his. "The countess speaks similarly, but sometimes I fear she might withhold criticism from me, lest I grow apprehensive of the position."

O'Sullivan positioned his hand so as to now be holding Abby's. "No fear of that, my dear girl, for 'tis from people whom I know well that I have heard words of the highest praise, that being, I believe, what the countess is repeating to you, so she is speaking the utter truth."

Abigail leaned back, her hand slipping out of the young officer's as she sighed. "Ah, so very good it is to hear that, *my love*. . . ." Her mouth dropped open, her right hand covering it, and her eyes were round, her cheeks scarlet.

O'Sullivan smiled broadly, but neither moved nor said a word.

"I mean . . . I meant . . . oh, dear, I . . ." Abby attempted, finally managing, "Oh, my, I have really done . . . I have said . . ."

As so she had: In the complex eighteenth-century Irish world of interpersonal relationships, women of a certain class—such as Abigail and Eileen—would constantly, effusively address each other, as well as close friends and servants, as "my love" or "my darling," but Abby had suddenly now trod on to new ground.

O'Sullivan leaned forward and then knelt at her knees, a hand resting on one of them. "Could it be that you have said what you have been thinking, perhaps even how it is that you feel?"

Abby's whole face was scarlet; her mouth opened, but all she could do was nod.

"Perhaps what you have said is that which we *both* have been thinking, perhaps how we *both* feel."

Abigail's face returned to its natural glow, though her eyes gleamed, and she nodded, just nodded.

His folded hands resting lightly on her right knee, Denis O'Sullivan looked into her gleaming blue eyes. "So that being the case, 'tis for me, then, being the one tested in battle."

Abby sat, rigid, happily, wonderfully terrified, and nodded again.

"Lady Abigail O'Connell, I love you. I believe I have loved you for a long time. 'Tis the only possible condition that could explain my utter and complete peace and joy in your presence, and the fact that you are near constantly in my thoughts."

Her hands at her mouth, Abby burst into happy tears. "Oh, Denis, I love you, *I do*, as well. I have so told the countess even . . ." she babbled joyfully.

And they stood and embraced for long moments, Abby's tears long past, replaced by both of their radiant smiles.

As they stood closely side by side, both leaning on the balustrade, Abby placed her palm on the back of Sullivan's as it rested there. "'Tis a confession I must make to you, sir," she began softly.

O'Sullivan continued looking out towards Hungary and whispered, "Yes?"

Abby took a deep breath. "I have told the countess more. . . . I have said that 'tis an understanding of sorts that we have, though perhaps I should not have, sir. . . ."

O'Sullivan moved his hand, so now Abby's was resting on the stone, his hand covering hers. Still looking ahead, he said, "Abigail, have you ever told Her Grace, the Countess von Graffenreit, a serious untruth?"

Abby's golden brown curls bobbed as she shook her head in the negative. "No, sir, I have not, not ever."

Finally turning his gaze on her, he added, "Indeed you have not, not about anything. 'Tis indeed an understanding we *do* have, one I believe we have had for quite some time." He smiled as she nodded gently.

When the hour of his departure finally came, O'Sullivan rose reluctantly and drew on his uniform coat, and Abby facing him smilingly brushed his shoulders, his sleeves, as she had seen Maire do to Donal Mór innumerable times. It felt as natural to both of them, as if Abby had done it often.

Taking Abby's arm, O'Sullivan led them unenthusiastically towards the wrought-iron doors and stopping, turning and kissing Abby forcefully, a kiss Abigail O'Connell returned with all of the ardour she felt for the man whom she now fully realised would ultimately be her husband. When finally they stepped back, both of their cheeks were scarlet.

Arms linked, gazing at each other, they continued slowly towards the door.

They could not have seen the two figures standing in an obscure upper window of a small, rarely used room, gazing benignly down onto the balcony. Had the young couple been able to look closely, they would have seen that it was the Empress Maria Theresa and the Countess Maria von Graffenreit, smiling.

Derrynane—October 1762

For many years, even prior to the flight of the Wild Geese at the end of the seventeenth century, there had been a steady, surreptitious flow of young Irishmen of varying stations into the armed forces of Catholic Europe. Many had departed in groups from remote locations in the south and west, though few of them, if any, provided a more spectacular setting than did Derrynane Harbour on the chill, brilliantly sunny, windy morning of 13 October 1762, as Daniel, along with four young O'Connell relatives and fourteen other young men from the vicinage of Derrynane, departed for France, aboard one of the O'Connells' sturdy seagoing sloops.

Derrynane, remaining largely untamed, nevertheless or on account of it, was breathtaking, dominated by the today restless Atlantic, made ever more stunning by the intimidatingly awesome sweep of the grey mountains looming behind Derrynane House itself provided the setting for this particular leavetaking.

Flanked by their mother and Maurice, Daniel Charles walked straight and tall this morning as he joined his cousins and the neighbour boys on the beach, the sand still warm under the morning's benevolent October sun. It was at best a bittersweet occasion, all of the families being fully aware that a not-insignificant number of young Irishmen had never returned from such service; instead they now lay—restlessly, many believed—in graves in France or Austria or Spain. Daniel nevertheless appeared buoyant and eager, though neither his mood nor his demeanour proved sufficient to dispel Maire's sadness as she sang the ship out of Derrynane

École Militaire, Paris—October 1762

Within moments of the small ship's arrival at Le Havre, Daniel found himself in the midst of a colourful, milling crowd, one, save for a handful of flirtatiously enterprising prostitutes, otherwise all male, an incredible array of seafarers, merchants, gentlemen, tradesmen, servants, thieves, virtually all of undistinguished dress.

Dragging his own battered luggage along, Daniel's eye caught sight of a young blond man of middle height in a military uniform consisting of a striking dark blue coat with buff collar and cuff, a white ruffled shirt, a blue waistcoat and buff breeches, his high boots gleaming in the brilliant October sun of Normandy.

The wearer of the uniform was Lieutenant Jarl Stensland, who had been ordered to meet a "tall, fair, very young Irishman, most likely carrying his own baggage, as no servant is said to be accompanying him," a fact about which Stensland, who came from a family of moderate means near Stockholm, strongly approved. Similarly, Daniel had been told, via a letter to Maurice from General Dillon received just prior to his departure, that a "young Swedish officer, in uniform, shall be at La Havre to meet the lad."

Daniel saw the lieutenant first and lifted his free arm, calling out, *"Hej, soldat!"* the Swedish immediately catching Stensland's attention. He raised an arm as well, the young men now walking towards each other.

As he approached the young officer, Daniel extended his hand and smiled. *"God dag, län. För* Daniel O'Connell."

Stensland grabbed Daniel's and vigorously pumped it, "You speak Swedish, excellent!" he exclaimed in French.

Laughing heartily and still gripping the Swede's hand, Daniel replied, *"Je crains d'avoir entièrement épuisé mon vocabulaire,"* and the men both laughed.

Stensland grabbed one of Daniel's satchels. "*Francais?*"

Daniel nodded an emphatic *oui*!

The young officer fraternally clapped him on the back, saying, "The horses are this way, my friend."

An orderly, in a uniform substantially similar to, though the product of a considerably less exquisite level of tailoring than, Lieutenant Stensland's stood beyond the throng through which the young men shouldered their way, holding four saddle horses and a stolid-looking packhorse, the latter fully readied with straps and panniers to haul Daniel's luggage. The other rank saluted to Stensland and quickly loaded the horse, and the three young men headed off, "*à Paris!*" as Stensland proclaimed.

The three-day journey to Paris followed basically the same route as that taken by Abby and Eileen approximately a year earlier and was similarly pleasant and unremarkable, although the men, who slept in the open, shared flagons of wine and were pleased to note similar, somewhat ribald senses of humour.

By midmorning of the second day, after what for Daniel had been a relatively comfortable, restful night with his saddle as his pillow, Stensland began to educate the young Irishman, speaking in precise, almost militarily clipped French.

"So, O'Connell, you shall know that the École Militaire is located in Paris, southeast of what is called the Champ de Mars. It is relatively new, founded by His Majesty Louis XV only in 1750, with the original aim of creating an academic college for cadet officers, primarily from the nobility, but also including some from poor families." Stensland looked across at Daniel, riding along on his right side, and smiled. "As you are not of French nobility, are you from a 'poor family,' O'Connell?"

Daniel nodded *no* a bit sheepishly; he replied, "I am not" in a level, matter-of-fact voice.

The Swede smiled. "Nor am I, though certainly I am not of the wealth, the prestige, of the O'Connells of Derrynane, which, according to General Dillon, are both vast, yes?"

Daniel merely smiled and continued to ride a bit in silence, falling slightly behind. Gently booting his horse, Daniel caught up. "Lieutenant, please permit me to be fully candid."

Stensland gently reined his horse, and both of the men's mounts slowed to a walk.

"Now 'tis the first time I am ever in my life travelling alone outside of Ireland, and whilst there, in my whole life since birth, I was to Dublin, its major city—like Stockholm, I believe—but once, to Cork City twice. We, the O'Connells, live in a wild and remote place . . . whilst we live well, with ample food and drink, and"—he shook an arm—"fine clothing, but being of 'vast wealth and prestige,' I know not of the world's standards, but my most recent Jesuit tutor said, just prior to my leavetaking, that I am, I believe he phrased it, 'educated to my age and position' . . . perhaps that could be a form of 'wealth,' yes?"

Stensland pulled his animal to a halt and looked for a moment at Daniel.

"O'Connell, I like you. Your response is a fine one, one an officer, a gentleman, would give," and, smilingly, he tugged off his glove and extended his hand. Having shed his own glove, Daniel grasped it, and they shook firmly, as would officers and gentlemen.

Continuing the lesson, Stensland went on. "Construction began in 1752 on the grounds of a farm of a family named Grenelle, but the school did not open until 1760, only two years ago, so it is very new, very nice, I feel. It has one extremely large building, many stables, parade grounds—you shall spend much of your time there—marching, marching and marching." He laughed heartily.

"You shall immediately be formally attached to Le Royal Suédois," he said with a broad smile, "and I shall thence be your superior, Monsieur Cadet O'Connell," and he booted his horse into a gallop, laughing in a not unfriendly manner back at Daniel, who hurried to catch up.

Entering Paris, Daniel's awe, bordering on a degree of disbelief, was not dissimilar to that experienced by his sisters. "'Tis incredible," he finally managed to say, his escort having permitted him to remain silent.

"It is indeed; it is certainly not Stockholm," Stensland agreed. "I am still in a degree of awe, but I caution you, O'Connell, it is the palace of Versailles that may silence you for days."

"How so, Lieutenant?"

"I shall not even attempt to describe it, my friend. We shall share observations after your first visit there."

As the little group moved in a northeasterly direction, the urban scenery gave way to what, at first, appeared a thick forest, through which they passed quickly, opening onto an open plain, instantly dominated by a massive, baroquely ornate building, itself dominated by a neoclassical dome of sorts, which now loomed ahead. Stensland extended a gloved hand, pointing. "Your school, your new home, *bon ami*."

As they quickened their pace, rounding the building on its right side, they drew near a guarded entry gate through which a young man on a very fast horse approached, from the direction of the interior of the École, bearing what Daniel would quickly learn to be the standard of the Royal Suédois: a striking flag of blue, gold and white. Reaching the group, which had slowed on his approach, the young soldier rendered to Stensland a sharp salute, which the lieutenant returned in an equally elegant manner, and they entered into a hurried conversation in Swedish, at the conclusion of which Lieutenant Stensland waved him off with his gauntleted right hand.

"He was sent out to identify us. He advises your patron, General Dillon, awaits; a kind gesture, I should say. It speaks well for him and, friend, for you!" He smiled at Daniel, and then nodded, as if to reaffirm what he had just said.

Stensland and his young charge galloped away from the solider and the packhorses, entering a courtyard that itself opened onto a massive open space. Turning left, they approached the massive building they had first seen and shortly drew up before its ornate interior entrance, where a group of dazzlingly uniformed officers, older gentlemen for the most part, milled about.

They reined in with a clatter of gravel stones, as several young men, referred to as *ordinannces* in the French army, in this case being attached to several staff officers, appeared and immediately grasped the bridles of both horses, and the men dismounted, almost in unison. Stensland draped a seemingly protective, certainly reassuring arm over Daniel's soldier and led him the several paces to the cluster of officers, away from which stepped two quite tall men.

Stensland leaned to Daniel's right ear: "General Dillon, on the right; Marachel Alexandre Toffeta, Comte de Sparre de Kronenberg, shorter fellow, same uniform as mine, just more braid and gilt, on the left."

It was not until he was standing but a few feet from the two senior officers that Daniel became acutely conscious of how slovenly he must appear in his dusty brown travelling suit and unchanged shirt, the ruffles at his throat and cuffs undoubtedly soiled, his boots dirty, dull and scuffed, his hair not even properly tied, much less dressed. He felt a massive knot in his stomach, his throat and tongue suddenly dry. *What if I am unable to speak?*

Theobold Dillon had been around young men, young soldiers, since he himself was a young soldier, and instinctively he understood the thoughts racing through Daniel's mind. Magnificently arrayed, his white-lined, below-the-calf-length uniform coat a brilliant red, the facings, chevrons, cuffs and trim a dazzling golden yellow, General Dillon stepped to Daniel, removing his gauntlets and extended his hand.

"Young Master O'Connell, 'tis been quite some while since you permitted me to briefly hold your carefully crafted sword, has it not, sir?"

Stensland smiled openly; Daniel had told him about meeting Dillon for the first time when the officer had come to Derrynane, Daniel then a very wee lad. *Beautifully done, General. How perfect*, the Swede thought.

Taking the proffered hand, Daniel smiled and gripped it firmly. "Indeed it has been, sir. How kind of you to recall that, General, it having been so long ago."

"An impression it made on me, lad. When I received your brother's letter and reached the topic that has brought you here, our first meeting immediately came to mind. 'Twas the last time I was at Derrynane, sad as that is to say. But to be a soldier you have always aspired, and," he gestured broadly, "now here you are, my young friend."

Stepping back from Daniel, the general turned to the Swedish officer on his left, and as Dillon began to speak in French, he gestured to Daniel, who immediately stood to an approximation of attention.

"If you please permit me, Your Grace, I am pleased to present to you Master Daniel O'Connell of Derrynane, the Kingdom of Ireland. He gratefully acknowledges that you have done him the high honour of receiving him into your command, sir."

The Swede smiled, gently saluted to the Irishman and, to Daniel's amazement, to him as well.

"Monsieur Cadet O'Connell, I welcome you to the army of His Majesty Louis XV and to the Royal Suédois. I have heard much good about you," he nodded, smiling, "and as I was just advising my brother Dillon, I have once, perhaps twice, had the pleasure of being in the company of your good uncle, General the Baron O'Connell. I know much good about him, much good!"

Though he felt awkward doing so, Daniel nodded and smiled pleasantly but thought it best to remain largely silent, managing a gentle, "Thank you, sir."

The Comte de Sparre de Kronenberg then unexpectedly clapped Daniel smartly on the shoulder and stepped back. "I am happy to have you in my command, young man. Now, you will please go with Lieutenant Stansland. There is much to be accomplished before tomorrow."

Stansland linked his arm in Daniel's and, as they began to step away, General Dillon nodded and, to Daniel's delight, winked.

The day following was, for the young Irish cadet, a dizzying, virtually mind-numbing series of events, beginning with a predawn awakening by a shrieking whistle in his largely unoccupied barracks, a hurried toilette and, unshod, clad only in his shirt and breeches, a foot race of sorts to a vault-like room at the far end of the magnificent building, where he was greeted by a stocky non-commissioned officer, who briskly introduced himself as Sergeant Holstrum.

Gesturing to a rack of regimental uniforms, as well as hats and boots, Holstrum, speaking in a Swedish-laced version of French indicated, "We shall find some garments that approximate your size, Master O'Connell, and then later the tailor will fit you, so . . ."

At Holstrum's direction, Daniel moved efficiently to and through the array of coats, waistcoats, breeches and boots, and within the hour Daniel Charles O'Connell of Derrynane had been transformed, at least in appearance, into Cadet Daniel O'Connell of the Royal Suédois Brigade of the armies of His Majesty Louis XV—his uniform a wholly-satisfactory, though less elegantly-tailored version of the striking raiment worn by Lieutenant Stensland.

As Daniel brushed one buff-coloured coat cuff against the other, the sergeant stepped back. "Is good!" he exclaimed in English.

Daniel nodded and smiled in response. *"Det är mycket bra,"*/It is very good, to Holstrum's delight.

"Now that you are properly attired, you may eat," Holstrum said casually, and they walked briskly to a bustling dining hall, Daniel consciously standing up as straight as he could, his head high, his eyes straight ahead.

The Hofburg—Winter 1764

The joyous tumult of the Christmas season having given way to a deep, snowy Austrian winter, a quiet, largely uneventful late February Wednesday morning was unfolding predictably in the apartments of Maria Carolina and Maria Antonia. Following her customary supervision of their rising, toilette, prayers and a light breakfast, Eileen and her little archduchesses proceeded as they did most days to join Countess Brandeiss in the girls' playroom cum classroom.

It was at this point and place that, since she first began in the children's service, Eileen ceded full authority to her superior and, as frustrating as she had come to find it, each day generally stepped back into a supportive role.

This particular morning, however, began differently. The usually pleasant Brandeiss seemed uneasy, ruffled in a way that Eileen had never seen her. She gestured to Eileen to join her to one side, whilst the girls took their places at writing tables.

"Her Imperial Majesty has requested a representative portfolio of Her Imperial Highness Maria Antonia's written work and drawings," the countess said softly.

Eileen nodded, understanding the countess's unease. Brandeiss was beloved by both girls, especially Antoine. She was an effusively loving, gentle woman, though, Eileen observed, and others had quietly confirmed, not a terribly bright one. Eileen had also noted that the archduchesses did not appear to work very hard at basic literacy, whilst both, especially little Antoine, appeared to thrive at drawing, embroidery and music, arts the mastery of which—save for the harp—had largely eluded an otherwise quite talented Eileen.

"We must assemble a portfolio, Eileen, as we have done previously."

Eileen took a breath and slightly lowered her eyes. "If I may, Your Grace, is now not perhaps an appropriate time to, shall we say, advance Her Imperial Highness's skills in writing and reading? She is now closer to nine and she is proving most talented in the arts. I thought perhaps . . ."

Brandeiss's cheeks flamed. "What are you suggesting, young woman?" A marked alteration in the countess's mood and demeanour was evident. "I do not fully understand . . ." she stammered uneasily.

"If I may, Your Grace," Eileen continued softly, her eyes remaining deferentially lowered. "Most respectfully, I am concerned that Her Imperial Highness might be said to be lacking, at least to some measure, in terms of her command of the read and written word." Eileen paused as she noted the countess's expression clearly was not a pleasant one. "Given that she is now approaching nine," Eileen concluded, and stood quietly.

"Lady Eileen," Brandeiss began archly, "I have schooled her Imperial Highness prior to your arrival here. I believe I understand the level of her education."

Eileen nodded. "Yes, Your Grace."

"I have thus begun to assemble some materials," she gestured to papers spread neatly on a side worktable, "on which Her Imperial Highness has laboured in recent months. In an effort to preserve her original work, whilst providing Her Imperial Majesty with representative samples of the same, these documents are to be copied, obviously most efficiently by their original author, yes?"

Eileen sighed and nodded, her cheeks a bit bright now. "I shall begin to assist Her Imperial Highness in their reproduction at once, Your Grace."

"Very well, then. Your assistance shall be noted and is deeply appreciated," Brandeiss said quietly, her tone a subtle mix of authority and plaintiveness.

Accepting, although with some difficulty, the reality that it was not her place to have raised the issue and, indeed, fully aware that she had, very soon after her arrival at court, unquestioningly assisted in what was a much less extensive reproduction of such work, for the remainder of the day and much of the one following, Eileen sat patiently with little Antoine whilst the child carefully, methodically and unquestioningly traced pages of the alphabet, simple sentences and sums, short bits of uncomplicated poetry and several penmanship exercises, the vast majority of which had been painstakingly prepared by Countess Brandeiss herself. Indeed, Eileen had to grudgingly admire her efforts to reproduce Antoine's childish scrawl. *This must have taken hours!*

By Eileen keeping her continuing thoughts to herself, the atmosphere in the small schoolroom lightened considerably, the countess's mood improved accordingly and the portfolio of work was delivered by the countess herself to Her Imperial Majesty early Thursday evening, whilst Eileen and the two archduchesses were riding in the open countryside near Schönbrunn.

It was late Friday afternoon, after the children had been dismissed for the day, whilst Eileen was, uncharacteristically, casually strolling slowly to her own apartment to prepare for what sounded as if it would be a lovely ball, when a cryptic, unsigned note in Abigail's handwriting was delivered to her in the corridor by an expressionless young page.

Her Imperial Majesty requests your immediate presence in her audience room.

Eileen folded the stiff card into a pocket of her afternoon dress and redirected her steps towards the empress's location.

Even though her presence was pointedly being requested as opposed to being commanded, her heart thudded audibly as she slowed her steps, having covered the distance between the archduchesses' apartments and those of their mother. She approached the massive, dazzlingly white double doors, flanked by two liveried footmen. Despite her many kindnesses to Eileen and Abigail's warm relationship with the empress, Eileen found Maria Theresa to be an imposing person, one of the rare individuals to whom Eileen felt herself to be totally inferior, indeed fully subject.

Reaching the door, Eileen stopped and nodded, and one of the young footmen gently flung it open, simultaneously announcing, "The Lady Eileen O'Connell at Your Imperial Majesty's request." As Eileen stepped inside, before she had begun her curtsey, the door closed with a deep but soft thud.

"Lady Eileen," she heard Maria Theresa's soft tones from across the room. "Please approach." She beckoned with her right hand.

As Eileen approached her, Maria Theresa took note, as she had for the last year and several months, of the Irish girl's regal bearing, in which the empress delighted, though at the same time finding it to be a bit disconcerting, on more than one occasion reflecting, *I find the tall one's overall demeanour far superior, in ways, to that of several of my daughters.*

The empress remained seated, turning slightly in her gilded and cushioned chair. Though there were several less ornate ones near her writing desk, she did not offer her guest a seat, nor, Eileen correctly surmised, would she, so the younger woman stood in respectful silence, her arms at her sides, her eyes slightly lowered.

"I have received from the Countess Brandeiss a portfolio of the Archduchess Maria Antonia's recent schoolwork," began the empress.

Eileen nodded and smiled tentatively.

"I find her progress to be acceptable, though in no way extraordinary."

Eileen remained silent.

"How do *you*, Lady Eileen, find Antoine's progress to be?" the monarch inquired pointedly.

Lifting her eyes, Eileen's cheeks reddened slightly, and she involuntarily took a deep breath. "Her Imperial Highness progresses, Your Majesty, yes, although she is more accomplished in the fine arts than in *these*," she gestured delicately with her right hand towards the open folio, resting ominously on the otherwise bare side table, "I believe."

Maria Theresa nodded slightly, her expression now more one of maternal frustration. "I see . . ." The empress nodded. "Are you saying that you believe she perhaps may have room for improvement here?" She tapped the pages with a fingertip.

Eileen's heart pounded. "Your Majesty, if I may, I have come to learn that there are differing ways in which a teacher instructs his or her students. The tutors to whom my own education was entrusted were, if I may say, quite demanding, but then they were primarily Jesuits whom my father had—there is no other way to phrase it, please forgive me—smuggled into Ireland."

A smile flickered now on the empress's previously impassive face.

"I see . . . and you are saying that Antoine's principal tutor is . . . perhaps less demanding than the good Jesuit fathers, yes?"

"That would be correct, yes, Your Majesty," Eileen said, her voice firmer now, despite the fact that her heart continued to pound and her mouth remained dry.

A seemingly lengthy though not wholly negative silence hung in the already quiet room, the women, whether involuntarily or not, eyeing each other.

"Well, then . . . I understand," Maria Theresa finally said softly and paused, her voice continuing a bit louder, a bit firmer. "Though I do appreciate what you believe, Lady Eileen, *you* must also understand that the Countess Brandeiss is the individual primarily charged with the care and education of the Archduchess Maria Antonia; it is to her that this role has been entrusted and it is to the countess that you must at all times defer. Do you understand this, Lady Eileen?"

Eileen did not hesitate. "Yes, Your Imperial Majesty. I fully understand, yes."

Maria Theresa smiled ever so slightly as she stood, adding as a carefully calculated afterthought, "I am aware of your own love of books, my dear, and your fluency in the languages of your country, my country and this court. I thus realise I may be asking much of you." She extended her hand, and Eileen stepped forward and curtseyed, her lips brushing the smooth back of the empress's right hand, finding the subtle fragrance of the French-made hand lotions she used daily to be agreeable. As Eileen lifted her lips, Maria Theresa gently placed her fingers under the young woman's chin, raising it slightly and, leaning forward, continued very softly, "I *do* understand, Eileen, and I should be most grateful should you be able to assist the archduchess as you see fit . . . within the strictures of which I have spoken." Both women nodded simultaneously.

The empress resumed her seat, gesturing for Eileen to rise. She then indicated that the imposing Irish girl was to withdraw; as Eileen deftly backed out of her presence, Maria Theresa added, "I trust you will fully enjoy this evening's entertainment, my dear. I believe you have not had an altogether easy week."

Eileen answered with her eyes. Then, reaching the door, she curtseyed once again, the door opened and she backed out into the corridor. She turned, and without acknowledging either the doorkeepers or a tall young officer who smiled at her, she stalked—her stride one familiar at Derrynane and Ballyhar but rarely seen in Vienna—up majestic staircases and down imposing corridors to her own apartment, her mood such that she fumbled with the small gleaming brass knob before opening her own imposing door.

Though she had stopped herself from slamming the door, once inside her sanctuary Eileen permitted herself a heartfelt "Damn! Damn! *Damn!*" as she dropped onto her sofa.

After closing her eyes for perhaps half an hour, Eileen summoned Anna, who gently extracted her from her afternoon dress and assisted her into a magnificent, wine-red velvet ball gown, with a full skirt, a flowing train and, as Eileen, smiling wickedly, had noticed, a more than ample amount of décolletage. "My lady, it is striking, yes?" Anna said as she stood back.

Carefully studying her image in the full-length looking glass, Eileen smiled. "Striking, yes, my dearest Anna, 'tis striking indeed," and, almost casually tossing her hair over her shoulders and turning to see that some of it had come to rest at the small of her back, she bent and kissed Anna's forehead. Lifting her skirts with her right hand, she stepped through the door the girl held open for her.

The evening was indeed an exceptionally dazzling one, with copious amounts of food, an extraordinary array of champagnes and wines, both French and German, and two orchestras, alternatingly providing the empress and emperor's court and guests with a near constant presentation of what Eileen found to be the most glorious dance music she had perhaps ever heard.

She sipped champagne and danced several times with her beloved uncle, but also, at his urging, the general saying with his typical candour, "'Tis time, my darling, for you to savour all of what Vienna offers," with several young infantry officers in their magnificent regimental dress raiment. She finally shared a late-evening plate with one major, Wolfgang von Klaus, a statuesquely tall—his height exceeding her own—blond, ruddy man of, she guessed, thirty-five, perhaps older, with whom she danced several of the newly-popular figure dances called *contredanses,* which were slowly replacing the complex and, many thought, difficult *danses à deux* in Viennese ballrooms, the major protesting—without sound basis, Eileen felt—his inadequacy at the still-novel dance form. He was far more comfortable as they danced an Austrian favourite, the *ländler,* both the major and Eileen laughing playfully as they executed the various hopping and stomping steps, smiling warmly into each other's eyes as they stepped more lightly, .twirling, spinning, switching and holding hands.

At approximately ten o'clock, as the evening quieted ever so slightly and, after sharing subtle nods with Abigail as she departed behind the empress, Eileen rejoined the major, her arm in his, the gentle clink-thud of his sword against the top of his gleaming left boot, in a gentle stroll about the periphery of the ballroom, even stepping out onto the long balcony for a brief moment in the chilly air, chatting amiably in French on a variety of light but, she found, interesting subjects. By parsing his language, she concluded that, in addition to being regarded as a brilliant field engineer, he had several times commanded units of mounted infantry under General O'Connell during the Seven Years War and had been wounded twice.

As they walked, the major finally confessed, nodding in the direction in which Abby had been standing, "I have several times inquired of the Lady Abigail as to your identity and precise role here. She is quite adroit at rendering an already intriguing individual such as yourself even more, may I say, *mysterious,*" and he laughed warmly.

Eileen's hand patted his arm gently and, intentionally, she began to flirt. "Intriguing? Mysterious, you say! I? Ah, just a girl from deep in Kerry I am, good sir." She laughed, and his handsome face was wreathed in a glowing smile.

"Ah, the Irish. I love the Irish!" he exclaimed, in, to Eileen's smiling surprise, precise English.

Approximately an hour later, wondering whether she still retained her air of mystery, Eileen was, in the luxury of her high bed, playfully perched astride Major Klaus, the flames of a low fire dancing on the walls of her bedroom, a single candle shedding seductive, magical shadows on her face, her already tousled hair streaming down her bare back.

His right hand cupped her left breast, his thumb teasing her hard nipple, causing her to laugh softly, as she, with her elegant right forefinger, traced a serpentine scar, which began frighteningly close to his neck and had been inflicted, he told her, by the wild thrust of a Prussian sabre. Her fingertip continued down his left shoulder and upper arm, her eyes widening slightly when he advised her, almost playfully, that he had rendered his attacker "quite dead." She laughed aloud as he then immediately pinched her nipple.

They had tasted champagne on each other's mouths, had laughed and played, touching, exploring, teasing; had begun and stopped and now begun yet again. Eileen was fully enjoying her role as *provocateuse*, marvelling at the ever-so-slight befuddlement of one who commanded men in battle, as, displaying what he felt to be a remarkable degree of ease, she straddled him, listening as he quietly spoke.

"My dear, in all honesty I feel that you must know that I am not one who is fascinated by the defloration of young women, so should you require that this experience be somehow a significant one for you . . ."

Eileen smiled gloriously, her fingertips and then her soft palms on his shoulders, and she momentarily leaned her head back, arching her breasts as she did. "Ah, sir, whilst I am most grateful for your candour, 'tis married I have been and widowed I now am, so that particular *experience* is one I have had and is now of no matter to me." She smiled wickedly and, her hands now behind his neck, leaning forward and sliding down slightly, pressing her bare breasts, her naked body against his own, Eileen pushed him back against and deeply into the down-filled pillows.

What ensued was a series of highly erotic, powerfully athletic and lengthy passages between, Klaus happily discovered, two experienced, extremely sensual individuals, both of whom revelled in and thoroughly enjoyed each other's shameless passion. When it was finally concluded, their sexual tumult had left them both gleaming, breathless and, as passions ebbed, quietly, warmly laughing, following all of which both had slept soundly.

With the chill, grey dawn of a Viennese February Saturday in the offing, Eileen, who after slowly awakening, had been lying quietly on her back, sleepily turned and faced her just-waking lover. Gently, she stroked his slightly rough cheek with the tip of her right thumb after greeting him with a languid kiss and inquired in a whisper, "So, my kind sir, in no way meaning to hasten your leavetaking—indeed, I should prefer that you delay as long as you are able—but what is the protocol in such instances," she laughed, "of a gentleman's departure?"

Without responding, remaining beneath the puffy quilts, von Klaus rolled on top of Eileen and kissed her passionately as her arms and legs instinctively wrapped about him, and she returned the kiss, opening herself to him yet again. Conscious that it was no longer deep in the night, though they were only slightly less physical, the lovers were considerably less vocal, especially as they were concluding their lovemaking.

A few moments later, lying on his side, his forefinger slowly tracing the outline of his lover's lips as she faced him, Klaus smiled affectionately. "Now, as to your inquiry concerning one's departure, it involves one becoming a 'ghost,' my dear. I confess I do not often do such as this, but . . ." Taking note of the weak grey light outside her windows, he lifted himself up on an elbow and softly kissed Eileen's proffered lips. "As the dawn does relentlessly approach, I—most regretfully, I assure you—must," he turned and quickly stood, elegantly taking his silk drawers from the bed with him and covering himself, "a Viennese ghost I must become, departing properly clothed, silently and neither offering nor receiving any acknowledgement of the fact that I see or am seen. Properly executed, 'tis quite simple."

Eileen found herself shamelessly giggling, her fingers to her lips.

He held his finger to his own lips as he gathered the parts of his uniform and moved gracefully, Eileen observed, into her dressing room, emerging within minutes, slightly rumpled but once again fully clothed, only his boots remaining to be drawn on, this being accomplished in the parlour.

At her lover's insistence, Eileen had remained grandly abed, the downy quilts not quite covering her full breasts, her broad shoulders seeming, to the major, tantalizingly bare, as he stepped to her and bent. As she offered him her lips again, his own grazed them, barely, gently. "Thank you, my lady," he said softly in English, kissing her again just a bit more firmly as her outstretched hands pressed his lips to hers, after which he slowly stood.

"Ah . . . thank *you*, kind sir," she whispered, leaning back, watching as Wolfgang Klaus quietly left her, smiling at him as he turned to playfully wave from her doorway. She listened for the tugging on of boots, their gentle padding across her thick parlour rugs and the almost elegant *click* of the door of her apartment being closed by this most elegant man.

Following the major's ghostly departure, stretching under her covers, she gloried in the sensations she felt and quietly whispered aloud, "Yes, thank you, kind sir . . . very much so!" and slowly nodded back to sleep until Anna arrived with her breakfast two hours and some minutes later.

Though she had not at the time planned on doing so, during the ensuing years Eileen would continue to enjoy the handsome major's more than occasional company—in the bedroom but also elsewhere. Discovering that they had in common a love of books, conversation and horses, aside from his skill as a lover who shared her appreciation of an athletic, sensual form of sex, Eileen felt him to be both bright and inquisitive, traits not universally applicable to handsome officers at court.

As time progressed, Eileen laboured on, deftly navigating the obstacles that the empress had placed in the way of her efforts to advance Antoine's literacy. She quietly tried to enhance the child's interest in reading, sharing with the nine-year-old archduchess her own fondness for books.

"A book can take you far, far away, as we have seen, yes? To Ireland and beyond."

"Oh, but Lady Eileen, *you* always read to me!" the little girl had responded, smiling her most beguiling smile.

"Would you not like to be able to lay abed on a cold night and read of the South Seas, where 'tis always warm and magical, they say, or of far, distant Cathay, perhaps even learning of the lives of that monarch's children?" Eileen asked.

The archduchess sighed. "I believe that I shall *always* have someone to read to me, so . . . no, no, I do not think so, but thank you." She smiled, in what Eileen knew to be her totally sincere, very sweet way.

Eileen's cheeks nevertheless glowed red. *You shall always have someone to open a door for you, but do you not want to know how to turn the knob yourself? Or to dress you, but would you like to forget how to slip your foot into a slipper?* She forced a smile, stood, curtseyed and quietly left the child.

"Let us now have *fun!*" she heard Antoine exclaim as she scooped up her kitten, and together they scurried down the long corridor. "Let us find the new puppies."

Eileen watched the beautiful child scamper away and sighed. *Try again tomorrow, I shall.* And so she did the following day—and for many, many months thereafter.

She also began regularly joining in the child's musical practices. Though Eileen was a fairly well-accomplished Irish harpist, she made it clear to the archduchess that she had not reached that level without "much hard and diffi-cult work, work done when out with the horses I would far rather have been," she said, stretching the truth. It was also quite apparent that Eileen lacked ability in terms of the complexities of the classical harp, and she struggled to improve, the child taking notice. Eileen also permitted her to see— and hear—that her talents did not extend to the harpsichord.

Near daily, Eileen worked alongside her younger charge, under the gener-ally stern eye of a master harpist, receiving praise when it was deserved but much more often criticism, of which she made certain the little girl was aware.

She struggled as well with the child's efforts at writing, her penmanship being poor and laboured, accompanied by much sighing, blotting and frus-tration. More than once, Eileen would kneel next to Antoine's writing desk and chair, her long, thin fingers gently on the child's hand as she struggled impatiently to write.

"It is so difficult, my lady!" Antoine would exclaim, putting down her pen.

Sitting back on her heels, Eileen looked up at her young mistress. "So was dressage, so was jumping the high barriers, yes? But you kept trying and now you are excellent in the saddle. You are brilliant at music, at needlepoint, and neither are simple arts. Were you to apply the diligence, the patience you display with these efforts, you would both read *and* write with the ease with which you express yourself so beautifully in art and music, singing even."

Antoine scrunched up her nose. "It is not the same. Music and doing needlepoint are fun, reading and writing not!"

Eileen sighed. "Music and the arts beautify one's life and gladden the world all about a person, but unless one is able to continue to learn by reading, and to express oneself in the written as well as the spoken word, one is frighteningly limited, my darling, in sharing one's talents, one's thoughts with the world all about."

The young archduchess, her expression serious, nodded, saying nothing.

Though the conversations—and the repeated attempts to improve the archduchess's reading and penmanship that they led to—were frequent, despite Eileen's efforts, Maria Antonia would enter adolescence and embark on the path to the awesome role she would very soon begin to play with the quality of her literacy being such that Eileen retained a permanent sense of failure and frustration.

Schönbrunn—August 1765

For months, and then weeks, first the Hofburg and then Schönbrunn had been bustling with an extended round of fêtes and balls, all in anticipation of the impending marriage of the Archduke Leopold to Maria Luisa de Bourbon, the Infanta of Spain. Abigail and Countess von Graffenreit had together been fitted with magnificent new gowns especially for the occasion, as they would be closely accompanying the empress throughout the joyous festivities, in connection with which they laboured in tandem to assure all would progress as perfectly as possible for Maria Theresa.

Whilst the younger Imperial children and their servants would not be journeying to Innsbruck, the site of the wedding, even they were involved in a number of celebratory events prior to their parents' departure, accompanied by a huge retinue.

On the morning of the Imperial couple's actual leavetaking, along with their siblings and their own households, Countess Brandeis and Eileen flanked the youngest archduchesses as they gathered to see their parents off for the happy occasion, all surrounded with much laughter, mirth and the bustling activity of children.

Finally, just as he was about to join the empress in their carriage, the emperor suddenly stepped away from his wife, racing back to little Antoine and, as Eileen deftly stepped aside, gathering the child in his arms, kissing her over and over and over again, in a wrenchingly tearful farewell.

As the emperor finally released the little girl from his embrace and, still in tears, was slowly returning to the carriage, even then looking back and waving, Antoine stepped close to Eileen and reached for her hand.

Looking up at her governess, "Why is Papa so sad, Lady Eileen?" whispered Antoine, her voice tiny, plaintive.

Before Eileen could answer, Countess Brandeiss, who had already released Charlotte's hand and despite the fact that she had begun to walk away, turned and placed her hand on the younger woman's lower back, standing on her toes to do so, she murmured into Eileen's ear, "It is almost as if he *knew* that he was never going to see the child again."

Eileen shuddered, a chill coursing up her spine.

"*Sssh*, Your Grace . . . please! One must *never* speak thus on a leavetaking," she whispered softly but firmly.

"Oh, my dear," the countess smiled, speaking now in a normal tone of voice, "you dear, sweet Irish . . . you are so wonderfully superstitious. I find it so very charming, positively delightful," and she strolled away casually, shaking her head, and smiled back at Eileen, who remained standing now with both little girls, holding their hands.

That evening, after she and the children knelt to pray, as she kissed Maria Antonia good night, Eileen said yet another silent prayer for the emperor.

Some eight days later, a solitary rider was spied racing towards Schönbrunn, his uniform dusty and spattered with mud, the young man himself winded, breathless. As he drew closer, it was seen how heavily foamed his black horse was, the animal's heaving flanks pasted with a coating of congealed dust and sweat. It would quickly be learnt that the cavalryman was the last of a series of such riders, who had covered the approximately 295 miles between Innsbruck and Schönbrunn.

"The lord high chamberlain! I must . . . I must see . . . him!" the rider cried out to no one in particular amongst the typical gaggle of servants, courtiers and visitors, into the still summer morning, even as he was reining in his exhausted horse.

General O'Connell was just then arriving as well, albeit from another direction and at a far more leisurely pace.

He walked his massive white warhorse to where the young rider stood, both horse and rider still gasping, breathless.

"Young man," the baron began, disregarding protocol, despite that, on seeing O'Connell, the rider had already snapped to attention.

Sensing anguish on his part, instead of returning the salute, the general lay a huge right hand on the rider's suddenly drooping left shoulder, his tone gentle. "My boy . . . what . . ."

"It is the emperor, Your Grace. He has died, died at Innsbruck! On the eighteenth. Horsemen, of whom I am the final one, have ridden straight here since then, General, from there to here, Your Grace. The Emperor . . . he is dead!"

Now resting both of his large hands on the young man's shoulders, O'Connell's mind was racing. The pulses in his temples spontaneously beginning to pound, he immediately assumed command, as to do so was his nature, as well as his position. Quickly escorting the rider inside, he secreted him in a small anteroom and immediately sent one of the ubiquitous pages racing for the lord high chamberlain, Prince Johann Joseph Khevenhüller-Metsch, who, having been ill on their departure, had not journeyed to Innsbruck as part of the Imperial couple's large retinue.

In the meantime, believing that more senior individuals, in possession of more definitive information, would at some point be arriving, he gave terse orders that they should immediately be brought to Prince Johann.

Some few moments later, hastening down a side corridor, the general strode to meet the lord high chamberlain himself, reluctantly greeting the prince, despite their warm personal relationship, almost abruptly, immediately preceding to brief him in his clipped battlefield-proven manner of conveying difficult information as quickly as possible, and directed him to the anteroom in which the young rider awaited him.

Having thus done all he could, O'Connell knew with whom he must next speak and straightaway stalked to the left wing of the palace—the wing of the archduchesses—as quickly as his long legs would carry his heavy body, his sword swinging, barely touching his boot top.

Greeted warmly, profusely, by a magnificently dressed and bewigged elderly gentleman whose name he could not remember, the general leaned over, as the fellow was also an extremely short man, and said softly, "I must see the Lady Eileen O'Connell at once, and *not* in the household of the archduchesses who are in her care, do you understand?"

First bowing gracefully and nodding in acknowledgement, the man escorted the general to a tiny, elegant parlour with but a settee, two chairs and a low table; then, after bowing himself out of the suddenly bleak room, he in turn sent yet another page, racing this time to locate Eileen.

Such was the distance between the two spaces that it was fully twenty minutes before a delicately sweat-sheened Eileen knocked sharply once and immediately entered the small parlour, to which yet another group of pages had directed her.

Her uncle was already standing and enveloped his niece in one of his bear-like embraces, though she immediately sensed a notable degree of unease in the usually stolid soldier.

Wriggling from his arms, she said, "Uncle, something is wrong. Is it Maire? No, is it other bad news from Ireland? Is it *Hugh*?"

The general gently gestured her to the settee, then sat heavily in a facing chair, leaning towards her, his hands resting on his knees as he softened his normally rumbling voice, speaking in English. "Though not from Ireland, not involving the O'Connell family, 'tis very bad news, sad family news, though, indeed. His Imperial Majesty the Emperor is dead," he said, his voice flat.

Her hands went immediately to her mouth. "Oh, my dear God . . . no!"

O'Connell rested his head against the high back of the chair, causing him to momentarily look directly up at the ceiling. "Ah, dear girl, 'tis true; so sad, but it is indeed true."

Eileen's face had gone ashen and she seemed overwhelmed; *something quite unlike her*, he thought immediately.

It was at that moment that she began to relate the particulars of the Imperial couple's departure, and Francis Stephen's painfully sad, unsettling, indeed eerie return to his youngest daughter. It was also then that the general fully grasped the feelings with which his niece found herself beset.

"When Brandeiss spoke thus, Uncle, chilled I was . . . immediately and powerfully chilled . . . and . . . *'superstitious'* she says, *och*! 'Tisn't superstition, 'tis having a certain feeling, just as Maire says; having a certain feeling . . . is all."

The general was, at the moment, less inclined than his niece to reflect on the value of and whether Eileen shared at least to a degree Maire's prophetic musings, a Dark Woman of the Glen though she might be.

"Sadly, 'tis of no matter now, none of this. The will of God has been done; 'tis not for us to know or question; what 'tis for us—for *you*, my darling girl— to do is to hasten to your little archduchesses and as gently, kindly, as sweetly as only you are able . . . to tell them their papa . . ." the oft gruff soldier's voice trailed off ". . . that their dear papa has gone to heaven." He sighed powerfully. O'Connell abruptly stood, now anxious to leave. "I do not envy you, my girl; were I able, I would ease this for you, but I fear I am not. . . ."

Catching his sleeve, Eileen ventured, "Uncle, could you not at least walk me to them? *Please?*"

The general could not suppress a slight ironic smile, "You forget, Dark Eileen, we share more than a name; we share a certain manner of thinking. I know precisely what it is that you are thinking . . . and thus again I say *no*."

Eileen smiled weakly and nodded. "'Tis utterly obvious, the scheming, conniving O'Connell mind, is it not? . . . At least to another O'Connell." She shook her head.

The baron nodded in reply. "Whilst perhaps I might lessen your burden, I fear that I would not soften this blow for either of them, but 'tis you alone who may be able to do so. They associate me with fun, hah . . . even a wee bit with buffoonery. . . . Now 'tis not a time for me. If I thought otherwise, my darling girl, with you I would indeed go."

Eileen gently wrapped her hands about the back of the neck of one of the few people at court markedly taller than she and softly kissed her dear uncle's cheeks. *I know. Thank you*, so said her eyes and, sighing deeply, she slowly stepped out of the tiny, sad room.

Lapsing as she did only rarely at court into her once customary long stride, Eileen swiftly though sadly made her way through what were suddenly eerily still, almost unfamiliar-feeling corridors, up a majestic, multi-storeyed staircase to the floor on which the archduchesses' and her own apartments were located.

Her mind raced. *Donal Mór Ó Conaill, John O'Connor . . . two men were never less alike, and yet two men in my life died sudden, shocking deaths. As Uncle suggests, I am thus perhaps better prepared than most here to do what I must, to say to my darlings what I must.* Though, as she strode down the last passageway leading to their apartments, tears streamed down Eileen's cheeks. Stopping before she reached the door, she wiped her eyes, her cheeks, and took a deep breath.

She had left the girls—Charlotte reading and Antoine working on a detailed needlepoint—with a young servant girl sitting quietly in the adjoining room. Eileen gently dismissed her with a nod of her head, and the girl closed the door softly behind herself.

The girls smiled up at Eileen, and the tall young woman knelt on the floor, opening her arms to them. As she gathered them to herself, the children sensed something was different, for often, even though Charlotte was now thirteen and Antoine ten, after doing so typically Eileen would still lean back and they would all three tumble together onto the thick carpet, but not now.

Holding the children, Eileen began, "My darlings, I do not know . . . I cannot . . ." She sighed, frustrated at her fumbling. She released the girls and sat back on her heels, so she could look at her archduchesses, and sighed again, resting her hands in her lap.

"My darlings, I am sorry, but I must tell you something that I myself have once been told . . . and, sadly, have myself twice experienced. There is no tender way to say it; your dear papa has . . ." she choked, caught herself and completed, "your dear, beloved papa has gone to join God in His heaven. . . . Your papa has died at Innsbruck. . . ." Opening her arms again to the shocked children, she pulled them to herself, and all three dissolved in deep, bitter, profound tears.

What seemed like hours passed, and Eileen finally loosened her embrace and sat back once again on her heels. As they had come to do over the years they had been with Eileen, both Charlotte and Antoine positioned themselves the same way, their hands folded in their laps, and so they sat, a sad, tear-stained trio, in silence until Eileen spoke, her husky voice even deeper, softer, markedly slower than usual. "I would not say it were it not true—you know that of me, yes?—so I say to you both, *I do know how you feel . . . .*"

"How do you, *how can you* know, Lady Eileen?" Charlotte softly but pointedly almost immediately demanded, her eyes red, her cheeks damp, as her younger sister sat in silence, her sorrow-filled eyes, too, now on Eileen.

Eileen nodded, her tone more certain now. "I *do*, I *can* because when I was not much older than you, darling Charlotte, my own papa . . . I saw him as he prepared to leave our home, he kissed me on the top of my head, and one hour or even less afterwards, my mama spoke to me of what, and in the manner I just have to you . . ."

"*Your* papa?" Antoine asked in a tiny, plaintive voice.

Eileen nodded, her eyes dim with tears. "Yes, my darling, *my* papa," she managed. Pausing, then clearing her throat, she continued, "Also . . . do you recall when first I came to you, we sat at the Hofburg and I told you then where I had come from, about Derrynane and my family, about Bull and . . ."

The girls both nodded gently in the affirmative.

"Do you recall that I also told you I had been wed and only recently widowed?"

Small blond heads bobbed again in unison as Eileen drew another deep breath.

"My husband—he was an older gentleman, older actually than, than . . . the general, but in seeming good health. One evening I returned from riding Bull and I came into the room where he was writing. I remember removing my big straw hat with a broad flourish in an attempt, perhaps, to make him laugh, and he looked at me as if he were going to speak . . . and then . . . as gently and quietly as one of your dolls tumbling to one side, he . . . he toppled onto the floor and . . . and by the time I knelt by him, he was dead. . . . So I *do* know, I *do* understand. I am so . . . very . . . sorry. . . ."

Her shoulders shaking, Eileen then unashamedly wept, the girls both reaching around her and she about them, and they cried until they stopped.

The days—indeed the weeks—that followed were a series of painful unbroken tableaux of grief, beginning with the return of the emperor's remains to Vienna, along with the removal of the empress and much of the court to the Hofburg for the lying in state and funeral.

An unseen but acutely felt heavy veil of grief, of genuine wrenching sorrow, descended on Schönbrunn, where the younger archdukes and archduchesses and their servants remained, along with the numberless throng of cooks, cleaners, door minders, candle lighters and the like, all dealing with their own thoughts, their own varying levels and degrees of grief, all going through the motions of court life absent the sovereigns.

On the third floor of the archduchesses' wing, the cluster of Charlotte's, Antoine's and Eileen's apartments took on a strangely, otherworldly air. Though she would have clearly wished to remain with the children, protocol dictated that Countess Brandeiss be included amongst the throng of nobility required to be in attendance at the emperor's funeral. So as not to further upset either girl, after a brief early morning stop in Eileen's apartment, where she said, "I am certain you will know the correct thing to do, to say at any time, in order to ensure the archduchesses' stability," Brandeiss entered a carriage with several other nobles, and it lurched heavily off to Vienna.

With Brandeiss gone, Eileen felt the mantle of grief, of unreality, descend on her own shoulders, heightened when, as soon as she had responded to a sharp rap on her door, a page she had never before seen wordlessly lay a soft, carefully wrapped, rectangular parcel across Eileen's extended arms, which she instinctively positioned as she had seen the page's own.

It was only when she lay the package on her settee that Eileen realised what it contained: simple though elegant black dresses for the archduchesses and for herself. Pressing her own to her bosom, she began to softly cry. *'Tis perhaps as much because of the too-recent memory of my own becoming a widow, and pity for these dear children, as 'tis grief on this monarch's passing, is why I weep.*

When Anna responded to her summons, Eileen saw that she, too, was freshly clad in black. Together, they quickly rendered Eileen in the same fashion, and genuinely dreading the moment, Eileen walked slowly toward the girls' apartments, their smaller dresses draped across her arms, Anna following quietly behind.

Once the archduchesses were in formal mourning, an oddly comforting routine began: Rising, retiring and meals provided some sense of normalcy, whilst recreation of any form—save walking—was prohibited. The archduchesses' informal summer instructions ceased, though Eileen, sensing the strength of their ability to distract, to even entertain, resumed her seemingly endless repertoire of Irish stories, a number of which she made up as she went along—later racing to her desk to make notes, so as to be able to remember them afterwards—and she insisted that the girls join her in morning and afternoon walks, which Eileen deliberately caused to be longer and thus more time-consuming.

Additionally, seeking any activity that would distract, hopefully consume—at least for a time—the archduchesses, Eileen had begun to teach them Irish.

"Why must we learn *another* language?" queried Charlotte, her grief showing itself in the form of a suddenly petulant, oft-times openly quarrelsome adolescent.

"Why should we not?" tried Eileen valiantly.

"Will you take us to Ireland, Lady Eileen?" Antoine had inquired, a suggestion of hopefulness in her soft, weary voice.

"Would that it were possible, my little darling, I would take you both today, departing this very moment, off to the sanctuary, the powerful peace that Derrynane offers," Eileen responded, tears suddenly streaming down her cheeks. "Perhaps someday, but for now . . ." and she began counting, holding up her long, elegant fingers as she did: "*A haeon, a do, a tri . . .*" and soon the girls joined in, ". . . *a caithre, a cuig, a se, a seacht, a ocht.*" The planned distraction, the hoped-for absorption in something, *anything*, new and different had begun. It would not last, but it would help for a while, which, Eileen understood, was the best she could have hoped for.

Meanwhile, in Vienna, the pageant and panoply surrounding the death of a Habsburg emperor had slowly unfolded, with the Lady Abigail O'Connell finding herself at the very epicentre of each wrenching stage. To Abby, now clad in the most elegant of mourning robes, it seemed that, upon her return to the Hofburg, Maria Theresa had ceased to sleep, as at all hours Abigail found herself with the prostrate monarch, sitting or kneeling, initially at her consort's catafalque and then, following his internment, at his tomb, beside which the grief-stricken widow had commanded her own open casket be laid.

Whilst initially Countess von Graffenreit stolidly intended to do everything possible to assume the responsibility for seeing to the empress's needs and care, it soon became apparent that, as the hours of such filled most of each day, with Abby being more than twenty years her junior and of a more vibrant constitution, it was, after a gentle though candid conversation between the two, agreed that it would be upon the Lady Abigail that the bulk of such would immediately come to rest.

After the emperor's entombment, Abby spent countless hours in the dim confines of the gloomy, almost-cramped Habsburg crypt, which lay beneath the simple church of the Capuchin Franciscans—on the square known as New Market, not far from the Hofburg. She alternated between kneeling on a velvet-cushioned prie-dieu and sitting on a small, thickly padded chair that one of the younger monks had thoughtfully provided for her. *Dear God, forgive me, I cannot pray constantly. You understand. I know You do.* She felt she could neither read nor walk away for any appreciable time. *I am here because the empress needs me to be, and because God in His wisdom has decreed that I should be*, she reflected, fighting sleep, boredom and resentment. *I cannot imagine, I cannot in any way conceive what that dear lady is enduring,* she thought many more times than once. Occasionally, she would stroll quietly amongst the various Imperial sarcophagi, dating to those of the Emperor Matthias and his wife, the Empress Anna, who had established this as the place of imperial entombment in the first decades of the sixteenth century.

Though the empress had requested that she do so only on several occasions, and despite that Abby found it exceptionally painful to join her in the recitation of the Office of the Dead, she nevertheless offered to do it whenever asked, being most grateful when eventually it appeared that she would not be again. Abby could never reflect on those grim days without almost hearing the seemingly endless responsive refrain, *"Timor mortis conturbat me*/The fear of death confounds me." As she would discover so many other Irish had, Abigail eventually came to conclude that she did not fear death.

Abby's presence and her service did not go unnoticed. Late one night, as the empress rose from her place at the tomb, she gestured to Abigail, putting her arm around the younger woman's waist as they silently departed the crypt, slowly climbing the narrow stairs.

As they emerged onto the small square outside the church—deserted save for their waiting carriage, the darkness diminished only by the flickering tapers held by the outriders—"I am so grateful, Abby," Maria Theresa whispered, her voice brittle, dry. "I shall never forget what you have done for me these days, these weeks . . . and before, and after . . ." and she hugged her waist even tighter, as Abby instinctively and against all protocol stretched her own arm about the empress's waist, and together they slowly took the few steps remaining to the waiting carriage.

During the endlessly long, crushingly depressing days and weeks, Abby wept as well, though, she acknowledged to herself, only rarely was it for the dead emperor, being much more so for his empress and their children. She also shed tears as she desperately missed Denis O'Sullivan. She wrote plaintive letters, to which he gently and immediately responded, as well as writing his own notes, a dutiful young corporal serving as their link. She had only caught sight of him on a few occasions in his magnificent full-dress raiment, in brisk command of some of his Hungarian Hussars, as they participated in the various observances and displays that seemed an integral part of mourning a Habsburg emperor.

Vienna—Autumn 1765

Though both Abigail and Eileen promised themselves things would improve, some normalcy would return, it must return, it was a difficult promise to keep.

The empress did not return to Schönbrunn. Whilst the other Imperial children remained there until almost Christmas, later on in the summer, Charlotte, Antoine and their retinue were moved to Laxenburg, a palace Maria Antonia loved above all others. Though Laxenburg shared with Schönbrunn a warm place in the hearts of the empress and her children, especially Maria Antonia, in addition to the colour of its gentle pale yellow stone, Laxenburg was unique in that its mass lay in its breadth as opposed to the more common palatial heights; to Eileen, the less ornate palace thus had the appearance and comfortable feeling of being an exceptionally large home, as opposed to an Imperial palace.

Eileen had first been to Laxenburg shortly after she had arrived in Vienna, during the course of a lengthy, day-long riding expedition with a debonair Spanish officer named Jose Maria d'Alvarez y de Castro; she had found the relatively smallish palace and grounds to be lovely, far more compelling than her companion, whose favourite words in English, Eileen had laughingly written to Abby, "appeared to be 'I' and 'me'!"

Her brief visit there notwithstanding, Eileen was pleased by the news of the removal and, indeed, the change of place—especially to one adored by the younger archduchess—had an extremely positive impact on the overall quality of life of the little household.

Though Charlotte's petulance seemed at times as if it would be at least semi permanent, Eileen skilfully navigated around her moods and occasional outbursts of temper, recalling from her own not-at-all-long-ago early adolescence both the physical and emotional aspects of this tumultuous period of any girl's life. Eventually, Eileen understood that the older of her archduchesses wished primarily to be left alone, that she would seek out Eileen when she wished to—as she did, but only occasionally.

As a result, Eileen began to spend considerably more time with Maria Antonia, who, though she expressed a continuing desire for her mother, appeared to be slowly recovering from the shock of her father's death and indeed was able to speak with Eileen about how she felt.

"I feel emptiness, Lady Eileen," the girl had said one flawlessly warm autumn afternoon, as the two strolled the gentle gardens at Laxenburg, holding hands. "Is it not horrid enough that my papa has died, but the empress—I have seen her but twice since July, and then only for minutes."

At that moment, Eileen drew the girl to her and held her whilst she cried—yet again.

The girl's tears stanched, Eileen draped an arm gently around Antoine's shoulder and nudged her to continue their walk.

"The situation in which you are, 'tis far more complex than any young girl should be: Your beloved father has died and you want—you *need*—your mother's presence, her love, yes? I understand this, yet I am helpless to act."

The girl looked up and nodded, keeping step.

"Your mama, she . . ." Eileen's voice drifted in the gentle, warm air, "she is also an empress, *the empress*; the most powerful woman in the world. I have no doubt, Antoine, that she loves you, she treasures you, yet her world, too, has been shattered, and she cannot be here"—she gestured, spreading her arms—"or any other place of refuge, but must at the Hofburg remain, to rule, to govern the empire. I am certain she would rather be here, darling."

The young girl nodded softly. After they strolled in silence, Antoine touched Eileen's arm. "My world, it is not the world of almost all people; I am only beginning to understand this."

Eileen smiled gently, maternally. "It is good that you are; I have come to understand the same: Upon a throne you shall sit—and rule . . ." *and I shall not*, she shook her head in silent irony—in her heart a profound sense of gratitude that she would not.

The Hofburg, Vienna
7 November 1765

My darling, dearest Sister:

I have so longed for you, for your company. I shall never again feel so alone, so helpless as I have these weeks and months since August.

Lest I forget, Uncle advises that soon—perhaps even within the coming week— you and your young ladies are to return to Vienna. Please say not a word, nor even suggest this possibility; it is all subject to Her Imperial Majesty's decision, and Uncle says there are days when she is unable to decide. This, sadly, you shall see for yourself.

I am sorry my letters have been so terse, so brief as to be undeserving of even the appellation "letter." I have longed for the chance to write you; 'tis only yesterday that Uncle sent a message that the empress would be in council all of today; he wrote that I would "thus be free," and as guilty as I feel being grateful for the respite, I am indeed grateful.

I sense that your life has not been one of ease either; I cannot imagine how difficult it must be even for one as creative, as resilient as your good self, to be mothering two girls whose father has died, and whose mother has been largely absent from their lives. We shall at some point be able to share our experiences.

For now—I am glad to have the time to write you, my love. I must prepare you for a changed place, a different world it is here:

The empress has had her beautiful hair cut short; she of course is in full mourning, but the countess and I have seen that her clothing—it has all been removed and that the seamstresses work on nothing but more and many more black dresses and gowns, as if she will never emerge from her mourning.

The palace is funereal: Crepe and other black draping are throughout much of the palace; chandeliers are hung, mirrors covered or at least obscured. One rarely hears laughter, instead a deafening silence, at most an equally unsettling sound of whispers. 'Tis eerie!

Abby sat back, read what she had written, and finished by briefly describing the hours she had spent in the crypt of the Capuchin Church.

I have said all this so that you can be prepared as best one can.
I so long to see you, Abby

Though not as soon as the general and Abigail had believed or hoped they would, Eileen and the children—along with their siblings and their own households—did indeed return to the Hofburg within several weeks of Abby's letter, and indeed saw it to be as Abigail had written. The invariably joyous atmosphere that had traditionally settled over the palace—indeed, over all of Vienna—as December arrived was cruelly but understandably absent this Christmas of 1765.

As the sad year of 1765 sombrely slipped into 1766, black remained the dominant, indeed the only colour at court; the low, gentle murmur of multi-lingual voices that flavoured daily court life continued as the primary sounds, indeed virtually the only sounds, that were heard; quite plausibly, other than quietly behind closed apartment doors, there was no music, no laughter—not even a momentary cessation of the process of mourning, such that many, who, though they knew it would eventually end, now began to wonder whether it was to be a process at all, occasionally considering that, rather, some signifi-cant variant of it might become the new way of life in this once bustling and vibrant, once merry, once exciting place.

Vienna—January–May 1766

For Eileen, indeed for much of the family and their servants in the immediate orbit of the empress, one of the very few bright moments in both the overall desolation that was the Hofburg in January 1766, as well as in the sad, stressful situation with which they had all been dealing since the emperor's death, was provided—in her mind, wholly fittingly enough—by Abigail . . . and Denis O'Sullivan.

After quietly seeking out General O'Connell and receiving, as he felt he must, the senior officer's consent to do so, O'Sullivan had similarly approached Abby and, in the course of a brief conversation—the contents of which, she told Eileen, she could not remember—made and received Abigail's effusively-positive response to his proposal of marriage.

When, early one morning several days after she and O'Sullivan had announced their betrothal to a wholly-unsurprised but overjoyed Eileen, Abby had quietly advised the empress of O'Sullivan's formal proposal, Maria Theresa sat quietly for a moment, before her face brightened, appearing momentarily radiant to Abigail. A faint suggestion of her prior joyfulness momentarily returned as the empress rose and took Abby's face in her hands, looked into the young woman's bright eyes and gently kissed her on each cheek. Stepping back and pointing Abby to her customary chair and resuming her own seat, Maria Theresa looked warmly at her servant, her dear young friend, to whom she had grown in many ways closer than to most of her daughters.

"You shall wed in the spring, yes?" she inquired; *or was it something of a command?* Abby wondered as she nodded *yes*.

Gesturing again to Abigail to sit, the empress continued, "Spring shall be lovely, yes; at the Augustinerkirche it shall be, yes? Shall we then say later on in May, my dear?"

Abby felt herself unable to speak, so she vigorously, smilingly nodded *yes*, her hair bouncing on her shoulders.

"Please have the Count von Stemweitz come to me, perhaps tomorrow afternoon? I shall begin then to make the necessary arrangements with him, as our master of ceremonies—if that is satisfactory to my lady?" the older woman said softly.

Abby could only manage a whispered, "Of course, Madame . . ."

The empress then gently indicated with a customary nod of her head that Abigail was free to return to whatever she had been doing, though, as Abby rose and began to turn to depart, as she was permitted to do in private settings, Maria Theresa added, "You will please request the Countess von Graffenreit to arrange for Madame Schullheimer to come to you as soon as possible so that you may discuss with her exactly how you desire your gown to appear, so as to permit adequate time so that it will be perfect. I shall see that *everything* will be perfect for you, my darling."

As Abby left the empress and walked back to her small office, she did not sense that her slippers at all touched either the thick carpets or the marble floors upon which she trod.

One evening a week or so after Abigail had advised the empress of her betrothal Eileen had invited herself to her sister's apartment, appearing at the appointed hour accompanied by a young page bearing a large oval tray upon which rested a silver coffee service, cups and a large plate of pastries.

After Abby settled herself on the sofa directly in front of the pastries, she daintily helped herself to one and gestured for her sister to do the same.

"How is it, my love," Eileen began, gracefully licking chocolate glaze off her fingers, "to be a betrothed woman now?"

Balancing a small coffee cup on her knee, Abigail smiled. "'Tis lovely—yes, very much so. I feel quite *content*, I believe."

"I am glad, darling; it seems quite natural, you and the 'dashing Captain O'Sullivan.'" Eileen nodded. "You two fit quite nicely together."

Sitting quietly for a few moments, Abby's eyes fell on the now-gentle fire before them. Whilst not redirecting her gaze to Eileen, she did pose a very pointed question. "Can you say whether you had come to care for Mr. O'Connor in much the same way I do for Denis?"

Eileen, too, remained gazing into the fire. She instantly felt that her face had become pink, as if she had been slapped.

Abby noticed the brightness in her cheeks. "My darling, I did not . . . I do not know from where . . . how is that . . ." She struggled, quite unusually, and then rested her hand on her sister's knee. "I am trying to say that I did not mean to disturb . . ."

"No, no, my love, 'tis not disturbing, 'tis just a wee bit of . . . something I had not thought of recently," Eileen began, her voice soft, thoughtful. "Some time goes by when I do not even think of those months at Firies at all, much less about my feelings . . . for . . . for my husband." She rested her head again the high back of the sofa, sitting quietly.

With some difficulty, Abigail sat quietly as well, gently nibbling on a small crème-filled pastry.

"Yet, when reminded of those months, of him . . . I *do* have feelings, sister, yes, and—allowing as it is betrothed you now are, 'tis not inappropriate for you to inquire of me these things. After all, I *was* married, albeit under rather different, very different circumstances than you are to be, but wed I was."

Abby poured a bit more coffee, sipped and listened.

"So, yes . . . yes, somehow . . . fond it was that I most unexpectedly had grown of John O'Connor, quite fond, truth be told, though I believe the depth of your emotions for Denis are far deeper than were . . . are . . . *were* mine for . . . for my husband; but yes, fond I was of him. By a certain time— I know not exactly when—but by this time, whenever it came about, I had come to feel warmly towards him, and I felt . . . I still have difficulty applying the proper word . . . I believe I felt *secure* with him, being near him, *comfortable* being his . . . his wife.

"After . . . the *beginning*, as I told you that day on the mountain, I had seized power and gained some control, and by doing so, I felt that I had made the place safe for myself . . . and I had come to feel in that way secure. After all, I went about my business with a loaded pistol at the ready; I had been prepared to kill the man—I had reminded him of the fact—so when I say I felt 'secure' with him, I believe 'tis a different type of security, a different feeling altogether perhaps. *Whatever it was*, when John . . . when . . . when he died, I felt a sense of loss—not as when Papa died, not when we learnt of Conaill's drowning at sea last year, those were different—but I felt as if something had been torn from me.

"At first, I believed 'twas my status alone that I had lost; a gentleman's widow, especially a young widow, soon ceases to be the mistress of the house, of the lands. . . . Mama's situation was far different; by custom if not in fact she will always be mistress of Derrynane, no matter that Maurice has wed. . . . I knew that would not be *my* situation." She sighed.

Abigail maintained her silence, her body now turned towards Eileen, her legs curled up on her side of the long settee, her bare feet hidden by the volume of her skirts.

"By the time of his funeral I had come to understand, to accept that 'twas John O'Connor whom I had lost, not merely the place I had by being his wife, and I mourned him, I mourned that; I believe at times I still mourn. . . ."

Abby noticed that her sister's eyes were brimming, and she rested her hand on Eileen's leg. "I am sorry. I did not mean to . . ."

Eileen gently waved her hand in an equally gentle, dismissive gesture. "You have done nothing for which an apology is required, my darling. . . . 'Tis just feelings . . . nothing more."

The fire had revived itself slightly and the flames were suddenly brighter; having reached a pocket of resin within a log, it had fed itself, and it popped loudly several times and hissed before quickly blazing.

After a moment, Abby asked, very softly, "Would you wed again, Eileen?"

Eileen at this moment sighed deeply, her gaze thoughtfully fixed on the now blazing logs. "I would . . . I may . . . but, were I to do so, I should very much wish to feel what I believe you feel, and *how* you feel. I was wed under rather odd and difficult circumstances, and whilst at its end 'twas far better than at its commencement, were I to ever again wed, I should like to feel *more*. . . . I should like to feel it is a special thing, as I believe what you and the good captain are and have is a 'special thing,' a *very* special thing." Kicking off her slippers, she assumed a position mirror to her sister's on the long settee, and her toes playfully sought Abby's. They giggled like little girls for a moment.

Abby was tempted to inquire about the dashing Major Wolfgang Klaus, in whose company she had seen Eileen at several glittering occasions before the emperor's death, but about whom her younger sister had said nothing more than that he was "utterly charming . . . and wonderful company." The elder sister strongly suspected that Eileen might have shared a bed with the handsome officer on at least one occasion—quite probably more.

The remainder of the winter itself seemed to pass quickly, uneventfully, though, despite being more fully engaged in government, in more actively ruling her complex empire, Maria Theresa seemed to have slowly returned to the sad, dark and inevitably lonely place in which her consort's death had placed her. Some days she appeared distant, others engaged but wistful; on rare occasions, at times she would even be ill-tempered, for which she invariably and immediately apologised.

Amongst the empress's principal distractions remained the planning for Abigail's wedding; she met weekly with Count von Stemweitz and inquired frequently of Madame Elisabeth Schullheimer, the renowned Viennese dressmaker and the court's continuing preferred couturière, as to the progress of Abby's gown. It was only when Abigail inquired that the empress provided any details. "All is being cared for, all provided for, my darling," Maria

Theresa would say, seeming then to almost immediately return to her own melancholy place.

With the coming of spring and the arrival of an exceptionally lovely May, so great was her affection, indeed her love for Abigail, that Maria Theresa summoned an inner strength sufficient to permit her to emerge, howsoever briefly, from the dark place where her emotions, her very spirit itself, had continued to dwell. On a flawlessly sunny, cool Viennese Saturday morning, the fifth of May—the date itself chosen by the empress—the Lady Abigail O'Connell, in Madame Schullheimer's creation, a magnificent creamy white silk and satin gown—made, at the empress's direction, to Abby's exact specifications—its exquisite, near aisle-length train carefully gathered in front of her, arrived for her wedding at the Augustinerkirche in the empress's own coach of state, drawn by six magnificent white horses, trailed by six horsemen, with four Hungarian Hussars as outriders.

Abby's journey had been largely ceremonial and relatively brief, as the Augustinians' church, its simple, almost nondescript exterior in no way suggesting the magnificence awaiting one within, was, as was the Spanish Riding School—its neighbour up the street, facing Michaelerplatz—virtually part of the sprawling Hofburg Palace complex. At one point Abby had, only partially in jest, mentioned to her sister that perhaps they, and the young archduchesses, might just walk to church, Eileen responding that, given the weight and construction of her wedding gown, such might prove to be a "wearying experience."

As it was, the gown's volume had permitted only Abby and the Archduchesses Maria Carolina, now aged fourteen, and Maria Antonia, approaching eleven, to ride in the state coach; Eileen followed in a stately but far from magnificent carriage which she shared with General O'Connell and Countess von Graffenreit, whom, Eileen noted, held hands during the brief ride—wondering if the couple might be the next to wed.

As the carriage jangled to a halt behind the state coach, the countess gestured for Eileen to step out first. "You must lead the way to the altar for your dear sister, darling!" the countess said, genuinely happy. The couple then proceeded into the church.

Herself attired in a magnificent deep blue satin gown, also the product of Madame Schullheimer's salon, featuring a lengthy train of its own, the Lady Eileen stepped to the side of the state coach as the footmen handed down the two young archduchesses, their dresses perfect smaller versions of Eileen's. The three of them eyed one another with broad smiles. "We are all so very pretty!" exclaimed Antoine.

As directed by Count von Stemweitz, the master of ceremonies, Eileen stood and awaited her sister, who, preceded by some of her train, being gathered and then held by several young pages, emerged on the count's hand. He gave her over to Eileen, who smiled, her eyes deep blue pools of joyous tears, and bent and kissed her sister softly on each cheek, taking approving note of Abby's soft hair resting simply on her shoulders, rather than being done in a complex arrangement, and the expression of sheer joy on her face.

"Now . . . be about your business, girl," she commanded Abby in an affectionate whisper, the homely, familiar idiom spoken in Irish, as she stepped to retrieve the remainder of Abigail's train from the coach, gesturing to the archduchesses to each take a corner of the magnificent garment they would bear into the church.

Leaning down to the train bearers, Eileen spoke softly but precisely, using her hands for emphasis, as she often did. "The Lady Abigail will begin to process, when and as the count directs," she explained. "As she goes forward, her train will straighten out and the pages"—she gestured—"will see that it remains straight, and when we are directed, we shall then begin to walk forward."

Antoine suddenly appeared anxious. After their years together, Eileen immediately recognised the expression and quietly bent to her. "I shall be directly behind you both, walking between where you are, *directly behind*."

Thus reassured, the younger archduchess looked up at Eileen and smiled. Charlotte, in contrast, fully taking in the spectacle of pageantry and seeming to relish people's eyes on her, appeared already regal, fully self-assured.

From within the church, a blare of trumpets sounded and then another, longer and louder, joined by a full suite of brass instruments, the continuing music of which, combined with the cathedral's organ, soared. The count fluttered in the open doorway, dramatically gesturing that, with this musical accompaniment, Abby had begun her walk up the grand aisle. The little pages straightened and smoothed out the extraordinary train and stepped back and away, the creamy satin gleaming softly in the late morning sunshine. Suddenly the fabric began, ever so slowly, to move. Eileen gestured to her archduchesses with her right hand—*go*—and deftly holding the train in their hands, they did, Antoine beaming proudly, Charlotte smiling regally.

As someone handed her a sheaf of flowers, Eileen stepped behind the girls and together they—and Abby's train—made their slow, elegant way up the steps and into the dazzling church.

As Abby entered the building, she initially tried to focus her eyes on her seemingly far distant husband-to-be; satisfied that he was there, she quickly broadened her line of sight to look about the church itself. It was at that moment that her eyes went wide: The church was full.

She and O'Sullivan would later learn that, by a quietly circulated Imperial Decree of Welcome, the Imperial family and the nobility had joined with the entire court for this moment. Guards and doormen, room servants—including, of course, Elena and Anna, wearing new gowns for the occasion and seated together in specially chosen places—maids and outriders, pages, grooms, footmen, candle-lighters and -minders and individuals from the various Imperial kitchens—the literally hundreds and hundreds of people whose lives Abigail O'Connell had daily touched in her years at court, not to mention virtually the entire Konigkrantz Regiment of the Hungarian Hussars, officers and other ranks alike, in their breathtaking full-dress uniforms: all had come together in an astonishing, historic and brilliantly colourful tapestry unlike any such assembly in Vienna in memory, perhaps even, as was said by more than one person, in history—to honour Abby and her Denis, now *Major* Denis O'Sullivan. Abby could see him in the distance, his six-foot four-inch frame ramrod straight but largely eclipsed, now but a tiny figure at the end of the magnificent aisle, the cardinal archbishop of Vienna, Christoph Anton Migazzi, at his side, awaiting her as she was slowly, surely making her way to the altar, her eyes straight ahead, her heart thudding, her mind a sweet, wonderful blank upon which she made every effort to impress her recollections of the magnificence all about—and, she numbly thought, *for*—her.

It was not until the very moment that Abigail was preparing to take her final steps in approaching the cardinal and Denis at the foot of the altar that, as skilfully directed by the count by a delicate sweep of von Stemweitz's white-gloved right hand, the brass and tympani suddenly fell silent, the entire church itself instantly, breathlessly, still along with them.

According to a plan that had just that morning been finalised, with a gentle motion of his right hand, Cardinal Migazzi directed Abby's attention to the left front pew. She immediately stopped and turned sharply to her left, her eyes suddenly wide and her mouth momentarily half-open.

It had been suggested that the empress might possibly attend, but, as with so many events involving Maria Theresa now, it was uncertain. Realising what was about to happen, Eileen frantically gestured to the archduchesses, whispering, "Release the fabric, my darlings, and come forward—now!" And they did, and they and Eileen lifted the heavy train at Abby's feet, at least in part enabling what would be Abigail's most gracious gesture to the woman who was primarily responsible for this day.

Taking a breath, and with the utmost grace, a brilliant smile now on her face and her eyes brimming, Abby executed a flawless deep curtsey to Her Imperial Majesty, the Empress, as she sat, clad in a simple though elegant black gown, her son, Joseph, who had succeeded his father as Holy Roman Emperor, at her side, the emperor standing and gently bowing to her as Abby knelt.

As Abby rose, so, too, did the empress, extending her hands, her arms, embracing Abby.

"God bless you, my darling. God bless you and your bold knight," she whispered, "and bless you both with beautiful children and a beautiful life."

Tears streaming down her face, all Abigail could do was nod and whisper, "*Merci*, Madame," at which point the empress, her own eyes moist, directed the bride's attention to her groom, whilst everyone nearby smiled.

A final blare of trumpets sounded to accompany Abigail to her designated place, the left of a pair of high-backed chairs and cushioned prie-dieux. Eileen and the archduchesses waited for her to move forward, lifting and arranging the massive train, then taking their own seats at the left front of the church.

The couple knelt and smiled at each other as the cardinal archbishop, a spare man beneath his magnificent layers of vestments, began, as had the Roman Mass begun for centuries, intoning, in a resonant voice, half-speaking, half-chanting, *"In nomine Patris, et Fileii, et Spiritu Sanctu,"* to which the magnificent boys' choir responded in flawless tones, *"Ahhhhhh-mennnnnnn."*

Vienna—January 1767

Early one snowy Monday morning in January, elegantly lettered heavy, cream-coloured note cards had been delivered to Eileen, Abigail and Major O'Sullivan and, they believed, a number of others, requesting the recipients to join the Countess von Graffenreit and General the Baron O'Connell for what was indicated to be a gala on the following Friday evening at the countess's small castle, its very existence still known to only a few, though it was not far from Vienna itself, tucked into the gentle mountains off the road to Laxenburg.

The O'Sullivans and Eileen shared a sledge, the sisters each wrapped in her own striking winter cloak —Eileen's red, Abigail's purple —both fur-trimmed and wonderfully warm. As they departed the Hofburg, Abby wondered aloud, "Should there not be other sledges, or men on horseback, this being a gala?"

Her husband and sister nodded. "Curious it is," said O'Sullivan offhandedly, in his own mind thinking he would have preferred an evening with Abby by their own fireside to a cold sledge ride.

As they arrived at their destination, Abby spoke for all three. "Now 'tis beyond being curious, as I see no one, no one but us!"

Nevertheless, a footman stepped to the sledge and handed the sisters down on to an entryway freshly cleared of snow and, O'Sullivan stepping down himself, the three entered a brilliantly lit entrance hall, which, whilst glimmering with candles, itself was strangely, almost shockingly silent. The only thing that seemed normal was the covey of servants accepting their cloaks.

Whilst Abigail, looking warily about, was just about to step away and, as she said, "explore," the wonderfully officious Count Von Stemweitz, the court's ever-present master of ceremonies, appeared, this evening elegantly attired in a wine-coloured velvet suit, his wig dazzlingly white.

"Velcum, velcum, Major *und* Lady Abigail, Lady Eileen." He smiled, laughing at his limited, heavily accented English, then continued in his customarily flawless French, "Please, if you would follow me."

He conducted the wondering trio to a large, thickly carpeted gallery—the room was used for receptions and similar occasions where there would be no dancing—which was ablaze with light, though largely empty save for an assemblage, in front of a massive fireplace, itself brilliantly blazing, of gilded, padded, high-backed chairs, in which appeared to be already seated two, perhaps three individuals, though even O'Sullivan's line of sight was blocked by a group of servants, lined up behind the final grouping of chairs. He did note a piano set before the chairs and to one side. "A small concert, perhaps?" he whispered to his wife.

Abby nodded. "Perhaps," she said and, taking her husband's arm, followed the count, on whose arm Eileen travelled.

As they arrived at their seats, Abby gasped and Eileen involuntarily broke out in laughter, shocking the count but not the empress and Emperor Joseph, who, having turned in their seats, now both stood and smiled.

"My dears, why how lovely to see you!" Maria Theresa smiled, her expression warm, even joyous, despite the severity of her elegant black gown and wrap.

"Your Imperial Majesty . . ." Eileen managed, though the empress indicated that curtseying was not necessary.

"A select group it appears we are, yes?" the young emperor asked into the room.

The count indicated they should all be seated; as they did, some six chairs remained empty.

A bit of a clatter resonated at the rear of the long room, the unmistakable sound of one or more small children in evidence, this being confirmed as von Stemweitz led Countess von Graffenreit's two daughters, Elisabeth and

Maria, their uniformed husbands, both barons, and—each holding his mother's hand, two little boys—all to the seats with the O'Sullivans and Eileen and the royals.

Eileen had early on *sensed something* and was finally about to burst out in news, just as the general, magnificent in a full-dress uniform, his hair powdered, as it rarely ever was, and his hat under his arm, accompanied by Father Stanislaus Tyminsky, a rotund Polish Augustinian priest who had served as his personal chaplain when on campaign with his regiment—and who, in the process, had been twice wounded—a striking lace surplice laid over his simple heavy grey woollen habit and a colourfully embroidered stole draped about his shoulders, strode forward. The general was beaming.

At that moment, whilst not meaning to do so aloud, Abigail spoke a now-obvious word: "Wedding!"

The empress smiled broadly. "Insightful indeed, my darling girl!" and they laughed whilst the emperor rose and walked stiffly, precisely, to the rear of the room, the priest indicating the others should rise and stand in place.

A single bell rang, a deep, almost profound *bonnnnnng*.

As the empress, the three younger Irish people and the countess's family turned in the direction of the sound, they all broke into broad smiles as Maria von Graffenreit, attired in a magnificently embroidered gold and deep blue court dress, a sheaf of fresh flowers in her arms and a brilliant smile on her always lovely face, entered on the arm of the Holy Roman Emperor. She nodded regally at the tiny congregation and stepped forward as he relinquished her to the arm of the general, her very-soon-to-be husband.

The actual ceremony, the simple Roman Catholic Rite of Marriage, was purposely brief and the aftermath intimately joyful as the adults mixed and mingled as at a simple family gathering, with Eileen and Abigail, the countess's daughters and several times the empress herself taking turns entertaining the squirming little ones whilst champagne and a light supper was served in a much smaller, still comfortable library, warmed by fires blazing in a pair of facing hearths.

The supper consumed, and coffee and pastries being on offer, along with more champagne, two young nurses entered quietly and scooped up the countess's grandchildren. The adults had a pleasant remainder of the evening, the gathering and their conversation continuing informal and family-like—until, at precisely nine o'clock, the empress quietly rose from her chair by the fire, the young emperor doing the same, all those who were seated then rising as well. Within moments the empress and her son had departed and were quickly followed into the still, bitterly-cold but brilliantly-starry night by the remainder of the guests, General O'Connell and Countess now-von Graffenreit-O'Connell bidding them all a good night at the main entrance.

Vienna—Winter–Early Spring 1767

Even as Anna, with her customary chatty efficiency, extracted her from the elegantly-heavy purple velvet robe she'd worn to the wedding, Eileen began to experience *something*—she told herself at various times in the days—and weeks—that followed that she sensed herself feeling odd, off-kilter, even "a wee bit askew," as she finally said aloud to Abby.

She did not often dwell on the subject as the winter, albeit largely uneventful in any significant way, was nevertheless proving to be a busy one for a number of reasons—not the least of which being the fact that Easter would fall on April nineteenth, thus rendering Lent's penitential arrival an early one. The winter days were long—oft-times both beginning and ending in the dark—but invariably fast-moving. They were filled with the archduchesses' lessons—academic, musical, equestrian, the weeks punctuated by the occasional minor crises typical to the household—a series of colds for Charlotte, a muscle pull one day, a nasty bump on the forehead on another, both whilst riding, for Antoine; dresses failing to arrive when promised, their mother's seeming all-too-frequent absences from their lives. As she had since arriving in Vienna, Eileen managed, with her usual finesse and signature mix of good cheer and dark humour, to navigate them all.

As an unusually cold and snowy January wound towards a blizzardy close, the alpine winds proving themselves this year exceptionally brutal, creating mountainous three- and four-foot-high snow drifts in Vienna and the countryside alike, Eileen felt she had reached at least a partial rationale for her unusual feelings:

In mid-February, as illogical as the timing seemed to anyone who'd given it a thought, Major Wolfgang von Klaus was due to depart Vienna for what was generally understood to be a multiyear posting at the Austrian mission to the court of the Empress Catherine in St. Petersburg. In her small leather book-like desk calendar, Eileen had written in her broad, elegant script, on the page for that month, *Au revoir, mon cher Wolfgang!* At some point afterwards, in a slightly different-coloured ink, she appended a hopeful *À bientôt!*— though, from what she knew of the Habsburgs' relatively recent unpleasant, even stormy relationship with Russia, Eileen had come to accept that his time there would most likely be indeterminate and could prove to be lengthy.

Von Klaus had explained to her that the countries had fallen out in 1762, during the very brief—until he was overthrown by his wife, Catherine—reign of Czar Peter III, the strange, many felt mad Russian autocrat having, as part of his desire to reach an accord with Prussia, declared that he was "resolved to get free of all commitments to the Court of Vienna." The Austrian envoy at St. Petersburg, Count Mercy Argenteau, who had dedicated years of diplomatic effort in Russia—and who would come to be ubiquitous in representing Austria at the highest, most complex levels of diplomacy—had immediately requested that he be recalled from Catherine's court. The Habsburgs having followed his advice, he had been succeeded by a series of lower-level diplomats. Von Klaus advised Eileen that, as a confidant of Emperor Joseph, he was— with the empress's full concurrence—being dispatched to St. Petersburg as the sovereigns' personal representative, possessing *carte blanche* to deal with the Empress Catherine's government as he saw fit.

Since they'd first met—and immediately become intimate—in October of 1764, the relationship of the two tall, striking, athletic individuals had been the object of more than the usual, though not the malicious variety of court gossip: *They will wed soon, see how in love they are. . . . How can that be? The girl is a mere commoner, the von Klauses amongst the oldest, the leading families of Austria. . . . I doubt if they've even shared a bed. . . . Hah, I doubt that they do not frequently do so!*

The incomplete truth of the matter was that the two were, as Eileen had first admitted to her sister, "friends, *very* . . . good . . . friends," ultimately expanded, under Abby's relentless elder sisterly questioning, to Eileen finally blushingly conceding, "Yes, yes . . . we *are* lovers," though even then she immediately disavowed any serious romance, firmly maintaining there was nothing approaching an "understanding."

The full truth was that Eileen had to some degree grown fond of the tall, husky and handsome noble—fonder than she'd ever intended to. Though she believed that von Klaus might share her feelings, she'd never pressed the matter—nor had he.

Nevertheless, as January unavoidably progressed, the two sought each other's company frequently, almost anxiously: It seemed they attended every ball, and there danced every dance. At dinners—"protocol be damned," as von Klaus put it—they had the seating rearranged so they could dine together, so too as to their seats at the opera, the symphony.

On the rare mild day, they would ride about the city, Bull as always appearing smug that von Klaus's magnificent palomino Andalusian stallion, El Dorado, was not as large as he. More typically, they—once or twice a week—went sledge riding, von Klaus taking the reins of the team himself, the pair cosily sharing heavy blankets and robes as the conveyance lurched through the gritty, icy-grey streets of Vienna until it reached the snow-covered open countryside beyond. There they would skim for hours through the powdery snow, the horses' bells jingling merrily, the couple feeling warm, merry even—Eileen herself feeling fully at ease, her fur-hooded head resting against von Klaus's broad shoulder, as it often did, as the sledge hurtled gaily towards Schönbrunn one sunny, frigid morning, the palace appearing a fairy-tale castle, heavily dusted with snow, encrusted in numerous places with ice, their shared hope being the availability of hot coffee, hot cocoa, perhaps even brandy.

And frequently—more frequently than ever before—their days—be they ones of labour or play—were ending in Eileen's bed, the massive piece of furniture seeming a sanctuary, providing at least a temporary haven against the inevitable passage of time. Once abed, their near-immediate lovemaking would commence—their usual athletic passion, their customary verbal fervour had begun to take on an unspoken urgency, a shared desire to extract as much—could it, both wondered silently, be some form of *love*?—out of each passage, more than from the ones prior, less than those to come.

Eileen—and von Klaus perhaps, as well—would long remember the night of the seventeenth of February, two days prior to his departure for Russia, as one marked by a wildly-howling snowstorm and a pair of comic events on their arrival: Anna was at first nowhere to be found, and when she ultimately did appear what she saw on her humming unannounced entrance was Eileen perched on her lover's lap, causing von Klaus to reflexively rise, tumbling her mistress to the floor in a swirl of heavy skirts. Anna's face ablaze, her mouth agape, the trio could not help but laugh as Eileen scrambled to get up.

Within minutes of Anna's departure, as von Klaus padded towards Eileen's dressing room in his heavily-stockinged feet, pieces of his uniform—though including neither his breeches nor his shirt—strewn on the furniture in the parlour and the carpet heading into her bedroom, a wailing Archduchess Maria Antonia burst into the parlour, blood dripping from two fingers, sobbing, "App . . . app-felllll," she managed in German. As she began again in French, Eileen put her hands up, indicating she understood what had happened, the archduchess nevertheless sobbing, *"Je essayé de couper. . .* ohhhhhhhh, Eye-leeeeeeeeeeeen!" Von Klaus diplomatically remained in the bedroom as governess and archduchess stanched the flow of both Imperial blood and tears, and Eileen had located and tied on a small cotton bandage strip with a neat little bow, that made her patient laugh weakly, as she was led back to her own apartments—and her blood-spotted fruit.

As Eileen returned, closing her door with a gentle click, von Klaus playfully peeked out of the bedroom, inquiring, "Who is to be next? Perhaps it will be Bull—distressed by an inadequate oats bucket," his booming laugh filled the room. Eileen could only shake her head.

An hour later, the storm still raging beyond the heavily draped, thickly glassed windows, firelight flickering against the bedroom's crème-coloured walls, the pair lay entwined under a rumpled mass of puffy down-filled quilts, their skin moist, their breathing slow, deep—the aura of just-spent passion heavy in the room.

Her arm stretched across von Klaus's scarred—on separate occasions by two different sabres—chest, Eileen's head rested against his shoulder, her mass of tousled hair fallen to one side on the bed's mountain of feather pillows. She began to speak and, yet again, she grew unusually tongue-tied. Wolfgang stroked her hair, until she finally managed, "I was just thinking, this is . . . it is . . . our final night, *ja*? Tomorrow, your brother officers, your regiment, they must . . . they will, they . . . you . . ."

"*Ja* indeed they must and they will—dispatch me to an even more frigid 'Mother Russia' with a grand banquet and much drinking . . . and I fear you are correct, that this is the final time we shall be abed for some time, my dearest friend."

Eileen snuggled closer, her mind somersaulting with words such as *love* . . . most definitely *passion* . . . *affection* . . . *friendship, companionship* . . . her whirring thoughts resting again on, perhaps settling on *friendship*—saying nothing of any of the others, she finally whispered, "I shall indeed miss you, my own dearest friend."

After a long moment, he managed, ". . . and I you . . . I shall miss you, Eileen, my dearest . . ."

Wordlessly, he abruptly rolled onto his back, pulling her almost roughly atop him, her hair streaming over her breasts, down her own back, her hands on his chest. His hands on her bottom, her lower back, Eileen moved instinctively and arched, and settled on him, a loud *Aaaaaaaaaaah* . . . as he took her . . . as she took him . . . as they joined—almost violently, thrusting and writhing, thrashing—for how long neither knew.

As they climaxed roughly as one, von Klaus lay atop Eileen, their bodies glistening, looking into each other's eyes, lips close though not touching. Finally, Eileen's hands found his neck, beneath his semitied queue, and drew his mouth to hers in a silent, powerful and lengthy kiss. Von Klaus finally eased off her and they lay facing each other, gently touching, saying little—until first she, then he, both reluctantly fell asleep.

The following evening von Klaus had indeed been fêted by his brother officers, a number of colonels joined by several generals. The emperor himself was the evening's surprise guest, unsuccessfully attempting a series of "bitterly cold Mother Russia" jokes that produced little laughter. Joseph, who was fond of von Klaus, finally said, "Your cheer—good or forced—in accepting this posting shall not be forgotten, my friend." Then he left.

In the morning, von Klaus himself departed. That it was windless rendered the air not-quite-bitterly cold, as a small group gathered on the gritty, grey-iced cobblestones of the *Schweizerhof*'s snowy courtyard. A sombre though composed Eileen, unintentionally resplendent in her brilliantly red full-length cloak, had previously gifted von Klaus with the fur-lined gloves of the finest Spanish leather that he now removed to bow and formally kiss her hand—and Abigail's, and that of Maria Antonia, as well. With yet one more nod to Eileen alone, the officer mounted and—a last, long look—led his modest procession away from the Hofburg.

Turning to her sister, Abby remarked, offhandedly, though it seemed to Eileen *coldly*, "So . . . your *friend*, he is gone now, *ja?*" Her expression almost harsh, Eileen shook her head, muttering the obvious. "He *is* gone. . . ." After purposely appending a firm *"aye"* to her response, she took her little archduchess's gloved hand in her own. As her governess led her away in atypical silence, the little girl looked up at her solicitously.

Several weeks passed. With Ash Wednesday Lent had arrived and Eileen continued to feel "off kilter." Spending time in deep thought on the subject, she began to understand that she was feeling much the same as she had at Ballyhar following John O'Connor's death; similarly, what she had experienced after she'd been back at Derrynane for a time thereafter: *I am restless, bored, wondering if I even belong where I am. . . .*

She'd occasionally touched on whether perhaps it was von Klaus's departure—*I have no illusions; I do not love Wolfgang, nor he me, but . . . nevertheless I do miss him*—she would finally permit herself to accept it. Yet even then she qualified her emotions, *though nowhere near as much as I would Anna, were she to leave.*

One afternoon whilst walking the length of the vast palace alone, she thought, *I could be no happier for Abby and Denis or for my beloved uncle and the sweetest of noble ladies than I am, but could it be that I am envious* Giving it more than casual thought, she would finally shake her head, refusing to accept the sin of envy as being amongst hers, concluding firmly, *though I have many failings and though I commit—and regularly confess—*she smiled ironically, *more than a few sins . . . I envy no one, no one at all!*

As Easter drew ever closer, Eileen sought out her sister for some uninterrupted conversation. Arriving at Abby's ornate office, adjacent to the empress's, late one still, gloomy afternoon, Eileen began speaking even as she was settling her extensive grey satin skirts. "Do you ever consider returning home, sister?" she inquired bluntly in her husky voice, speaking Irish for the first time in a number of months.

Abigail's mouth fell open, though she quickly composed herself, clearing her throat, purposely responding in English. "Truth be told, my darling, in our early years here . . . I did, but with the passage of years, with the empress . . . and now Denis, I have come to think of Vienna, of Austria, as being *home.*"

Eileen nodded, saying nothing, her expression thoughtful.

"Is it that you are possibly considering . . . a return to Ireland, my darling?" Abigail probed, her own expression evidencing incredulity.

Eileen shook her head. "I—I do not . . . perhaps, yes . . . but . . ." and her voice trailed off.

"Dearest sister," Abby began, her tone firm, definite, "what is it of what you call *home* that you feel is lacking here?" Without giving Eileen the opportunity to respond, she declared, "Here we worship freely and openly—joyfully even—as loyal children of God and of His holy, true Roman and Catholic Church, *ja?* And at *home,* our holy faith remains outlawed, we ourselves being 'out of the law' by even believing, much less practising it."

Eileen began to speak, but raising her right hand gently, Abigail charged forward. "I would say also that it is *here* where we are truly free people. I have come to understand that at Derrynane for our entire lives we were shielded; we were protected by our wealth and by Papa and his men, by their cunning, their daring. They killed men to protect us!" Abby's voice suddenly filled the ornate room. "Killed, I said!"

Eileen nodded, again remaining silent.

"The only reason we are not illiterate, why our family is not hopelessly impoverished or landless like most native Irish Catholics is the armed, guarded, impenetrable sanctuary that is Derrynane. Beyond it, life is . . ." She shook her head.

"No, my darling, I strongly believe I *am* home, as I do that the general is home . . . as so, too, are *you*. We are *all*—O'Connell, O'Sullivan—home here, here . . . in Austria. Though Irish we shall forever remain, so, too, shall we stay put, at home . . . *here*." She gestured resolutely to the floor, to the ground of Imperial Austria beneath it.

Eileen sat quietly, her hands folded in her lap, her eyes warm on her sister. After several moments she finally stood, smiling warmly at her beloved Abigail. She turned to leave, took several steps towards the entry and turned back. As the door minder held the massive white door ajar, lifting her head slightly, her expression appearing to her sister to be so like a little girl's, Eileen softly said, almost whispering, "Aye, then"—and slipped otherwise wordlessly through the opening.

On the final Thursday in March, Eileen took Antoine alone for her regular riding lesson. It being a sunny afternoon and—Charlotte remaining unhappily in bed with yet another heavy, noisy, feverish cold—as it was just the two of them, Eileen had decided they would make the short journey to the Riding School on foot, to be accomplished by partially traversing the vast Hofburg, exiting the palace complex near the Augustinerkirche and strolling up the narrow street, also named in honour of the Augustinian friars, to the Michaelerplatz, there re-entering the palace and thence the school.

Eileen having advised the appropriate authorities in advance, the street was cleared of people and under full guard as the pair stepped outside. Attired in an elegant grey wool habit, nearly-identical to that worn by her riding mistress, looking up the silent, empty street, the young girl wondered aloud, "Are people *never* permitted on the streets when we are present?" Rather than attempting to summarise the various security protocols in place—governing instances where an archduchess is being driven as opposed to her being mounted, both of which differed from walking, as they were now—Eileen matter-of-factly indicated it was for her safety. "The empress would never want anything to happen to you, my darling."

The mention of her mother seemed to have instantly caught Maria Antonia's attention as she immediately reached for Eileen's hand and they halted abruptly. "I dined with the empress last evening, as you know." The governess looked down, indicating she did. Continuing to speak, the archduchess lowered her voice such that Eileen had to lean closer so as to hear what she was saying, actually missing her first words. ". . . and she was unaware that I practise my writing every day now and even of my progress with dressage . . . and . . ." Her words tumbled out breathlessly, a painful litany of how the empress's singularly demanding schedule prevented her from knowing things important to an eleven-year-old girl, whilst making it virtually impossible to spend any significant time with her. ". . . all of this caused me to think again of something I have often thought, especially of late, but have never told you." She was looking directly into Eileen's eyes, her own soft blue ones wide and brimming.

Sensing the importance of the moment, Eileen gently took both of the young girl's elegantly-gloved hands in her own, listening intently as Antoine continued. "You seem more . . . you *are* more like my true mother than is the empress." The tears that had been in her eyes fell, a pair of slow, shiny rivulets on her fair cheeks as the young archduchess began to cry in earnest as she spoke. "I love you so very much . . . and I know you love me. Please, *please* promise me that you will never leave me, *Mama*," she finished plaintively, her trim shoulders shaking under her soft grey wool riding coat, her tears falling visible on the tightly-woven fabric.

Stunned, shooting glances at the closest of the young sentries on each side—who instantly stepped back, averting their gaze—Eileen quickly knelt in the street and the child threw her arms around her neck, sobbing as if her heart would indeed break. Eileen held Antoine close against her bosom, whispering softly in her ear as the now-seeming little girl's tears slowly, very slowly ebbed.

Still kneeling, Eileen gently eased the young archduchess back slightly, holding her upper arms, looking deeply into her moist eyes. "I *do* love you, my darling Antoine," she said softly, her throaty voice even, calming, ". . . as much as if I had borne you myself, as if *I* had brought you into this world. Fear not, my darling love, I shall . . ."

Before Eileen could finish, Antoine again embraced her tightly, her head against Eileen's shoulder, murmuring over and over, "I was certain you would not, *Mama* . . . I knew it, I knew it . . . I love you, I love you . . . I love you so very, very, very much, my dearest, dearest Mama. . . ."

Quietly shaken, Eileen finally stood; again hand in hand, the pair walked slowly, virtually silently towards their destination, the little girl's head resting against Eileen's right arm. They barely halted as the huge doors to the Winter Riding School swung open on their arrival.

The lesson was unremarkable, their return walk largely the same—save that they spoke little and that Antoine clung more tightly than usual to her *Mama*'s gloved hand, again occasionally resting her head against Eileen's arm and smiling dreamily any time the governess looked down at her.

It was not until after she'd seen to both girls' bedtimes and returned to her quarters in midevening that Eileen had any opportunity to reflect on the powerful events of the afternoon.

Ah, love her I do! I adore the child, she admitted effortlessly, *I believe I love her more than I do anyone, even more than my darling Hugh.*

I should perhaps have immediately spoken up for Her Imperial Majesty, should I have not? Eileen wondered. *Is it that I have committed some form of treason, embracing the Imperial child as were she my own?* She rolled her eyes, finally resting her head against the high back of her wing chair, gazing into the low fire, and exhaled deeply.

Permitting her mind to wander, Eileen recalled proclaiming—frequently and, she smiled—loudly, with regard to her having gone to John O'Connor's Ballyhar, *"I have done my duty!"* Telling herself, *I have many failings, yet never have I turned my back on my duty . . . at least to my family . . . but now, this duty to a still-very-young girl, how can I? Is it that I am expected to . . . ?*

The following morning, whilst Antoine was occupied with a dancing lesson taught by a diminutive, doll-like little Hungarian master who always reminded Eileen of one depiction of the *wee little people who dwell beneath the ground and inhabit the raths—the fairy forts—in Ireland,* despite that she was without an appointment Eileen hurried to speak privately with Abigail, who quickly closed her door as her sister advised breathlessly that "'Tis a matter of some urgency."

Rarely behaving officiously with her sister, despite the significant difference in their respective positions, Abby apologised for not asking the younger woman to sit. "I am so terribly busy, my darling," she said softly, gesturing to the door that connected her office with that of the empress and then to the mounds of papers on her writing desk.

"I understand the limits on your time, sister; I only desire to ask, if I may do so without stating my reasons, is it that when the ultimate decision as to Her Imperial Highness Maria Antonia's *future,* if I may phrase it thus, is made . . . is it that I am to accompany her, to wherever it is that she may be bound?"

The question caught the empress's principal lady-in-waiting wholly by surprise—as, to her knowledge, the topic had never been raised with her sister. Whilst she did have a general idea as to what the protocol might be in such situations, she was certain of it in only one of them.

Leaning against her desk, Abigail spoke very softly. "You are aware that preliminary 'conversations' amongst the diplomats have begun regarding several of the archduchesses, including both of your charges, yes?"

Eileen nodded affirmatively and Abby continued, "The kingdoms of Naples, Parma and France—each different, each important in its own way to the empress—they are the ones with which the conversations go on.

"Truth be told, I understand that one possible scenario would have either of the Archduchesses Maria Carolina or Maria Antonia betrothed to the dauphin of France, the grandson of His Majesty Louis XV. I myself believe that that is highly likely, but it is at least two, perhaps even three years away—and there is no clarity in terms of which archduchess it would be. In any case, I must caution you against discussing *any* of this further with *anyone* . . . no one at all!" She nodded firmly at her younger sister, who returned the nod silently.

"Now, my darling . . . as to your inquiry, I am able to advise that in the event that either of your little archduchesses was to be chosen, it would be impossible for you to accompany her . . . even if you wished to do so, as French protocol prohibits it."

Sensing a subtle change in her sister's expression—though unsure whether it was an indication of relief or one of puzzlement she saw in Eileen's eyes—Abigail now relaxed, sitting back on the edge of her desk, her hands resting on the gleaming surface alongside her bottom, her tone less formal, speaking more as an elder sister to her cherished younger one. "In fact," she shook her head, surprising Eileen by laughing softly, "French protocol even prohibits such a princess from entering France in non-French clothing!"

Eileen's eyes widened and she could not help but laugh as well. "So naked as a wee babe she would go?"

She laughed again, Abigail explaining that some type of a wardrobe change was accomplished, "Though I am unaware how it is done."

Her question seemingly answered, just as Abby began to mention something further concerning Maria Josepha, Eileen leaned forward, thanked her sister warmly with a hug and withdrew.

Schönbrunn—Easter 1767

In what was a decidedly minor—though, as it marked the culmination of the massive annual logistical miracle that was the removal of the Imperial court from the Hofburg to Schönbrunn—not wholly insignificant event, a caravan of coaches bearing the young archdukes and archduchesses and the members of their various households was to set out for the smaller palace in the gentle countryside outside of Vienna on the Wednesday before Palm Sunday. There the family would celebrate Easter and remain through the summer, though some, including the youngest archduchesses, and with them Eileen and Anna, would also spend part of the summer at the slightly further-distanced Laxenburg.

The young royals were aware only generally that the transition involved, amongst a number of other incredible feats, the actual movement of most of the smaller palace's contents, not the least of which was virtually all of its furnishings from the massive Vienna warehouses where they had been stored since autumn, including their individual rooms of furniture.

Eileen had unexpectedly found the frenetic activity of these days of preparation to be energising; she did her share of the sorting and packing of the youngest archduchesses' clothing and belongings, playfully cajoling Charlotte into helping with the process. Antoine, having already decided it was fun, was merrily sitting on the floor of her bedroom folding and stacking clothing, making Anna laugh as she proclaimed, "We are *working*!"

As they prepared to finally depart the young girls' apartments, Anna having just done the same for her, Eileen then directed the footmen and haulers in terms of what trunks were to go to the cargo wagons, which to the archduchesses' coach, as well as showing the laundresses which clothing was to be washed, cleaned and packed away, as well as those numerous dresses and cloaks, gowns, robes, shoes and miscellaneous millenary—which, she noticed, actually constituted much of the girls' wardrobes—were to be disposed of. *Both of them are growing so quickly, little of this finery, or anything else, will fit them come autumn.*

To her surprise, Eileen also felt the entire process had been in many ways cathartic, as if she were perhaps shedding winter's gloom along with all of their heavy cloaks and wools.

Certain that all was in readiness, at least to the extent that it could be for their relatively short trek, Anna quickly assisted her mistress into her riding habit. As Eileen finished dressing, she accompanied the girls to their coach.

The distance between the palaces being perhaps five, at the very most six miles, Eileen had obtained, as she had since her first such journey, permission to ride Bull from the Spanish Riding School, where he resided whilst they wintered at the Hofburg. As the procession due to transport the archdukes and archduchesses was forming, Eileen appeared from the direction of the Riding School's stables, heads turning as the strikingly-elegant young woman in her fine hip-length black wool riding coat and flowing matching skirt, a black tricorn hat, trimmed in a subtle gold braid, perched jauntily on her head, her hair loose and gleaming, a gloved right hand gripping his bridle, walked Bull towards the archduchesses' coach. People smiled as the powerful chestnut stallion theatrically tossed his thick black mane, flicking his long, wavy black tail. Eileen was smiling as well, because she knew she herself cut an arresting figure—or at least she hoped she did!

Eileen mounted and positioned Bull next to the girls' coach, letting them know she was present as the caravan was being made ready for final departure. As she sat comfortably back in her Spanish saddle, she could only laugh at her beloved horse's continuing antics—but she was also now thoroughly enjoying herself, enjoying that people's eyes were resting on her, revelling even in the flirtatious glances of the young officers. Looking about, she nodded at some people, smiling at the more handsome of the cavalrymen, feeling their gazes warmer than the morning's dull sun.

Suddenly, orders and immediate acknowledgements rang out sharply down the line, the first of the coaches lurched forward and directly so, too, did the archduchesses', Anna laughingly calling out, "*Schließlich, geht es los!*"/ Finally, here we go!—both young girls cheering and clapping in response.

As the cavalcade clattered out of the city and wended its way on freshly-smoothed roads towards Schönbrunn, Eileen trotted alongside the coach, occasionally leaning in to chat through the carriage's open windows.

Mainly, however, she rode in blissful silence, the immediate atmosphere alive with the soft creaking of coach wheels and springs, jangling tack and the steady rhythm of thudding hooves—the gentle squeak of her own body, her bottom, her thighs against the thick leather of Bull's saddle, all seeming to her comforting, timeless sounds. A light wind came up as they were perhaps two miles gone from the Hofburg, diffusing the morning's thin cloud cover; the sun was growing brighter, warmer. More than once, she lifted her face to it, feeling the rays on her cheeks, the gentle breeze tossing her hair, sensing her spirits rising—beginning to feel in a way as frisky as Bull continued to behave.

By the time the distinctive façade of Schönbrunn appeared in the distance, smiling as she heard both archduchesses call out as they saw it, Eileen felt a sense of lightness—as if she'd somehow finally jettisoned those which had lingered of her strange, detached feelings, the quirky emotional discordance of the prior months seemingly evaporating in the pleasantly-altered setting of the Austrian countryside.

The cortège approached the palace at an almost deferential pace, the drive broad and smoothly-gravelled. As the archduchesses' coach in turn creaked to a halt, Eileen leaned back slightly, lifted her right leg over Bull's head and slid off, her boots crunching in the stones, a young groom immediately grasping Bull's cheek strap. Striding around to where its three passengers stood, Eileen took a deep breath as she looked up at Schönbrunn's always-welcoming entrance, its main and secondary doors flanked on the far sides by a pair of striking curved stairs, leading to the portico that protected the breadth of the entry on which today she saw gathered in greeting the majority of the household staff not directly involved in the logistics of the archducal arrival. As the young girls finished waving and calling out to their favourites amongst the group, Eileen placed her hands on their shoulders, indicating they should follow Anna inside, commanding softly, "Now, let us settle in—and prepare for Easter."

After a gloomy Palm Sunday and a fittingly dreary Holy Week—it had flurried snow on Holy Thursday and rained heavily on Good Friday—Easter Sunday dawned gloriously, with a magnificent, multihued sky heralding the festive singularly-holy day.

Despite that they all had been up late for the traditional Holy Saturday Pascal bonfires symbolising Christ's victory over death, His rising during the deepest hours of the night, Eileen and her charges awakened and were dressed early in their Easter finery.

For the day, Anna assisted Eileen into a new, striking two-layered court dress, à pannier, with significant décolletage. The underdress was of crème-coloured silk, with a subtle wild floral pattern, its graceful three-quarter-length sleeves plain. The outer dress was of heavy, striking gold satin, its own sleeves ending just above the ones beneath, creating an appearance of elegantly-flowing cuffs. Her hair was gathered into a thick, waist-length coil, and she wore comfortable crème-coloured French silk slippers.

Thus attired, she joined the archduchesses as they were being dressed in smaller versions of her own outfit—Charlotte in wispy sky blue and Antoine in a soft, mossy green over their own crème floral silk underdresses.

As the empress awaited the arrival of all her children, she could only smile at the striking appearance her two youngest daughters and their very tall governess made as they glided towards the end of the long hallway where the family was gathering for the brief walk to the chapel for Easter Mass. The archduchesses flanked Eileen, the three holding hands. As they reached the empress, Eileen softly said, "Now," and, releasing their hands, they curtseyed almost as one, deeply and *flawlessly*, Maria Theresa observed.

Watching Maria Antonia greeting her mother in a less than effusive manner, Eileen experienced a sharp pang of guilt as she mused again whether her own maternal relationship with the young girl, and Antoine's filial one with Eileen, was some form of *infidelity* in terms of their relationships to the empress. She quickly dismissed the feeling as Antoine again took her hand to walk to Mass, then nestled close to her throughout much of the lengthy service.

The Easter Mass was beautiful, the incense heavily-fragrant, the choir's voices soaring. The weather being fine and growing warmer still, they gathered outside. The day's foods and wines proved to be extraordinary. The young archdukes and archduchesses mingled amongst themselves, their relatives and guests, most of the children playing as much as they could in formal court dress. Major Denis O'Sullivan being away on manoeuvres, Eileen and Abby shared a bench and plates of food, enjoying each other's company and conversation.

Later, in the sunny, almost warm afternoon, Abigail joined the empress on a ground-level terrace, the panorama of slightly-greening grass and gardens just beginning to bloom sweeping away in all directions, the fountains gushing joyously. As Abby walked up, the empress slipped her own arm through her lady-in-waiting's and gestured silently with a gentle nod of her head.

Following the sovereign's gaze, Abby immediately saw that, not far from where they stood, Eileen and Maria Antonia were walking hand in hand, their arms swinging playfully, in the direction of a group of younger Habsburg relatives and the children of certain courtiers. Suddenly the archduchess swung around, extending both of her hands, which Eileen took and, both leaning back, they whirled together—first slowly, then faster and faster—their laughter audible to the monarch and Abby, who laughed as well until Eileen tugged Antoine to a halt.

She bent teasingly to her young charge and, after saying something to Antoine, Eileen flashed a dazzling smile and broke and ran, laughing.

Her arms out in front of her, the young girl sprinted after Eileen, lowering them as soon as she realised she needed to lift her skirts in order to run. She called out something that sounded like "I can catch you!" as her nimble governess, her hair now falling loose, streaked as best she could in her own cumbersome outfit, across the lawn, responding approximately, "No, you can't!"—both speaking in German.

The pair gambolled half the width of the palace, Eileen well in the lead until she abruptly turned, momentarily halted and began to race back towards the archduchess, who loudly feigned shock and surprise and then turning, shrieking as she tried to elude her pursuer.

The empress pointed out to Abby that a number of the gathered had stopped doing what they had been to watch the playful race, both women smiling as some of the children cheered on the archduchess.

Not surprisingly, Eileen's long muscular legs carrying her faster than did the not-yet twelve-year-old's, she caught Antoine. Laughingly, as she wrapped her hands around the archduchess's midsection—crying out "I've got you now!"—Eileen halted her in her tracks. Spinning her around playfully, in a fluid motion she lifted her up with surprising ease—the still-in-many-ways little girl shrieking, laughing gleefully, swinging her legs so hard that her slippers flew off—until Eileen finally set her down, Antoine's arms going immediately around the woman's waist with a massive hug, until Eileen knelt on the grass and the two embraced, the archduchess finally laughingly collapsing on her back, her bare feet arched in the sunshine—instinctively, primly holding her skirts close to her legs—until Eileen righted her.

By this time the empress was laughing heartily and aloud, something she rarely ever did since Francis Stephen's death.

"They are so happy together, *ja*? Antoine, she is always so happy with your dear sister." The monarch smiled, as did Abigail.

"There will come a time," the empress sighed deeply, "I fear they will no longer be able to be such."

Abigail nodded. "'Tis true, Your Imperial Majesty . . . though I believe that day may well be some years away."

Her expression brightening, the empress smiled softly. "*Years*, you say? *Ja*?"

Abby nodded. "I believe so . . . *ja*," Abby smiled, "Not until such time as Her Imperial Highness finally leaves us," she said with a firm, very certain nod.

Glancing again at the still-laughing pair strolling away across the lawn, again hand in hand, the women looked at each other and smiled. Momentarily pensive, Maria Theresa turned her gaze towards the gentle hillock, a break in the tree line in the distance, the mid-afternoon sky crystal blue and cloudless.

"When that time ultimately arrives, each shall then follow her own destiny," she observed, her voice soft but definite. Abigail nodded, aware of the archduchess's, wholly uncertain of what Eileen's would be.

Dropping Eileen's hand, the archduchess scampered ahead to join a group of young girls. Walking away in the same direction, Eileen glanced back at the empress and Abby, thinking, *What a conspiratorial pair they appear! For all the world, do they not seem to be deciding the fates of nations on this blessed beautiful day?* She laughed, but then slowed, turned slightly and eyed them again more intently.

She then knew, or she was fairly certain she did. *They are talking about me! 'Tis guaranteed they are, as sometimes, like Maire, I have a certain feeling about things, I just do, is all.* . . . More than that, she knew her cherished Abby as well as she knew herself.

"Ah, 'tis no matter!" she said softly aloud, her deep blue eyes twinkling. "None at all!"

Whatever their speculations, whatever their plans, indeed whether they were even speaking of her or not – and no matter her own uncertain restlessness in recent months, Eileen felt happy, content in this place – and, once again, very much at peace with her own good self.

As if to unconsciously confirm the fact, as she resumed walking towards the young archduchess and her friends Eileen slipped into the long, confident stride by which she had been known at Derrynane, at Ballyhar, but which was rarely seen in Vienna. That she'd done so, Eileen hadn't noticed; had she, she would not have altered her gait – but, rather, simply continued on, as she was:

Her step certain, her bearing regal . . . moving forward.

An Deireadh

Though this is a work of fiction, the tantalisingly few facts that are actually known of Eileen's and the other O'Connells' lives provide the basic threads around which the tale itself is woven, into which strategic additions of numerous fictional and historical personalities and events have, hopefully, seamlessly intertwined.

I have been a serious student of selected (including especially the eighteenth century) periods of the history of Ireland for most of my life; one significant aspect of this has been a continuing scholarly as well as personal interest in my extended family (Daniel O'Connell spoke of there being "many outcroppings of the O'Connells" who dwelt about Derrynane), many distant, and long-ago members of which, especially the characters of whom I write, I have "known" intimately since childhood. I have literally grown up with countless tales, a number of which have been the genesis for parts of *Derrynane*.

This notwithstanding, the book could not have been written absent a near-lifetime of reading and studying the works of a number of extraordinary historians and other authors, to all of whom – living and dead – an immeasurable debt is owed, especially to those noted below.

In addition to family materials, old notes and the like, my formal research has included standard works such as the still-brilliant *Course of Irish History*, by T.W. Moody and F.X. Martin; *Contested Ireland (Ireland 1460-1630)* by S.J. Connolly and *Gaelic Ireland (1250 – 1650: Land, Lordship & Settlement)*, edited by Patrick J. Duffy, David Edwards and Elizabeth Fitzpatrick.

Raymond Gillespie's *Seventeenth Century Ireland* as well as Ian McBride's *Eighteenth Century Ireland*, both volumes in the Gill New History of Ireland series, and Patrick Moran's *The Catholics of Ireland under the Penal Laws of the Eighteenth Century* proved invaluable in permitting me to immerse myself in the period and, hopefully, to write as the seanachie told tales of ancient Ireland – as had the events unfolded only recently, rather than centuries before.

Daniel Corkery's *Hidden Ireland*; volume one of Mrs. Morgan John O'Connell's classic *The Last Colonel of the Irish Brigade, Count O'Connell and Old Irish Life at Home and abroad, 1745-1833*, Richard Hayward's *In the Kingdom of Kerry*, Malachi McCormick's detailed, indeed poetic notes to his new translation of *A Lament for Art O'Leary* (his Stone Street Press's hand-made book being a work of art in itself); Patrick M. Geoghan's two-volume biography of Daniel O'Connell, *The Rise of Daniel O'Connell, 1775-1829* and *The Life and Death of Daniel O'Connell, 1830-1846*; Sean O'Faolain's classic *King of the Beggars: The Life of Daniel O'Connell* and *Daniel O'Connell's Childhood* by Brian Igoe, which appears on *The Irish Story* website have all played the same role for me concerning the O'Connells, Derrynane and County Kerry.

These works have been augmented by John Crowley and John Sheehan's breath-taking *The Iveragh Peninsula: A Cultural Atlas of the Ring of Kerry* and *Derrynane House National Historical Park: A Guide to the Country Home of Daniel O'Connell* by Jim Larner (vice Alain Craig's prior version)

Jim Ryan's *Carrauntoohil & MacGillicuddy's Reeks: A Walking Guide to Ireland's Highest Mountains* was priceless in enabling, amongst a number of other things, my being able to trace Eileen's fictitious trek to Ballyhar.

Invaluable background for the lives and careers of the Irish officers who appear in the book has been provided by John Cornelius O'Callaghan's massive classic, *History of the Irish Brigades in the Service of France*; Stephen McGarry's *Irish Brigades Abroad, From the Wild Geese to the Napoleonic Wars*, George B. Clark's *Irish Soldiers in Europe 17th-19th Century*, and the *Wild Geese – The Irish Brigades in the Service of France and Spain*, written by Mary McLaughlin and beautifully illustrated by Chris Warner.

In connection with the Vienna period, I have relied on *Maria Theresa: Biography of a Monarch* by Elfriede Iby, along with the biographies of Marie Antoinette by Evelyne Lever and Antonia Fraser, as well as Munro Price's *The Road from Versailles;* Carolly Erickson's *To the Scaffold* and Caroline Morehead's *Dancing to the Precipice: The Life of Lucie De La Tour Du Pin* (whose father was General Arthur Dillon – who deserves an insightful biography of his own).

Robert K. Massey's *Catherine the Great: Portrait of a Woman* suggested Count von Klaus's mission to St. Petersburg, as well as providing the rationales for the Emperor dispatching him thus.

I have collected and consulted copious numbers of booklets and smaller books, as well as notes made, at numerous locations in Ireland, France and Austria. The experience of wandering over the years from the sanctuary that Derrynane remains, in many ways little changed from the eighteenth century (many thanks to OPW for preserving and enhancing the area), as well as through the streets of Paris and Vienna, of Dublin and the countryside beyond these cities has proven invaluable. Few experiences were as a fascinating as an afternoon "stables tour" at the Spanish Riding School in Vienna, its impact rendered even more permanent and vivid by the extraordinary book, *450 Years of the Spanish Riding School*, written by René Van Baken and Arnim Basche, published on the occasion of this milestone in this wholly-unique institution's colourful history.

It being the twenty-first century, I have resorted on an as-needed basis to non-copyrighted, largely-obscure Internet-available sources for a vast range of minutiae, ranging from the detailed construction of an eighteenth century flintlock pistol; finer points and details of items of men's and women's fashion; to the availability and titles of books and periodicals published for children in English and other European languages.

ABOUT THE AUTHOR

KEVIN O'CONNELL IS A NATIVE of New York City and a descendant of a young officer of what had—from 1690 to 1792—been the Irish Brigade of the French army, believed to have arrived in French Canada following the execution of Queen Marie Antoinette in October of 1793. At least one grandson subsequently returned to Ireland and Mr. O'Connell's own grandparents came to New York in the early twentieth century. He holds both Irish and American citizenship.

He is a graduate of Providence College and Georgetown University Law Centre.

For much of his four decades-plus long legal career, O'Connell has practiced international business transactional law, primarily involving direct-investment matters, throughout Asia (principally China), Europe, and the Middle East.

The father of five children and grandfather of ten, he and his wife, Laurette, live with their golden retriever, Katie, near Annapolis, Maryland.

Made in the USA
Middletown, DE
26 March 2017